FADED FRAGMENTS

The Nexus Series
Book One

Mandi Kontos

DFA Press

Paperback ISBN: 978-0-6459077-0-4
Ebook ISBN: 978-0-6459077-1-1
Hardback ISBN: 978-0-6459077-2-8

Edition: 1
First Printed: 2023

This novel is a work of fiction. The names, characters, and incidents portrayed
in it are the work of the author's imagination. An resemblances to actual
persons, living or dead or localities is entirely coincidental. The exploration of
identities is the work of the author's imagination and is no way historically
correct, just an adaption.

This story comes with the trigger warning of self harm, gore and the use of
Ancient Egyptian deities with a spin.

Edited by Emily Marquart
Proofread by Beth Atwood
Cover Design by Miblart
Created with Vellum

For Dad.

Who supported me the most with my move away from the nest to follow my dreams. He was my biggest fan and so proud of the woman I became.

I wish you were still here to see this book through.

CHAPTER ONE

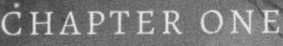

Nefertiti
Paoni 1358 BC

I AM A QUEEN.

I had people who waited on me hand and foot—hand-maidens who made sure I was fed, bathed and never alone. Except for when I wanted space.

Like tonight.

The hallway to my chambers was quiet at night. Flickers of light threw shadows against the ornate walls that were covered in rich, earthy colours, gold trimming and scripture markings, the code by which every citizen in Egypt lived. In the torchlight, Karrept's skin shimmered. Dark chestnut-coloured eyes stared back at me as his skilful hands pulled me flush against his body. I gasped and wrapped my arms around his neck. He held me tight, his strong arms making me feel safe and wanted. I smiled as I leaned up for the kiss that I knew was coming.

Karrept kissed me like there wasn't anyone else for him—and there wasn't.

He was a priest breaking a sacred law.

'What are you doing to me?' I whispered as I broke off the kiss.

'Driving you insane,' he replied with a smile. 'Is it working?'

I laughed. 'Yes, but you have to stop. Aten will be on his way soon.'

'Do not be so absurd. He will not be back for days. We have time. So much time, Nefertiti.'

My name on his lips sent a shiver down my spine; he always had that kind of effect on me. I sighed and pushed him away. He took two steps forward and spun on his heel so he was facing me. Karrept walked backwards and I grinned as I tilted my head and took in every inch of him. His dark curls, the heated gaze that mapped my body, those kissable lips that made me shiver with anticipation.

In the distance, I could hear the shuffle of feet. Even though I knew it was just Karrept's understudies, my heart leapt at every sound—maybe *this* would be the time that Aten caught us.

Aten was not stupid, though. My husband would have seen the small instances when Karrept and I touched for longer than we should have or when we spoke to one another more than necessary. Aten's superhuman senses would have picked up the differences in scent when we had been in the same chamber together, yet he said nothing.

I could not stay away from Karrept. I needed him in my life, and there was a magnetism between us that I did not have with Aten.

The shadows from the torches slinked into the darkness and faded as I watched the way his body moved, watched the pure strength and sex appeal in that powerful form. I ached to touch him, but he moved just out of reach as we walked down the hallways that led to my chambers.

It thrilled me to be so close to him, yet so far away.

'What if what I want has nothing to do with making our

bodies one?' I teased. I wanted nothing more than to have his weight pressed against mine. It was the only time I felt safe.

Karrept's baritone laugh filled the hall, and I did everything in my power not to lean into him as my body tingled with excitement.

'I will have to request your husband come back immediately, if that is the case.' The smile that lit up his whole face distracted me from the heat in his eyes temporarily. 'I need you.'

Need. Karrept needed me. Aten never *needed* me. He only wanted me because I was pretty to look at.

And because I kept his secret.

As we entered my chambers, Karrept's eyes never left mine. We moved around the bed—there would be time for that later—and to my favourite chair. The backs of his thighs touched the lounge and he sat down without a word. I lifted my skirt and sat on his lap so our bodies could be unobstructed by flimsy material. His fingers drummed a melody against my thighs and he grinned at me.

'What is that grin for?' I asked, feigning ignorance.

Karrept chuckled and looked down at our bodies before he spoke again. 'I remember when I had to coerce you into doing this, and now you want to do it all on your own. Akhenaten is oblivious to it all ...'

'Aten,' I murmured. 'He prefers Aten now.'

'Perhaps, but he is still Akhenaten to me.'

'Not to his face, he is not,' I replied. 'You like to test his patience, do you not?'

'He loves me for it. And you are not letting me finish my story ...'

I leaned back and called on my magick to stitch a line over my lips to seal them. I could have made it invisible, but I didn't. It was intricate and detailed, the lines of individual stitches catching in the torchlight when I tilted my head. I wanted him to see it, but as soon as he did, it disappeared. The magick still held the stitches in place even if he couldn't see them.

He dragged his teeth over my chin. He wanted to get a reaction and was rewarded with a sigh of frustration that I couldn't stop even if I wanted to. He knew me better than my own husband did.

'Now, how am I supposed to kiss you like I mean it, my light? Undo it.'

With a shake of my head, I rolled my hands in the air as a sign to keep talking. I loved listening to his voice.

Karrept snickered and tapped my arse before he pressed me into his lap harder. I could feel his bulge stirring to attention. My eyes widened at the change in pressure, and it took everything in me not to moan. He did this to me every time we were together, and I always reacted the same. He knew that no matter how many times he did it, I would always crumble.

He brushed his lips against my cheek and sighed into my ear. 'Do you know what I love the most about you?'

Karrept nibbled at my lobe as his nails dug into my butt. His nails were sharp but never pierced my skin. He liked to drive me insane with small, teasing touches, and time and time again, I gave in to it. With the same magick I used to stitch my lips shut, I unstitched them and dragged my nails down his bare chest. He was strong, and I loved that it was a strength defined by hard work and persistence. It took years of training to become a priest and achieve the physicality that came with it. To be the one that the king doted on was no small feat. Karrept worked daily to have the same strength as Aten, but he missed a single gene that only Aten had. He compensated, though; his strong arms were almost as big as Aten's.

'No. Do tell me what you love about me?' I asked.

'Everything. There is nothing I would change.' He leaned in and hovered his lips over mine.

'That is a lie,' I whispered and pulled back to look at him. His

4

eyes swirled with lust, and it tightened things down low. I could never refuse him when he looked at me like that. He gave me everything that Aten didn't.

'Oh?'

I adjusted myself in his lap and ran a finger over the bridge of his nose. 'You would want me to be your wife. Not his.'

Karrept kissed me hard, and I wrapped my arms around his neck to silence all the words that lingered on the edge of his tongue. Holding me tight, he switched our position and slipped so seamlessly inside me, my body ready for him to complete me. He was there inside the cracks, inside the broken memories and the hurt. He made me feel like I was lighter than air. I wanted to hold on to that feeling, but I knew I couldn't.

I knew what was about to happen.

And I couldn't tell him.

Phaopeh 1340 BC

OUR LAUGHTER VIBRATED through the halls as we snuck around the corner and stole a moment, a kiss that took the breath from my lungs. As he held me tight against the wall, Karrept ran his hand down my side and lifted my leg. He was good at kissing away any conscious thought from my mind, but there was a constant reminder that these moments were stolen when Aten wasn't home. Karrept led me away from his sleeping chamber and towards the grand hall, where we would stop playing and go back to our respected hierarchy within the realm.

Months had passed, and with the Illuminate Year to prepare for, we had to get the timing right or we would miss our opportunity to be together. We would miss the chance to be in a world without Aten. And that was a world I wanted to see.

The grand hall was decorated in gold, with two thrones a

step above the rest of the floor. In one corner there was a statue of Aten; it was solid gold and one of his proudest achievements.

Aten wanted everyone to remember his name.

Karrept guided me deeper into the great hall. He held my hand up above my head, and I twirled under his arm. Before I could say more, he pushed me into the wall. I gasped, and his whole body melded against mine. The warmth of his body dissolved any reservations I had.

'I missed you,' he said. 'There is too much time between our meetings. I need more. A whole season is too much time.' He intoxicated me with his words. I wanted to drink all of him in.

'You know that we can only do this when Aten is not around.'

He knew it; I knew it too. But I wanted more. I wanted to spend every waking moment with him because he made me feel. He wanted me to be the one who quietened the voices when it all got to be too much. The only way to stop him from saying much more was to silence him, so I kissed him and pulled him close—until Aten's voice cut through the silence.

'What is *this*, Nefertiti?'

I froze and broke the kiss. I tried to hide the gasp, but he would have heard it with his superhuman hearing. I swallowed hard and was about to reply, but Karrept turned to shield me from him. That was the biggest mistake he could have made.

'You are back already?' he asked. He aimed for surprise, for something other than smug, but it did not work.

Those words snapped me out of my stupor, Aten knew, but Karrept seemed to not care. Or he was being oblivious on purpose.

'I was not speaking to you, priest.' The venom that dripped from his words was enough to make even me cringe. 'I knew you were with someone, Nefertiti, but I did not think you would pick the priest. How long?'

The identity of the man had been a secret I was careful with.

'Long enough' was all I could say.

He refused to look at me, and that hurt. A part of me that I thought was long gone ached for him. 'Aten?' I took a step closer to him.

He slapped me, the pain immediate as my jaw rattled. 'No, you do not get to say my name in that tone. You are a promiscuous woman. I knew that there was someone, but I did not think that it would be *him*. I will not allow this to continue. Karrept, you will be going down to the tomb for a week. Perhaps a week of flesh being ripped from your body will be enough time to rid thoughts of you from my wife's mind, and the reminder of her flesh out of yours.'

Karrept leapt at him and pushed Aten into his own statue. His power slammed into the pharaoh, hot as a midday stroll, blistering but still calm. It rolled over my skin and felt like a comfortable blanket. Karrept stepped back and clapped his hands before he pulled them apart slowly. A small ball of wind built between his palms, but I could see Aten's move before Karrept.

'Karrept, *no!*' I screamed. That was the opening he needed.

Aten scratched a line across Karrept's stomach with his shifted hand, the claws sharper and more dangerous than any sword. Aten was a werewolf and that was why his people were so loyal to him. They sensed the beast that roiled beneath his skin.

Karrept doubled over in pain, and Aten held me tight as I tried to help him. I could help ease the pain. I could slow the decay with my magick and Aten knew that. The tips of his claws never broke my skin, but the pressure of them was a reminder that he was more powerful than I was. Aten's guards flocked around him, and he pointed to Karrept.

'Clean up this mess. Nefertiti, we are leaving.'

He pulled at me and tried to guide me away, like he wanted to prove who was in charge, but I wrenched out of his grip. 'No.

Go and see our daughter in Alexandria. I do not want to see you again.'

Aten raised an eyebrow at me. Instead of fighting, he took one look at the expression on my face and sighed. 'You mistake this for malice, but I am just looking out for you. For us.'

'No. You are not. You want to make sure it is known that you are the only one who has the ability to ruin others. Now leave.'

On the inside, my whole body was shaking. I had never taken a stand against him. This new level of confidence had everything to do with Karrept and nothing to do with me. Aten looked from Karrept to me. I was catching my breath from the magick that still lingered in the air and the force it took to break free, but I held my ground. It was all I could do to not fall apart as I watched the scratch bubble and decay.

Werewolf marks were deadly if the body was not prepared for them.

Or if you weren't me.

I was immune.

Aten stared between the two of us and turned on his heel. I knew that his gaze lingered on me over his shoulder, but my attention was firmly set on Karrept. He sighed and motioned to his guards to follow him. I should at least be allowed to mourn my lover in peace. As soon as Aten was out of sight, I rushed to his side.

'Karrept. Karrept. No, what are you doing? Do *not* try and magick it away,' I quickly reasoned with him. His magick would make it worse. He was trying to heal it and it wasn't going to work. I could only imagine what sort of pain he was in right at that moment. 'Werewolf claws are toxic. You will not be able to heal it. Stop wasting your energy.'

'Then tell me what to do? I am not about to die. You let him do this.' The pain in his voice was almost too much to bear.

'I did not. I love you. This is why I could not be with just you. He promised that any man that touched me would die, but he was so good at looking the other way. Do you think it is easy for me?'

I clamped my fingers on the wound to try to stop what was happening. It helped ease his pain, as though my touch was all he needed to heal. He smiled up at me, his fingers cupping my cheek. 'Your touch will always be beautiful. I can die knowing I loved you.'

A werewolf scratch made him move through the stages of grief fast. He was accepting his fate. My whole body shook as it mourned him. There had to be something that I could do.

My mind filtered through the different spells that could help. One to stop the pain, one to help ease his mind … but there was one spell that was different to all of them.

It was *the* spell, the one he said would promise us a life during the Illuminate Year. Without Aten and without any responsibility. It would be the ultimate spell and would require a direct descendant.

'No. You will not die. The spell, the one you told me about. Let us do it. Where are your priests? We can get them to help.'

He mustered up the strength and whistled to call his priest understudies. They were all sturdy men, most of them with an affinity to a god. They wore nothing but a loincloth and some had bands of black around their biceps to indicate how far along they were in their training.

'The spell. We need to do it. Now.' My arms shook as I kept the pressure on his wound.

Aten was a smart man and made sure that he could mark me after we were married, but he had not been ready for me to cheat on him, and he retaliated the only way he knew.

I wasn't about to let my lover die. Even if it meant that I would die first.

CHAPTER TWO

Lucy
Epep 2014

I NEVER THOUGHT I would be back at this house without my siblings.

I felt the tension creep into my body, and my shoulders felt like they were touching my ears as I reached into my pocket, hand stiff. I held the key inside my pocket and stared at the door. Maybe it wasn't too late to back out of this trip. Right?

As though he knew exactly what I was thinking, Travis spoke up and I jumped.

'It's just a key, Luce. It goes in the door. See?' Travis' warmer than usual hand coaxed mine out of my pocket. He helped pull some of the tension out of my body as he covered my hand and together we put the key into the lock. It opened with no resistance. We were greeted with a rush of cool air and the smell of pine and alcohol. The floorboards had been recently repolished.

Dread settled in the pit of my stomach as I stared at the threshold of the house. The memories that were etched into the walls were eerie, and while they were all good memories, it was still too much. Two years ago I stepped out of this house without my siblings and never looked back. Their disappearance was still a mystery, and being back meant that I needed to find out what happened. I had to know if they were still alive.

'Luce? Are we going in?' Lili asked.

I looked over my shoulder and swallowed past the lump in my throat. 'I'm seriously thinking about just turning back and going home. I've got a bad feeling about being here.'

Most times that was enough to drive me back, but Lili and Travis wanted a holiday. They thought that it would be a good idea to come here.

I didn't.

We couldn't stay outside forever. We would melt, and our rude taxi driver was long gone. I wanted to show him who he really was dealing with but it was illegal to use magick and Egypt was far more strict with their laws than Australia was.

I stepped across the threshold of the house, and memories rushed through me. They tried to fill that empty pit in my stomach, like it would help the dull ache that had been permanently there since the funeral two years ago. I stumbled, but Travis caught me in a blur of speed. His touch scorched my skin, but that was what happened when you were best friends with a werewolf. I was breathless from the rush, but he held me tight.

Lili's face hovered in front of mine. 'Luce! Are you okay?'

I stared at her and tried to form words. 'I think so. I didn't think that the house would have any more power over me. I thought I could do this without them.'

Travis helped me steady me. 'What do you mean?'

'Devin and Destiny, their presence is still in the house. I thought it would have been long gone.'

'I thought that there was nothing special about the house,' Lili said.

I wanted to tell her she was right, but there was so much that was special about this house. 'It wasn't supposed to be. But the

11

memories are stills fresh. Something that I thought would have been long gone.' I held Lili's gaze and frowned.

Travis distracted me and helped make sure I was steady. His green eyes stared at me with an intensity that I had only seen once before. And we were much older than that time.

'What are you doing, Matthews?' I asked Travis, using his last name to remind him where we were.

'You,' he said.

In my mind, through the Bond I shared with Lili and Travis, I could feel the desire, the heat in that single word. I knew I was in trouble.

Don't do that. You promised you wouldn't, I said to him telepathically through our Bond.

Liliana Tisiano and Travis Matthews were my best friends. We came from families who were wealthy, educated and had a strong hold on so much of the world within Melbourne, our hometown in Australia. We shared a bond; one that allowed us to talk telepathically to one another, feel one another's emotions and know what the other person was thinking. It all started when we met at the beginning of high school and got to know each other better.

It seemed that our friendship went deeper than high school, and there was a sense that we had walked the earth together long before this lifetime. As we learned more about the Bond, we'd figured out how to shield most of our feelings and emotions from one another, but there were times where we didn't. Or couldn't.

'Let's get inside, and out of this heat,' Lili said and pushed her way between Travis and me and into the hallway of the house that I had grown up in during my summers as a child.

'Good idea, Lili,' I said and pulled my arm away from Travis. He smiled at me, almost like he was mocking me. I pushed past him and let him close the door behind him.

The taxi driver had put me in a mood. I may have looked like a foreigner with my lighter skin, but my mother was Egyptian, and while I took after Dad's side of the family, I spoke Hebrew and Arabic fluently.

'Earth to Lucy Ryder,' Lili said as she waved her hands in front of my face.

'I'm here. Sorry, I zoned. The living room is down the hall.' Like that would settle Lili's mind about where my head was.

I guided my two best friends down the hallway. On the walls were pictures that were taken by Dad of me growing up with my siblings, my parents, grandparents and photos of the very first Ryder Hotel. A hotel that was only a few blocks away from the house. Further down the hallway, there were more images of the other hotels located all around the world. Melbourne, LA, Singapore, Greece, Italy, South Africa, Dubai, the list went on. Dad's chain of hotels was almost in every city in the world.

'Is this the latest one that's being built?' Lili asked and pointed to a picture on the wall. It was only in the beginning phase of construction, and as the hotel was finished that photo would be replaced with one of the completed building. The simple black frame held Mum, Dad, and me, all smiling in front of a building that was half together. There was scaffolding all around it, and we were all wearing hard hats. An appearance I'd been forced to do only a month ago.

'Yup, that's Scotland. The one that Dad keeps trying to get me involved in.' I sighed.

'Is he still trying to get you to take over?' Travis asked.

'He sure is. This was supposed to be Devin's job. I don't know anything about business. I want to stay home and write.'

'You do know how to talk your way out of almost anything,' Travis said with a smirk.

I narrowed my eyes at him. 'You're only saying that because you're not getting your way.'

'Look, he's not wrong,' Lili said, 'but we all know where your heart lies and it's definitely not in the hotel chain.'

'And where is that, Miss Tisiano?' Amused, I walked away from the frame and past the last one down the hallway. I turned to the left and was greeted with the open-plan living space.

Mum had an eye for design, and it was why she always had the last say on any sort of decorating, whether it was the hotel or a room in the house. Here the living, dining and kitchen were all on show. My favourite thing about the room? The huge looming windows. They were bi-fold doors that opened to the deck, so there was the whole living outside-inside look; it was the main feature that had seen many parties celebrating special occasions. Although it had been more than two years since anything of the like had happened. The space still looked immaculate, even with the curtains closed.

'Obviously with the player werewolf.' She winked and put her bag down by the kitchen bench.

'You're hilarious,' I said as my own bag hit the ground and I avoided Travis' attention. I kicked off my shoes and walked behind the kitchen bench. Once upon a time, the bench had decorative lights hanging over it, but Mum had changed her mind a year ago and put in surface-mounted downlights instead. They looked like long cans on the ceiling. I wasn't sold on them, but she said they were all the rage and she was the designer.

'Are we eating?' Travis deflected.

'How can you think about eating?' Lili asked.

'I'm a werewolf, it's all we can think about.'

'You're not tired from the flight?' I asked as I got myself a bottle of water from the fridge. Before I closed it, I thought again and grabbed two more. I put them on the bench and twisted the cap on my own water bottle. I walked to the dark grey couch, which was the only hint of darkness in the room, and sat down. The pale greens and shades of white were all one hundred per cent Subira Ryder.

'Nope. I'm sure that the kitchen is fully stocked for me to go crazy, hmm?' Travis finished.

I nodded and watched him walk off to the left and open the fridge to survey its contents.

'This place is Subira. But it's got a different edge to it. I like it, Luce,' Lili said, her designer eye scanning every inch of the place, although she looked purely at the aesthetics. Lili was the only daughter of Roberto Tisiano, the *capo* of the Italian Mafia in Melbourne. Not that we were meant to know that, and we only knew as a by-product of the Bond. We were sworn to secrecy. Her mother, Chiara, was the only one of our mums who was a traditional stay-at-home mother, but when you had Tisiano Incorporated to run, you didn't need to work.

'I'll be sure to pass on my compliments to Subira. She'll love it,' I said.

'I doubt that.' Lili walked over to the curtains. 'We should open these to let some light into the house.' She looked over her shoulder at me. 'But only if you're up to it. How are you feeling?' *Because that rush of power wasn't normal for you*, she finished in my mind.

I pressed my lips together and looked at Travis, who had begun to pull things out of the fridge. As the son of Aria Award–winning artist Sarah Matthews, he had learned that his love language was feeding the wolf inside as well as the people around him; we would need to top the fridge up tomorrow. I felt his dad in his life had something to do with it too. Maybe he was compensating for the lack of a father figure and, as a result, decided to feed people with love.

'I'm okay. Let's bring some light into the place.'

Lili helped with the heavy drapes and together we opened them and let in the sun that was shining high. She rested a hand on my arm, as if to say that it was okay to be sad.

You're safe with us. We won't let anything happen to you.

I wanted to believe her, because she was the one who

was always right, but something felt wrong. Like now that I was here I *needed* to know what happened to Devin and Destiny.

Because there was no way that my twin brother and older sister were dead. They wouldn't leave me, and I was going to prove everyone wrong.

'Do you have good memories here?' Lili asked.

She would be the only one who would ask. Travis was getting stuck into making a meal that would consume all of his attention until he was done.

Plus, he's a guy. He can't concentrate on more than one thing, Lili said telepathically.

I grinned at her. I could shield from her if I wanted to, but I didn't. Because her words weren't harmful. They didn't say anything but the truth.

'Loads, but I also have some not-so-good ones. Especially from the last time I was here, two years ago. I'm scared I'm going to relive them.'

'Why?' Lili asked.

'Because there's a weird sort of power thing that happens in Egypt. Maybe it's the history, or maybe it's because there is so much raw power here.'

Before she could answer or ask me to elaborate, I was hit with a memory.

Egypt
Paoni 2012

'Luce, I'm coming to get you,' Devin yelled from somewhere in the house. Probably upstairs. Or closer, it seemed.

I watched as my twin brother came at me. A squeal left my lips as I scrambled to get away from him. He pounced on me and pinned me to the floor. I laughed hard as he tickled me. I tried to push him away, and I accidentally poked him in the eye.

It made him squint down at me, but the tickle attack never stopped.

'Will you two cut that out? Are you, like, five or something?' Destiny said as she looked down her nose at us on the floor.

While I caught my breath, Devin spoke up for the both of us. 'Dest, you're missing the point of a holiday.' He tickled me again and I kicked out, but this time he was faster and blocked it.

I gasped. 'Stop being so lame and a spoilsport. Josh looks so bored over there. I'm pretty sure your boyfriend, or fiancé-to-be or whatever, didn't come here to be bored out of his mind. Show him some excitement, or he'll leave.'

I should have kept my mouth shut—a problem of mine—but I had enough common sense to keep from goading her further. I liked Josh, he was fun to be around, but Destiny was a little bit like just before summer storm; she was hot, scathing and would change temperature without notice. I didn't want to risk the lightning that would come with that storm.

'Why you ... I should ... what the hell?' It was Destiny's turn to squeal, and I caught a glimpse of Josh's fingers trailing over her sides just as Devin started up again. I squirmed out from under him and got to my feet before I ran outside. The doors were wide open, letting in the summer breeze. This was my favourite time of the year to come to Egypt.

There was a moment of sheer exhilaration. I was free.

'Oh no you don't, Lucy-Bell.' My nickname was enough to slow me down, and that was when Devin attacked. He jumped on my back and dragged me to the ground, but I used his momentum to turn us so that I pinned him down under me.

'Jeez, Luce, that hurt,' he wheezed.

My vision flickered; it was like someone was playing with a light switch. 'Wh-what?' Was that a laugh that bubbled in my throat?

Devin gasped. 'Luce, your eyes, they're not grey anymore ... what the fuck?'

Fear filled his eyes, and a part of me liked it. Really liked it. Why shouldn't men be beneath me? They *should* be afraid when they cast their eyes on me.

'What colour are they?' I asked calmly.

'Golden,' he replied.

I pushed off his body and got to my feet, quicker than I ever could, and stamped my foot on his chest. My body was doing the exact opposite of what I wanted it to do. I tried to pull it back, but I had no control. I pleaded in my mind, I screamed, but something had a hold of my body. It had control.

The Force applied more pressure to my foot. I clenched my teeth, as though it would help stop the motion, but it didn't. Instead there was laughter in my head.

'Are you afraid, Mr Ryder? You know the person I seek.' The words out of my mouth didn't make sense because they weren't my own, but seeing the fear in Devin's face excited me.

'Lucy. What are you doing? *Stop.*' He gasped.

The Force inside me laughed; she was excited, drunk off Devin's feeling of powerlessness. I looked down at my brother and saw him, really saw him. He was my twin. The other half of me. His eyes were more blue than grey, and he had a smile that mimicked my own. There was a dimple in his right cheek whenever he truly smiled, and his eyes sparkled. His brown hair was wavier than mine, almost bordering on curly. He was always the one who got me through anything I needed. He was the reason I was so grounded.

Who was this Force, and why did they want to hurt my brother?

I pushed at the power inside me. They were looking for someone, a boy, or something of the like, but it seemed to think that Devin knew. The Force tried to keep the reins but I pushed back and finally it got to be too much before they fled. I felt my legs give out on me, the adrenaline leaving my body. I shook with exhaustion.

'Luce!' Devin screamed. He was by my side in an instant. He gathered me into his arms and held me tight.

Feeling disconnected from my body, I let my brother hold me. I looked up at him and he exclaimed, 'Your eyes, they're grey again.'

Well, that was a good sign. I closed my eyes and buried my nose into his shoulder.

'What happened?' Destiny asked. I looked up to see her face becoming pale. I hadn't felt Devin walk me back into the house.

There were no words. I just looked at Destiny; the worry on her face was foreign, at least when it was directed at me, and it made me want to run away. Devin laid me down on the couch. Time seemed different. Everyone was moving in fast-forward mode because in the next instant, I was being forced to drink a glass of water I didn't remember being put in my hand.

I did it anyway—they weren't going to leave me alone until it was all gone. I couldn't figure out why there was a lingering taste in my mouth. It was metallic and rusty. Why could I taste blood on my tongue?

Egypt
Epep 2014

I blinked out of the memory and found Travis and Lili staring at me. I looked between them and the glass of water that was now in my hand.

'What happened?' Travis asked.

'Memories. I didn't think the house was going to do this, but it looks like it wants me to remember all of the things I thought I had buried.' I took a sip of the water, and it seemed to help with the weird hoarse feeling in the back of my throat. It was like I had been back there with Devin and Destiny, yelling all over again.

'I'm guessing that this is something that isn't meant to

19

happen, yeah?' Lili asked. 'Because I know that we have this Bond, but us being able to see memories like that, almost like we were there, shouldn't happen, right?'

'No. I thought that learning how to shield from one another should have stopped this.' I looked at Travis. 'Did you ...?'

He nodded. 'I saw something. Devin was there, under your foot, but I couldn't tell why or how that happened.'

'I don't know either, but that's weird that you guys saw it.'

'I think I need to call Mum and talk to her about this,' Lili said. 'She'll be able to let me know if there is something that we can do, or something that we missed. This shouldn't happen.' Lili's mother knew more about the Bond than we did. She had called Lili a Watcher and informed us that Lili was the one who held the three of us together with her abilities. But everything about it was so secretive. Our Bond, even though it was something that we had been used to for the last five years, was still new to us and we were still figuring out what it all meant.

'Maybe we need to figure out how to stop it. I'm going to have a shower in the meantime.'

'Want any company?' Travis asked.

I sighed as I looked up at him. His bright green eyes stared back at me, and I shook my head. 'I'm good. Just ...' I wanted him to not look at me like he was. I didn't want to complicate our relationship, and ever since the party, he had tried to. 'Just try not to break anything. Mum will know, even if we replace them.'

'Luce ...' Lili started. It was like she knew that there was more to say, but she held it back. Like it would make it all better.

'I'm okay. Really. I need to find a way to just move past this.'

The metallic taste of blood was also another thing I couldn't forget. And to have that same taste again, after the memory of first having it ... I did everything I could to try to keep my heart rate at a normal level. Travis would hear if it wasn't. And I was going to try not to worry about what the taste of blood in my mouth meant.

This house was full of many memories, most good, some bad, and I knew that memory was only the beginning. Hunter had helped me get a handle on this side of my magick, and I was sure that I still had it. I should have been able to be here, without him, and not have to worry about it, but maybe the ability to see these memories again was the key to what had happened.

Once I was up the stairs and locked in the bathroom, I turned on the water and thought about the protection circle Hunter had taught me for times of need. I focused on the water and envisioned it wrapping a protective barrier around me. As I stepped into the shower and let the warmth of the water wash away the travel mess and the residual energy, I could feel Travis and Lili thinking about me.

If I was still talking to Hunter, this would be when I called him for his help, but he'd made it clear he didn't want to talk to me. Not after our breakup.

After two years of grief and silence, I was here, moving through the painful memories to understand what had happened to my siblings. There was no going back now.

CHAPTER THREE

Nefertiti
Phaopeh 1358 BC

THE SPELL we had weaved together was going to stop this. It had to. I was not going to lose Karrept like this.

My gaze shifted from Karrept to his priest understudies and I felt powerless. He was bleeding and in so much pain, but I could not do anything to help. Would my blood immunity stop the wound from getting worse? Or would it speed it up? My magick would do nothing; there was no remedy for werewolf scratches.

I was immune to Aten's claws, and by default our children were, but I had never tested the effect my blood had on anyone by myself.

The fear that he would be found out was too big.

'Karrept, stop it!' I said as I felt the flicker of power shiver across my skin.

'I cannot.'

Dark lines appeared around the scratch site. The magick was making the poison spread through his body faster.

'You have to, or you will be dead before we can finish the spell.'

The spell would be the catalyst for us living our lives together.

A ceremonial knife was handed to me. The hilt was mother-of-pearl, iridescent in the shimmer of the light from the torches, but the blade itself was solid obsidian. It was spelled to capture that which we needed.

'My light, it burns. I have to keep going.'

'No. Stop, call Nephthys. The spell will fix it. The one that we spoke about. It has to be done today.'

As if my half-sister had been within earshot, she appeared. But she was part goddess, so her hearing was superhuman.

'You called?'

I looked over my shoulder. Her makeup was impeccable, but underneath it her skin was kissed by the sun in a soft bronze, her black hair curlier than ever. Her eyes were a vivid blue, the only tell that she was part goddess.

'Do you have your cards with you? We need to do the spell—now.'

With a wave of her hand and a shimmer of power, the cards were in her hand and she smiled at me.

'Of course, dear sister, I never leave my chambers without them.'

I turned to Karrept and his eyes widened. The pain had started to take over more than his physical body. His beautiful chestnut-coloured eyes darkened with agony. Soon the pain would take over and he would not be able to think straight.

'We are doing this and doing it now,' I said.

He smiled, his blood-free hand brushing a strand of hair out of my face. 'This is not how I wanted us to end. I did not want to put you in this position.'

'I am volunteering for this. You know how I feel about you.'

'Can we cut all the mushy stuff? We have a spell to prepare

for.' Nephthys waved her hand and Karrept's priests made a circle around us. One by one they interlocked fingers, and when we were in the enclosed circle, I gripped the dagger tightly.

I looked around at the grand hall. It would be the last time I would see the throne in this light.

'I will find you. I promise, my light. I will always find you and come back to you,' Karrept choked out.

I swallowed back the urge to fight him. Did I really want to end my life for his? I did not care for much. This was the perfect way to get back at Aten, to make sure he knew that he was not going to be able to control me any longer, but I was about to lose the man who I loved in the process, and that was something I did not want to do.

'You have to, Karrept, or I will make sure that none of my descendants see the light of day.'

With a smirk and a playful look, he grabbed the back of my head and crashed his lips into mine. The kiss was fierce, it was hot, and I wanted to take all of the pain I could from him. I wanted to keep him around because it was in moments like this that I felt most alive. He broke the kiss, which brought me back to the room. Then I heard the chanting.

He had done it as a distraction so that I would not hear the start of the spell.

'Karrept,' I whispered.

I love you, he mouthed.

I took a moment to take a breath, step back and tighten my grip around the blade to the point that it was almost painful. Karrept held out his hand, and I sliced my palm with the blade before I sliced his. Our hands found their way to one another—I could not stop it even if I wanted to—and as they joined, I felt the jolt of power. It rushed through my body and tapped at the power deep inside me.

Being a queen was not my own calling; the power that resided within me was one that I had mastered early on in my marriage to Aten. It was this power that he wanted to use to make himself a god.

'I call upon the lines of Watchers to keep Karrept and Nefer-titi safe,' my half-sister's voice rang through the hall. 'To keep them from dying, to be reborn during the Illuminate Year when the moon is covered by the sun and blood in colour to signal the beginning of the becoming.'

Nephthys pulled three cards from her deck. One to signify Karrept; one to signify me, and one to signify the beginning. As she drew the fourth card, she slammed it on top and the power activated the spell.

'*Now,*' Karrept said, and I drove the dagger into my chest.

CHAPTER FOUR

Lucy
Epep 2014

ONCE I WAS all showered and dressed, I went back downstairs and found Lili and Travis chatting and laughing over food. Food had always been the icebreaker.

Lili looked up first. 'Hey, how are you feeling?'

'Better. That was what I needed.' I sighed and tried to avoid Travis' gaze. They were quiet, like I had come in and interrupted some private confession. 'I was thinking about that party in the shower … the one where you let the wolf get too much in control.'

'The party?' Travis frowned.

'Yeah. The one right after Hunter and I broke up.' My fingers danced over the stool. I clenched my jaw as I avoided eye contract, not quite sure if I should sit down or not.

It was supposed to be a fun party, something to celebrate the end of our school years and ring in new and exciting times. But it hadn't been.

'I remember it,' he said. 'I don't know what came over me. I think my wolf and I just wanted to claim what was ours.'

'But I'm not yours. I'm my own person.'

'I'm fully aware of that,' he said before he shoved some chicken into his mouth.

'Just checking.'

I pulled out the last of the rattan-backed stools next to Lili and Travis at the kitchen bench. It was a much more relaxed option than the ten-seater dining table.

'I don't think I want to relive your memories, Luce,' Travis said. 'You know that magick gives me the creeps.'

'Trav, it's not like Luce can help it,' Lili said. 'We're going to have to just deal with it until we can get some answers from Mum and see what else gets thrown our way. You know that this is not something that we can help.'

When I looked at Travis, I half expected to see purple wolf eyes, like at the party, but they were just plain green. I took a deep breath and my shoulders dropped down from my ears. I opened my mouth but closed it again. Looking at his face was too much, so I stared at Lili's food while I spoke.

'We keep you shielded from most of the metaphysical things that happen because we know that you hate anything to do with magick, but this isn't something we can hide from you. We don't have a choice here. I know that you hate the idea of not being in control of what happens around you, but I don't know what being here is going to do. I've … this sort of reaction isn't something I expected, and to have this happen after two years … it's scary.'

Lili handed me her fork, and I picked at her food. The silence that filled the room was odd. Like Travis was trying to understand what was happening and couldn't find the right words to explain what he was feeling.

Lili glanced up at me. 'The Bond is something we barely understand. We know the basics: we share emotions, we can talk to one another and we know where we need help. But we've never been able to share memories with each other like watching a movie. And that's what it feels like, Luce. It's like we're watching the memory as a movie. Maybe it's tied to the house or maybe it's just you, Luce, but we are going to have to try and live with it.' Lili directed her final words at Travis, and I tore my gaze away from her.

'It's so hard to get a read on you, Luce,' he said.

It was a weird sentence coming from him, because he never checked the Bond—or at least that was what I'd thought.

'I think it's better to keep my shield up. I'll try to minimise the amount of run-off you get.'

This was a trick Hunter had taught me when I told him about the Bond. It had begun as a way to help my own sanity as we went through high school. But it was more than that; it was a safeguard to help with the hormones and keep one another safe.

'Do you think if we drew from our sign that we would have more protection?' Travis asked.

I peered at Travis. He'd never been interested in knowing more about the ankh Lili and I wore around our necks as a symbol of our friendship and the Bond. The Egyptian cross had been my idea and Lili loved it. Travis didn't wear jewellery, so his ankh was in tattoo form on his back, but he didn't give much thought to it. Until now, it seemed.

'We might be able to,' I replied.

An ankh was a symbol of life. We used it to help us take control of our own lives and the Bond. We thought we'd been going crazy and it was the only anchor that held us together. The circle, to us, symbolised the Bond, and the spokes were each of us.

'I think I need to check the journal. Might have something more to help with,' Lili said.

Lili and that journal went everywhere. She was trying to

finish her training as a Watcher, and the only person she had to guide her was her mother, who was always busy. It meant that she had to do a lot of the learning on her own. Harder that way, but she was getting good.

'Could also tie us over until we can call your mum at a decent time,' I reasoned.

She just grinned and pushed the seat back, leaving the remnants of her food in favour of the journal. I pulled the plate over to me and continued eating.

There was nothing left to say, and Travis and I fell into an uncomfortable silence.

'Sometimes I wonder where my brain and mouth filter go,' he said finally.

The fork dropped out of my hand. 'Don't start. Trust me.' I didn't want to get into this here. 'I know what your feelings are and you know what mine are.' I pushed out of the chair, trying to give myself some space, but Travis was there, pinning me against the counter with his hips.

His eyes had flecks of purple in them now. That bloody wolf.

'Why are you resisting?' He trailed his fingers up my arm, and I pushed them away.

'I've been over this before. Hunter. Ex. Do not want another.'

'Blah, blah. That's all I'm hearing,' he said.

'Soulmates. Soul. Mates. Travis. *Adelphi Psychi*. Why can't you understand that?' I had told him before. When Hunter and I came to the realisation that we would be tied together forever, it was also when I realised that Travis could only ever be my best friend, not someone who wanted to sleep with me.

'That stuff is bullshit.' He leaned down and hovered his lips over mine, his hand coming up to cup my face. 'If it was true, he wouldn't have broken up with you. We wouldn't have had to put the pieces back together.'

He wasn't playing fair. He knew my weaknesses and he was using them against me. I missed Hunter so much, but I missed having someone treat me like a princess, having them hold me, hug me, kiss me. The little touches. Travis' all-too-warm skin made me want to give in and let him do whatever he wanted.

'You keep refusing to believe. Why won't you just—'

He interrupted me with a kiss. I moaned into his mouth and kissed him back. My body tried to melt into his, but my head got the best of me. I pushed him away and slapped him. 'Fuck you.' I wiped my mouth on the back of my hand and stared at him.

'Come on, Luce, you loved that.' The smirk on his face was all wolf. His aura had changed, and he had let the menace slip through the cracks, his eyes now a vibrant purple.

'Don't "come on, Luce" me. I'm not available. Get over it. If you even think about kissing me again, I'm going to castrate you and then curse you so you can't grow your balls back. Now move.'

I had threatened him enough times that he probably thought I was bluffing, and most of those other times I had been. But not this time.

I meant business.

He moved out of my way, and I walked past him, trying not to touch him, and ran up the stairs.

I THREW myself onto the bed and screamed into a pillow. The wolf would still be able to hear it, but at least it was muffled. Why was he doing this? Emotionally unavailable women seemed to be his forte, or those that were just too easy. I was the former; Kali, his ex, was the latter. I sighed and punched the pillow. Just as I thought about wanting to throw it against the wall, the pillow flew out of my hands and across the room.

That was new.

I blinked at the pillow and panic rose in my body. I had always been known for my control. Being back here had taken that from me and I didn't like that. Without control, what would my magick do and how would it change?

There was a knock on the door and I jumped.

'Luce?' Lili's voice was soft.

'Come in.'

She pushed the door open and picked up the pillow. 'Are you okay?' she asked as she hugged the pillow to her chest.

'I guess you heard?' I said as I crossed my legs, yoga style, under me.

'Some of it. I had the music going, but I felt your panic. What happened?'

'This.' I thought about the pillow in Lili's arms being pulled from her and slamming into the wall. It was plucked from her arms and hit the floor with a soft thud.

'What's new about that?'

'All I did was *think* about that. I didn't have to put any effort in, and that's not normal. I'm always so good with my abilities, but that's not something I could do before.'

'Um ... what?'

'Yeah.' I glanced down at my hands and tried to come up with something to say. Something that would make it all seem less real.

Lili waited patiently. She was a listener—a *watcher*, in truth.

'Why does he have to do *this*? Who the hell did he talk to before we left? We had this sorted. Did he say anything to you?'

She shook her head. 'He didn't talk to me. If he did, I would have told him it was a bad idea, but he still does talk to someone.'

'Who?' I shifted forward and resisted the urge to grab her shoulders and shake her.

'You're not going to like it.'

'I need to know.'

'Kali.' She paused. 'He still talks to Kali.'

'What?' I uncrossed my legs and stood up before I started to pace. 'He said he'd stopped talking to her, that they were finished. Why would they still talk? What the hell?'

Lili was suddenly tight-lipped.

'What? You can't go all silent on me now. Why are they still talking?'

'I can't tell you. Don't make me, Luce,' Lili pleaded.

Those were words that Lili never uttered to me. She told me everything—*everything*. I couldn't get past this.

'Did you swear? You swore, didn't you?'

She nodded.

'Dammit, Lils. Why did you go and do that?'

Swearing an oath to one of the three of us, or all of us, meant that you were unable to tell the other party or those outside of us what the oath pertained to. If you tried, your tongue literally became tied and the words would spill out of your mouth all jumbled.

'Fucking hell. I hate him right now. What am I supposed to do with this information? I can't just go and ask him, because we both know what'll happen if I do.'

'He's going to clam up and make you angry. His specialty.'

'What do you know about Kali?' I knew I was going to push too far.

'Gurantula wants a toy poodle to get through it,' Lili uttered.

I closed my eyes. 'Okay, so I'm not going to get anything out of you. I'm sorry.'

Kali was the high school bully who had made my life a horror story, but she hadn't stopped there. She would pick on me and make sure I knew that she was better than me. I could never understand why she did that. Why was I so special? Was she envious of my friends? Or was I just the flavour of the year —or years—because I was the daughter of someone who was well-off? She was an only child to a single mother and maybe she was jealous that I had siblings and a happy family.

'Yuck, don't make me do that again,' Lili said and shook her head, almost like she was trying to clear the mess in her head.

'Probably better not to. I think I'm just going to cancel the rest of today and give in to the sleep deprivation from the trip. It's probably a better option to just go to sleep and hope that tomorrow will be better. Did you finish journaling or finding anything out?'

She shook her head. 'Griffin texted me and distracted me, but I was halfway through Mum's journal and I couldn't find anything. This could be related to just us, and if so, then my ancestors won't know anything, which makes it hard.'

I sighed. Nothing was ever easy for us.

'Why can't we get a break? Just once.' I stopped pacing, finally, and sat down on the bed. I hugged Lili and she squeezed me back. I held on a little longer and tried not to think too much about what could have happened if I'd kept pushing the issue.

I changed the topic. 'Are we ready for tomorrow?'

'Yup. I have the list; we just need your geological knowledge and we'll be good to go. Oh, and a car.' There was a shine in her eyes. She got way too excited when it came to making lists.

'Devin's Porsche is still in the garage. Easy,' I replied.

'Great, then everything is ready. I'll let you get some sleep, and please don't try poking for answers. You know what will happen. I don't want to be speaking in a jumble for the next two days.'

'Noted.' I laughed. 'I'll see you in the morning.'

'Sweet dreams, Luce. Try to get some, yeah?'

'I'll definitely try.'

She left the room, and I lay back on the bed and stared at the ceiling. I willed myself to sleep, but my brain had other plans.

CHAPTER FIVE

Nefertiti
Paoni 2012

THE DESCENDANT's body was here in this year. I could see it and she was beautiful. She was the perfect vessel; every part of her looked like me. She was ready, and as I watched her run around with her brother and sister, playful and joyous, there was an innocence to her that I never had at her age. I was already a mother by then.

I took a deep breath. I had one chance to do this. Karrept had made sure of it. As I focused my attention on her body, I hovered just over her before I slammed my energy into her. She ran after her brother and I smirked. She worked out—I could feel the way her muscles moved. She was an athlete, that was for sure. How different that felt to my own body.

As I moved her body to make sure that no one knew she wasn't herself, her brother jumped me and brought me to the ground. He was strong. Karrept had whispered to me about what he was like. And I had almost used his body for this, just to have a taste of what it would be like to be in a body again, but my descendant's was better.

I wanted to caress my hands over her, to remember what it felt like to be in the flesh, but I resisted, and instead of letting him drag us down, I used his own momentum to flip us. I pinned him under me.

'Jeez, Luce, that hurt.' His wheezed words gave me power and I pushed through, trying to force Lucy back into her body, willing her to let me take over, but she was too strong. But even with her strength, I watched the fear fill her brother's eyes and I loved it. I wanted to pull that fear out more. He was going to make sure that this worked for me, him and the older sister. They needed to be gone to make this body mine.

I pushed myself to my feet, using some of the strength I had learned while I was dead, and instead of letting Devin get up, I stamped my foot on his chest and proceeded to press my weight onto it.

Stop it. Let him go, she screamed at me, her voice high-pitched enough to give me a headache, but instead I pushed down harder.

'Are you afraid, Mr Ryder?' I asked, the words coming out in my tone instead of the descendant's. The fear delighted me and I wanted more. Needed more.

Who are you? What do you want?

I avoided her questions. She was in my land now, and things were not the same. I pushed at her, trying to coax her into giving me full control, but she was too strong.

She would not stay that way.

But as she screamed and pushed at me, she was too much. I couldn't do anything, so I let go of her body, vowing it wouldn't be the last time the descendant would see me.

CHAPTER SIX

Lucy
Epep 2014

I STARED at the open fridge and found nothing jumped out at me to eat. Sleep had been dull, dreamless and almost peaceful. When I finally got to sleep. Travis had tried to be as quiet as he could, but he was still loud, especially for a werewolf; stealth was natural to them. He had a way of making himself the centre of attention even when we fought. Luckily, he was now tucked upstairs sleeping, just as Lili was, and I was able to bring my shield down a little before anyone else disturbed me. If it was a spell, there would've been a price for doing magick, but because it was my own personal protection, I was able to drop the shield I was grasping on to. It kept Lili and Travis safe and out of my mind.

I felt empty.

It was like there was a big, gaping hole in the centre of my chest. I missed Hunter. As much as I wanted to hate him, I couldn't. It was hard to hate part of your own soul. Being back in the house, I was reminded of my siblings, that they were gone, but being here made it seem like they weren't. I felt like the house had a secret it was trying to tell me and I couldn't understand what it wanted to say.

Not yet.

I sighed and gave up on the food thing and shut the fridge. I found Travis staring at me and I jumped.

'Shit! *Trav*, what are you doing? I thought you were asleep.'

He tilted his head and there was no sign of the wolf in his demeanour. I liked it that way.

'I heard you.' His voice was rough and sleep-hazed, even if he didn't look it.

The wolf inside him didn't need a lot of sleep. Sometimes it ran on an hour's sleep, sometimes twelve. It was all up to how he felt. I shook my head and went to the pantry. There had to be something for me to eat. When I found nothing, I shut the pantry door and sighed. Maybe I'd just make a smoothie or something.

As I moved, I could feel Travis' eyes on me. His heated gaze made me squirm, but I didn't let it show, because then the wolf would win. And I didn't like to lose. Werewolves were funny creatures; they didn't like being challenged but they hated weakness. Dealing with them was a perpetual game of silent negotiations. Or screaming matches.

'Okay, you know what? You suck. You fucking suck.' I pointed at him before I grabbed the frozen berries out of the freezer.

'Oh, come on. Are you still mad about the kiss?'

'Yes.' I turned around to look at him.

'Oh, look at you, all huffy. It's been coming for so long, Luce, you just refused to see it.'

'I'm not ready for this. I don't want to ruin what we have,' I said as I dumped a cup of berries in the blender and grabbed a banana.

'What we have? Are you kidding me? I've loved you for as long as I can remember. We ...'

I added some coconut water to the blender, as well as some chia seeds and flaxseeds. I snapped the lid on before I pushed the button to start it. I closed my eyes and drowned out his words. After a few moments, I opened them and took my finger off the button.

'... have something,' he finished.

I turned to look at him, my body shaking with the need to have his stupid, idiotic words out of my mind. 'We're best friends. Do you know what the statistic is for people who go out with their best friends?' He shook his head and I sighed. 'We won't be friends after, and I sure as hell don't want to risk that. Plus, we have this Bond; no matter what happens we won't ever be out of each other's lives. Not unless one of us is dead, and you're going to outlive us both. I don't want to acknowledge that at the best of times.'

I picked up the jug of the blender and a glass. I poured the smoothie into it before I stared him dead in the eye. 'You're the only guy who has never hurt me like the others and you want to change that? Do you want to be just like Hunter?'

He growled and stormed up to me. I could smell his cologne as he looked down at me, his anger bubbling just under the surface.

'I am *nothing* like Hunter,' he said, voice rising.

I held his gaze and didn't flinch. Being friends with Travis meant that I was used to his quick emotional changes, but I was always prepared for what would come next if I did flinch.

He took a deep breath and backed up, his voice lowering. 'You said you were over him. The Bond says so too.' He sounded hurt, and I knew he didn't deserve to sound that way.

'I'm not over him. I've said that before too.'

I could show Lili and Trav what I wanted when it came to the Bond. They didn't know that I could manipulate what they saw. It was something Hunter had helped me work on as soon as we could put a name to the Bond. Lili knew me well enough to be able to read me without needing the Bond, but Travis had always had a problem. His hot-headedness and temper always got in the way. He wasn't very good at reading signs. The Bond helped him cheat.

'You are,' he confirmed again as he backed up further.

The space gave me just what I needed to pour my smoothie into a glass and put more distance between us.

'I'm not. But it seems awfully odd that you're over Kali so soon. She didn't turn out to be what you wanted?' It was a low blow, and I knew it. I took a sip and put the counter between us.

'Leave her out of this,' he growled and stalked to the fridge. He started getting out food and refused to meet my gaze.

'Why? I thought you guys were on again. That's what Lili said.' Okay, verbal manipulation was not a tactic I liked to use with Travis, but sometimes it worked.

'Lili didn't say anything of the sort. I know what she would have said.' He turned to face me, a flash of purple in his eyes before it was gone again. He knew I knew about the oath.

'Whatever. Where's Lili's list?' I was done with the conversation. If he wasn't going to tell me about Kali, he didn't have any right to try to cross the friendship line between us.

He pointed to the piece of paper on the dining table. Smoothie in hand, I went to look it over. Her handwriting was neat and in a cursive I always wished I'd been able to master. On her list: Tutankhamen, the Temple of Giza, the Sphinx, the pyramids, the Valley of the Death. All great places, but we wouldn't be able to make it to everything in one day. We might have to go back tomorrow too.

I felt Lili stir and thought it was only fair to warn her. *Good morning, sunshine. I'd be careful when you come down. Travis is a little volatile today. Approach with caution.*

39

Dammit, Lucy, what did you do? Lili was going to be down quicker than I'd thought.

Nothing. He started it, I replied.

I sipped at my smoothie. Travis looked up from his prep and stared at me.

'Poached or scrambled?' he asked.

I wanted to reply neither, because I couldn't stomach anything, but it was his white flag. 'Poached, thanks.'

He nodded and went back to work. Lili slipped into the room and nudged my back. I rolled my eyes at her.

'So I'm thinking of taking you guys to the Valley of the Dead first. I have an ancestor who I think you'll be excited to see.' I pointed to the list and Lili stifled a yawn.

'Sounds like a plan to me. Trav, is there bacon? Tell me there's bacon.'

Travis laughed and it set something inside me at ease. 'Oh, come on, like I would be cooking breakfast without bacon. Of course there's bacon, Lils.'

'Good. I'm not on this weird meatless thing that Lucy has going on.' Lili poked Travis in the ribs and he squirmed.

I smiled at the two of them. I wanted their kind of relationship without Travis' need to ruin it. 'Hey, Trav, do you want to try out Dev's car? It's a Carrera.'

The room fell silent. Even the cooking stopped temporarily.

'You have to be kidding me? Like I'm going to say no to that.' He glanced over his shoulder at me, and for the first time in a while, I saw my best friend staring back at me and not some hybrid of a person.

'Good. I'm going to go and check out some things, but you can take her for a test drive before we leave, yeah?' My white flag to Travis, and he nodded at my words. Lili's telepathic high-five lingered in my mind, and I tried not to show the smile that I could feel creeping into the corners of my mouth.

'Still thinking of going to culinary school instead of uni next year, Trav?' Lili asked.

'Mhm. More so now than before, because food.'

That was the last I heard of the conversation before I left the room.

IN THE SAFE haven of Dad's study, I took a seat behind the sturdy mahogany desk. It was lined with gold detail, green leather and was clear of any clutter. Unlike my own desk at home that was filled with notebooks, sticky notes, pens and random crystals. But Dad had to run an empire and he was good at what he did because of it.

The office held some heavy memories. I was trying to make sure that none of them resurfaced because they hurt too much, but I also didn't want to relive being power raped. Spells that were intended to play with the will of others were a form of power rape, and as practicing witches, using magick was a jail-able offence among the humans. Practicing magick was illegal, just as much as much as being a metaphysical being. Power rape was punishable by stripping the power of the witch in question, or even death. I had never seen what that looked like or what it even felt like but I had heard about it from Hunter, whose family came from a long line of knowledgeable and powerful witches.

I was a descendant of Nefertiti, the first female pharaoh. The history books left out that she was a witch, it was left out history because her husband Aten, wanted to unite the people under a single god and magick wasn't a part of that, but my family was living proof that she was.

My attention moved away from the desk to the walls, where there was a painted portrait of myself. My brown hair, grey eyes and sun-kissed skin stared back at me. It was eerie to see a younger version of myself. My attention moved from my portrait to the next one and I came face to face with my twin brother, Devin. His eyes were a tad darker, just as his hair was, but his skin was not as touched by the sun as mine, but had enough colour to tell that we were twins. The last picture was of Destiny, her flame-coloured hair the only tell that she took after the Ryder family and not the Lebashky family.

Behind each portrait was a safe, put in place to help us get excited to hide trinkets and take responsibility for our own things. Dad had always had a funny sense of humour, but also a weird way of teaching us lessons. The portraits were two years old and had been completed while we were back in Melbourne, after ... after the loss of Devin and Destiny.

The house echoed the sadness that I felt when I looked at the picture of Devin. It was like a part of me was missing, and as cliché as that sounded, it was true. I had never been able to put my finger on why, but part of me knew that he was still around. He wouldn't leave me. He wouldn't dare.

Almost as if the house knew I was thinking about him, his portrait swung open and a chill ran down my spine. Could Devin's spirit be haunting the house? The back of the portrait was blank, just like it always had been.

'You know, it's creepy that you're doing this,' I said out loud. I hoped that whoever was around, heard. I pushed myself out of the chair and walked towards the portrait and stared at the safe in the wall. The code would be random, but I knew my brother well enough that it wouldn't be. As I keyed in our birthday, it didn't budge, and my whole body froze. We never kept secrets from one another. It was hard when you had a weird twin-bond thing where we could always tell when the other person lied, so we just stopped lying. Or at least that was what I'd thought.

I tried our mum's birthday next. Nothing.

Dad's birthday came up with the same thing. Just as Destiny's birthday.

It had never been this hard, and I knew that there was something I was missing. I searched around the room to see if there was somewhere he could have left a clue. I backed away from the safe and stared at it.

Devin would have changed the code the last time he was here in the house, and that last time was just before he disappeared.

'The last time I saw him alive,' I muttered to myself and walked back over to the safe. I turned the dial to eighteen, then six, then eleven. June 18, 2012, or *Paoni*, which was pronounced Ba-oo-neh in the Ancient Egyptian months, which was scratched into the backing of his portrait. I was an idiot. How did I not see that? I ran my fingers over the scratching and realised that he had glamoured it. A glamour held in place as long as the person who had cast it was still alive or you didn't stare too hard at it.

Could this be proof that he was still alive? It had to be.

The safe clicked and the door released. I pulled it open and inside there were trinkets, cards and memorabilia from times past, but what drew my attention was the letter that was addressed to me.

Devin's handwriting was illegible; the scratchy block letters always felt like home. Even when I had to ask him what it said.

My fingers shook as I held the letter in my hand. I wanted to open it right then, but I didn't know if I was strong enough to handle what was inside. Could there be a lead as to where he was? Or what had happened? What if it had something more in it?

More questions spiralled through my mind as I stared at it. This couldn't be real. I had gone so long without a clue about what happened to them and this could be something that could change all of that.

'What's wrong?' Lili said as she burst into the room. The Bond came in handy in times like this; I didn't need to say anything and she just got it.

I turned around and held the note up to her. I didn't know how to find the words to tell her, but she could recognised Devin's handwriting just as well as my own.

'Holy shit,' she said as she covered her mouth in surprise.

She knew exactly what this meant.

'I felt your spike in emotion and I came. What do you need?'

'I don't know if I want to read this, or what it will say. It could be an innocent note, but it could be so much more. Lili, this note could have been there the whole time. The whole fucking time. And I have avoided coming back here for two years because I didn't want the memories that the house had to give to me. And if this was here the whole time ... Lili ...'

'I know, but we're here now, and there has to be a reason why now is the right time. You can't beat yourself up for this. You didn't know.'

On some level I knew she was right, but I also knew that she wasn't. This had been here for a long time, or at least it could have been. The last time I was here I hadn't seen a note, and I could have sworn I opened his safe, could the magick of the house have hidden it from me? There was no way that I could be sure. I couldn't trust my memory two years ago. Not when it came to Devin and Destiny. It was clouded by grief. Not that the grief hadn't disappeared. I still had flashes of deep, hot pain. I missed them more than I could put into words.

'You know that's not going to happen, Lili.'

'I know. I could say something, but I knew that you probably won't hear it. Are you okay?' she asked.

'Can you close the door?' I asked her, and I made my way to the leather couch against the wall. I had to read the letter now, or I would lose my nerve.

'Sure.'

It would be easier for Travis to lose track of what we were saying, because he wouldn't be able to hear. It was the only place that I knew a shifter couldn't hear a word. Dad had made a passing comment about this being the only safe space he could talk, and I had never understood it until now.

'Why does Travis want to be such an arse about this?' I really wanted to know, and if Lili could give me some insight into his behaviour it would make way better.

'He wants his shot. I did tell him that it wouldn't be a good idea, but you and I both know what Travis is like when he sets his mind to something. It's not going to be easy for him to back down. What's the cliché that we use?'

'He's like a dog with a bone.' I sighed. This wasn't what I wanted.

A weird silence fell between us. I turned the letter around to open it. No words were needed from Lili, but she wrapped an arm around my waist to give me support.

Lucy,

If you're reading this, then it means that what Destiny and I tried to do has failed and we're gone. I'm sorry. We had a choice and we had to keep you out of it. I hope that you can forgive us for that. We are just being protective older siblings. It's really important that you read this letter really carefully. Dest and I are about to leave to try and stop a force that is making life difficult for us and for you. They want to make sure that you're weakened; we don't know why, we just know that you're the ultimate target. If you read this, go back home. They can't get you when you're in Melbourne. I hope that you can go on with your life, but if I know you, I know you won't. Just remember that we love you, we always will, and I stand by my promise of never leaving you. I'm always right there next to you. Always making sure that you're going on the right path. Even if I'm not breathing.

But I know you and you're reading this letter when you shouldn't be, and you're in Egypt when you should be back home. In saying that, the house will be working weirdly; you didn't notice it when we were here but it will make sure you're reliving memories. Some of them will be good, some of them won't be. I know that Lili and Travis won't be far from you. Keep them closer than you ever have. The Bond is going to save you; try not to let it go.

There is an evil coming. It's linked to our descendants. The descendants of Nefertiti. Destiny and I checked through the whole line and there is an evil out to get us, I don't know why. We're going out to find out, but if we don't come back ... be careful.

I love you.
Devin

The letter dropped out of my hand like it was hot.

'They didn't die. Or maybe they did. Fuck,' I said. Lili was staring at me like I was going crazy, but I wasn't. The weird twin thing that everyone asked about had always been a sort of crutch, and when Devin was gone, I didn't have that feeling where I knew what he was thinking before he was thinking it. In fact, there was an empty void where I used to be able to feel him. That was what had made their disappearances so hard; it felt like they had died and I was alone. And they promised they would never leave me. It was different to the Bond because there was a weird magick to that, and the bond Devin and I had was always just so natural.

'Luce?' Lili said. 'What did the ...?' She picked up the letter, and I gave her a moment to read it. 'What the shit? Are you ...? Lucy, what does this mean when it says you're a descendant of Nefertiti? Like the pharaoh Nefertiti? The legend?'

My shoulders rose to my ears and stayed there. I didn't like that I had lied to her and Travis, but then again, it wasn't really a lie—it was more of an omission.

'Yeah ... only it's all real. My mother's line are direct descendants. So ... I'm a bit like royalty when people figure out who I look like.'

'Wh-why didn't you ever say anything?'

I stared at her and wondered how much of the truth I could tell her. I mean, I had never really kept anything from her, but this was the one thing that I never shared because I didn't want her to look at me like I was different. I wasn't. I was still the same woman who was her best friend.

'I didn't know how to. It wasn't something that ever came up in Melbourne. Only when I'm in here. I ... I just ... it's a lot. I don't like to really talk about it.'

'Does it make you any different?'

'Not really.'

'Does it change who you are as a person?'

'Well ... no.'

'Then you really don't have a good reason to say otherwise. You are still you, and you're still my best friend.'

Instead of saying anything, I just pulled her into a hug. Some things were better said with actions than words. I was lucky to

47

have Lili as a friend, and for the last two years she'd been like a sister to me after everything we had been through. The loving sister I'd always wanted and never gotten from Destiny.

There was an evil out there that wanted to do something truly terrible to my family and to me. If Devin's words were true, Lili and Travis were here for the ride.

Whatever this evil was, it would be no match for a werewolf, a Watcher and a witch.

CHAPTER SEVEN

Nefertiti
Epep 2014

I OPENED my eyes for what felt like the first time in a long time, and I could feel her. I could feel my latest descendant for the first time in two years. She was close again.

This time I would not let her get away. I could not.

In my dreams, I had known she would come. She would not be able to stay away, and in the Illuminate Year, she would not be able to resist.

She would want to know what happened and that was all I needed.

I waited for Karrept to bring me back and he would. Two years ago we tried, but it was not the right time, she was too strong. I remembered feeling her body and just how powerful she was.

Her body had felt like home, something that I ached to feel after being displaced for so long. The new age, the new way of moving, made her different. It made me want it more.

I would have her body.

I could not wait to feel Karrept's body again. And while the years had changed and the language had changed, there were two things that would be the same: I would be free of Aten and would be able to finally be with Karrept.

I could hardly wait.

CHAPTER EIGHT

Lucy
Epep 2014

'ARE YOU ALMOST READY, LUCE?' Lili said from the doorway. I looked at her through the mirror. Her strawberry blonde hair was pulled back in a bun and she had on leggings too, except she wore a white singlet with a blue shirt over it. It was almost too proper for the tombs, but she liked her clothes. Her clothes mimic mine, minus the shirt. I had a t-shirt, legging and heavy steel capped boots. They would be hot but would save my feet.

'Yeah, I am. Where's Trav?' I grabbed my phone and the letter before I turned away from the mirror. I picked up my shoulder bag and walked out of my room without a second thought. It took everything in me to not adjust

'Kitchen.'

'Where he belongs, hmm?'

'I can hear you, you know,' Travis yelled from downstairs. I rolled my eyes. Of course he could—he had werewolf hearing. *Selective* werewolf hearing.

This was one of the times he wanted to listen in.

I shook my head and we made our way downstairs and into the kitchen.

'Didn't your mother tell you it was rude to eavesdrop?'

'Yup, but I'm a wolf; she also told me that I couldn't help it all of the time.'

I raised an eyebrow at him. 'You have excellent control.'

He grinned at me. 'I know, but sometimes it's fun to pretend I don't.'

I took the letter out of my pocket and put it on the kitchen bench. 'You might want to read this.'

'I don't need to. I heard you and Lili last night.'

'You didn't say anything,' I said.

'We weren't exactly talking last night and I wasn't going to push it.' Travis nudged a plate that had a sandwich on it.

'They're not dead. They can't be,' I murmured and picked up a triangle. There was spinach and some sort of white meat in there, but that was all I could see from this side. I took a bite and tasted mayo and a hint of cheese. Delicious.

'Maybe, but I'm more interested in the part that says you're a descendant of Nefertiti. You're practically royalty here too? That's pretty cool. Why was the taxi driver so rude to you, then?'

On the way here, the taxi driver had called us tourists, and rightly so. If I hadn't been in the car, Lili and Travis would have been tourists. But I'd spoken back to him in perfect Arabic, and he'd left in a hurry.

'That's just the way people are sometimes, but it's fine. I prefer it that way. You know I don't really like the attention that much.'

'Yeah, but what's the difference between here and home?'

'People don't bow in front of me at home? I mean, it's possible. But here, if I'm recognised, it's a pretty big deal. The culture here is a mixture of Muslims and really old worshippers who think that the gods and goddesses of Ancient Egypt are still present.' I shrugged. It was a weird dichotomy of religion in the city centre, and it was obvious which part of the city was which. Even without the Nile separating the sides.

'Okay, *that* is weird.'

'I thought you'd be used to that sort of thing, Trav. Don't the wolves do it for you?' Lili said with a smirk as she popped a blueberry into her mouth.

'That's not even funny,' Travis said and rolled his eyes.

'What am I missing here?' I asked.

'Nothing,' Travis said quickly.

'Well, Trav gets some sort of special treatment when he's not getting challenged. He pulls rank and people bow to him.' Amusement coloured Lili's eyes as she looked at me, and I caught on to what kind of bowing people were doing.

'Gross,' I said and took another bite out of the sandwich and walked over to the console that had a bowl of keys on it. Inside were various keys for doors, cabinets and safes, but there were also the keys to cars. I shoved a few blueberries into my mouth with one hand.

'Heads up, Trav,' I said with a mouthful of blueberries as I tossed the keys at Travis.

'Ohhhhhh. Let's go see this baby purr.'

Lili raised an eyebrow. 'It's weird hearing that come out of your mouth ... shouldn't it be bark or something?'

Travis snorted. 'What am I, a dog?'

Lili and I looked at each other and nodded together. 'Yes.'

'I'm offended. I'm a wolf. Much more intelligent.'

I don't know about that, I thought. He could do better on that front.

Egypt
Paoni 2012

I WOKE up and padded downstairs to grab some orange juice. From the kitchen window, I could see the car: black, sleek, beautiful. The Porsche 911 Carrera was sitting in the driveway. *Our* driveway. There was a big red bow on it, and I knew exactly who it was for.

'Dev. Devin! There's a Porsche in the driveway, have you seen it? It's, oh my god, gorgeous.' I ran into his room to tell him.

'What do you mean there's a Porsche?' he murmured, his voice thick with sleep.

'Wake up, wake up, sleepyhead.'

'Go away, Luce, it's not time to get up.'

'Come on. It is. It's time, very much so, there is a car in the driveway.'

Devin was resistant to waking up, which wasn't new; he needed his sleep because he hardly got any. Too busy dream walking, or that's what Mum said.

'Dev, you can sleep later. There is a car. Get up. Get up, get up!' I chanted.

It felt like hours passed with me pestering him, but the more he woke up, the more excited he seemed—which was better than trying to murder me.

He got dressed and rubbed the sleep from his eyes before he bolted outside with me at his heels.

'Wow, does it work?' he asked and Dad grinned.

Devin ran his fingers over the hood of the car, his touch gentle, loving, caring. It was like he didn't want to break it. *It's a damn Porsche, it's not going to break if you touch it*, I wanted to tell him, but he was too engrossed in the car.

'What sort of question is that? Of course it works. Do you want to take it for a spin?' Dad threw Devin the keys.

He blinked at the keys in his hand. 'This is for me?' he asked.

Dad just grinned with a glint in his eyes that was all too knowing. 'You really think I'm going to drive that thing? I'm too old for that.'

'You're never too old for a Porsche, Daddy,' I commented back as I hugged him and stared at the leather seats. It was almost too beautiful to get into.

'Hey, Dest, come and see what Dad got Dev.' She was probably on the phone somewhere. I didn't care what she said, she needed to get herself out of the stupid friend funk she'd been in for the whole trip. She only wanted to spend time to with her friends and not with the family. It was like I was invisible to her, but then again, what else was that something new?

'What?' she said as she walked closer. Her eyes rolled and I saw red.

'Why do you have to do that? You have to ruin everything with your attitude.'

'What are you talking about?' Destiny said as she whipped around to look at me.

'I saw you roll your eyes. What are you rolling your eyes about?' Anger crept into my voice, and I felt my cheeks start to burn.

'Josh's best friend has a car just like that,' she said, matter of fact.

'Are you serious? Are you actually serious right now? Who are you?' She was a cold-hearted bitch and I wished, really wished, that she would just get over herself. Why was my older sister like this? Sometimes I wondered if she had been dropped on her head or if she was adopted. It would say a lot about her if she was.

'Girls. That is enough,' Dad said, trying to stop the fight before it happened. 'Devin wants to take it for a test ride, and that's only going to happen if you decide to play along with one another. Or I will have to make sure that both of you don't do anything for the rest of our trip. Understood?'

'Yes, Dad,' we both chorused.

'And, Destiny, that does mean your phone. It will be mine if you don't listen to me.'

'But Dad—' she started to complain and was cut off with a hand.

'Destiny. No. You are both going to be nice. You're sisters and you need to start acting like it.'

I looked at Dad and could see that he was disappointed in us, and I felt guilty. I was willing to try to be nice if Destiny tried too. Otherwise all bets were off. I didn't want him to be upset. He was just trying to be a good dad.

Egypt
Epep 2014

'It really does work, doesn't it?' Travis said with a smirk, and it pulled me out of the memory. I had forgotten to put my shield up again and felt the memory slip through.

Lili and I stalled in our movements and watched Travis run his hands over the car like it was the most precious thing in the world. What was it with guys and cars? Watching Travis do that made me ache to talk to Hunter.

'Pretty sure it does. Are you going to get in it or just keep worshipping it like a woman?' Lili commented saying what I was thinking.

'I'm sure I could ...' he started.

'Matthews, if you finish that sentence, I will make sure that you are in a world of pain. Understand?' I could already hear where that sentence was going, and I was not up for an image of him worshipping my body. We just got past it.

'Oh, come on.'

'If you keep it up, I will take the keys from you and drive *my* car. Actually, give them to me. I'll drive there, you can drive back.' I held out my hands, and he protectively held the keys close to his chest.

'No way. You gave them to me. I've earned this ride.'

'Fine, fine, but get in quick or I'll take them from you. I'm calling shotgun, though.'

'But ... the seats are so cramped,' Lili said.

I laughed. 'Gotta be faster next time. You're out of practice.'

Lili's brother had been murdered, and she was an only child now, but it was a good enough excuse to be out of practice with the whole sibling thing.

'Guys, I want to leave this century. Just get in,' I said.

Travis unlocked the door and I moved the seat forward for Lili. She poked my side and I squirmed before she climbed into the back. I pushed the seat back and slid into the car. Travis did the same as he put the key in the ignition and gunned the accelerator. This was going to be a fun drive.

I DIRECTED Travis to the stables that weren't far from our family's first tomb. Mum had left her dear friends Moe and Aziza in charge. I had loved talking to them as a child, and they had been here forever, but today it was someone I didn't recognise. Aziza had just given birth to her third child and they were out for the month.

'I wish you guys could have met Moe and Aziza, you would have loved them,' I said.

'Uhhh, I have a question.' Travis scratched the back of his neck. 'What are we doing here? I thought we were going to see some tombs today.'

'We are, but we need a horse to get to where we really need to go today.'

'Horse?' Travis' voice rose an octave higher than normal.

'Yeah, we can't get there by foot. I mean, technically we could use a camel, but a horse will be faster.'

'A camel would be better.'

Lili stopped fiddling around with her bag and stepped closer. 'Are you afraid of horses, Trav?'

He pulled down the collar of his T-shirt and avoided eye contact with me or Lili.

'You are!' I couldn't believe it. He'd never said anything about what he was afraid of, and we were about to get on horses and he was scared of them.

'You have to be kidding me,' Lili whispered. 'Trav is scared of horses.'

'Shhh! Don't say it any louder, will you? It'll ruin my image.'

I snorted and was about to say something when my eye caught a sun catcher hanging from the door.

That was new—I didn't remember it being there last time. Curiosity took over and I brushed my fingers over it. I gasped as a vision clouded my view.

'THIS IS IT. We have to do this. You know we do,' Destiny said as she hung up the sun catcher.

'No way,' Dev said from the base of the ladder Destiny was using. 'We made a promise, Dest. We can't go back on it.'

'Lucy will be okay. This is for her safety. We're making sure she doesn't have to go through this.'

'What about ...?'

'No, don't. Don't think about that. The sun catcher is enchanted. It should make her walk away, gush at Aziza and Moe and forget she was even here.'

'What if her powers go wonky ... like ours?' Devin commented and tightened his grip on the ladder as Destiny came down it.

'I'm hoping they won't. It shouldn't affect her. She's different.'

'I'm not so sure about that, Dest. She is stronger than we both give her credit. She's going to really hate us, you know that, right?'

'She already hates me. It doesn't make much of a difference.' She glanced out past the door to the stables and sighed.

I JUMPED BACK from the sun catcher like it burned me. It fell to the floor of the stables, and I stared at it incredulously, hoping what I'd seen wasn't true.

'They were *here*.'

Travis and Lili looked at me oddly. 'Luce, what are you talking about?' Lili spoke up first, while Travis bent down to pick up the sun catcher. He held it up by its string and it twirled on its own.

'Devin and Destiny, they were here. They must have got horses and gone to the tomb too, but they enchanted that'—I pointed at the sun catcher in Travis' hand—'to make me turn back.'

Lili frowned and took the sun catcher from Travis. It was an Eye of Horus, with a crystal in the centre of the eye. It shimmered in the light and threw rainbows inside the stall.

'That's such an interesting thing to enchant. I can't feel anything from it, but I believe you. Maybe we should take this with us.'

Part of me wanted to take something that my siblings had enchanted, but the other part didn't want to look at it.

It was a reminder of them being gone. I shook my head.

'We should get going. We don't want to burn any more daylight.'

And I didn't want to get caught in the desert when dusk fell.

CHAPTER NINE

Nefertiti
Athor 1348 BC

MY MOTHER WALKED into the room, her body paint flawless and shimmering in the flicker of the flame. Her bright eyes were lined with kohl and her wig was meticulously straight, the long raven locks held in place with a headdress that was just for decoration.

'Nefertiti, you are not ready! We are due to be at the celebrations now. You are going to make us late.'

I did not care for the party. It was supposed to be for potential suitors—like I had any choice in the decision.

The choice was already made: I was to wed Akhenaten. My mother had chosen him to be my husband, and I had to abide by her choice. It may have been different for someone who was not of noble blood, but I was not so lucky. I looked at my mother and sighed. She did mean well, but I wanted to avoid this.

She fussed over my face and I let her; it was easier to do so than fighting her. She would not be around for much longer—I had foreseen her death—and to help her feel as though she was still a mother to me, I let her fuss. I did not want to explain what I had foreseen.

No one knew about my abilities, or what else I had seen; it was like it was a secret that I couldn't tell anyone.

As Mother finished my makeup, I sat down so that she could fit my headdress. Once I was adorned with crystals and the best in the land, she dubbed me ready.

'Was that so hard?' she chastised me.

'Yes,' I said and raised an eyebrow at her.

She clicked her tongue and shook her head. 'Nefertiti, you are always the only one I worry enough about.'

'But there is no need.'

'A mother will always worry. You will learn that with your own children when it comes to them.'

Children ... I was still a child myself; I could see it in the way that my breasts were still growing and my hips were not yet wide enough to bear a child. My bleed was consistent every season, so it was no surprise that I was to be wed soon.

Without another word, we left my chambers and walked through to the great hall. The light cast by the first torch was enough to see through to the main ball area. As we entered there was a hush in the room, and all eyes turned to me. I tried my best to not squirm in my skin; that much attention was a little much, not that they would be able to tell. The pretence I wore was one of confidence, even when I was not remotely confident. I looked around the royal room and found familiar faces, that of my brothers and sisters, but there was one that was new. He still had his hair, which meant he was new to the priesthood but also that he was yet to be paired with a prospective ruler.

Our eyes met across the room and things down low tightened. I wanted to have his skin pressed against mine and I wanted to know what he tasted like. The rest of the party fell away from me and as I moved from Mother, she hissed for me not to go anywhere, but I didn't care. I walked over to him and stood in front of him. His chestnut-coloured eyes smiled as I moved closer, and he rubbed his nose with his thumb and grinned at me. There was a boyish charm to it that reminded me of my brothers, but there was a hint of mischief that they never had.

'Princess,' he cooed, and I had never wanted to push someone against the wall before and ravage them so.

'Please, just Nefertiti. You are new.'

He smiled. 'I am. You are very observant. I am meeting with Akhenaten to be his priest. Are you here to have your suitor chosen for you, Nefertiti?'

'I am. And your name?'

His smile grew to a grin, lighting up his whole face.

'Karrept,' a voice said from behind me, and I turned to see Akhenaten jog up to us. 'You are here. I do hope your travels were easy. Nefertiti, I hope you are not bothering my new priest.'

I blinked and looked between them. Karrept seemed to want to reach out to touch me, and my body swayed closer to him, but I was looking at my brother. 'Not at all. I was curious about the new arrival. It is rare to see a priest with his hair before it's gone.'

Karrept chuckled. 'I wanted to hold on to my hair for as long as I could.'

'It is a good head of hair.' Akhenaten laughed.

'Indeed it is.'

'Nefertiti, are you ready for the ceremony?' Akhenaten held out a hand to me and I stared at it.

Was I? This ceremony would name which of my suitors would be my husband. My brothers would be there to help raise my status, but I knew that it meant that one of them would be my suitor, to keep the blood pure. I wished that I had more of a choice than this. Maybe my children would get the chance to have a say in who they would wed.

'I am.' I took his hand, and even as I did, a small shiver ran down my spine, and I did everything in my power to hide it from him.

'Good. I think you suitors will be infinite.'

'Do you? I think we both know who will come out on top, though.'

Akhenaten laughed. It was deep and rich, almost like he had practiced how it was exactly meant to sound when he was alone.

'You are too wholesome sometimes,' he said.

'I am sure that there will be a suitor you will admire more than the rest,' Karrept said.

I was drawn to his energy, the boyish look in his eyes and the way he seemed to look straight through me. His fingers brushed my elbow and I wanted to moan in delight. That simple touch said more than anyone else could or do.

I wished he would be a suitor, but as a man of the priest-hood, he would be off limits. No matter what.

'That is kind of you, Karrept,' I said. Akhenaten guided his priest away without another word, and I watched them go.

Karrept turned to look at me with a smile on his face. My knees felt weak and I knew that smile would be the end of it all.

CHAPTER TEN

Lucy
Epep 2014

TRAVIS CLUTCHED me tightly against his body as we rode to the tomb, my mind spiralling about Devin and Destiny. They had been there and tried to ward me off with magick. I couldn't understand why they would do that. It seemed like their whole time here was spent making sure I didn't follow them, but if they really thought that was who I was, my siblings didn't know what I was willing to do to get them back.

I came to Egypt to find them and so far … they were making it difficult. The memories that surfaced like a movie, the secrets and now finding the sun catcher. What was going on? Some would stop and go home, but this just made me more determined. And I wasn't going to stop until I found out the truth.

As we came to a steady stop, Travis' grip still held tight. As a pre-shifting wolf he was trampled on by a horse. I could see that memory loud and clear in my mind, and I should have had him ride with Lili but he had jumped on the horse with me. Most animals knew that werewolves were dangerous and it was easier for him to ride with me because my horse—Stardust—knew me and she trusted me, and by default would trust anyone who rode with me. Travis was a born wolf, but as he hit puberty he shifted for the first time and was still learning to control it.

He was better about his control, but strong emotions and hormones made it difficult.

'I am riding with Lili on the way back,' he said as he dismounted from the horse, his legs a little shaky.

'Horses don't like wolves, Trav. Hector might not let you on him,' I said and dismounted next, taking Stardust's reins and tying them to the fence. Lili pulled up Hector next to us and she dismounted and did the same with him.

'But he'll understand that I won't hurt him.'

I raised an eyebrow and smirked. 'Trav, you are a werewolf who can kill a horse with a twist of a wrist. They're going to be more scared of you because of it.'

He straightened up and glanced between me and the horse. 'Well, when you put it that way ...'

'I'm sorry, I'm mad at the sun catcher and Moe and Aziza who weren't even there. And I took it out on you. I just pushed Stardust really hard, when I shouldn't have.'

He wrapped an arm around my shoulders and pulled me into a hug.

'I forgive you, this time,' he whispered into my hair. He was six foot two and I was five foot six.

I let him hold on to me, and when it felt natural, I pulled away and looked at Lili, who was taking the tomb in. I was sure she was memorising what it looked like so that she could pull up an image later. Maybe work it into some sort of inspiration when it came to a fashion collection. Loads of sand and pillars with hieroglyphics, ornate carvings and weather-rotted stone.

'Where are we?' Lili asked.

The tomb was mostly untouched. It was old, just like all of the others, but there was a difference. It was my ancestor's tomb; Nefertiti was buried in here, and until she was ready for the world to see where she rested, it was a coveted secret that my family held on to so tightly. It was why we had to get horses exclusively from our own stables. They were the only horses who knew how to get there, and as each horse was laid to rest, a new one was trained to know the exact position. It was why we kept the stables. With all of the beauty of the tomb, it didn't stop me from thinking back all of those years ago when there were people here who made this with their bare hands and then entombed a dead Nefertiti inside.

'Welcome to Nefertiti's tomb,' I murmured and motioned to the entry.

It was sandy and dusty at the same time, lit by the concave discs that caught the sun outside and filtered through the enclave. The tomb opened up to a room that was the official waiting room for tourists, or it would be if we let anyone in.

When she was ready to be found, we would be the first family to willingly allow visitors inside. If we didn't, people would die, and having that on our conscience was a good enough reason to open it up so that no one trespassed in the tomb.

The walls of the tomb—on the inside, at least—had once been filled with brightly coloured paintings of gods and goddesses, although the deeper you dived into the tomb, the scenery changed and the paintings that covered the walls were tales of Nefertiti's life, including those of her lovers and her abilities.

Lili whistled and Travis coughed, their noises pulling me out of my thoughts.

'Come on, we should take a look around. Pay special attention to the walls; the deeper we get into the tomb, the more you will be able to decipher about Nefertiti's life, if you look close enough.'

'It wasn't very well known, but as you can see, we kind of

decorated it to help keep people from mysteriously dying. Human curiosity and all keeps them coming back. But we have kept it a family secret. It's not on any of the maps. Remember the article about Nefertiti's tomb? They were really close to finding it then, but the wards went back up before they could. Trav, did you feel any magick just before the tomb came into view?'

'To be honest, I was too busy holding on for dear life, but now that you mention it, yeah. There was definitely a shiver from the magick.'

'That's to make sure people don't find it. Nefertiti's tomb is off limits or well...hidden from the public. Eventually it'll be found, but not until she's ready.' I looked at Travis, who just nodded. Lili's eyes were huge with excitement.

'It's amazing. Can we go inside?' she asked, not hiding the awe in her voice.

'Yeah. We just have to make sure that ... Oh. Hello, you're n —' My jaw dropped as a man with perfectly chiselled features and deep green eyes hidden by black curls stared back at me. He was wearing the typical guard attire: khaki pants, a beige shirt and a black scarf that was wrapped around his neck—when a sandstorm kicked up, it was often wrapped around the Guardian's face to protect them. There was also a staff on hand and a sickle, not to mention a jacket in case it got cold.

'Miss Lucy. You are here. This is a surprise.' His eyes were wide; he was just as shocked to see me as I was to see him.

'Sam? Samjate Jr, I can't believe it.' I wanted to hug him but a deep stone of regret settled in the pit of my stomach. 'Why are you here? Wait. No. *No*. It can't be true.'

'You did not hear? I thought your mother would have told you.'

'Oh god. I'm sorry. Are you okay?'

He nodded. Typical stoic Tomb Guardian response.

'Luce?' I felt Travis at my back and squeezed his hand.

'This is Sam. He's the Tomb Guardian; it's a job that's passed down from father to son, and the last time I was here, his father was the one guarding it.'

I wanted to push for more information. How long had it been since his father's death? I wanted to find out why no one had told me, but most of all I wanted to do was comfort Sam. He would still be mourning the loss of his dad, and the heaviness I felt in my heart made me want to cry. I'd grown up with Sam; we used to play in the tomb together as kids. Our families had spent a lot of time down here making sure that the wards were in place, because we all knew that one day the public would find this site and we wanted to protect as much of it as possible.

Sam was the first boy to kiss me too. We were three.

'Hello. You are most welcome to come and take a look around.'

'Thanks, Sam,' I replied for everyone. Lili and Travis didn't wait for me as they moved deeper into the tomb. I stood off to the side and awkwardly squeezed Sam's shoulder. He nodded at me again, but I saw the sadness in his eyes. He was nineteen and too young to be here. Tomb Guardians were trained to take over from their fathers at any age, but mostly they waited until they were older than twenty-one. Most Guardian trainees married early so that the next Tomb Guardian would already have a family and a son to pass on the legacy.

Samjate Jr was now married to the tomb.

He wouldn't get a family. The tomb would not have another Guardian if he died.

BITTERNESS FILLED my body and I kicked a stone. It skidded in the sand and hit the wall. 'This sucks,' I murmured.

'What do you mean?' Travis asked.

I looked up from my shoes and found the werewolf looking

back at me, his eyes purple to see better, but there was enough light in here that he didn't need to. It was probably a safety precaution.

'Sam's father is dead, which means that he is here to keep an eye on the tomb and is able to help if something goes awry. But he's our age and won't get to have a family. Destiny and Devin were the last ones here. I don't know if they had anything to do with Sam's dad's death, but if they did, I feel even worse.'

Lili searched the room, and I watched her as I sat down on a fallen stone pillar. We were in the main area of the tomb, surrounded by all the things that were buried with Nefertiti: jewellery, goblets, plates, books, clips; anything and everything that Nefertiti would need in her afterlife. There was also no shortage of gold. There were pieces scattered between my mother's family that were all locked up and away from prying eyes. Through the door was a hallway that led to where Nefertiti's corpse lay, dormant and alone for so many years.

'What makes you think that?' Travis asked.

'The sun catcher was spelled to make me turn around. The house is doing something weird, and I get the feeling that we're not alone.' I pulled my knees to my chest and rested my chin on them. This pillar had been where it was for years. Some time ago, there had been an earthquake hard enough to rock the tomb and bring a few down.

'This is turning out to be a different kind of holiday, hey?' Lili said.

'You're telling me,' I murmured.

Lili picked up the trinkets and was in awe. I knew she would love the tomb, and I figured coming to Nefertiti's tomb was a better option than going to one that was already discovered; she could touch what she wanted before seeing other tombs where she wouldn't be allowed to touch anything.

'You need to release some of the tension,' Travis said. 'Maybe you should voice what you feel.'

'How?' I raised an eyebrow.

'Scream.'

I shook my head, but I couldn't hide the smile. 'I can't do that. This is a place of resting, I would get shot.'

Or Sam would come running in and try to kill whatever was making me scream.

'Scream, Luce,' Travis pushed again.

'In your dreams.'

He smirked. 'You're right. In my dreams, but you need it.'

I shook my head again, and my eye caught on something. It wasn't there before when I'd swept the room, but all I could think about was that very spot. Travis opened his mouth to say more, but I held up a hand to silence him.

'What are you doing? Lucy?'

I wandered away from him and he was forgotten as I bent down to pick up a piece of paper. It was old and dingey and looked how I imagined papyrus would, but there was more than one. As soon as I touched it, something settled in my chest and I felt like it was mine. It whispered to me, like it was begging to tell me a secret. My fingers skimmed over the page and I could read the words, the images as familiar to me as my own writing.

'They're pages from a Book of the Dead,' I said in awe.

'Like in *The Mummy?*' Travis commented.

I went to respond at first but I unable to take my eyes off the beauty in my hand. It made everything I had ever seen look dull in comparison. 'That was based very loosely on mythology and stuff, but this is a Book of the Dead. There are many. Everyone was given a Book of the Dead to take with them to the next life or afterlife. It's supposed to have sacred spells to help them on their journey.'

'That doesn't look like a book,' Travis noted.

His comment made me do a double take before I stared at the pages.

'I know. I wonder where they belong,' I replied. 'I don't feel comfortable with this. We all know books aren't so innocent.'

The Mummy movies and Harry Potter didn't do anything to dispel that notion.

'Oh hey, that's treasure. Old, musty treasure, but treasure nonetheless. Can I see it?' Lili had a brush in her hand. She was determined to uncover something.

It had been a long time since there was anything of value to uncover in this tomb. That much was for sure. She excitedly took the pages out of my hands before I could tell her no.

'Lils. What are you doing?' I asked.

She sat down on the ground, crossed her legs under her and opened the first page. She handled the page with care, like she was touching the most finest of silks, and skimmed her fingers over the first page.

'It's read from right to left, isn't it? Not like we do, left to right, yeah?' She glanced to me for confirmation and I nodded.

'It's so beautiful,' she murmured.

I felt eyes on me and found Travis staring at me, instead of Lili, and I frowned.

I felt a hand brush against my chest and I shivered. It made me bring my fist up to my chest and clutch there, almost like I could hold my heart in my hands.

'Did you feel that?' I whispered to Lili, but she was oblivious.

Something wasn't right. The air changed, and I peered at Travis. He was on his feet, his eyes glowing a vibrant purple.

'Lili. You might need to put those pages down,' I said, this time feeling a chill in the air.

'Hang on. I'm trying to figure out if I can take a photo of this. It's so ...'

'Liliana, you're going to need to do it *now*.'

She glanced up at me and must have seen something in my face because she put them down.

I opened my mouth to speak, but the air was knocked out of

my lungs as I hit the wall. Spots exploded behind my eyes. I slid down the wall and landed on my side.

'Luce, can you hear me? Are you okay?' I could hear Travis' voice, the wolf thick in every syllable.

'I'm … fine,' I wheezed out as I tried to remember how to breathe.

'You were just thrown against the wall. You don't sound fine,' he replied.

'Are you guys okay?' I didn't have superhuman sight, so while they were in the part of the chamber that had light, I was in darkness.

'Yeah, we're fine. Where are you?' Lili answered for the both of them.

'Dark corner,' I replied.

'That's real descriptive,' Travis said.

A shuffle of feet sounded to my left.

'Who's there?' I called out.

An invisible fist hit my stomach and I doubled over. I wheezed as my back hit the wall again. A force swept my legs from under me, and I cried out with whatever air I had left.

'Lucy?'

I tried to find my voice, but the spots in my vision were worse, even in the dark, and I was having a hard time breathing. Every inhale felt like knives digging into my throat.

'Talk to me.' I could hear the worry in Trav's voice.

I was caught completely off guard.

'Luce!' Travis called out again.

Finding my voice, I called back, 'Tra—'

'Lucy! Where are you?' Sam's voice filled the tomb, louder and more demanding than Travis' own, and it was impossible to hear anything else. I closed my eyes and tried to focus on the rush of movements while I found Travis through our Bond. In my panicked state, I hadn't thought to reach out until I heard Sam's voice.

There is something in here, Travis. It's attacking me.

Fuck. Can you see anything? Are you okay?

No. Can't see a thing. I'm down and winded.

Hands gripped my arms and slammed me into the wall. I screamed. Or tried to. The entity breathed on me before it made a sound that filled my entire head. It was close to a scream but something else altogether. I tried to lift my hands up to cradle my head to stop the noise but I couldn't move them.

Nails clawed at my arms, and I tried to kick out to push it away, but I couldn't. I couldn't seem to get any momentum.

Light flicked in the corner of my vision. It was brief but enough.

'I can see you. Luce, are you ... oh god, that is ugly.' Travis' comment would have made me laugh if I wasn't being held against a wall.

I whimpered. 'Tra-vis.'

'Sorry. We're coming.'

I focused on the entity in front of me. It was angry, ugly and persistent. The entity was disfigured, with wisps of hair barely covering its face. It had hollowed and sunken cheekbones, no eyes and no teeth. As its nails dug into my arms, I could feel my energy getting pulled from my body. Fighting back was starting to seem useless, and I closed my eyes to make the pain go away.

A scream filled my head again, and when I opened my eyes, I saw light, bright as the rising sun, flash before it was gone. I could feel heat and saw a hint of fire. I looked up and saw Sam, who was breathing hard. He held a sickle sword in one hand and a torch in the other.

'Are you okay, Lucy?' He was all business and there was no sign of the happy-go-lucky boy I had grown up with.

I nodded.

Travis wrapped an arm around my waist and pulled me in close. 'What was it?'

'It's a spirit guardian. Specifically for a book, but I'm not sure which. There are a few books left in here.'

'We found—' Travis began, but I stepped on his toe to stop him from saying anything. If Sam knew about the pages, he'd be honour-bound to take them from us. And I wanted to look at them. There was no harm in looking at one. 'A cover. But no books. That's so odd.'

'Indeed. Are you okay?' The concern on his face made me want to hug him.

'I'm okay. A little shaky. That was … intense. It was like it was sucking energy out of me.'

He frowned. 'That can only come from one book. Are you sure you didn't find a book along with that cover?'

'We're sure,' Travis spoke up again. I think he got the point I was trying to make.

'Maybe you should call it a day. Find another tomb that is less likely to hurt you. This one has always been unlucky for descendants of Nefertiti, and I cannot afford to lose you.'

His version of saying I miss you. I squeezed his arm and smiled. He was all lean muscle and strength, a far cry from the scrawny boy that I'd grown up with..

I'D FORCED myself to get on Stardust and we made it home in one piece. Travis drove home with guidance from Lili as I sat in the back seat. Once we pulled into the driveway and Travis and Lili helped me out of the car, they led me inside to the couch where I was currently lying. Feeling useless.

'Well, that was anticlimactic. Sorry we couldn't do any more than the one tomb.'

My joints felt like they were on fire, and any time I moved a muscle, they creaked as though they needed a good oiling. The claw marks ached. They were deeper than I'd realised, and I was putting up with the pain because I didn't take pain meds, I didn't like that they masked the pain and didn't help fix the root of the pain. Travis had tried to talk me into letting him heal them. The look I gave him said more than any words. I didn't want to take a gulp of werewolf blood. Wulfie was the latest drug on the market and was also known to make you fly high, higher than any other drug in existence. In bigger doses, it also turned you into a werewolf. I would never let myself go to that extent, I didn't want to tempt my addictive personality and I didn't want to be closer to becoming a werewolf, if I could help it.

'Don't stress. It's not like you were expecting to get attacked by a spirit that wanted you dead,' Lili said as she sat down and pulled the pages from her bag. 'These are so beautiful.'

She handed them to me, and as I touched pages, I gasped and was hit with another memory.

'OH MY GOD, Dest, do you know what this is?' Devin marvelled.

'Are you ... is that what I think it is?'

'It's Nefertiti's Ode. It's what her lover made for her.' Devin turned the Book over in his hands. 'I think his name was Karrept.'

'Weird name. Wait, why does it look like a Book of the Dead? Like I could have sworn that this is what they looked like.' She poked at it with a finger, as if afraid that it would jump out at her.

'It must have been a cover for the Ode, so it would get into her burial chamber. It's gorgeous,' Devin said as he opened the cover.

'You seriously need to get into archaeology or something. You're good at this shit.' Destiny picked at her necklace and twirled it between her fingers.

He beamed. 'That's the plan.' He paused and ran a finger over the edge of the book. 'We can't leave it here.'

'Why not?' Destiny asked.

'Because it feels like it belongs to us. Hold it.' He handed her the Book. As soon as she had it in her hands, her eyes widened.

'We have to get it out of here, Devin. It can't get to where it needs to go,' Destiny said as she hugged the Book against her chest.

'Yeah, that's what I thought when I touched it.'

THE PAGES FLUTTERED out of my hand. I expected them to crumble into a million pieces as soon as they hit the floor, but they didn't. They were still there, page-like and all.

'Devin and Destiny touched these. They had them in their hands. These are part of a book. Something bigger than these pages.' I rubbed my hands together to warm them, suddenly feeling a chill spread up my spine. I studied Lili and Travis, wondering if they felt cold too.

'What do you mean they touched these? They look like they haven't left the tomb in years,' Lili commented. She peered at the pages, then looked at me. She grabbed the throw that was draped over the couch and wrapped it around my shoulders.

'I don't know. But they definitely touched them. It just came to me. Like at the stables, a sort of vision.'

I glanced past Lili to Travis, who was shifting from foot to foot.

'Just … you have to believe me.' I stared at the pages, and Lili shuffled closer to them. She picked them up and we held our breath. I waited for the wind to make some kind of ruffle, or for another spirit to attack, but there was nothing.

Nothing that would come out and take me hostage. Or Lili.

I breathed a sigh of relief.

'Can you read something from it?' Travis asked.

I shook my head. I leaned against Lil and poked at the pages in her hands. 'It's not safe. I mean, Harry Potter and *The Mummy* are prime examples as to why reading obscure texts is really dangerous.'

'But they're fiction. Movies and books are made up. This is

real.' Travis had a glass of orange juice in his hand and took a sip as he sat on the edge of the couch.

'Sometimes even real life can be scary. Do I need to remind you why?' I pointed to the pinpricks on my arm, and he just shrugged. 'Who knows how these pages got into the tomb in the first place. I think they're there for a reason.'

'It's in Ancient Egyptian, isn't it?' Lili asked, her fingers still so delicate as they skimmed over the pages.

There were pictures, inscriptions and what looked like doodles. It was not like anything I had seen before. I could read each of the phrases as well as Travis and Lili could read English, but I knew enough to know that it was not something to be toyed with. Hieroglyphics were a whole other script that didn't make sense to a lot of people, but there was a richness to the text that I could never put into words.

'Yeah. It's sort of a lot more formal, though, like whoever wrote it was well educated, which leads me to believe it was a priest of some sort. You can see here.' I pointed to the mark on the current page. 'This is flawless, no line is ever broken. He practiced a lot. Or had some sort of position that allowed him to.' I was leaning towards a priest, due to the complexity of spells and poems on the few pages we had.

'Karrept.'

The name was whispered in the air and I froze. Maybe it was nothing and I was mistaken.

'Did you hear that?' Lili asked.

'Yeah,' I replied.

As she turned the page, I saw the name: *Karrept.*

'Lili, can you hand me the pages?' She did with a care that was reserved for small animals. There were at least five pages, each double-sided. They felt so right in my hands, like they were made for me; just for me. 'This is Karrept's. He was Nefertiti's lover and her husband Aten's priest. Shit. The pages are part of something bigger, but I don't know where the rest of the

Book is, because it's more than a Book of the Dead. It's like some sort of love bible.'

'Love bible? If it's just a love bible, maybe you could read something. I mean, I'd love to be able to hear the language roll off your tongue. I know it would.' Travis was closer now. He was changing his tactics. He thought that by being closer to me and gentler, he might get his way.

It might have started to work if I wasn't so stubborn.

'I really shouldn't. It's not that I don't want to, but I don't know what this will do.'

I put the pages down and a few fell off my lap until there was a page that stood out. Every symbol and picture was immaculate and precise. I had never seen anything like it.

'That's not cool. There is no way that it did that,' Travis said and stood up faster than I could follow. Werewolf reaction speed sometimes scared the shit out of me.

'Okay, I didn't do that.' I was scared to move. 'More reason not to read from it.' I stared at the pages for a moment before I looked up at Travis. 'Are you cooking again, Trav?'

Give the werewolf something to do and he would leave me alone, at least for a little while.

'Yeah. I think so.' He was back in the kitchen and already prepping ingredients to work with.

'Are you okay?' Lili asked. She was by my side, this time not worrying about the book.

I rubbed her arm. 'I'm okay. Although, I'm just going to nap for a bit. Do you think that you can make sure Travis doesn't get into any trouble while I'm out?'

She laughed. 'Of course, I'll make sure he doesn't try and sneak into your room while you're asleep.'

'Liliana!' I scoffed at her and tried not to look at Travis. I could already tell that he was pretty damn smug. Jerk.

'I'm sorry, you had it coming.'

'I'm going to kill you. Go and find something to do. Better

yet, go call your boyfriend and tell him that I may murder you before we get home. He'll need to plan your funeral.'

'He'll get a kick out of that,' Lili said as she laughed and grabbed her laptop.

'That's what I'm afraid of.'

CHAPTER ELEVEN

Nefertiti
Athor 1357 BC

THE BOOK in my hands was one that was written by Karrept. He was pacing the room and biting his nails as I looked over every symbol, every image, like I was trying to find the words to tell him what it meant to me, but I could not.

'Karrept, I have no words. This is beautiful,' I gushed.

'Really? You think so?'

I nodded and closed the book. My hands ran over the cover; it looked just like a Book of the Dead, and it was on purpose. I wanted a piece of Karrept for when I died, because I knew that I would; everyone did. But at least this way I had a part of him that would be with me always. It would be spelled, because that was what we needed to do to make sure that no one else would be able to find a way to decode it.

'I do. What will the spell look like?'

Practicing the kind of magick that would be attached to the Book was punishable by death. Aten had made sure of it the moment we wed, but there was a loophole. I was the loophole;

my abilities were unique to me. The way that I could move things with my mind and concoct magickal elixirs, the true mastery would come with the joining of Karrept's power, his bloodline and mine would become the most powerful witches the world would see.

'It will be a mixture of a depression spell and a bad spirit spell. Anyone who is not meant to see it will be haunted by it, but those who are meant for it will find that the Book instantly feels like it is theirs. They won't be able to help themselves.'

I smiled. The Book would serve its purpose to make sure that there was someone to wake me up. But more importantly, they would make sure that Karrept would be living and thriving.

'Is there more to be added to this?'

'Are you trying to get rid of me before you are ready for this? Because if you are, then I am going to have to start a new book. It might be closer to a Book that will take the edge off all of the pain I will be going through.'

Karrept moved closer to me. I was on the bed and he was standing across the room, an arm's length away. Akhenaten was away on a business trip; now that he was pharaoh, it left me alone, so very alone.

'I would never tire of your presence. I like it too much,' I said too honestly, and he closed the distance between us faster than I would have thought. He did not have the speed or strength like Akhenaten, but he had it in his own way. There was a way that he moved, power dripping from his body.

'Do you now?' he said and leaned over me, his arms on either side of mine.

I swallowed hard and stared into his chestnut-coloured eyes, unsure of what to say next. In a year, he had shaved his head. His beautiful brown locks were no more, but I thought he looked better without the hair. It was a part of the priesthood that wouldn't bend for anyone, no matter how much their hair suited them.

'Yes,' I whispered.

Karrept smiled wider and leaned down, his lips a hair's breadth away from mine. He was waiting for me to lose control and take him. Because if I instigated it, he couldn't get in trouble. It would be me who would ruin it all.

'Yes.' He mimicked my breathy voice.

The tone made my body ache for him. The first time had been by accident, a little too much wine, but the second and third times were a blur. His body was perfect and I was insatiable. Just like his attention was.

I could not hold it back any longer and I pressed my lips against his. They were soft, inviting and demanding. He kissed me back, and I wrapped my arms around his neck, deepening the kiss. He moaned into my lips and that was when I lost all decency. In that moment I was not married to the pharaoh. I was just a woman with a need that Karrept knew how to fill.

The spell in the Book would make sure that this heat would always stay with us through the generations to come. He would wait for me.

CHAPTER TWELVE

Lucy
Epep 2014

LUCY. Wake up. You need to wake up now.

With a start, I bolted awake. Disorientation took over, and I searched my environment to figure out where I was. I found Lili on her laptop and Travis making food. I didn't even realise I had fallen asleep, still on the couch.

'Luce?' Lili frowned as she tried to hide the concern on her face.

'Bad dream or something. Don't worry about me.' Who called me out of my sleep? It had to have been important because I was sitting up. The voice sounded like Devin, but everyone believed he was dead. He couldn't pull me out of a dream. Not anymore.

'You were out for all of, like, ten minutes. Are you sure nothing woke you up?' Lili asked.

I must have had a haunted look on my face because Lili promised Griffin that she would call him back and ended her

FaceTime call with him. She crawled over so that she was sitting on the same couch as me and I swung my legs over her lap.

'What happened?' she asked. Travis was busy listening to music as he chopped and sautéed, or whatever he was doing.

'I heard my name. And they told me to wake up. That was all that I heard, but it was so familiar, yet so different at the same time. I can't explain it and you think I'm crazy.'

'No, I don't think you're crazy. I just think that it's ... odd.' Lili rubbed her hands over my legs, her touch warm, kind and caring.

'It is odd, but now I can't get it out of my head.' I pressed my lips together and studied the pillow at the end of the couch. 'I had a weird dream.'

'Like what?' Lili asked.

'I'm not sure, but it was some sort of, like, sexy dream. I felt like there was a guy that really liked me and was kissing me.'

'Was he familiar?'

I shrugged. 'I think so, but I can't quite put my finger on it.' The dream was now dissipating from my memory, but I couldn't shake the feeling that it was important.

'Hey, Luce. The pages moved again when you were out for the ten minutes or so.' Travis pulled an earbud out of his ear and pointed to the coffee table where I had left the pages.

I looked over and found a different page face up, which was weird because I would have known if someone had touched the pages. Or at least that's what it felt like. The page in question wasn't as detailed, but it held a simple incantation. I heard warning bells go off in my mind. Picking up the page would make it hard to put down because it felt so familiar, so warm. It was, rightfully, *mine*.

'What does it say?' Lili asked. She wasn't pushing, but she was just as curious as Travis. I didn't blame them. If the roles were reversed, I would be just as antsy about finding out what a foreign page said.

I felt drawn to it, like the pages knew more about me than I did. I wondered where the actual book was. It had to be close because I felt that it was close. I felt Travis' gaze on me. His eyes were tinted with purple—leftover from the tomb—and said more than he wanted to.

'Travis,' I warned.

'What? I'm not doing anything.' He held up his hands. In one hand was a knife and in the other was a carrot. Like that was going to get him any brownie points.

'Don't,' I pleaded.

'Come on, what's the harm in just telling us what it says? It's probably just a poem, anyway. You like poetry.'

'I like stories. *You* like poetry,' I retorted.

He shrugged and I sighed. Maybe he was right. Maybe nothing would happen.

'Fine.'

I crossed my legs under me and held the page loosely. I was scared it would crumble, but maybe that was a deterrent. I took a deep breath and focused on the page. The incantation was there; I could read it like it was in English to me, the Hieroglyphics as second nature as the Hebrew I could speak. I bit down on my lip as a shiver threatened and read from the page, the words flowing out of my lips like we were old friends catching up.

'Anok so ah fou la house la vou, touka ro pouse na mou. Le jou ve aman fakous napoua she ahn.'

Almost instantaneously, there was a rush of wind; it made branches scratch the windowed doors and howled to be let in. I jumped and Lili shifted across the couch, almost sitting in my lap. I touched her and an inhuman howl filled the room. I covered my ears and leaned into Lili. I watched Travis and Lili as they tried to clear their vision, both of them blinking rapidly like there was sand caught in their eyes.

'What was that?' Travis asked.

'I don't know. But you heard the scream?' I asked.

'Yeah, I heard it,' Lili said. 'What the hell?'

The page changed and revealed a passage just underneath the incantation. It was almost as if it had been waiting for me to read from it to reveal itself.

Lili read the passage out loud: 'To all of those whom read this book, you must read it the wrong way right. But a warning to those who don't: You will not live very long. Choose wisely.'

I couldn't turn away from the page and Lili's voice wavered.

'The Unclean thing will be unleashed. Forever undead and walking, never satisfied, waiting for revenge. The Illuminate Year is here.'

'What the fuck?' Travis was there in front of us and I jumped. I hadn't seen him move.

'Shut up,' I whispered.

It started with a tightening in my chest and a dimming around the edges of my vision, as breathing became harder. And I looked at Travis.

'This is all your fault.' The words flew out of my mouth without a filter. 'You wanted to hear it, you wanted me to do it, and this is where we are now. This thing ... whatever it is, is going to haunt us.' I knew that I was a little over the top about it all, but I was scared. I didn't like knowing that I could have just put us all in danger.

'Are you trying to blame this on *me*?' Travis exclaimed.

'I don't need to try to blame this on you, but I do blame it on you.' I was being irrational, but I couldn't stop the words that came out of my mouth.

'You were the one who read from the pages.' He reached out to me.

I stepped back so fast that I nearly tripped. 'You're the one who was all like, "Lucy, come on, you have to do it" at me.'

'So if I told you to jump off a cliff, you would? Is that what you're trying to tell me?' he threw back at me and stopped trying to touch me.

'No. You just care about you and no one else.'

'That's bullshit. I care about you. If you haven't noticed, I've cared for you longer than anyone else has. I'm still here. Unlike everyone else!' he shouted.

Lili was trying to break through the stubbornness. I felt her pushing at my shields; she wanted in so that she could tell me something, but I didn't want her in. I didn't want her to see anything. I just wanted Travis out of my face before I broke him. The anger bubbled inside me and I wanted to throw him across the room, but that was what the old Lucy would have done. She would have used magick first, then thought about it later. Hunter had helped curb that reaction. Or at least I thought he had.

'You insensitive jerk. I don't want to be with you, yet you push it. What is your fucking problem? You never take responsibility for what goes wrong. You just make it all about you. It's not always about you. Go fuck yourself.'

'Kali is your half-sister,' he blurted out.

The next sentence died on my tongue. I felt a hand clamp around my heart and squeeze hard. That was a low blow. I stared at him, trying to figure out if he was serious, and when I found his eyes, they were his human green and not wolf purple. My stomach dropped.

'You're lying.'

'Travis!' Lili jumped off the couch and pushed him out of touching distance, and in doing so she confirmed his words.

'You knew, that's what you couldn't tell me. You made her take a vow over Kali Shaw?' I stepped back to put distance between us. 'Do you know what she did to me, how much I had to suffer because of her, and you tell me she's my half-sister? I hate you, Travis.'

I fled the living room and ran up the stairs. I headed to my room, slamming the door as soon as I was inside.

My phone was on the bedside table and without giving a shit about the time difference, I called the one person who could confirm this. If Dad didn't pick up, I was going to get back on a plane and find out the truth.

'What's wrong?' Dad answered the phone appropriately. There was an eight-hour difference between Melbourne and Cairo.

'Why didn't you tell me about Kali?' I didn't sugar-coat it. It was too late for that.

Dad sighed and I heard him lean back in his leather chair. He was already at the office. I couldn't miss the creak in that chair even if I wanted to.

'How did you find out?'

'Travis.'

'That boy is always too hot-headed for his own good.'

'Dad, I'm sure he can hear you.'

'Oh, I'm fully aware that he can hear me, Lucy.'

'So …?' I sat down on my bed and crossed my legs under me. I didn't have to call him, and I'm sure that he would have left a letter in place of an explanation. But I was the youngest and only daughter now; he didn't stand a chance to say no to me, not anymore.

'Kali's mother and I are—were—old friends. We went way back, like high school way back, and there was always something there. I'm sure that if I hadn't met your mother, she would have been the woman I ended up with.'

'Ugh.' The thought of me being closer to Kali was sickening. I didn't think that I wanted to know more, but this was why I had wanted to talk to him and not read a letter. I had done this to myself.

He chuckled. 'You're so dramatic sometimes. Your mother and I went through a really hard patch. We were dealing with a lot of pressure from your grandparents, on both sides, as well as scaling up the business.'

'If I know where you're going with this, these are excuses.'

'Lucy,' he said. His tone held authority, and it told me to shut up without saying the actual words.

He couldn't see it, but I was rolling my wrists, a sign to keep him talking. 'Keep going.'

'Anyway, your mother and I had a horrendous fight, like we have only ever had one of these fights, and we vowed to never have it again. She shipped herself off to Egypt to escape. She was in the very house you're staying in tonight, and she cut off all communication, so I couldn't even see Destiny, who was three at the time. It wrecked me. I got in touch with Kali's mum and we picked up our friendship where it had left off. We were best friends.'

I swallowed, already envisioning what had happened—not that a child wanted to think about their parents being sexually active and all that. Gross.

'We were close for months, until one night we went too far. Too much bourbon was involved, and I imagine you don't want me to continue with that story.'

'No, Dad, very capable of filling in the blanks with this one. I think I'm scarred for life just doing that.'

He laughed and I heard him tap away on his keyboard before he continued. 'Well, your mother finally seemed to forgive me and came home. We talked it all over and then we were back to normal. After our routine was back, your mother and I ...'

'Yeah! Dad, thanks, move on, I get it. Devin and I were conceived. Double gross there.' I scrunched my nose at the image of my parents doing stuff. No thank you.

'You are so squeamish sometimes.'

'About my parents having sex? Yes, always yes, Dad.'

He laughed again. Part of me felt like I was back home and he was telling me this to my face. Was I less mad? Not really, but it helped that this wasn't as bad as I thought it was going to be. The familiarity was something I needed, and I hadn't realised how much. But I could feel the anger bubbling underneath the surface.

There was a knock and the door opened slowly. A hand holding a tub of ice cream came into view and I grinned. Ice cream always made everything better. Or mostly, anyway.

'Anyway, your mother found out she was pregnant and so did Kali's mother. She decided to keep her, and I guess we're here.'

'Why didn't you tell me yourself?' I asked and there was silence on the other end. I could see him rubbing the bridge of his nose like I was standing right in front of him.

'Ego. Pride. I don't know. I thought I was protecting you, and after everything that we've been through in the last two years, I thought that I could save you from more pain.'

I snorted. 'Yeah, save me from the pain? Kali is a monster. She made my life a living hell and has for more than the last two years. I never knew why, Dad, now I do. Is she a witch too?'

'Yes.'

Great, another witch in the family.

'You should have told me, Dad.' I let that sink in. 'Maybe school would have been easier. Better.'

He sighed and I looked up as Lili came into the room with a spoon and the ice cream. Behind her I saw Travis hovering just outside the doorway, waiting for me to let him in. I didn't want to see him, but the look he gave me? That killed me. His eyes were so sad and he slumped forward; he looked like a hurt puppy. And maybe he was.

'I could have. I had a letter ready for you, for when you found out the truth if it didn't come from me. I didn't expect to have to tell you this over the phone.'

'You should have told me in the flesh, Dad. You can't do this to me.'

'I know. I promised you no more lies when you were six and I broke that promise.'

He really did.

'I should go. I'm really upset at you and the time difference doesn't make it a day that isn't a work day there.'

'Luce, the work meetings don't matter to me.' he asked.

'You lied to me my entire life about a sister I never knew I had. I kind of don't want to talk to you for a bit, Dad.' The words hurt coming out of my mouth but the pit in my stomach felt deeper, but I couldn't hold onto the pain.

'I know. I deserve that. I know I do.' He said and sighed.

'Are there any more secrets you want to tell me?'

'Just that I'm going to leave the hotel business and become a crazy cat man.'

'Dad,' I said, and tried to picture him as a crazy cat man. I couldn't.

'No more, I promise.'

'We'll have to talk more about this later, when I'm back. I have to go.' If I stayed on the phone any longer I was going to say something I wouldn't be able to take back.

'I'll make sure it happens. Bye, Lucy-Bell.'

'Bye Dad.' I hung up the phone and turned to Lili, who was holding the ice cream and the spoon.

'You can never say no to ice cream,' she said.

'You know I can't. Why ... why was this some big secret from me?' I asked Lili as she opened the ice cream and handed it to me with the spoon.

'Probably to protect you. Trav, why do you think that no one told Luce?' Lili glanced over her shoulder to Travis, who was still hovering outside of the room.

'Lots of things have happened—you of all people should remember them—and that's made people scared to tell you things, Luce. Do we need to remind you?'

I shook my head and dug the spoon into the ice cream. The

last two years of our lives had been too surreal. Between deaths, suicide attempts and learning about long-lost fathers, it was a lot. If we didn't have the Bond, I didn't know what would have happened to us.

'Trav, just come in,' I said with a mouthful of ice cream.

With the invitation, he walked into the room. His shoulders were hunched up near his ears and he was trying to make himself look smaller than he was, which was almost impossible for a man who was six feet tall.

'I am hot-headed. I'm sorry,' he said as he looked at me. In his eyes there was no hint of the wolf, just the boy who had said something without thinking it through first and he was sorry for it. I sighed and patted the spot next to me on the bed as a sign of peace.

It would take time for me to come to terms with Kali being my half-sister—she hadn't made my life easy in the least. Now the bullying made more sense, but it didn't make it right.

'We all say things we shouldn't and that's okay.' I handed him the ice cream and the spoon and he gleefully took them. He didn't like sweet things, but occasionally he was okay with sharing ice cream with us because he knew how much we loved it.

'No, it was uncalled for. I need to stop doing that thing where I say shit that hurts because I'm frustrated. It's going to get me in trouble.'

'You know that one day you'll learn and you'll be able to use that as your power,' Lili muttered.

Both of us looked at Lili like she was speaking a different language. She felt our eyes on her and shrugged.

'The cards said that it'll be a strength to you. You just have to get there.'

Lili's tarot cards were beautiful, and we learned the hard way that we needed to listen to the guidance or it could bite us in the arse.

'Do you think we can just all make up and have a sleepover? I feel weirded out about the inscription thing and I would feel way better if we were all together,' I said and took the ice cream back from Travis. It would be the last spoon before crashing, because if we ate the whole tub, we wouldn't get any sleep and I was still exhausted.

'I'm down with that. Let's finish the ice cream another day and I'll grab the extra pillows,' Lili said, and I wasn't about to fight her.

CHAPTER THIRTEEN

Nefertiti
Epep 2014

THE WORDS MAY HAVE COME from the living, but I heard them loud and clear in the astral plane. They were uttered yet again. In the right year and the right time. Not like the last time.

We were ready. The plan was in place.

The descendant was ready.

Butterflies fluttered in my stomach at the thought that I would have a solid form again. One that would look just like me and would be as familiar as my own body. She would be glorious to be in.

We waited. We knew that it would be a long way away, but the love I had for Karrept would make sure that our plan came to fruition. The hiccup two years ago was by chance.

I would take over the descendant.

CHAPTER FOURTEEN

Lucy
Epep 2014

A CREAK PULLED me out of my sleep and I bolted up in bed. The almost full moon lit the room up brighter than any light could, and I searched the room to see if there was a thing out of place. I held my breath and strained to hear anything out of the ordinary. I heard nothing. There was no one in the house besides us, and I'd made sure that all of the doors and windows were locked. But I felt sick to my stomach and I trusted my intuition; it was screaming at me about the reading.

The inscription had awakened a knowing inside me that made this all too real. I didn't know why, but I knew something was coming for us. When Lili and Travis had agreed to the sleepover, I was grateful. It meant that I didn't have to be alone, but it also meant that we were easy to pick off if someone was coming after us. I looked beside me. In the dark I could see Lili sleeping comfortably next to me. Travis was spooning an extra pillow on the window seat. I'd bet he wasn't asleep—he didn't need to sleep a lot, thanks to his wolf.

Slipping back under the covers, I closed my eyes, expecting sleep to take me back into its familiar embrace, but instead I heard a creak. This time I *wasn't* dreaming.

I nudged Lili to wake her up. She groaned and mumbled something incoherently before rolling over. Not the reaction I was hoping for.

'Lili, wake up. Someone's in the house,' I whispered urgently. That got her attention and she practically jumped out of bed.

Another step and another creak. It sounded impossibly loud now that Lili and I were both listening and expecting it.

She opened her mouth to say something and I shook my head. Talking would attract the intruder to us.

Bang. Bang. Bang.

I clapped a hand over my mouth as I quietened the squeal that rose up my throat. Lili wasn't so lucky.

Bangbangbangbangbangbangbangbangbangbangbang.

The thumping got louder and harder. I waited to see a fist burst through the wood. The noise alerted Travis and he climbed onto the bed and settled at our legs protectively. I could feel the wolf in charge, and for once I was okay with it.

No one had ever lived to tell the story of when they came up against our wolf. At least, not figuratively. I didn't want to think about who Travis had killed, or was willing to kill.

The Bond between the three of us was instantly magnified now that we were all within touching distance. I could feel Lili's fear as vividly as my own; Travis was just a wolf. He was ready to kill anyone who came into the room.

Something shifted in the corner of my eye and I saw glowing eyes staring back at me through the window. I yelped and fell off the bed. I scrambled to get to my feet, just as Travis mouthed *What?* at me. I pointed at the window and he followed my guide.

I don't see anything, he whispered through my mind.

The banging stopped, and I slipped my hand into Travis' as I felt a tickle in my throat, like there was something trying to crawl up it. I coughed to clear my throat, hoping it would help. Instead there was a buzz, almost like a flutter of wings brushing against my oesophagus. I coughed again and saw a bug fly out of my mouth. With wide eyes, I stared at it, just as the feeling started up again.

I gagged as I clawed at my neck. Like it would free the flutter of wings in my throat.

The buzzing didn't stop. The evil eyes were back at the window and they were glinting with amusement. I opened my mouth and screamed. Hundreds of locusts climbed out of my throat. They filled the air as I choked.

Lili dived off the bed and flattened herself next to me.

As soon as they came, they were gone.

I licked my lips and swallowed hard. My mouth was dry and I felt like I was it was so dry and felt like sandpaper with each gulp of saliva.

'What the *fuck* was that?' Travis asked, rubbing his fingers through his hair, trying to shake loose any bugs.

I shook my head and clenched my jaw tightly, afraid to open my mouth.

Lili sat up and helped me into a sitting position with her. She wrapped her arms around me and just like that, my body started to shake.

'Shh, it's okay. You're okay,' she whispered into my ear.

'Do I need to state the obvious?' Travis asked.

Lili clicked her tongue at him. 'I don't think you do, but you're going to do it anyway.'

'Where are they? They were here and then they weren't. Bugs don't just disappear.'

'Locusts,' I coughed.

I wanted a glass of water to help with that; better yet, a shot of tequila, or three. It would warm me up and chase away the feeling of dread that had settled heavily in my stomach. I focused on my breath. *In and out. In and out.* And as I did that I began to count them: one, two, three. It would calm my nerves and maybe the dread. My eyes burned as I struggled to not blink. I could see the glowing eyes with the same amusement sparkling in them. Like they were tormenting me with what was to come.

'C-close the curtains,' I stammered.

'What?' Travis seemed to be taking things in a little slower tonight.

'Trav, just do it.' Lili spoke for me and he closed them without asking again. Lili pulled back and held my face in her hands.

'Luce, come back to us. You're far away. What's going on?'

She was one of the only people who could bring me back from the point of no return.

'There were eyes, at the window. In the window and they were smiling,' I said.

Travis was looking at me like I was crazy. 'Luce, we're on the second floor.'

'I know that,' I snapped. 'They were there. Glowing.' I rubbed my throat and buried my nose in Lili's neck. I let her soothe me for once. I was so tired of always being strong.

'It's okay. You're safe. We're here. No one is going to hurt you, not as long as you have us,' Lili murmured.

Her words soothed, the pounding of my heart eased up a little and forced me back into the present. Just as my heart started to really settle, the banging started up again and everyone jumped. Travis stared at the door and Lili held me almost too tight. I pulled myself out of her arms and got to my feet. I let them carry me to the door. I wrapped my fingers around the handle and with unwavering confidence, I wrenched it open.

'Will you *stop*,' I said.

I expected to find someone with a knife and a creepy clownlike smile, ready to gut me, but there was nothing. No one. Just silence.

A scream tore through the silence, and I spun on my heel to see bandages, sand and rotting flesh bending over Lili. The thing was kissing her. I tried to lift a leg to get to It and pull It away from her, but I couldn't move.

I looked at Travis and he was scrunching up his face.

'What are you *doing*?' I was panicked. My best friend was being attacked and I couldn't move, and it seemed like Travis couldn't either.

'I can't move. I'm trying to lift my leg, but there's nothing. I … we need to get to her. Lili. *Lili*, talk to us.'

'Stop. Just stop what you're doing,' I called out to it.

She was fighting, trying to push It away. Her nails tried to break skin, but the creature's strength was too much for her. Her arms went slack and when It pulled away, I saw a pile of dust. It was in that moment that I got the use of my legs back and I collapsed to the floor. I searched through our Bond to find her, to see if this was real. I couldn't find her.

She was gone.

I tore my gaze away from the pile of dust and the face that peered back at me was soft, full of love and … familiar. He looked so familiar and I didn't want him to. How did he go from grotesque to beautiful? What kind of magick was that? There was still a hint of dirty bandage left in weird places.

He came towards me and kneeled down. His fingers brushed over my cheek and my breath hitched in my throat. His touch was cold, smooth, delicate. *'Nefertiti, it's been so long.'*

'Luce. *Lucy*, what did It say?'

It took me a second to realise that the creature hadn't spoken in English; the words sounded like second nature to me. He was speaking Ancient Egyptian.

Grief wracked my body, and I couldn't think of anything but the pile that was my best friend. I couldn't even reply to Travis.

She was gone. Taken from me when I needed her the most. I tried to move, but I couldn't.

The Bond was gone.

Empty.

Barren.

Decimated.

I tried to get to my feet but I was weak, and the creature caught me before I toppled over.

'Don't touch me.'

On command, he dropped me, and I tried to scramble away.

'Nefertiti, I know that you're in there. I can see you. I will free you,' he said to me.

'Luce? What is he saying?' Travis called out again. I had almost forgotten he was in the room.

'He thinks I'm Nefertiti. Wait. What—no, no. Stop. What are you doing?'

The creature turned around and started towards Travis. My heart jumped into my throat and I clawed at the floor, trying to pull myself over to Travis.

'What is he doing?' Travis, for the first time, looked panicked. The purple haze in his eyes deepened.

'Travis. Trav. Look at me. You know how you're an arse all the time? Well ... I just want to tell you that I love you and that you're my best friend.'

'Lucy, you better not be giving me a goodbye speech, because I will murder you.'

'Not a goodbye, Trav, just a see you soon. I'm sure I'm joining you next.' The words tumbled out of my mouth faster than I wanted. I was paralysed, my breathing shallow as I tried to move a limb. And I could see Travis was scared.

It was weird not to be able to feel his emotions.

'That's the kind love I want.' He was still an arse in the face of death.

'Why do you do that?'

'To compensate. I love you, you know, even if you don't believe me. I really do and I think that you're amazing. Hunter was lucky to have you and still have you.'

And then there was no more talking; the creature was kissing Travis, and from my vantage point, I couldn't see a thing. Travis tried to push It away but couldn't. Tears ran freely down my cheeks as I watched him disintegrate.

When the creature turned back to me, but he wasn't a creature at all. He was ... he really did look like Hunter. He had the same chiselled cheekbones, light brown hair and soft lips that always made me want to kiss him, even when I didn't want to kiss him. How was that possible? He had been so ... dirty, old and impossibly ugly. At the core of it he was a creature, but he looked so much like a man.

The creature was more familiar to me than I wanted him to be, but the colour of his eyes was wrong. Not Hunter's.

'*Nefertiti*,' he said again.

'I'm not Nefertiti. Stop calling me that.' *My name is Lucy.*

Lucy.

He leaned into me. '*I will show you who you really are.*'

I leaned back from him but I still couldn't move. I didn't want to have him kiss me. All grossness aside, looking at a carbon copy of Hunter was unnerving.

He kissed me, scorching my lips with a ferocity I'd never felt before. I resisted for a moment before my lips gave way and I kissed him back. It was then that I was pushed back inside my body and chained.

'*My light.*' The words were out of my mouth before I could keep them back, and my fingers were exploring his face. He let me go, freed me of the magick that had been holding me down. My body no longer moved the way I wanted it to, and with the chains holding me back, I could do nothing but scream.

'*I told you I would bring you back.*' There was sincerity in his eyes as his hands worshipped my body.

I felt ill. I didn't want his hands all over me. Not when I couldn't fight back.

'You did. You very well did. What year is it?' my voice asked.

'It is 2014. The Illuminate Year,' he said.

'It is time. It really is time. Oh, my light, it's going to be our new beginning. We have waited for this.'

The joy that radiated from me, joy that was not my own, was weird. Terror pulled at me, just as I pulled at the chains. They were not going to chain me down, especially not in my own body. I had worked too hard to let them just take it all over.

I pulled at the chains hard. If my wrists broke because of it, I didn't care, I just needed to be out of them. I screamed again just as the two went for another groping kiss and I was greeted with a scream, one that was out of my own mouth, but it sounded older, harsher, rough. Good, I'd made Nefertiti scream.

'Karrept, she is too strong. I thought she would have been broken. Everything went to plan, did it not?'

I pulled again and she screamed louder.

'It did, but she had help. She should have been perfectly ready for this, but she is not,' Karrept said. I could see him trying to peer through Nefertiti's eyes to find me.

'It is the Watcher and the wolf. They made her stronger, stronger than she ever would have been without them. They were not supposed to be together. The curse ...'

Curse? What was she talking about? I needed her to elaborate.

'I know. She was supposed to be ready, easy to take over,' he said again.

I pulled at the chains again and one snapped free. It disappeared from around my wrist and I stared at the skin. Metaphorical chains held me in place and I could break through them with enough pull.

'You need to make a switch. Her body is not weak enough. Try the Watcher, she is a descendant of Nephthys. But bring the wolf back *first, then the Watcher, then take my soul and place it in the Watcher. Do not try and bring back my half-sister now, will you, my love?'*

Karrept smirked at me and I wanted to rip that smirk off his face. He was not going to touch a hair on Lili's head after he brought her back. I would make sure of that.

I pulled at the chains again and Nefertiti cried out. *'Karrept, go. I cannot fight her for very long.'*

He nodded and I watched, through her eyes, as he brought Travis back, dust moulding into bone and flesh, reversing what he had done. I wanted to know how he did it, but from where I was, it looked like all he did was touch his remains. Travis was disorientated and blinking rapidly. Karrept brought Lili back next, and she stumbled back to life, pushing him away.

'Lucy? Are you ... what's wrong with your eyes?' Travis asked.

I screamed at Nefertiti. I wanted to warn them, wanted Lili to get out of the room. I wanted to protect her, but I was so powerless. Useless to try to do anything but scream from inside my head like a crazy person. I tried to reach through to them. Maybe the Bond would be back in place because they were alive. I could feel a flicker underneath it all.

Karrept kissed me and sucked Nefertiti out of me. I could feel the chains tearing away and I took control of my body. I slapped Karrept and he grinned at me.

'You were always good at playing rough.'

His tone made me shiver.

'Lili, Lils, you have to go, get out of the room. He's going to try and chain you away. Lili, look at me,' I pleaded.

'I can't move, Luce. I tried. Trav?'

'Oh god,' I whispered just as Travis answered her, and I missed everything he said.

'You kick this guy's butt. I don't know what he is doing, but I need you to. If you don't, I'm coming back to haunt your arse and I'm going to make it painful as anything.'

Lili stared at me. Tears clouded her eyes, but there was a resolve in her face—she was going to fight. But being unable to move, she knew there was nothing she could do to stop him. Even when she wanted to.

My heart sank into my stomach, and through the flicker in the Bond, I felt her slide out of reach and the power that was holding me hostage sink in as Karrept kissed her. I cried out. I scrambled on my hands and knees towards Travis, and he wrapped his arms around me. He was shivering, still trying to recover from being dead. I could feel his emotions again because Lili was alive. The pair pulled apart, and Lili's beautiful caramel-coloured eyes were replaced with vivid blue. They weren't golden, so that meant …

'Well, well, hello there. I didn't expect this. What a great body.' Lili's voice held no malice in it. Just wonder.

'You're Nephthys,' I murmured.

'Got it in one, honey. You're Lucy, right? There are people waiting for you to save them. And you know that they're alive. Devin is so much nicer to look at these days too. Mmm.'

My stomach twisted into a knot. I stared at her, unable to form words, and before I knew it, I was trying to lunge at her. Travis grabbed my arms and held me close.

Destiny and Devin were *alive*.

'How do you know about them? What did you do to them?'

Karrept tried to move towards Lili, but she shook her finger at him. She had some power over him it seemed. This was good; maybe we could keep her around. 'You're asking the wrong questions, Lucy. Find the right one and I might just answer you. What is it with you and your family reading from a book when it says, clearly marked, *Do Not Read*, hmm?'

I stared at her. What book was she talking about?

'You don't know? Yeah, I thought as much. Just watch yourself. You never know what's around the corner.' With that, she tilted her head at Karrept with a smile on her face. 'My sister is not going to be happy with you. Come on now, let's get this over with.'

'What? No. *No*. Don't let him do this,' I begged.

She spun on her heel and stared at me. 'I wish I could, but this is the price you have to pay. Come and find me, Lucy.' She kissed Karrept, and I watched as light exchanged between their mouths. When Lili pulled away and opened her eyes, they were golden, glimmering in the little bit of light there was. I clung to Travis and he held me tight.

'Give us the Book and she will live,' Nefertiti/Lili said.

'The B-Book?' I stammered.

We only had a couple of pages at the most.

My head felt like it was filling with fuzz. What was happening?

'Never mind, we will be back for it. *Karrept, let us go.*' And with that, Lili and Karrept vanished.

'No!' I cried out and ripped from Travis' embrace. Gone. She was gone.

My best friend was gone.

CHAPTER FIFTEEN

Nefertiti
Epep 2014

IN THE STREETS OF CAIRO, I twirled in this body. It was ... wonderful. Everything felt surreal. The world was unlike anything that I was used to, and even as I had watched it change, it was so much different than being locked away, floating incorporeal, and being her.

The streets were quiet for this time of night; the humidity of the day still lingered and it was glorious. I remembered the sweltering heat of yesteryear and it made me miss home, but only for a moment. The ecstasy of being in a body that was flesh and bone was beyond words.

'My love, this body is wonderful. She is older than I was when we ended it all. This is a different feeling,' I said as I ran my hands over her body.

Liliana was Nephthys descendant. I could feel it. She even looked similar to her. She was the whole reason I was here; if she hadn't done her part of the spell, this wouldn't even be possible.

'He looks just like Aten. The boy,' Karrept said. He wrapped his arms around my waist, pressing me against the wall. The breath caught in my throat and I gasped.

I smiled as he leaned closer, his lips hovering dangerously over my own. 'He did. Did you enjoy taking his life from him?'

I knew that it would be different. Karrept might be a priest, but he had years to hone his magick and his vendetta against Aten. Travis was the spitting image of him, and I wondered if he also had the wolf gene. The memories in Liliana's mind were jumbled. I didn't know how much of that was her trying to distract me or if that was really how her thought process worked. Whatever it was, I could see snippets of their life through the Bond. It was that Bond that I had quickly cast a disappearance spell on. It was still in place; they could talk to one another and sense each other, but there was a wall between Liliana and Lucy and Travis. They wouldn't be able to tell where she was or what she was feeling, because I had full control over her body.

Just the way that we needed it to be, because I wanted my body. This one was okay, but I wanted to be back in what was rightfully mine.

'I did enjoy taking his life,' Karrept said. 'It was joyous. I'm sad that it didn't last as long as I would have liked. But my magick seems to be limitless now. It is different.'

'It has been centuries, my love, I do not see how magick would stay the same it would have some sort of limit. You will get him,' I said and kissed him. His body was firm and powerful. There was a different kind of power to it than that which was once there. I could hardly believe it.

He still made my body clench in need for him, and if we didn't find a place to settle, it would be hell in the middle of the streets. I broke the kiss, my gaze finding his.

'We need to find new clothes too. These nightclothes are not what I would have expected,' I said as I motioned to the shorts and T-shirt that adorned this body. It was strange that I knew what they were, but I was even more perplexed that women wore items of clothes like this. I had watched clothing evolve, but living it was totally different. I wondered if I could put it into words for Karrept to understand. I didn't think that would be possible.

'I will just cover your body with mine. We will not need attire to adorn your body.' His smirk was devious and I wanted to lean into him, but there was the other part of me that was revolted by him.

Liliana was shouting inside my head. She did not want to touch him, or be near him, but with me at the helm of her body, she did not have a choice and that was where we differed. But it was her body too.

'And I can not wait until you do so, but that is going to have to wait. This vessel doesn't fit like the glove, or at least not like the descendant's body would, so we need to take it slow.' I trailed my fingertips down the side of his face, his eyes closed, and stared at him. He had not aged and still looked like the man I loved. But there was something different. I could feel it in the way that I touched him.

Maybe that was because of Liliana and not me, but it was like I was looking at him for the first time through new eyes. His green eyes and sun-kissed skin always made me fall deeper for him; his hair was still gone and it would stay gone because he died with it gone, but I loved it. All of it. I loved him.

But there was a whisper that made me doubt all of that. And I was not sure where that voice came from.

CHAPTER SIXTEEN

Lucy
Epep 2014

MY VISION BLURRED and my head throbbed. I had been staring at the stupid pages for hours and I couldn't find a single thing in them to help me. Maybe I was looking at them too hard. The tea in my hand was supposed to help with the throbbing; it was full of pain-alleviating herbs like ginger and lavender.

'Luce, give it a rest,' Travis called from the couch.

I jumped and spilled tea on myself, but shook my head in response. 'We need to get Lili back. What the hell is the Illumi-nate Year, and why can't I find it? Why is this so hard? It's like there's something blocking me. I fucking *hate* this.'

Two days had passed since Lili had been taken from us. The first day I didn't remember at all. Travis said I was coming in and out of consciousness all day and night. You'd think I would have felt rested, but I just felt even worse and it wasn't getting any better.

I pushed back the chair and cleaned up the spilled tea. 'What are you doing?'

'Trying to sleep. I'm exhausted, you are hard to look after,' Travis commented.

We were both getting testy.

'This isn't funny. We need her back, Travis.' I rubbed the tea towel over my top.

'You think I think this is funny? They took our best friend, Luce. She's gone and all we have is a few stupid comments from some ... thing, or whatever she is, and a few pages, not even a book. They're just pages that we can't get *anything* out of. Yeah, I think this is real funny.' He was standing in front of me and blocking the light now.

'Don't patronise me, Trav.'

'Don't be so stubborn. I'm trying here. I just don't know what to do. I want her back as much as you do. I need her back.'

His fingers guided my chin up so that I could see the look in his eyes. The greeny blue in them swirled with lust, and I pushed him away. 'No,' I said. It was the only word I could say.

I threw the tea towel in the sink and gave up.

'Why did he look like Hunter?' Travis asked.

I knew the question had been coming, but hearing it out of Travis' mouth didn't make it any easier to swallow. 'I don't know. I'm as confused about that as you are.' I turned around to watch as Travis closed in on the pages. There was nothing there that could help us, but I knew there was something I was missing.

Travis touched the first page and hissed.

'What?' I asked.

'It zapped me. Like it knows I shouldn't touch it. It's ... that's magick. It's magick, Luce.'

'It's magick. That's what's stopping you from getting very far. And ...'

'Trav, it's not telling me anything because the spell is blocking me, but there's also something more to it. There is a whole book, there has to be, and that's why it's blocking me.

You can't read something that's incomplete. Like, you can't start reading a book when you just have a few pages—it doesn't tell you the whole story. Oh my god. That's why they wanted to know where the Book was. It's a part of something bigger.'

'There's a whole book,' Travis repeated and I nodded. I pushed him out of the way as I picked up the pages.

'I can't remember a locator spell, but if the pages are here and they're doing their thing, why wouldn't the Book have to be close enough?'

Gripping the pages, I closed my eyes and took a deep breath. I tried to clear my mind and hoped that the pages would talk to me. If I could tap into whatever residual magick there was in the pages, maybe I could use that to find the rest of the Book. The pages felt like home, like it was meant for me but it wasn't mine. The page knew me, which made a lot of sense now that Nefertiti was back in the flesh. Granted, she was in the wrong body, but she was back. As I held the page close, I realised that it was pulsing. It was faint but it was there.

'Tell me what I need to know,' I whispered to the page, willing it to show me what it needed to show me. And with those words, my body tingled and I saw a bookshelf that was more familiar to me than my own hand.

It was upstairs.

'The Book is here. It's in the house,' I gasped and turned to stare at Trav. 'It's been here the whole time.'

'What?' he said. 'You mean the *whole* time?'

'Yeah, I bet that's why the house is doing this weird shit. It has a foreign object inside it and it's trying to protect itself. And thinks that anyone with any sort of magick is a threat. It makes sense,' I said and got to my feet. I wanted to say more but there was no time. I needed to find the rest of the Book. I had to figure it out.

'Where do you think it could be hidden?'

I knew that it wasn't in the safes, there was no way that it could be, and I didn't think that Mum and Dad would hide it in their personal safes. I wouldn't be able to get into those.

'I'm thinking the study. Let's try?'

Travis nodded to me and we walked out of the room and into the hallway. The office was just to the left of the stairs and always felt like home to me. No matter what happened.

As soon as we stepped into it, the Book's pages seemed to hum, like they knew they were so near to the rest of their pages.

'Can you feel that?' I whispered.

'I can hear it. It's humming really loudly.'

'It's faint, but your wolf ears pick up everything. Aren't you lucky.'

'Not always,' he said, and I glanced at him over my shoulder. We gave him a lot of shit for being a werewolf, but I knew that it would always be hard for him.

If someone found out what he was, he would be dead. Sent to jail without a trial just on the basis that he wasn't human. But then again, I wouldn't be far behind from that experience either.

The pages flew out of my hand and landed on the floor in front of the bookshelf.

'Okay, that's freaky. I don't care how much I'm used to magick, still freaky,' I murmured and kneeled down to pick them up. As I did, a spine caught my eye and I knew that it was the Book. I could feel it. I picked it up from the shelf and took it to the desk.

'I thought it would be mustier, honestly,' Travis said.

'Me too, but it looks almost brand new,' I whispered. I opened the cover, and as soon as I did, the pages slipped from my hands and fastened themselves into their home.

I inhaled sharply at the magick in the air.

'That was fast.'

'It nearly gave me a paper cut,' I joked, but with the pages in the Book I could still feel something around it, like it was telling me to turn away and look somewhere else. Like it was trying to save me from what was to come. But it was far too late for that. I couldn't put the Book away even if I wanted to.

I turned the first page and was greeted with neat handwriting. I knew it was Karrept's—the priesthood would have drilled into him about the neatness and what was expected of him, but there was more to it. The love that was attached to every stroke … he really loved making this for Nefertiti. The ode to their love story was hidden between the pages.

Travis touched my shoulder, and I was about to say something witty when I was hit with a memory. One that I had tried hard to forget, but the scars wouldn't let me.

Melbourne
Tobi 2012

The shadow of who I used to be flashed before me. She was happy, her hair perfectly styled, her clothes immaculate. But the girl who stared back at me in the mirror didn't have any makeup on, her hair was an unwashed mess and she was sad. Miserable. Inside I felt dead, abandoned and forgotten.

Devin and Destiny were gone. Dead to everyone else, but I knew they weren't. Devin would never leave me on my own. Not with our mother. He promised me. I stared at my reflection, scanning my shoulders and down to my arms. They were covered in little white scars. Previous scratch marks, searching for something to feel good.

'Ugh.' I clawed open the mirrored medicine cabinet door. Lining the shelves were common girly things: tampons, makeup, waxing strips. But my eyes snagged on the razor. It wasn't mine, a leftover from when Devin used to use my bathroom. I picked up the blade and pressed it between my thumb and forefinger. It was cool to touch, but the warmth of my skin melted that coolness away. I shut the door and took a few steps back, then slid down the wall.

An empty hole replaced my heart, and I wasn't sure I wanted to find a way out of it. It was safe here. No one cared about me; no one bothered to try to find out where I was.

I unfurled my arm and stared at my wrist. The right way to cut was down. If I hit the correct vein, I would bleed to death in minutes. I could find a euphoric release and join them again. Or maybe I could find them.

Life wasn't worth living when nobody cared.

Hunter was gone, and Travis and Lili were too busy with their own things. Travis was dating Kali again. She'd made it clear that she didn't want me around her boyfriend.

I balanced the blade on my skin and danced it down my arm. I tested the waters before I positioned the blade over my wrist. This time, I put some pressure against the blade. I whimpered as the metal sliced the skin. It slid apart a lot faster than I would have thought possible, and blood trickled down my arm and onto my legs. I stopped just short of my elbow and switched hands. The blade was slippery now, and I could feel my head start to spin. I had gone too deep. I felt clumsy as I dragged the blade down my other arm. Pain vibrated with every movement and I stopped barely halfway down my arm.

I lost the will to hold the blade and it clattered against the tiles. Tears streamed down my face as the blood flowed freely.

No one would miss me.

'Lucy. Are you in there?' I could barely make out the voice. It seemed so far away. Then I felt something press against my arms, and I tried to pull away before everything went black.

Egypt
Epep 2014

I CRIED out as I was pulled from the memory and almost fell. Travis used his speed and strength to catch me from behind. He turned me around so that he could look at me, and I could see the tears in his eyes. Travis and Kali were waiting for something to snap, something to change, but all I could do was try to catch my breath.

'Luce. You're here. You're okay,' Travis soothed as he held my hips pinned against the table.

'*Okay* is a relative term. Did you just see that?'

'Yeah. I could feel the blood on my hands. All over again,' Travis mumbled.

The memory wasn't linked to the house but it was linked to Travis, and when Karrept brought Lili back, he brought the Bond back. Maybe it was a side effect of it coming back and after that I still couldn't feel Lili. It was just static on the other end. I looked from the Book to Travis; the memory was tied to it, and it was distracting us so that we would forget about the Book. It was about to win that battle, or at least it would for now. Travis stared at me, his green-blue eyes brighter than I'd ever seen them. Or maybe that was because his wolf was trying to break through and they were about to be purple. Blood brought his wolf to the surface often enough. Just like any strong emotion did.

'What?' I asked. He was looking at me weirdly.

Travis shook his head. 'I can't believe I almost lost you that day. It was the scariest day of my life. I don't remember ever seeing so much blood. And it was a fight between basking in it and saving you. I almost fed you some of my blood.' Travis held out his hands, a silent request to look at the scars again.

They were a reminder of something that I wanted to forget, and sometimes I did too.

'I didn't want to be alive. All I could think about was being with Destiny and Devin. I thought they were dead and I wanted to be with them. The feeling I felt ... it was different. I couldn't put it into words. I don't know what came over me, but I couldn't be in a world where they didn't exist. I missed them, it was all I had left in me.'

Travis brushed his fingers over my arms and I hissed. They felt raw, like they were new scars, but they were years old.

'I'm sorry. I never realised how much you hurt. Even during it all, after it all. Luce, I didn't get it 'til now,' he mumbled.

'You felt the feelings too?'

He nodded. 'I didn't get it then, I just thought that you were sad, and it would be something that you would move past. But there was something more, like a black cloud over you, and I can feel it now, more than I could then. God, I can't undo it. And I want to. I want to rid you of the memories and the way that they made you feel.'

I pushed away from the table and away from Travis. It was too much to be so close to him. I made my way over to Dad's leather couch and sat down, cradling my head in my hands. 'I don't want to remember that feeling, the way that blade moved down my wrist, the scars, it's too much. Devin and Destiny are alive, Nephthys confirmed everything I knew to be true. I knew they weren't dead, even when everyone else said they were. I need to find them. I *have* to find them.'

Trav followed me to the couch and sat down. 'We will find them, Luce. You know that we won't stop. And we'll get Lili back and everything will be okay,' he said as he guided my chin up so I would look at him. His eyes flashed with lust, his body coaxing me closer.

'What are you doing?' I tried to look away but I couldn't. The warmth of his skin chased away the chill that lingered from the flashback.

'I want you. I have wanted you for so long, and that memory reminds me of how close I was to losing you. I just want to try my shot,' he said, and his raw tone made me avoid his eyes.

'Trav. Don't.' The words were weak out of my mouth, but I didn't stop him. The memory of who I used to be was still fresh in my mind.

I never wanted to go back to that girl who had been alone

and hurting. I was afraid of what would really happen if I went back there.

'Just one kiss,' he said as pulled me into his lap. The warning bells were already going off, but I was tired and vulnerable. The memory was too much and I was tired of fighting it. 'You are just ... something else,' he murmured before he kissed me.

I bunched his shirt in my fingers and pulled him closer. A little comfort wouldn't hurt. I broke the kiss and held his gaze. His eyes flashed purple before they settled on green. Heat stared back at me and I kissed him this time. Harder, faster, needier. I wrapped my arms around his neck and pulled him in close.

Travis pushed me back onto the couch and settled above me, his fingers catching the hem of my top and sliding underneath. His hand burned a trail up my ribs.

'Travis,' I whispered into his mouth.

'Shh. We need to feel, just to wipe away the memory. I don't want to see you covered in your own blood anymore. I just want to stop thinking about that moment. If I hadn't been there at the right time, you wouldn't be here.'

Just to wipe away the memory. Yes. With the kiss he switched our positions, lifting me like I was feather. I made space for him between my legs and pulled his shirt up his body. As soon as it was over his head, I threw it to the ground and stared back at him. My fingers traced the ankh on his back from memory. A symbol we all shared.

I felt guilty that he had walked in when he had and saved me. For a long time I'd been angry because I wanted to die, but was that really my feeling? Were my emotions at the time my own?

His fingers, with much knowledge and skill, lifted my shirt up my body. Instead of tugging it off and being done with it, he took his time, his eyes taking in my body. I could see it in his mind and he liked every part of what he saw.

There was too much raw emotion running through him, and

I had half a second to doubt that this was a good idea. It wasn't. He made me nervous, but I was in too deep.

'Lucy, stop thinking. I can see you thinking and it's distracting. You need to just feel,' Travis said. His voice was hoarse with lust, and as he bumped his hips into mine, all rationality flew out the window. Wrapping an arm around his neck, I pulled him in closer and kissed him. I put all of my frustrations, all of my doubts and insecurities into that kiss.

Travis' fingers tugged at my pants, and before I knew it, I was naked under him. My nimble fingers pulled on his belt, a moment of sheer frustration as I had to take the time to undo the clasp, but it was enough.

I pulled back and Travis groaned. 'What? What is it? You can't be—'

I put a finger to his lips. 'Protection.'

He blinked and pushed himself off me. He ran up the stairs and into his room with a speed I had never seen him use. Travis was back before I had time to be embarrassed by my nakedness. In his fingers was a little square; if we were doing this, we were going to be responsible.

Travis kicked off his own pants, and with the crinkle of a wrapper was ready. He settled above me, his hands on either side of my head. No words came to mind as he slipped inside me. I wrapped my leg around him and he leaned down to kiss me. Something inside snapped, almost like a key locking into place. As he began moving I forgot about anything else but him and the way he felt inside me. His eyes bled to purple and I let myself get lost in that haze.

His lips fused to mine, and for a moment I forgot about the purple, or that he was a werewolf. I wrapped my other leg around him and pushed him deeper still, almost like I was trying to find a place for him to fit in better. As our bodies moved in sync, I rose to meet his thrusts with my own and moaned into his mouth as he changed the tempo and started to slam himself into me. He chased away the bad, and as I ripped my mouth from his lips, I held his gaze. The ferocity in his eyes was animalistic; he was claiming me. And in that moment? I let him.

'Trav,' I whispered, the pressure building with every thrust. I didn't think that the steady build-up would mount as quickly as it had, but there was something about the way he moved that pulled me right in. My breath hitched, and I cried out as his fingers raked down my sides.

'Too much,' I breathed, but that didn't stop him.

If anything, it made him pump his hips harder, almost as though he was trying to crack me in two, but I knew that he was trying to bury himself deeper, like there was an ending in sight.

'Never too much. Keep going.' He slipped a hand between us and started to rub the hardened nub that was on full display and I arched into him, moaning.

The pressure built and I threw my head back as my orgasm ripped through my body.

'Fuck, Luce,' he whispered before he buried his nose in the crook of my neck and moaned, coming just after me.

For a second, time stopped, and all I could hear was our breathing—and then there was so much noise. I could hear *all* of Travis. And that wasn't a good thing.

Fuck.

CHAPTER SEVENTEEN

Nefertiti
Epep 2014

THE MEMORY FELT SO REAL, I could see every motion, every droplet of blood, but it was not mine. I could see Lucy in the bathroom but it was like I was watching it through my own eyes. There was so much blood. I stared at my face in the mirror, or Liliana's face, and there were tears streaming down it. I touched the moisture like it was a foreign object, because they weren't my tears, but they were. I was in her body and she could feel it all.

'What is wrong, my light?' Karrept asked as he walked into the bathroom. His gaze went from my body to my face, and in the mirror I watched as concern filled his eyes. 'Are you hurt?'

I shook my head. How could I put into words what I was feeling when they weren't even my feelings?

'Is there some run off magick?'

'I can feel her,' I whispered, not quite sure on what he meant. 'All of her. Liliana is inside and she is screaming, kicking and fighting to come out. I just relived a memory with the descendant. She tried to kill herself. Ran a blade down both of her arms to bleed out. And she would have if Aten's descendant didn't save her. She was almost dead, because of something that we did. We took away her family.'

'We were getting her ready for what was to come, Nefertiti. This is everything we wanted. A time without Aten and a time where we could explore the world. It's our time now.'

Karrept leaned over to place a kiss at the top of my head and I lurched back. 'No. We took them from her. I don't know if I want to do this.'

'This is why it was meant to be the descendant. She would have been a better choice; she was supposed to be ready for this.'

'But she is not. She was not. There is a Bond between them. I think that the Bond was made when Nephthys created the spell. It was the price that was paid. I can feel them, Karrept. I can feel them, I can hear them, I can share memories with them. Maybe the Book is to blame, but we did this. This is on us.'

'No, it is not. We did everything right, we did it all right and Nephthys made sure of it. That is the end of it.'

I turned on my heel and looked at him, almost like I did not recognise him—and I didn't. I had been a spirit, wandering for thousands of years, while he'd been dead. Maybe he'd been in a sarcophagus or maybe he'd been floating; his army had learned tricks to keep him secret, to plant him just where he was needed. But he hadn't seen the world change before his eyes.

I had.

I was sharing a body with Liliana and her screaming was endless. My head pounded with the noise, but I was sure that whatever had happened we were the reason that there was this connection between them. It was a hard pill to swallow. I didn't even know what that meant, but by sharing her body I had access to the colloquial terms that I would have missed out on. It was weird to have all this knowledge and not have learned it.

'Nefertiti. We have waited so long for this moment. We

cannot let it go by. We cannot let this small change stop us from getting our way. The world is ready for us. I am ready for us.'

'I did not say that I wasn't ready for this, but the Bond was the price that was set when we made the spell, when you died and I sacrificed myself. It has been a part of them all along and they found each other in this reincarnation. It means something.' I felt Liliana scream, this time louder, and I cradled my head. It was too much. Like there was something she really needed to say but could not. 'I don't know how to make it stop, but this is where we are now. This is what we have to do. We need to quieten her voice, or this is not going to work.'

Karrept looked at me like I was going crazy. And maybe I was, but there was something different about being inside a body. It had been thousands of years since I was last flesh and bone, and it was going to take some time to adjust, but it meant that the plan had to change. I wanted to change. I want to help the descendant and Aten's reincarnation. But that wasn't why I was here. We were going to use the Illuminate Year to bring forth a time where gods wouldn't be feared—they would be revered. And it would start here. It had to.

'We need to find a way to make her quiet. I cannot handle having her screaming and trying to break through. She is not as together as the descendant, but she is still strong enough.'

'My light, we need to separate her from you. I can do that, but I need the Book to get the right spell. I cannot accidentally separate the two of you and lose you for good.'

'Separate?'

Noooooooo, Liliana screamed, and I pressed my eyes shut, but as I did, I felt something inside me snap. Like someone held up a stick and broke it in half.

'Something happened,' I said. Racing through my brain, I tried to find what was different. It was hard because everything felt so foreign, but it was there. Through the haze of Liliana, I realised it was the Bond. 'They broke it,' I whispered.

'Who?' Karrept said. I looked up into his eyes, my body tingling with excitement.

'The descendants. They broke it. I don't know what they have done, but I cannot feel them anymore. Or they altered it in some way. I cannot put it into words, but there is something missing. This is what we need. This is exactly what we need.'

Liliana was quiet. I could feel her slipping into the dark. Was she trying to find out what was going on? Or was she trying to slink away?

CHAPTER EIGHTEEN

Lucy
Epep 2014

BIRDS CHIRPED through my consciousness and I groaned. It must have been morning because my body ached and it was far too bright. I opened my eyes and groaned again as I threw an arm over my face to hide behind the gloom of the shadow.

'Hey, hey, don't *do* that. You're ruining my picture.'

Travis was sitting across from me with a sketchbook and pencil, frowning at me.

'You're drawing again?' I sat up on my elbows and he clicked his tongue.

'Yes. Now go back to sleep. I was nearly done.' He pointed back to the couch as he looked over the rim of the glasses.

'Get out. You got enough of a look. Do it from memory. I miss seeing you with your glasses. Wait, you don't need to wear your glasses.' He had perfect vision thanks to his werewolf genetics, but he did look hot. Really hot.

Travis smirked but the doorbell rang before he could say anything.

Shit, shit, shit. That could be my *savta* on the other side of the door, coming to check up on me, and I was naked. And I'd had sex last night. She was going to kill me. She always had a sixth sense when it came to us kids doing things that we shouldn't.

'Clothes. Where are mine?' I hissed at him. He just shrugged. It was easy for him; he was a werewolf, so he was used to nudity. He spent a good chunk of his life naked, running with the pack. I, on the other hand, was not, and if that was my *savta*, she would not be pleased at all.

'Fine. I'm taking this.' I grabbed his shirt and put it on. I also found my underwear, but nothing else. 'Put some pants on, it might be my grandmother.'

His eyes widened, but I didn't see him get up because I was skidding down the foyer to answer the door.

As soon as I did, I wished I hadn't.

Standing in front of me, with her brown hair tied back from her face and wearing denim shorts and a purple tank top, was Kali Shaw. She looked me over, and I felt the anger bubbling under the surface. It didn't feel like mine, but I don't know who else's it could be.

'I see it didn't take you long to jump on my seconds.'

Before my brain could catch up with my actions, I slapped her across the face. I should have slammed the door and stormed back down the foyer, but I didn't. I turned on my heel and saw Travis was wearing pants now and a singlet. Decent enough to deal with people. Or, well, a person. I pointed at the door on my way past him. 'You deal with Hurricane Kali. I'm going to go and get changed. And I'm not sorry.'

'Lucy, wh—?'

I didn't hear the rest of what he said because I bolted through the living room and back up the stairs, collecting my clothes from the office on my way up. Leaning against the door, I tried to calm myself, but it felt like there was an angry beast

125

under my skin. It was pacing, hungry, wanting. It wasn't mine—I didn't have that kind of anger—but it was there. It wanted me to make a home for it, though.

I pulled Travis' shirt off my body and threw it to the ground. I found some of my own clothes and settled for a skirt and tank top. I caught a glimpse of my hair in my mirror and gasped. It was messy, sticking up every which way. I looked dishevelled. I sat down on the stool and started to fix it when my attention snagged on a photo of my family.

Everyone was happy, smiling, *living* and oblivious to the secrets that we, as a collective, held. Anger unfurled from inside my stomach, and I watched the picture hit the floor. I blinked at it for a second before I leaned down to pick it up. There was no way that it could have been me. I had better control than that with my powers, and that anger …

'Luce?' Travis said from the door. The frame forgotten for a moment, I turned around to look at him. He was holding himself carefully. Almost like he was afraid he would anger me. It was more of a gesture I would make than one he would.

'What? I mean, sorry.' I sighed.

'Are you okay?' He took a step into my room and I held up a hand. He stopped instantly, and I knew that it was not my power but his own free will, not wanting to hurt me.

'I … don't know. There's this anger. You know I'm not an angry person, but it's there, under my skin, and it wants me to hurt things. Or it's doing weird things.' I gestured to the broken picture frame and Travis tried to come closer. 'Don't, please. I'm afraid of what I'll do.' *Or say*, I added silently.

He was expecting more. I could feel it and I just … I couldn't give him more and he wanted to try to coax it out of me. I wasn't ready for that, and I wasn't sure I ever would be.

'Do you want me to do anything?' he asked.

'Yeah.' I pushed myself off the stool and carefully started

picking up the pieces of glass from the frame. 'Keep Kali occupied. I'll be down soon.'

He nodded and lingered for a moment. I could tell he wanted to come and hug me or something. Definitely something. The heat in his gaze made me uncomfortable. It was like I had awakened a sleeping beast inside him and he was waiting for more. More I couldn't give him.

'YOU CAN'T BE SERIOUS,' Travis said.

'Deadly. What? The guy tried to grab my arse; you think I was going to let him get away with that? You've been out of my life for too long if you think I would,' Kali replied.

As I crept down the stairs, I had to fight the urge to run back up and away from what I was about to walk into. Two old flames catching up, my high-school-enemy-now-half-sister talking to my best friend, in *my* house. It was almost too much to bear. I was at the threshold to the living room when I turned away. I couldn't think of her as my sister, even though we shared blood. Not right then.

'Luce?' Travis' voice made me turn around and look at him.

He couldn't have been looking for me, but I felt him feel through the Bond. That never happened. He could never do that before. There was no way that I could have felt him reaching out for me. We could feel emotions and we could find where one of us was, sort of like a hunch, but we could never feel where the other was physically. Like being able to pinpoint exactly where they were. Something was wrong. It had to be broken.

'Hi,' I said.

How lame.

Don't go running away, Travis whispered into my mind, and I held his gaze. His eyes were a deeper green, calm, different to what normally stared back at me. Part of me was relieved to hear him, whatever happened he was still there. That shouldn't be reassuring but it was.

It's hard when you're playing house with the woman I hate, I retorted.

Travis snorted, and Kali looked up, her gaze moving from Travis to me and back to Travis.

'Okay, what am I missing here?'

'Nothing,' I said quickly. She didn't need to hear about the Bond that Travis, Lili and I had. If she didn't already know, I wasn't about to clue her in.

'Whatever,' she mumbled and tucked into her eggs. 'You're still a great cook,' she said to Travis through the mouthful.

'It's always breakfast time,' I muttered to myself as I slipped onto a bar stool and danced my fingers over the counter.

I wasn't sure how I felt about this. I wanted to run away. I wanted to slap her again. But most of all I wanted to climb into bed and not come out for a few days. Maybe I could stretch it to a few years. Everything would blow over, right? It would, yeah? I tried hard to put those barriers back up between Travis and myself, but I was struggling to concentrate on the wall of earth that was normally there to protect him from my thoughts. It was there, but it was just dirt. Drenched dirt. It was mud.

Stop thinking like we're going to hurt you. Or that Kali is the bad guy here. He paused. *Or me.* I could hear the hurt in his words, and it made me want to crawl under a rock.

We could feel emotions when the others felt them, but hearing emotion in their voice when they spoke, that was … new. Sleeping together seemed to have fractured the Bond. Or changed it.

What had we done?

More so, why didn't we know this was something that could happen?

'You deserved it,' I said to Kali. The words were out of my mouth before I could even try to police them. Oops.

'I probably did, but you didn't need to walk away,' Kali said.

'You're here uninvited. I wouldn't have expected any less!' My fingers tightened around the bench and Travis gave Kali a stare.

'What? You're not going to take responsibility for this, Trav? Really?' Kali said.

Then it clicked. Travis had called her here. Traitor.

'Hey, I never said I wouldn't. There is just no need to go about throwing insults and the like. She knows you're her sister now, you *have* to deal with that.'

'You *told* her?' Kali stood up, knocking the stool to the floor. My first response was to get to my feet too. Self-defence classes taught me that being at the same height as your opponent was the best offence.

'I was angry, it slipped out.'

'I made you swear. You broke it.' Kali walked around the counter so that she was standing near Travis.

It made my skin crawl.

'She was making me angry.'

'Lucy always makes you angry. She's always been the one you talk about the most, the one who is always perfect. Why the fuck do you think it was so hard to be with you half of the time?'

I swallowed hard before I backed away slowly. I didn't want to be here for the Kali meltdown.

'Oh, we're going to have that fight again? You broke up with me. I loved you as much as I could and you wanted more. I told you I couldn't give you more. Deal with it.' Travis growled—an inhuman noise that made me pause—but then he let out a sigh. 'Dammit, Kali, I didn't call you here to fight over shit that happened a year ago. I called you here to help, so sit down, finish those goddamn eggs you like and shut up. Lucy, sit down.'

I sat, and for a moment was completely dumbfounded that I did as I was told. It was like I had no will of my own. I stared at

Travis before I glanced at Kali. She was staring back at me and angrily stabbing at her eggs.

'Happy now? Daddy gave you everything and me, nothing,' she spat out.

'That's a lie,' I told her. My mind was still on the command, but I knew Kali's volatile attitude was going to be a problem.

'Excuse me?' She tried to get closer to me.

'I had to work for everything I got. Everything. I didn't know you were my sister and yet you still made my life a living hell. If I had known that Travis had called you here to help, I would have talked him out of it.'

She snorted. 'Yeah, like you talked him out of his clothes.'

That was enough. I picked up the knife that was within reach and went to throw it. Travis caught my wrist and grabbed the knife.

'Kali, please don't bait her.' Travis' touch was grounding, calming.

'She de—'

'No. Stop. Seriously. You're her sister. She *just* found out about that, so cut her some slack. You've known for way longer. Remember when you found out?'

Kali dropped her eyes to the plate and mumbled something I didn't hear. Travis put the knife out of reach before taking my face in his hands.

'What are you doing? You're a mess.' The words were so soft, I almost missed them. I pushed him back because I couldn't breathe—too much intensity.

'Do I get some eggs?' I asked, changing the topic. Food was always safe.

'Yeah, mushrooms too. And bacon. If you want it.'

'Yes, please.'

Travis held my gaze and asked me without words what was up. He couldn't understand. He was Travis. And a werewolf.

What did he know about being a woman? Or human? He was more beast than he was human most days.

I stared at Kali as she ate and I felt something tear. She had Dad's nose, and his ears. Why did I never notice that before? She felt my stare.

'What?' she said. Hostility radiated from her.

'You have Dad's nose.'

'Wh-what?' This time there was no malice in her voice. She rubbed her fingers over her nose and frowned.

The words *I'm sorry* fluttered to the tip of my tongue, but I knew better than to say them. She didn't deserve them.

'Here's your food.' Travis put a plate in front of me and I smiled.

'Thank you.' I picked up the fork and poked at the eggs.

'Travis said you guys had a problem.' Kali filled the awkward silence that had ensued with a question that made me glare at Travis.

'Yes, but I'm not sure what I can really say about it beyond the fact that Lili was taken by a thing. I want to say that he's a mummy, but I don't know what the hell he is.' I was hesitant about saying much else. Trust was a big thing with me, and Kali had neither earned it nor warranted it.

'So a mummy took Lili and you have something he wants. Or someone. There's details missing. What are they, Lucy? Travis mentioned a book.'

My glare deepened and Travis held up his hands before starting the clean-up. Stupid werewolf.

'Yeah, it's an ode to Nefertiti, who is an ancestor.'

'Wait, does that make me ...?'

'No. We share a father; Nefertiti is from my mother's side,' I replied and Kali's face fell. 'Anyway, the Book is full of spells, inscriptions and stuff.' I stared down at the food in front of me and wanted to dig myself into a deep hole. 'They wanted me. They couldn't get me, so they took Lili instead.'

I stopped talking and listened to the clatter of cutlery and the gentle tap of plates as Travis loaded the dishwasher. It was like no one wanted to say a word.

Maybe Karrept should have just taken me instead. Maybe I shouldn't have fought as hard as I did.

'Can I see the Book?' She leaned forward as I popped a mushroom into my mouth. I chewed it slowly before swallowing.

'Um … I'm not sure what you'll be able to get out of it. It's written in Ancient Egyptian. So if you're good at reading that, you're welcome to.' I didn't want her to look at the Book because I didn't want her to find something I missed. Or touch it. It was mine and I didn't want to share what was mine.

I already had to share Travis with her.

'I don't, but it won't hurt to have someone else look at it. What's the worst that could happen?' she said.

She could break it. Like she did Travis. I sighed. 'Okay, but after food. I'm starving.'

'Deal,' she murmured and went back to her breakfast.

We all sat in silence as we ate. I couldn't look at anyone.

WITH THE FOOD finished and the dishes put away, I went to grab the Book from its hiding place, which was in the study. But I had a feeling, deep in the pit of my stomach, that made me leave it right where it was.

There was a crash and my heart raced as I ran into the living room.

'Travis, did you just break something?' The glass door to the backyard was completely shattered. 'What the he—'

'Lucy! Duck.'

I dropped to the floor on my hands and feet in a plank position. A rush of air shadowed my body. I let my tummy hit the floor and rolled so that I could catch a glimpse of what it was.

'Are you kidding me?' I watched a throwing staff hit the breakfast counter, and with a loud clunk it bounced to my left, missing me by inches. 'That was a—' My words were cut short as I saw Karrept and Travis locked in a fistfight outside. I got to my feet and ran outside, stopping just short of the end of the porch as Kali came up next to me. Her fingers wrapped around my wrist and she shook her head.

'I wouldn't. Unless you have some kind of power.' Her eyes widened when I tried to pull on her hand. 'You do. What is it?'

'Telekinesis is the biggest one, and magick, but it's not really working that well in the house. I can't … I have to go and help.'

'Lucy, I don't know if that's a good idea. Travis is a werewolf, he can handle himself. You're going to be defenceless out there.'

I smiled at Kali. 'I could never be defenceless. Can you put up some kind of barrier around the house? And make it specific to who can enter? Is that something you can do?' I glanced at Travis, who dodged another punch before he tried to sweep Karrept's feet from under him, but he was fast. Almost as fast as a werewolf. Not good. 'Kali, there might be sigils already up, but I haven't checked that they're still there in a while.'

'I didn't think that would be something you would know.' And with that, Kali turned and started to walk around the house, muttering under her breath.

I heard clapping and saw Lili/Nefertiti sitting on the retaining wall. 'Hello, Nefertiti.'

'Oh, Lucy, look at this. Our two men fighting together. Isn't it glorious?' She pressed her fingertips together and smiled wider.

'Just your man. Not mine,' I said. I searched for vines or something that I could use to make my way up there, or bring her down.

'Oh, come on, you two did a naughty thing. He is your man.'

I stopped looking, fear freezing my entire body as I studied her. On her face was a look that straddled an expression Lili would make and something else; something much darker. 'What do you mean?' I barely choked out.

'You and Travis, you broke something. And you know it. That look on your face says it all.'

'Lucy, look out!' I had time to turn around before I was hit in the face. I didn't get time to think about the throbbing before Karrept was right there again, in front of me.

Karrept was fast, faster than I'd anticipated. He kicked me, and I was too late to dodge, distracted by his all-too-familiar face. He hit my ribs once before I got my bearings and blocked him with my forearm. I grabbed his leg and twisted him away from me.

He spun in the air before he slammed into the grass. I planted my hands behind my head and swung my hips up to kick up off the ground. My ribs screamed at me, but it was enough motivation for me to back up.

'Trav, are you okay?' He wasn't answering. 'Travis?' Frantically, I tried to sense where he was, but Karrept was on his feet and making his way over to me.

I dropped down into a defensive position and held my fist up, just like my self-defence master had taught me. A growl came from my left, and I watched Travis get to his feet.

'You two have been naughty. Have you not?' Karrept said, a smirk on his face that looked so wrong. All I could see was Hunter, and it made it hard to be afraid of him. Hunter would never hurt me, but I knew Karrept wouldn't hesitate.

'Your girl-toy said the same thing,' I said as Travis stood at my side now. I saw his hands twitch in the corner of my vision.

'Watch your mouth. That is your ancestor,' he snapped.

'She's in my best friend's body. She's a girl-toy,' I replied. I'd struck a nerve.

He hit me and pain throbbed harder through my face. I held up a hand to stop Travis from doing anything.

'Karrept!' Nefertiti said in Lili's voice. I hated that she

sounded so like her and so not at the same time. It made this harder.

I gingerly touched my cheek and blood covered my fingertips. The bastard had hit me hard enough to bleed. Fury raged through my body. If it left a scar, I was going to make sure he died a second time, or a third. No matter who he looked like.

Travis, get Lili. I'll take Karrept. We have to split them up.

Travis showed no exterior indication that I had spoken to him telepathically, but he moved. Lightning fast he pounced at Lili, but she jumped back. At this stage, I swept Karrept's legs out from under him with a low spinning sweep kick. He landed on his back and I kicked him in the ribs.

He smiled and got to his feet before he flicked me across the yard and into a wall. My shoulder hit it hard and I whimpered. Pain dotted behind my lids and I had trouble breathing.

'You are nothing. You're supposed to be powerful, but you're not,' Karrept said as he stepped closer. 'If I cannot have your body, I will kill you so that you know what it is like to have someone murder you before your time.'

Karrept wrapped his fingers around my neck, and with every second, he tightened his grip. I clawed at his fingers to try to make him stop.

'I think you might want to stop that.'

Karrept froze and peered over his shoulder. I followed his gaze and saw Kali had a knife to Lili's throat. The mummy dropped his hand and spun so fast a mini dirt storm kicked up under his feet.

'Don't come any closer or I will slit her throat,' Kali cautioned.

I rubbed a hand over my neck, and Travis flicked out his claws. He was going straight for Karrept. He jumped Karrept and had his claws within touching distance of his face.

'Kali! Whatever you've got planned, don't you dare hurt her,' I screamed at her.

'*She is mine,*' Karrept said. I weighed up the distance between where I was and the porch. Kali would slit Lili's throat before I could get there. I could focus on the knife if I tried hard enough, but the threat made Karrept stop.

'What did he say?' Travis said through gritted teeth as Karrept's knowing eyes stared at him. It was as if he knew he shouldn't move.

'That she's his,' I said. 'Kali, what are you doing?'

'Stop what you're doing, Karrept.' She pressed the blade into Lili's throat and I gasped, stepping forward involuntarily. It was in my nature to want to protect Lili. I needed to. She was the healer, the helper, not a fighter. I hated that I couldn't protect her now. She wasn't Lili. Lili was in there somewhere, but she wasn't going to come out right then and there.

'Kali. Stop,' I pleaded.

'First, we need to figure out why they're here. Why they decided to come right now.' Lili wouldn't tell her, not even as Nefertiti. If Lili did something out of character, she would never say so. We would have to discover what it was for ourselves.

'The Book and the curse,' Karrept said. And it was in English.

Nefertiti gurgled as Kali pressed harder against her neck. I moved a step forward without realising it.

'You're hurting her!' I said, panic creeping into my voice.

'That's the whole point.'

Travis' claws were dangerously close to Karrept's face; one scratch would be all he needed to make him a guy living with excruciating pain for the rest of his life. Or to kill him. Werewolves transmitted diseases in their wolf form and they were medicinally hard to cure. It rotted away bones and flesh before any form of antibiotic could get to it. The infection worked in reverse; it was how their own healing worked. It was the perfect weapon.

'Travis. Pull back.' I put my hand down and Karrept's eyes

widened as they focused on my chest. Almost like he was afraid of something. My hand came to the necklaces that hung at my throat. The tiger's eye and clear quartz crystals had fused together because they were close to one another. Destiny's necklace, the one that she had left behind, had always been an item of power, and when they were joined, like they were around my neck right then, that magnified the protection that came with the necklaces. Heirlooms we had been given from our *savta* with the promise of guidance.

He pushed Travis off him, with strength that surprised not only me but Travis too. It made him cry out. There was no way that was humanly even possible. There was an exchange between Nefertiti and Karrept, the words fast and almost unrecognisable, but they made sense.

'Kali, let her go. Right now. They're leaving.'

'What?'

'Right now,' I said.

Kali let go of her. She seemed surprised, but once Nefertiti was clear, they mumbled to each other before they disappeared in a haze of sand.

'What did they say?' Travis said as his fingers brushed my elbow.

'They were afraid of these.' I lifted the chains from around my neck for them to see. The necklaces sparkled in the light.

CHAPTER NINETEEN

Nefertiti
Epep 2014

'THAT WAS NOT SUPPOSED to happen. We were meant to get the Book,' Karrept growled. With the swipe of his hand, a vase on the coffee table shattered against the wall.

I would have been surprised by it, but I was too busy looking at the cut in the mirror. 'That bitch got me good.' I pressed a tissue against the cut on my neck.

'Are you okay, my light?' Karrept said as he rushed over to me.

His hands rubbed my shoulders and the warmth that came from them was enough to make my whole body relax. He still pulled the same reaction from my body regardless of time or space, and with Liliana quietened I leaned into his touch. It felt like heaven again. My other hand moved to his hips and squeezed.

'I am okay. It is superficial. But they were ready. You saw the necklaces, right?' I asked.

'Yes. I thought the other descendant would have had it on her so that this would not happen. She had it the last time I saw her.'

I stared at him in the mirror and searched his face; he had frown lines that hadn't been there three millennia ago and he looked tired. The fight took it out of him.

'I could have sworn the necklace was on the other one, I thought I saw it. But they have them. We need to get them away from the descendant or we are not going to be able to get what we want.'

Karrept smiled and removed the tissue from my hand to take over dabbing. 'It is a superficial cut.' He sighed, and his body seemed to lose steam. I saw his tired eyes: there was pain in them now that I looked harder.

'The spell did not heal it, did it?' I asked.

He seemed taken aback. Maybe, after all these years, he didn't think that I remembered, but I did. I couldn't forget the whole reason we were here. In that Book lay something more important than words, to me and to him.

'Let me see it,' I whispered. He shook his head and I took a step back, letting the blood drip out of the cut. I wanted to see what all this time had done.

'Nefertiti,' he warned.

'No, I am not the meek little wife that I was. I need to see it. You are meant to be at full power, and if what I believe to be true is there, then that makes this whole thing ... different.'

'You always had a tenacity that no one understood. Even as you rose to power. It is part of why I love you so. But I cannot show you.'

'Karrept, I am not going to ask again. Show me, or I will be forced to show myself. This body doesn't have access to the same power that the descendant does, but she is a Watcher and that has a different skill level altogether. Show me.'

He sighed again and pulled his shirt over his head, revealing sun-kissed skin. I was always obsessed with his arms; for a priest, he had honed his body well. I could feel my whole body react and tighten with a single glance. His skin was unblemished, rippled and so beautiful, but there was something there, something he was hiding. I tilted my head and clicked my tongue.

'Drop the glamour.'

And like that, the perfect skin was gone, replaced with a festering wound. I held back a gasp because I wanted to show that it didn't bother me, but it did. I did not think it would still be like this; we had started the spell to find a time where magick had the ability to heal something like this. Being incorporeal, I hadn't found anything, but there was more in the Book. And if I had the descendant's body … the knowledge I would have …

It would be unparalleled.

I wondered if the Watcher had the same knowledge, but whatever had been broken, I had a feeling that it also meant that she was locked up tight.

You could say that, I heard a voice in my head as I took a step closer to Karrept. My fingers gingerly brushed the edges of the wound and he winced.

'Did you hear that?' I asked.

'Hear what, my light?' He looked down at me and I shook my head.

'Nothing,' I murmured.

Yeah, he's not going to be able to hear me, but maybe, just maybe, we can come to some sort of deal. Because that looks pretty nasty.

The Watcher was not wrong. The wound looked the same as it did when it happened. It hadn't aged a day, but that wouldn't be the case forever. It would fester, and I would lose the love of my life. Again.

This time it would be permanent.

What do you know about it? I asked her. And instantly felt weird. The last time someone had access to my thoughts, he would use it. Or try to. Aten wasn't kind in the least.

I have access to things you don't. That's all. And with that, there was silence.

Just great. I was going crazy in a new millennium.

CHAPTER TWENTY

I HISSED as Travis pressed a bag of frozen peas to my cheekbone.
'Ouch, *ouch*. That hurts.'

'Mm, he got you real good.'

'Thanks for stating the obvious, *capitán*.' I pushed him back.
Even the gentlest of presses made my face ache, and he was not
helping.

Kali stared at me with a smug look.

'What? What's that look for? You could have seriously hurt
Lili. What got into you?' I spat out.

Travis' fingers slid under my shirt, and it distracted me for a
moment before I swatted them. 'Lucy, your ribs, let me see
them. You could have fractured something, and you don't have
the joy of supernatural healing,' he said.

I growled and lifted up my shirt. His fingers spanned over
my ribs hesitantly.

'Kali. Why would you put Lili in danger like that?' I asked

again, and hissed as Travis hit a tender spot, tearing my attention away from Kali and to him. I gave him a withering stare.

'You know, you think that you're so smart, but you forgot
one thing: Karrept is a man. He has the same impulses; attack
the thing he loves and he's going to cave,' Kali commented.

My attention was brought back to Travis.

'Bitch. *Ouch*, Trav.' He looked apologetic but pressed his
fingers over my ribs again in the same spot.

'I think it's just bruised, but without a scan we can't know.
We should really go to the hospital.'

I ignored his words. 'You were hurting Lili, and you could have
done some serious damage. That was not part of the deal. At all.'

'You were in trouble. Travis was in trouble. I did what was
necessary to save you *both*.' She uncrossed her legs and leaned
forward, her cup of tea now hovering above her lap. I willed it
to splash over the edge. 'Oh, come *on*,' she lamented as it did.

Kali stared at me and my cheek started to throb harder. The
power she pushed into me made me angry, and I cried out in
pain as it got too much.

'Kali, that is *enough*. Stop hurting her on purpose.' Travis was
different when he spoke to Kali. Like he had more power.

'She started it,' she said, standing as she tried to wipe the
liquid off her legs with her hands but it didn't do anything her
legs were still wet.

'Are you four, seriously? Just quit it, both of you. We're here
now we have to let her in, Luce. She did a bad thing. I'm angry
about it too, but being petty is not going to bring Lili back. Kali,
can you take a look at this? I assume a hospital trip is out of the
question, then?'

I nodded and shut up. A wordy Travis was rare, especially
when he was trying to make a point. The media would have a
field day with this; they would be tipped off by a staff member
wanting to get their fifteen minutes of fame. If I was at full

capacity with my powers, I could have healed myself, but personal gain and all.

'I felt her,' Kali said as she put the mug down and inspected my ribs.

'Who?' I felt stupid for asking, but I needed to know.

'Lili. She was under there. I have the ability to see auras, to pick them apart and put them back together. I can single out people in a crowd if I know them. I felt her, Lucy.'

I instinctively reached out for Kali, but Travis made sure that the peas went back to my cheek, distracting me. 'What do you mean, you felt her?'

'I know what she feels like. I've been around her long enough to know her. I can pick you out in a crowd too. I used to think that was because I hated you because you're my half-sister, but I know it's because I just get it. Genetics and all that.'

'Wh-what?' I winced as she touched the part of my ribs that hurt the most. I felt warmth spread through her fingers. 'What are you doing?'

'She was scared, terrified of what they were doing. But she's in there, and as long as she's in there, we can use that. I know we can.' Kali's explanation was clearly designed to distract me as her fingers felt like they burned a hole in my skin.

'What are you doing, Kali?' I asked.

'Helping your fractured rib heal a little. It's not much, but it's not personal gain to heal someone with your own aura. Don't think too much into it.' Kali shrugged and backed off. My torso still hurt, but it was less of a stabbing pain and more manageable.

'Thank you,' I said sincerely.

The shock in her eyes was enough to make me want to take it back. She didn't expect anything from me, and I seemed to expect more from her. Maybe because it was a grudge I had always harboured, but she was the better person right in that moment.

She recovered and the shock was hidden from sight. 'No sweat. Do you think I can take a look at that Book? You should rest. Have a nap or something. It'll help.'

A nap would be good. 'I'll get the Book. It's in the study. Maybe you'll find something I haven't.'

She nodded and Travis helped me off the couch. What a weird day this was.

THE SUN HAD long set and the full moon shone bright in the sky. There was a ring around the moon, a glow, the only tell that the earth was making its path between the moon and the sun. I really loved eclipses, I was always in awe of the event and the thrall it had a hold on my attention. Tonight, of all nights, there would be a total lunar eclipse. I leaned back and the hammock sighed softly as it swayed with my subtle movements. The air was still hot and dry but there was a breeze to it. I glanced over my shoulder at the door that was back in place; I called my *savta* and she'd been unhappy about the destruction, but she called someone and they would be here in the morning to fix it. She had good connections. I also had to convince her that I was fine and that she didn't need to come down. I didn't need a lecture about the cuts and bruises on my body.

'Is there room for two on there?' Travis' voice was soft, hesitant.

'It's big enough to fit, like, five. Of course there's room,' I said and shifted over.

He sat down next to me and the hammock swung a little harder. I looped my fingers through the holes and waited for it to stop. It was almost automatic—Devin used to try to throw me off it when we were children.

I pointed at the sky. 'Blood moon,' I said softly. 'A total lunar eclipse. At the climax, the moon has a red haze to it. It's my favourite part.'

He was silent as we watched. It was a slow process and the sun was only just starting to touch the moon, so the smallest hints of red were colouring the moon already.

'Doesn't that take hours?' Travis asked finally.

I looked at him with a smile. 'Yes.'

'And you're going to sit out here all night?'

'Yup. It's the only time that I've ever felt at peace. I don't know what it is about eclipses, but they soothe me.'

And after everything that happened in the last twenty-four hours, I needed to be soothed.

'Luce …' Travis started.

I held up a hand and shook my head. 'Please, don't.'

'I love you.' He said the words and I closed my eyes. 'I love you, and you're not saying it back. Or giving me anything. What is going on?'

This conversation was going to happen sooner or later. I would have preferred never, but that was asking too much. I knew that. 'I can't. Don't. Let's just drop it.'

'We slept together and you're barely looking at me. Did I do something wrong?'

Yes, I wanted to tell him. *You helped me cross a line I didn't want to cross.* Instead I looked at him.

'It's not you, it's more me. I love Hunter. I love him with all of my soul. He's my soulmate. And I mean it literally. We found out that we're what's called *Adelphi Psychi*. It's Greek. We're destined to be.'

I could hear his heart breaking. And I wanted to stop it but I was sick of him not listening to me.

I didn't want to have a lovesick puppy following me around instead of the werewolf I knew we needed.

'So sleeping with me didn't mean anything?' The hurt in his voice was a reason as to why I couldn't do this.

'It did, Trav. But I can't let it go beyond what it was.'

He stared at me before he laced his fingers through mine and brought my hand up to his lips. 'I can't take back what I did or how I feel, Luce. I want a fighting chance here.'

'You're going to lose. And the thought of breaking your heart kills me. I won't be responsible for that.'

'But you already are.' He pulled me closer, and my body betrayed me. Heat flushed my face and my stomach tightened with need. His hands gripped my biceps and he held me there. He looked so vulnerable, and I realised that there was no one there but him. No wolf, no family, just Travis Matthews. Just a man asking me to love him.

If I could love him the way he wanted me to, everything would be okay. But I couldn't.

'Trav. Don't.'

'What does he have that I don't?' He leaned up and his lips hovered a breath away from mine.

'He's not a wolf. Or my best friend who's always been there,' I whispered.

He kissed me like his life depended on it, like life had no meaning without me. I was taken aback by the feelings that radiated off him. The beauty of it was that Travis was always rough around the edges. He was popular, and I knew that he was vulnerable—I'd seen it—but this was different. He was raw.

He pulled back, and I sighed as I looked up at him. I expected to see eyes ringed in purple, but they weren't—they were green and lust-filled. How long had it been since I'd had a man look at me like that? Too long.

And that was probably why I stayed away from men in general after Hunter. It always got me into trouble.

I kissed him, cupping his face and climbing on top of him. I hissed into his mouth as the movement jolted my ribs. Travis pulled away and laughed. 'Luce, your ribs. Come on now.'

He guided me onto my back and I caught a glimpse of the eclipse. It was just hitting the halfway point and I had been out on the hammock for at least an hour. Time was slipping away, because it hadn't felt like that long, I looked back at Travis and brushed the pads of my fingers over his stubbled jaw.

'I can't love you like you want me to, Travis.'

Hurt clouded his eyes for a fraction of a second before he pushed it back behind the lust. He'd already come up with an answer to that. 'Just love me like this right now. Who cares about anyone else? Egypt can be our place.'

If only it was that easy. It would permanently damage our relationship, and leading him on was not okay. It just ... didn't work.

There was a cough and we both looked at Kali, who was clutching a cup against her shoulder and had a blank look on her face. Her presence made me think a little clearer—what had been about to happen?

'Kali?' Travis said.

'I figured it out. The Book. It has a depression spell over it, and that's probably why your mummy friend came out of the pages. Literally—there's a page missing from where the inscription was. But I think I can break the spell. Did you want to help?'

She was looking directly at me. She refused to acknowledge Travis, a look that I knew well. I forced myself to look at Travis and then back at Kali. Her blue-grey eyes stared back at me and there was a flash of hurt. *Shit*, I thought, realising she still loved him. Fuck. Travis had broken up with her and moved on; her ... not so much. My heart plunged into my stomach and I pushed Travis off me.

'Sure. Is it safe to do that when there's an eclipse going on?' I pointed to the sky and Kali looked impressed.

'Huh, would you look at that,' she said as she crouched down to see the moon. 'I completely forgot that was happening. It's just removing a spell with positive elements. And if anything, the magick will be heightened by the eclipse. I'm thinking that you can't handle another migraine from staring at the pages.'

'How did you kn—?'

Kali held up the glass. 'I got one. I got into your mother's wine. I'm sorry, but it tends to stop mine in their tracks.'

'It's fine. I'll be in in a few,' I said.

She nodded, her gaze lingering on Travis before she went inside.

I punched his shoulder. 'Ouch. What was that for?'

'She's still in love with you.'

'No, she's not.' He was in denial.

'You moron, yes, she is. I'm going to go and help. Stay put,' I said.

'You know, for someone who hated her, you're acting like a sister towards her already.'

I stared at him, realising he wasn't wrong. There was something innate about that. Maybe it was because I missed Destiny, or because it was just in my nature to care about people. 'Shut up.'

I got out of the hammock and slipped into the house between the curtains that blew in the breeze, a cool change from the blistering heat of the day. The house was sticky with humidity as a result. With the broken doors and opening any windows we could, it would help cool down the house as the air con was useless. I hoped that the cool change would stick around, but since it was the peak of summer, it wouldn't. No matter how much I willed it to.

'You know, he used to look at me the way he looks at you. When we first started dating and he didn't know I was a witch.' Kali interrupted my thoughts.

'I'm sorry,' I said.

'No, you're not, but thanks anyway.' I heard a crash. 'Ouch, fuck.'

I rushed up to the sink. 'You cut yourself.' Oh god, blood. *Not again.*

'Oops. I didn't mean to. I think it's deep.'

149

'What happened?' Travis came in and I turned to him.

'Oh no, no, no. Purple puppy eyes are not going to help right now. Go upstairs, I'm going to try and fix this.'

Kali laughed. 'Shouldn't puppy be shifting tonight?'

'Eclipse,' I reminded her.

'No bestiality for you tonight,' she said in a singsongy, shocky voice. Had she had more than a glass? There was no way she could be this drunk after one wine. And how had she hidden it so well?

'I guess you would know, hey?' I ran her hand under water to clear the wound. Thankfully, for everyone, it wasn't as deep as I had expected. 'How many glasses did you have?' I asked as an afterthought, knowing I wouldn't get an answer.

'You know it's not fair. He always wanted you, he never wanted me.'

'Kali. I won't have this conversation with you, so just stop. Seriously. What happened, happened. Let's just move on.' I picked out a shard of glass from her palm and she hissed at me.

'I just wanted to matter to him. I wanted him to love me like he loves you, Lucy. I was always jealous because you got everything. Our dad, Travis ... I got nothing.'

If I ignored her, maybe she would shut up. I grabbed the first-aid kit and flipped it open. Inside was a whole array of goodies to help. I started with the butterfly stitches; they would allow the wound to close up. And then I would put the gauze down, before wrapping her hand. I didn't know a lot about staunching wounds, but I felt like using all of those would definitely help. And echoing the steps in my head would drown out her words.

'You know werewolves are like poison. Everyone knows it. They have a system, a hierarchy, and you have to be born into it. Travis is the son of an alpha. His dad left him; he has a new family. A new wolf daughter that wants to rise up in the pack but can't because of Travis.' She leaned in closer. 'He doesn't like her very much. He doesn't like his father either. Oh well.'

Stick the butterfly stitch down and repeat with a second one before covering the cut with gauze and wrapping it. Avoid getting information I don't already have from Travis. No one gets upset.

Right?

WHEN I FINISHED PATCHING Kali up the best I could, she continued to stare at me. What did I do now? I averted my eyes and was saved by Travis, who was sitting next to Kali. I felt like I was intruding or something; the two of them were playing around, despite the fact that Kali just spilled her guts about Travis to me. I felt weird. I knew about his father. I didn't know about the werewolf culture that he experienced. He didn't talk about it much. I assumed it was to protect me, but maybe it was because he hated it.

'Let's do this,' Kali said and stood up. Her sway was minimal but the magick incantation she was muttering under her breath must have sobered her up. She lit the sage smudge stick and I grabbed the mason jar full of salt. Together we walked around in a circle to cast the spell. Travis opened his mouth, and I held up a hand to stop him. If he was going to talk, he could go into the other room. Distractions were not going to help us focus.

Once Kali finished smudging the circle and hopped inside it, I closed it with the salt. Then I forced my power out and visualised a golden circle of light. It settled around us and was strong, powerful. My innate ability to channel magick was still intact. A weight lifted off my shoulders and I sighed.

'Hunter is a good teacher,' Kali said. 'I've never seen a circle so strong before. Did you say that something happened to your other abilities?'

I nodded.

'Still amazing. Okay, so here's what we're going to do. The

raw amber, which is really rare—I'm impressed, by the way—is going to be the catalyst for the entire spell. We're going to burn it and drop it on the Book, then it should weaken the spell around it.'

'Then, I assume, the bergamot and black pepper are going to help break it down further?'

Kali nodded. 'You are good. Okay, give me your hand.' She held out her non bandaged hand, and I stared at it for a fraction of a second before taking it. She wrapped her fingers around my hand and I jumped as I saw her power rush to meet mine in my mind's eye. I could see her power in colours—very much like she could see auras, I assumed. Hers was purple, strong, darkened, whereas mine was golden, pure and a lot weaker in comparison. Our levels of training differed because mine was interrupted when Hunter and I broke up. The colours of our abilities met each other and meshed like they were a perfect match. And they were. We did share a bloodline, after all.

Hunter had told me that some powers refused to mesh together, and while it was rare, it happened and was dangerous. I breathed a little easier knowing that ours weren't opposing one another.

Together we focused on stilling our minds, our breaths and our bodies. Breathing in and out, I focused on the rise and fall of my chest. Sounds floated away like clouds passing in the sky, and Kali became an extension of my body, breathing in sync with me. Power spread through the circle, and when I knew I was ready, I opened my eyes. It happened to be the same time Kali opened hers too.

Without saying a word, she lit the incense as I uncapped the oil and shaker. We moved in harmony. It was as if we had been doing this all our lives; she dropped the incense as I shook the pepper and pinched a few drops of oil from the bottle. As they fell through the air, they hit a black circle of power, one that I hadn't seen before, until it shattered. The feeling that weighed me down when I read the inscription drained away. I picked up the Book and when I felt nothing, I grinned.

'Hex-free book, here we come,' I said and fingered through the pages.

'I think that this is why Karrept was released ... and you said you were attacked by a spirit?' Kali asked.

I nodded.

'Yeah, I think it's because of the hex. If it wasn't there, you probably wouldn't have a mummy running around and you wouldn't have been attacked by the spirit.'

I was about to reply when I gasped and dropped to my knees. The pressure in the air had changed and I struggled to breathe.

'Travis, no!' Kali yelled at Travis before she dropped to the floor, her hands ready to be a barrier to his foot.

'What?' he said as he stilled.

'You can't enter the circle when it's been cast, not without hurting Lucy. Back up slowly and we'll open it so you can come in,' Kali explained. She was quick, succinct and made sense. My words would have had an order and been laced with fury.

Travis backed up quicker than I thought was possible, and I took a deep, cleansing breath before I focused my attention back on the circle. I envisioned opening a box and pulled my power back into it, then I swept my fingers through the salt and opened the circle.

'Lucy, are you okay?' Travis was there in an instant, trying to comfort me.

'I'm fine,' I said as I shrugged it off. He held tight as I caught Kali's attention. Even though there were things that made him so wrong for me, he was still my best friend. But right now I was mad at him. He didn't need to step in just because the spell was done.

'Are you sure?' His voice was strained, like he was trying to stay calm.

'I'm sure. Really, it's okay. I'm okay.'

I closed my eyes and inhaled his scent. I could smell the musky wolf that was just beneath his skin. Most of the time he smelled like a forest, not this time.

'Trav?' I whispered.

'Mm?'

'Your wolf is so close to the surface.'

His response was to hold me tighter. I could swear he was trying to crack my bones. His silence said more than I wanted. And the wolf being so close to the surface meant that he was claiming me as a mate.

That was bad. Very, very bad.

CHAPTER TWENTY-ONE

Nefertiti
Epep 2014

THE ARRAY of foods brought to the room from the hotel staff was different from what I was used to. Food had changed and a lot of the little packaged foods confused me, even after watching it evolve it still confused me. Why were there grains that came in a box? And bread that was square in thin slices? And what was up with the glossy texture of that white stuff?

And there was brown liquid that smelled delicious but tasted disgusting.

That's coffee, the Watcher piped up.

Karrept was still asleep. We had worked on some spells to try healing the scratch. The years had been good to his powers, but being in the body of the Watcher made it harder for me to do magick. Karrept would be knocked out for hours, trying to heal and take in what we had done.

I ignored the Watcher's words and went into the bathroom. Closing the door behind me, I looked at the face that was now mine in the mirror. The Watcher was beautiful. She had strawberry blonde hair and perfectly sun-darkened skin, and I imagined she looked different from anyone in her family. Most Italians had darker hair, fair skin, but she seemed like an exception.

'Look, we need to talk,' I said to the mirror. Anyone else would think I was crazy. 'I know this is hard for you. I get it, I really do, but you need to be here. We need to be able to work with what we have, and I know that you know a lot more than I do. Especially about this world. But I just want to fix it all. All of it. And your body is a means to an end.'

I stared at the reflection in the mirror some more. My eyes looked weird in this body. The descendant was a perfect match; we were almost identical. The only thing that was different? Her age. She was older than I had been. But that was why we had waited so long. I wanted that body. I *needed* that body.

To get it, I had to make sure that I could get Liliana on board. Because the Watcher was the glue compound of the pyramid; she would be the one to help get them on our side. She was not only the peacekeeper but also the neck of the whole body. She could turn the descendant and the wolf whichever way she wanted.

Calling me by my name, that's a start. But also, my body is the body that you're currently in. You need to deal with that fact.

I could hear her voice clearly in my head. There was no static, no filter. It was just there.

'We need to work together. I want to help heal him, but I also want to be able to get out of your body.'

And into the body of my best friend. I think I'd rather die than let you do that. You do know that there are other ways to do this. I'm sure that your body, your real body, could come back from the dead. His did.

I shook my head. 'It is not that easy. I was mummified and my body, for all intents and purposes, is dead. It is done. I need *her* body to live.'

I have already heard you; you're not giving me much of a reason as to why I should even help you. You've got my body and you're basically using it to let me get raped.

I blinked at the mirror. What was rape? 'I do not know what you are talking about. I do not know what rape is.'

There was a snort in my head. I didn't think I had said something funny. *You're using my body without my permission and you're having sex with it. That's what rape is.*

'That is such an odd concept. Sex is never something to be coerced if the man—'

Let's not try and figure that one out. I don't know if I can get you to understand that one very much. Why are you here in this time?

'The eclipse ... it is in the right time. It's also the catalyst for the beginning of the way the world will change. It needs to change, again, like it did when I was ruling, though this is different. Magick needs to be different. I have watched how it changed and how magick has had to be hidden. This is why we are here. To free it.'

I wanted to truly free the world from the constraints on magick, but I also really wanted to live with Karrept. I wanted a time when I didn't have to be with Aten and be married to a man who was my own brother. I wanted to be with Karrept.

I can hear your thoughts. You do know that Karrept has a descendant that is alive and that Aten's descendant is also alive. He is also a wolf, but everything worked out in the end: Lucy is with Karrept's descendant. Why do you need to be here?

She did not get it. 'It is the way we wanted it, every part of this. We put it into motion. We worked it out so that you are the Watcher of the Bond, which was put in place because we needed a price so that there was balance for the spell that would save *him*. But we want more time together. We want to be together. Now, in this time and in this age. It is not about the descendants. It is about *us*.'

So basically you're just doing this because you're selfish. Yeah.
Fuck off. I'm going back down to where I can't hear you or see you.

And like that, I could not feel her. She disappeared. I knew
that her words were right—I *was* selfish. For the first time in my
life, I wanted what I had earned and I was going to get it.

No matter the price.

'WE NEED the help of the gods.'

Karrept looked at me from the bed with a bemused smile.
'You never cared too much about the gods.'

I ran a brush through my hair and adjusted my top. 'No, I
did not care for one god. Aten wanted to unite them all. I was all
for keeping them separate and using them. We should bring
them back. Use them to get to the descendant and the Book. I
think they will be able to get the gods to bring it back. To give
us the one thing we need to bring magick back into its rightful
place.'

He pushed himself out of bed, wincing as he sat up and then
stood up. The pain that lingered in each of his movements was
enough to make me want to stop him, but he would have found
a way to make sure that I did not interfere. Magick or
otherwise.

'You think we could do that?' he said. There was a sparkle in
his eye.

I nodded. 'I think you could do it.'

'But my magick ...'

I held out my hand. 'Use mine. I have it. The Watcher has
some, use that against them. We have always said that this was
our time. We need to make it our time, and the only way we do
that is if we actually use it. We can do this.'

He pulled me in close and pressed his body against mine. I
sighed and smiled up at him. There was still so much warmth in

his embrace, even as the wound slowly started to destroy him. How long would his mind last?

'I think I like this side of you. It is different from the side that I saw before we started the spell. Let us finish it.'

The talk with the Watcher had revealed that I was ready to make the most out of this situation. And this was just the beginning of what was to come.

'Let us start with the god of death.'

CHAPTER TWENTY-TWO

Lucy
Epep 2014

'THIS COULD BE A BAD IDEA. I mean, seriously. Going out, just the three of us? We've never done it before, why should we do it now?' I said as I pushed the earring through the pre-existing hole and stared at Travis in the mirror. He was walking around topless with his back to me. It made me pause my movements in getting ready, and I toyed with the ankh on the chain around my neck.

'Because you need it.' He was silent for a second. 'We all need it. When was the last time you went out? Even back home.'

He had a point; it had been way too long. We were of legal age back home but we didn't go out much, or at least I didn't. I was busy writing or trying to help Dad with the business. Or I had been with Hunter.

'It has been a while, but I like that I don't go out much. Plus, it means I'm less likely to meet a guy who just wants to get into my pants.'

His face dropped and he gave me puppy-dog eyes. Stupid mutt.

'Oh, come on, you can't be serious. Don't give me that look, Travis.' He kept it up and I sighed. 'Okay, *fine*, but I'm banning that face. You know how Lili and I feel about that face.'

We would give him anything he wanted when he gave us his puppy-dog eyes. And I was afraid he would ask for something I couldn't give him.

He waved his hands and slipped a shirt over his shoulders, the tan, toned skin disappearing along with the tattoo on his back. Hidden from sight. He took a step towards me and I turned away. I stared at my reflection in the mirror and gingerly touched my cheek, hissing at the sharp pain that vibrated through the cut when I put even the smallest amount of pressure on it.

'Kali said she was good to glamour that. Are you okay with that?' Travis leaned over me, his chest pressing against my back as he hovered his fingers over the area. I pushed him away; too close, too much for me to handle.

'I don't have much of a choice. There will be paps out tonight and I would rather not have photo evidence get back to my parents.'

He smirked.

'What?' I asked him. That smirk never meant anything good.

'Photo evidence and you. There is lots that your parents don't know.'

Yes, there was, and it was why he was sworn to secrecy and had a photo of me very, very drunk tucked away in his phone. He had one of Lili as well.

At the thought of Lili, I tried to reach through the Bond to find her. Even though I knew that I couldn't, the pang of hurt that settled in the pit of my stomach was a reminder of what we needed to do. It made me want to fight to find her faster.

I pushed him towards the door. 'And that photo evidence is

staying right where it is, or else, Travis Matthews. Remember, I know stuff.'

He laughed and laced his fingers through mine, pulling me away from the mirror and flush against his body. I hid the way that made me feel, but I remembered he was a wolf and already knew what I was feeling. Plus, the Bond. 'Trav,' I whispered.

'You look great. Forget about everything else and just be.'

I took back my hand and stepped away. 'No. We already spoke about this.'

'Are you guys ready?' Kali said as she came out of the guest room.

'Yup. You look great,' I said. It was true, she did. She was wearing a red dress that had cut-out pieces, chunks of golden skin peeking through. It brought out the brown in her eyes and she was vibrant and full of life.

'Thanks. You do too.' She waved a hand and I smiled. My black mini skirt clung to my body and the black and white spotted sheer shirt was tucked into the front of it showing off the black body suit underneath it. I paired it with black ankle boots.

'Okay, let's get going on this cheek so we can go.'

With the evidence gone, I could at least try to enjoy myself.

TAMARI.

It was one of the hottest and most exclusive nightclubs. It was right on the Nile—like most bars—and it was busy. The club was outside and boasted great food, even better music and an atmosphere that made you forget who you were. Or in most cases, anyway. Booking a table or even a booth was a nightmare, but dropping my name had ensured we got one.

As we were guided to our booth, I took in everything. Tamari had big pillars that were the same colour as the pyramids and they were decorated with speakers that vibrated with sound. Lights on the floor lit up the small podiums—right where the DJs would play their set—and each booth was dimly lit by lights under the seats. In the middle of each row of booths there was a tree and that too was lit up. In the background, you could see the city lights, a sight that was not to be missed.

The ambience in the club hadn't changed. The only thing that had? Me. I was older and legal now, which seemed to make this club all the more appealing.

This was also one of the places that I had been with Destiny and Devin on our last trip here. I was not of legal age and neither was Devin, but no one looked twice at our fake IDs because they were pretty lax with their rules. As long as no one got hurt, they didn't care how old you were.

'This place is gorgeous. I'm going to get drinks.' Kali was the first to hop up to the bar. I laughed and sat down in one of the big lounge chairs. Well, for a moment, anyway. I had too much nervous energy. I wanted to be back home, poring over the pages of the Book to find out everything and anything I could about Nefertiti and Karrept. The quicker I did, the sooner all of this could all go away and we'd get the holiday that we came for.

But did we really come here for a holiday? I wanted to know what happened to my siblings, and I was going to try to find out if anyone here would be able to help.

Going out may have been Travis' idea, but once I was on board, I thought about the possibilities of being able to get information about Destiny and Devin.

Travis leaned in. 'You're doing that thing again,' he whispered in my ear—although it was more of a shout, thanks to the music.

'What thing?' I murmured. He was a wolf and had super-human hearing; he could hear that just fine.

'Thinking. You need to stop doing that so much. Getting lost in your head is not a good career path. Writer or not.'

'Sometimes I like it better there,' I retorted. And I did. I always liked it better when I could rationalise things. This was irrational.

'Let go. Strip free of anything weighing you down. Go and dance.' Travis pointed to the dance floor. It wasn't as crowded with as many people as I would have liked it to be, but he did have a point.

'Fine. You stay here, though.'

I threaded through the bodies that were milling about. They chatted about work, life and everything in between, all of their words mingling together to make a smooth cacophony of white noise. I slipped between the people and raised my arms above my head as the beat dropped. I swayed my hips in time and twirled. Dancing out frustrations was a good way to change up energy; maybe I could try to dance through the emotions and find some answers. I let the music take a hold and do what I needed—take away all of the bad and bring in the good. I used to dance; as a kid, my mother enrolled me in dance classes, but I was an athlete who liked to dig balls, set them up high above the net and slam them in people's faces, volleyball was always such a rush. I wasn't built to prance around in pointe shoes. But I still had the leanness and the musicality that came with being a dancer. Well, most of it, anyway.

I almost blended in with the girls here, almost, but my skin had too much of an Australian haze to it that made me stand out. I wasn't quite dark enough to fit in.

'You are all grown up,' somebody said in my ear. I spun around to find Tyler Askew. I squealed and wrapped my arms around his neck.

'Tyler!' I shouted over the music.

He grinned back, all boyish charm and playfulness. He had always been cheeky. Last time I was here, he'd fed me shots, or helped stop me; the details were hazy there, but it was definitely 'time of my life' sort of thing.

'Lucy Ryder, look at you. How are you? Are Devin and Destiny here?'

My smile dropped and a shiver ran down my spine. He didn't know.

'Oh god, what did I say? Did I miss them?' He looked around, frantically searching for my brother and sister.

'They're dead. You didn't hear?'

His face fell. 'What? No. How ...? I'm so sorry.'

That was a question I wanted an answer to. 'Kidnapped and killed is the official assumption. Last time we were here, they left and never came back. I don't know much beyond that.'

But that would change. I was going to find out what happened and bring them home. Both of them.

'Who are you here with?' Without missing a step, Tyler changed the topic right away as he twirled me to the music.

I laughed. 'Some friends. Who are you here with? Wait, you're doing your freaky lonely man thing, aren't you?'

'You know me too well.'

I felt movement at my back, and Travis touched my hip, a show for Tyler.

'Who is this?' Tyler asked.

'This is Travis. My best friend. Trav, this is Tyler.'

Travis held out a hand, like any man would, and waited for Tyler to make a move. Their palms connected with a shake before they both went back to their own dance spaces.

'Great to meet you.' Tyler's voice picked up an accent; he always did that around new people.

'Tyler is an old friend, from when I used to go out when I was younger.'

He smirked and Travis dug his fingers into my hip. I was about to comment when there was a sudden change in the atmosphere. The music faded out and a hush fell over the club.

'Daughter of Nefertiti. I know you are here. Show your face,' a voice boomed over the crowd of bodies shuffling; the music may have faded but the people didn't stop. Goosebumps rose on my skin despite the sticky heat, and I searched the club, trying not to freeze as my eyes caught up with my brain.

Everyone in the club screamed and ducked, and with Travis' quick reflexes, he pulled me down so we would blend with the group. I looked for Tyler, but he was gone.

'That's you,' Travis whispered. I nodded and searched the room for Kali. She was at the table where we had been sitting, cowering under it. But from here, she looked okay.

'I know you are here. Show yourself and nobody will get hurt.' The voice vibrated through the club and sounded like it was coming from a chorus of people. I could see two rotting corpses, a man and a jackal, standing at the entry. Their words snaked through the room and settled in my bones. I watched them merge; together they were a monster, a creature with a jackal head—and that's when it made sense.

Anubis. It's Anubis. But I don't get how, or why. Travis blinked at me as I shared the information through our Bond. The words made his eyes instantly purple. *Down, boy. Not yet.*

'Daughter of Nefertiti, show yourself or I will rip every person apart until I find you. If it means we are swimming in blood, then it will be so.' Anubis grabbed a woman and she screamed and started to whimper.

He drummed his claws against the woman's neck and she screamed again, which promptly turned into begging. Her words flew fast out of her mouth—Arabic. The creature seemed unmoved by every single word. Or maybe too old to understand them. He tugged on her hair, and she tried to fight back as his nails dug into her shoulder.

'I'm *here*. I'm right here.' I stood up and moved out of Travis' immediate grasp. I heard him growl in my head because I was risking my life, but it wasn't about me.

'He never said you were the spitting image of her. Welcome

back.' Talons dug into the woman's shoulder and he shredded the skin as a warning.

'What are you doing? Let her go.'

Anubis tilted his head and stared me straight in the eye. 'What gave you the impression that I would let her go?'

I unconsciously lunged forward, only to stop as he started to pull the rest of the woman apart. With a sickening snap of bones cracking and a squelching of insides, he split the woman apart. Her bloodcurdling screams of pain were cut short as he used extraordinary strength; he made it look like he was putting in no effort.

The club was silent and nobody dared to move. I opened my mouth, ever so slightly, and started to breathe through it, so as not to smell the blood and gore that permeated the club. And I hoped it would stop the gagging feeling that was in my throat.

'What do you want?' My stomach flipped as I caught a whiff of whatever the fluid was, and I put my hand to my mouth, knowing that if it wasn't there I was going to vomit.

'You,' he said with no emotion.

He took a step forward, and it took everything in me not to flinch or take a step back. Showing a hint of weakness to a god was a bad decision.

'Karrept said if he could not have you then no one could, but I want you. I think we could make a good team.'

My chest tightened and my tongue felt like sandpaper in my mouth.

Lucy, step back right now, Travis said through the Bond. As he said it, I took a step back against my own will.

I wanted to look over my shoulder at Travis but I didn't dare.

'He wants me dead now?' I said.

'He said I could have you. Do you know how long I have waited to have a Lebashky woman? Since Nefertiti herself. I was not allowed to touch a human and Karrept had her back then.'

I swallowed hard and pressed my lips together as he settled in front of me and sighed. I gagged and took a step back. He followed me, but it was a start.

'Your breath smells like something died in your mouth.' The words were out of my mouth before I could stop them.

He smiled at me. 'That is not all that is going to die.' His hand came up to strike me, but I was pushed back. I kept my balance, but only just. It had all happened in an instant and now Travis was standing in front of me. He was still human, but I could feel the wolf energy emanating from him. If he wasn't careful, he would shift and there would be witnesses.

'Travis!' I hissed.

'You are letting a wolf do your dirty work. Now, that is not very queen-like.'

Every person in the room backed up. Except Kali and me.

Werewolves were illegal; those who were caught spent a lot of time in jail waiting to be executed by a specialised hunter. Anubis had just opened a door that was going to be hard to shut for Travis. It was only lucky that no one here would remember his face. Or his name.

'No,' I said and tugged Travis back with me.

Don't try anything. Ask Kali to work on a memory spell, like now. We can't have anyone knowing about you, even if they don't know your name yet.

Travis looked at me. *Are you fucking kidding me? Let me kill him.*

I shook my head. *Not right now. Just trust me.*

He sighed and moved back towards Kali as inconspicuously as he could. I could tell that Kali was already in damage mode; I snuck a glance over to her and saw her lips moving ever so slightly. She was working a spell.

'I don't let anyone do my dirty work. You should know how that feels.'

'You are all talk, Daughter of Nefertiti. The wolf could have tried to kill me, but he would not get very far in his human form.' There was a smirk on his rotted face. 'I am going to kill you now.'

'Thanks for the warning,' I muttered and sidestepped the punch he threw. I dropped into a crouch and swept his legs out from under him, or at least I tried to. He saw it coming and jumped. Back on my feet, I threw a jab out and he blocked it without straining. Anubis kneed me in the stomach, jolting my already sore ribs, and I screamed as I stumbled back.

Anubis didn't give me a moment to breathe before pinning me between the wall and himself. 'It is such a shame I have to kill you. I could have used you.' He wrapped his clawed fingers around my neck and squeezed.

The air was pressed from my lungs and I wanted to scream. This was not how I'd pictured myself dying. Ever. Images flashed through my mind: Hunter, Travis, Lili, Devin, Destiny. There was so much that I still had to do. I couldn't die here.

His fingers went slack around my throat and I watched, with wide eyes, as he fell to the ground. Travis was breathing hard, with a still-beating decayed heart in his hand—a furry hand with elongated claws. His eyes met mine and I saw the wolf in them; purple, hazy and angry. He wanted blood.

'Tr-Travis?' I coughed and held my hands up to show that I wasn't a threat.

His wolf was funny; he liked to be the one in charge, but he wouldn't hesitate, even for a second, to rip my own throat out if I moved wrong.

'I'm here. I just ... I couldn't stop him.' His fingers squeezed the heart in his hand and I gagged. Blood and dark, murky stuff oozed out of it.

'Are you okay?' I asked and willed my body to move. It didn't want to. The fear of getting in the way of the wolf was real in that moment.

'Lucy, they're really not dead,' he said, his purple wolf eyes wide with incredulity.

'What?' I stopped worrying about the fear and I gripped my stomach hard.

'Devin and Destiny. I saw them.'

I couldn't hold it back anymore. I bent over and vomited.

CHAPTER TWENTY-THREE

Nefertiti
Epep 2014

I STARED at the black obsidian crystal ball. It was the device that was showing me exactly what was happening. A mystery gifter had procured it for us from the magick shop in town, or that was what the note said when it was left outside our door. I watched the descendant … no, Lucy … as she danced. It was intoxicating. It was like looking in a mirror; the way her body moved, it was just the way mine moved too. I ached to be back inside her flesh, inside my own body, because while Liliana's body fit right now it wasn't my body.

'What are you thinking about, my light?' Karrept asked.

I looked past the crystal ball and wondered if he could read my mind. Or if there was something I could do to make him change his mind about trying to use his own magick.

'Just how much I can not wait to get back into my body. She seems to be having a lot of fun.'

'Can I see?' he asked, and I picked up the crystal ball and walked over to him. He was under the sheets in bed. He needed to conserve as much of his power and strength as he could, and I didn't mind being able to use some of my own power. It had been too long since I was last able to use it at all.

'Look,' he said softly, 'there he is.' Karrept's smile had always been one of his best features. It lit up his whole face and reached his eyes. I couldn't help but smile back.

Aten had always been a cold man; he never smiled the same way and he was the kind of person who was always so serious about everything.

Our marriage.

Our children.

Our rule.

The whole thing was a business deal to him, a term that I couldn't put into words way back when I was alive, but the Watcher had words for things that I did not. Or if she did, they were different to what I was used to. It unsettled me, but part of being in this time was knowing there was a way to make the transition into the twenty-first century easier. It needed to be easier because I didn't know how to survive in this world; it was vastly different to 1634 BC.

'Nooooo.' Karrept's cries pulled me out of my head and I stared at the crystal. Travis, who was the spitting image of Aten, had ripped Anubis' heart from his chest. It was in his hand and he squashed it.

That should not have been able to happen.

Anubis' flesh was strong, almost like he had invisible armour. He shouldn't have been able to come to a demise of any sort. Karrept locked eyes with me, and I forced my expression to be blank. It meant that his abilities were much weaker than we had anticipated. Anubis was a god. He should not have been able to be bested by a wolf.

'He … I do not understand.'

I wanted to tell him about the Bond. The one that I knew a

little about, thanks to Lili, but she stayed tight-lipped. I was sure Karrept knew a little, but not enough. Not like I knew.

Or what I thought I knew.

I did not understand how Lili could have this much power over me. Maybe she was stronger than we gave her credit for.

I could have told you that.

Karrept smiled and tapped his fingers on the crystal ball. 'That is okay. They can stop one, but can they stop them all?'

CHAPTER TWENTY-FOUR

Lucy
Choeak 2012

LITTLE GRANULES of salt spilled over the bar and arranged themselves into a mishmashed shape that resembled something like a cloud.

'Oops,' I snorted before I licked my hand. I dotted the damp part of my hand with salt, then picked up the lemon in the same hand and the tequila shot in the other. 'Here's to me,' I toasted before I licked the salt, downed the shot and sucked the lemon.

Hello, tequila.

'Hi there.' A tall, very Egyptian-looking guy sat down next to me.

'I'm taken.' Another shot was placed in front of me. More salt graced my hand and just as I was about to down the shot, it was taken from me.

'Hey! That's miiiiine. Give it baaaack!' I watched as the loser next to me downed it for me.

'I think you've had enough,' he said.

I wouldn't be drunk if Destiny and Devin hadn't dragged me

out when I didn't want to be out. The fuzzies started to take a hold of me.

'I'm still taken. That's not going to get you any brownie points.'

'I don't care that you're taken. You just need to stop. What's your name?' the stranger said.

'I'm not telling you. You could be a stalker for all I know.' Another shot was placed in front of me. I snatched it up and downed it without any salty help and grinned at him.

'That could very muchly be true, but I'm not sure you're old enough to even be here.'

He was right. I was fifteen. That didn't make me feel any better, though.

'I am too old enough to be here.' I crossed my arms over my chest and stared at him.

'What's going on here?' Devin said from behind me. 'Lucy, what are you doing?'

I grinned at Devin and didn't say anything. Instead I had the sudden urge to text Hunter. He was officially trying to give me a break or have a break from us ... or was it a break to explore? My head was fuzzy and I couldn't remember which one was the right one, but I did remember the look on his face when I'd tried to tell him that Antony had hit on *me*, even if there was some sort of magickal mysticism that made me flirt back with him. I couldn't remember. Fuzzy drunk feeling was good.

'Where's my phooonnne? Do you haaaave it? I need to text Hunter.' I made grabby hands at him and slipped off the stool. Devin caught me before I hit the ground, but that was what twin brothers were for. Or at least mine was. He was always there when I needed him.

'Whoops.' I snickered.

'I think your girlfriend had too much to drink,' the stranger said.

I snorted. 'We're twinsies, didn't you know? Can't you see the resembalenceness? I'm sure you caaaan.'

'Lucy, how much have you had?' Devin said.

'Shhh. Don't tell the stranger my name.' I pointed at the guy, who was waiting for his chance to talk.

'I tried to stop her from downing any more shots. I'm Tyler.' He held out his hand to Devin. I swatted at Devin's arm and he ignored me. 'Tequila seems to be her poison.'

'Thanks. Tequila is always her poison. She's going through a bit of a rough time.' He took my face in his hands. 'You are so dead. What are you doing?'

'Hunter doesn't believe me. He doesn't want to be with me. Do you know what that feels like? I bet you don't. You have your girlfriend, what's-her-name.' He did have a girlfriend, didn't he? Or maybe he didn't.

'Lucy. You are talking in jumbles. How much have you had?'

'You asked me that already. I told you.'

'No, you didn't.' He looped an arm under my arm and entangled his limb with mine.

'Yes, I did.'

Devin was there—and then he wasn't. He was gone and I was left in the new guy's arms.

'Who said you could touch me? Where did my brother go?' My vision blinked out for a second before I vomited on the new guy. 'Oops.'

'Ugh. Okay, I think we need to get you home. Let's go and do that, hmm?'

I didn't want to go home. That would make the pain come back. Being numb was good.

Egypt
Epep 2014

I jolted out of my sleep and was immediately welcomed with

fresh pain. 'Oh god, why does this keep happening to me?' I groaned.

'I always knew that you needed to stay away from fights, they've never been your forte.' Tyler's voice came from the window seat and I automatically covered my chest with the sheet. I had clothes on, but something about being in pyjamas always made me feel so vulnerable.

'Neither have bars. Tyler, you're still here? Wait, why are you even here?'

He laughed. 'Kali and I got talking, and after last night, I thought it would be better to be safe than sorry and stay the night. Here.'

He handed me a cup of tea and I took a sniff. 'Are you trying to put me into a herbed coma?' I took a sip of the tea. Instantly, the pain in my stomach subsided. Oh, he was good.

'I thought you'd need something with a punch to it for the pain. I heard that you got beat up before last night.'

I nodded. And narrowed my eyes at him. He had disappeared—how did he hear about the fight?

'Trouble seems to follow you,' he murmured.

'You're telling me. Aren't you meant to be at some rich prep school? That was where you said you were going.'

'You didn't hear? I'm a free agent these days. School's so not for me, too many rules.'

'And that's the best nonanswer I've heard.'

'I know. I've perfected it.' He laughed.

'So you and Kali, hey?' I saw him blush and I laughed. 'And you did more than talk, I see.' I didn't think he blushed so easily, but it seemed that he did.

'Shut up. I can't believe that she's your half-sister. How crazy is that? She's a Ryder, yeah?'

I sipped the tea and was saved from needing to answer when Travis walked in. 'Hey. I have some food for you if you're hungry.'

My heart plunged into my stomach as I gazed at Travis, the words from the night of the eclipse playing in my mind. Tyler picked up on the awkwardness.

'I think that's my cue to leave. I'll see you later. Call me if you need anything, Luce, yeah?'

Travis waited for Tyler to leave before he shut the door. He hovered at the door and looked everywhere else but me.

'What was that last night?' I finally spoke up to break the uneasy silence.

'The wolf?'

The wolf I could understand, that was the easy part. I shook my head. 'Devin and Destiny.'

He moved over to the chaise lounge in front of my bed and stared at me.

'I ... touching Anubis—god, this is going to sound so fucking strange—but when I killed him, something happened. Sort of like a sense of clarity. I could feel the dead. The fucking dead.'

He paused and I held my breath.

'Do you know how weird that sounds coming out of my mouth? I could feel the dead and I instantly knew that Devin and Destiny weren't a part of them. They were missing. I expected them to be there, but they just weren't. Instead, I can hear the voices of wolves I've killed, people who have been murdered, or even died of natural causes. There's like ...' He wiggled his hands either side of his head. 'A sea of people in my head that won't shut up.'

I took another sip of the tea to try to keep my head in the conversation. But Devin and Destiny were alive. They were *alive*. I was right ... all this time. And no one else believed me. Or wanted to believe me.

'They're not dead,' I murmured.

'They're not dead,' Travis echoed.

I stared at him. 'What do we do now?'

We needed to get Lili back, that was the first priority, but I needed to find out where my siblings were and how to get them back. I wasn't going to leave Egypt until I had them both by my side.

'I don't know,' he said. 'We have to find out what happened, and I know we need to get Lili back, but I don't know what this means. Does it mean I can sense the dead—what do I do with it?' He was rambling and mirroring my thoughts.

I took a moment to look at him, really look at him; the shirt he wore still had flecks of blood on it and his hair was a dishevelled mess. He was vain and never let himself seem like he was frazzled, so I knew he had been up thinking too much about what he saw.

'You're going to have a shower first, though. You look and smell gross. Then you're going to give me all the details. I'll get Kali to help and we'll try and figure out what we need to do here. Okay?'

He nodded.

I took charge because he couldn't.

BY THE TIME I made it down the stairs and into the living room, there was a bowl of muesli for me and Kali was sitting on the couch reading the Book. There was no sign of Tyler, and I was relieved to not see him.

'You're up early. Considering how much magick you used last night,' I said.

'Mm ... couldn't sleep. But it's only, like, eight thirty. How are your ribs?'

'On fire. Did you get everyone in the club with the memory wipe?'

She nodded. 'It was hard, but most of them now don't remember Travis. Tyler helped with Anubis clean-up, because that was one I couldn't do, but we're all in the clear.'

'That's a relief. I really hope it sticks as well. The sun is up—

can you open the curtains?' I motioned to the windows, and she sighed and got off the couch. She pulled back the curtains and was welcomed by a human-sized vulture. She screamed and threw her hands up as it bashed into the glass. It hit a barrier that Kali had put in place with the movement of power she pushed out. She was good in moments of crisis.

'Travis, you need to get down here now,' I called out, trying to stay calm. I didn't take my eyes off the vulture. 'Kali, what do you need?'

'Nothing. The barrier will hold. It's a basic barrier that'll keep that thing out, but it'll keep *us* inside. I don't know about you guys, but I didn't envision staying inside today.'

As she spoke, I watched two more figures approach the house, an androgynous being and a corpse. Rotting flesh dropped from the corpse with every step it took.

'Um … I don't think that the vulture is going to be much of a problem right now.'

'What?' Travis was standing next to me, his hair wet but dressed.

I pointed beyond the vulture.

'Oh,' he said.

Oh, indeed. More monsters Karrept had sent to kill us. Great.

'I'm sick and tired of people trying to come and kill me,' I said.

'There's only been four,' Kali muttered.

'Exactly! Four too many. What are we going to do?'

The vulture pulled back and we all watched as the three beings merged into one.

'Should we go outside?' I asked.

On the list of bad ideas I could have, that one was pretty bad. I wanted to stay inside and will the monster away, but I knew that wasn't going to happen.

Kali didn't answer, but her brows furrowed in concentration. When she looked away from the window and to me, she nodded. 'We might have to. I've pushed the barrier out so that it stops just in front of the porch. They won't be able to get any closer to the house.'

'Are you sure about that?' I couldn't rip my eyes from the rotting creature as they tried to peck at the barrier with their beak.

'It's either we stay here and die inside—can you imagine the clean-up? Something tells me going outside will make it less … messy.'

She wasn't wrong. The clean-up *would* be messy. I had a flashback to the club and Anubis, and I shivered at the thought of that happening to us in here. Of it happening at all.

'I don't know if I have anything that can help.'

'You have innate magick. It's okay,' Kali said as she opened the sliding door. She held out her hand and I took it. Jolted by the slice of power that came with the skin touch, I bit the inside of my cheek to stop the squeal. She caught it and smiled.

'You are the one we want,' the creature screeched. 'The others do not matter.'

'Sorry, but you're not getting her without a fight,' Travis said. He curled his fingers into a fist and dropped into a defensive pose.

'Then I will have to kill you to get to her. We want her. We do not want to kill her.'

'You'll have to forgive us if you think that we'll take your word on that. The last one seemed to want her dead,' Kali stated.

I took one step at a time until I hit the grass. Kali hissed my name and I ignored her. Travis was right by my side, ready to pounce.

'Why do you want me?' I asked. The fear I felt didn't show on my face; I was proud of that. There was no one else here besides Kali and Travis, both of whom wouldn't get too close. There would be no entrails on the floor today.

Or so I hoped.

'Because you are valuable, Daughter of Nefertiti. You are a person too. A child still. We protect children.'

'Nekhbet,' I whispered. The vulture-headed goddess of children and childbirth. The crown made sense now.

'You know us?' she said.

The crown on the vulture's head was familiar; I knew enough about mythology to be fluent, but there was a part of my brain that was refusing to work.

'I do. Karrept wants to kill me. He sent Anubis last night.'

'We know. He wanted us to kill you, but he said if we could get the Book, we did not need to kill you. Just give up the Book so we can protect you from him.'

We need the Book, Travis said.

No shit, Sherlock, I replied and I could feel his annoyance, but I had an idea.

'And what if I don't give it to you?' I replied. My legs walked me outside of the barrier spell. A normal person would be terrified. I was, but I had a feeling. And I followed my hunch: she wouldn't hurt me.

'We have to kill you,' Nekhbet said.

Well, crap.

'I can't give you the Book.'

'Please, Daughter of Nefertiti, do not do this. Please, we do not want to hurt you.'

'I don't want to hurt you either. You're a protection goddess. You are good.' She was polite too. But I couldn't help her. I wanted to.

I shook my head at her and she screeched—and attacked me.

In her fury, she swiped outwards, and I was too slow to move. Her claws dug into my shoulder and I cried out in pain, my other arm trying to push her away. If she pulled me into the sky and dropped me, I'd be better off dead. If my neck didn't snap first.

I grabbed a fistful of feathers to distract her. She screeched and bolted into the air, but not before she let go of my shoulder. It was going to be bloody to look at. Her big wings flapped, causing a mini hurricane in the backyard. Travis covered my body with his. I wanted to push him off but I didn't. Having cover while I caught my breath was just what I needed.

'You could have made this easy. Now we have to kill you. Just give us *the Book*.'

She swooped down and tore up Travis' back. He grunted on top of me before he punched and clipped her shin. An ungodly screech left her lips, and I cringed as I covered my ears. It muffled the scream temporarily, but it was hard to keep my hands over my ears with a hundred-kilo werewolf on top of me.

'Travis, get off me. Now.' I pushed at him and he pulled his weight off me. I ran back towards the porch to get out of harms reach. He hung back and twisted as Nekhbet swooped again.

Breathing hard, Kali looked wild as her eyes moved from the giant bird to me. 'You're bleeding,' she said and I instantly felt sick.

'Oh god,' I said. Blood! That was it. With the hand that wasn't full of feathers, I swiped my fingers across the blood. With sticky fingers, I crushed the feathers in my hand and focused on them. Kali said power was innate, and I was going to use it.

'With this sacrifice, I offer heat. Burn that which wants to bring harm to us.'

'Daughter of Nefertiti, do not make us do this. Please,' Nekhbet said at the time that Travis spoke.

'Lucy. Whatever you plan on doing, do it soon. I can't hold her off any longer, not when she's flying, especially when I'm on the ground.'

'I'm trying,' I threw back. My voice softened as I repeated the chant.

'Just believe, Lucy,' Kali said. 'I'm going to help throw her off the track.'

She was going to risk her life. Maybe it was to help save Travis, but it still meant something. 'Be careful. Don't get too hurt.'

She laughed. 'Don't worry about me. Concentrate.'

I did as she ordered and concentrated. I thought about heat, and if I focused on the warmth and pushed it into the feathers, I could feel the rising warmth as I held them.

Nekhbet batted at Kali and she ducked. Oh god, everyone was going to get killed if this didn't work. As I chanted over and over again, I felt the feathers heat up inside my clenched fist. On instinct, I opened my palm and watched the feathers burst into flames. Blood magick was powerful; it was also really dangerous. Hunter had always warned me against it because of the consequences, but life or death was as good a reason as any to tap into that. I pushed more of my power into my hand, and Nekhbet screeched louder than before. The feathers disintegrated in my hand, and just like that, her wings were useless. She hit a pile of broken logs and flipped up using her godlike strength, and bolted back into the air. It was time to stop playing scared—I was a witch. I had a werewolf and another witch with me. Nekhbet was no match for us without her wings now. I had power, and Nekhbet wasn't going to get out of here alive.

'Daughter of Nefertiti. We wanted to *help* you. Now we *have* to kill you.'

She circled around in the air, and Travis shadowed me, tightening the distance between us to make sure that she couldn't get a leg up. Nekhbet attacked, but Travis kicked and forced her back. I grabbed a broken branch with my good arm, and found a comfortable grip on it.

'Kali, watch out!' Nekhbet tried to swoop Kali but with her wonky wings, she missed, her crown falling from her head. Kali picked it up and threw it onto the porch—inside the barrier, where she couldn't reach.

Shit.

In the moment it took to watch the crown bounce, Nekhbet clawed at me and I deflected her with the branch. I swung it and connected with her abdomen, before I was on top of her, the branch poised at her neck. She gasped for air.

'You cannot kill me. You do not have it in you.'

I stabbed the branch through her throat. Gargling, her body went limp. On my feet, I found myself staring at Travis, who was blinking, wide-eyed, at me. I didn't like killing anything—not even spiders, even though they freaked me out—but if you told me I couldn't do something, I would. I'd make sure of it.

'So, she's dead,' I said. 'Now I can go—ouch, ouch, ouch.' My pain was returning, as if putting Nekhbet in her place had drained me of the adrenaline running through my system.

'Lucy? What is it?' Kali asked.

'Arm, she got it good.'

Kali's hands explored the wound and I hissed at her. 'The blood isn't stopping. We need to slow it down.'

'Ouch. That hurts. Travis, what are you doing?' I said shakily. My head spun, and I could feel my body starting to go limp.

'We have to get rid of the evidence.' He slammed an axe into Nekhbet's neck. It was the last thing I saw because everything went black.

CHAPTER TWENTY-FIVE

Nefertiti
Epep 2014

KNOCK, knock.

It wasn't a mealtime, so the person on the other side of the door wasn't room service. That left one other person who would be able to find us.

Karrept got off the bed and opened the door—he finally felt strong enough to move, which was a huge win in my book—then stepped out of my view so I could see who it was.

'Hi, Mum.'

'Khaldun,' I whispered.

His boyish charm, no matter what he looked like, always shone through. He was my biggest love and regret. The one who I had to keep a secret. He was the only one of my children who was not raised by me. He was the one who I wanted to be around in my body.

'Where have you been?' Karrept asked.

'Keeping an eye on the descendant. This Tyler seems to be still just out of arm's reach with her, and I've been in this body for far too long. She doesn't trust me like her siblings did.' He walked through the threshold of the room and I shut the door behind him. 'I couldn't find the Book when I was there.'

'You were inside?' Karrept closed the door behind Tyler.

'Yes. I even swiped this.' Tyler held up a key.

'You are definitely your mother's son.'

I smiled, knowing just how crafty I could be. I had hidden him away all of his life, before finding him and convincing him that life would be better if he added his soul to ours. He embodied Tyler four years ago to get close to the descendant and her family. The body was disposable.

'I thought you'd like that one, Papa. I think I can find out more.' He looked at me, and I wanted to wrap my arms around him and not let him out of my sight, but that wasn't the part we had to play. The Illuminate Year was here, and it was the perfect time to finish what we started.

'Their werewolf keeps killing my monsters.'

'He's the weak link, though. The tension between him and the descendant is palpable. He is her weak spot. Do you have a bar you can spell? Getting him drunk to distract her will be perfect.'

My biggest regret, when Khaldun went into hiding, was that I wasn't able to teach him the way of the world myself, but he grew up smart, cunning and full of ideas. His curiosity was nurtured, and his ability to think for himself was his biggest asset. It was what I valued the most in him. I would be forever indebted to the family that took him and raised him as their own.

'That is a really good idea. Nefertiti, can you find the right bar? We are going to do this today and make it last until he has his fill and then some,' Karrept replied.

He pulled out his old spell book and I watched him as he flicked through the pages. It was full of enchantments, hexes and potion recipes. I knew inside those pages was countless attempts to rid himself of the scratch Aten gave him in the moments leading up to our spell. It wasn't like a cough or a fever that could be shifted to someone else by magick. No matter how hard he tried.

'Would you like some food, Khaldun?'

'That would be great, thanks.'

Manners too. None of my daughters ever had manners—but then again, I had too many of them and they were always fighting for the attention of their father. Or, at least, who they called Father.

'Did you know that the house is acting as a conduit to keep the descendant occupied?' Khaldun said.

'What do you mean?' I asked as I busied myself in the small kitchenette. The food here was still weird, but I read the instructions on the little meal and put it into the machine that zapped. *Microwave*, the Watcher filled in.

'The hex on the house, I placed it there before they arrived. It's messing with the descendant's powers. She was supposed to be easier for you to inhabit, but the Bond that she has with the wolf and'—he pointed towards me—'the Watcher is incomprehensible. I don't think I've seen anything like it before.'

I smiled now. 'You have not. It was part of the original bond that happened when we did the spell. I did not think that it would manifest like this, though. They have some abilities between them, but the Watcher will not tell me what. I cannot get the information out of her.'

'I could fix that?' Khaldun rolled up his sleeves, like he was getting ready for something.

I shook my head. 'No, it is fine. I am working on it, but it is different to what was initially put in place. But it is okay. We can make it work.'

'Can we? I feel like it puts a dent in our work.'

'Do not doubt your mother, Khaldun. Trust her. She is good at what she does.' Karrept walked over to me and rested a hand on the small of my back. I looked at him and saw my whole life; the whole reason I was here and we were doing this. Nothing was more important than this. My family and the ability to have my body back. The Bond wouldn't take that away from me. I would make sure of it. But Lili was there to remind me that it wouldn't be easy, and the more I got to know her ... did I really want to destroy what she had?

CHAPTER TWENTY-SIX

Lucy
Epep 2014

MY HEAD ACHED. The bleeding finally stopped when I blacked out, or that was what I hoped, at least. Kali's haphazard stitches had kept my muscles from spilling out, but that was the least of my worries. The cut on my face was going to leave a scar because it was deep, and I didn't want to go to the hospital. I swallowed hard, and I could've sworn that the metallic taste of blood lingered on my tongue.

'And you're sure that's the right one?' I asked as I rubbed the bridge of my nose, trying to alleviate the headache that was only getting worse. 'We don't even have enough people for it.'

I'd searched the book and found a spell that could work, and Kali had confirmed the spell that would be *one* to help us.

'I know, but it's the right one. It says it's the best way to get rid of Karrept.'

I sighed and started to pace out of habit as Kali continued, every step aching. I tried not to move my shoulder too much.

'Okay, Lucy, you need to lie down. You still look pale, and if you pull out any of your stitches, I swear I'll magick them back in,' she said with a look in her eye that I had never seen before. I stared back at her and walked over to the couch.

She looked back down at the book and continued. 'We need someone to represent each of the elements. I'm fire, you're earth, Travis is water, and we need someone who is air. Do you know Tyler's temperament very well? Is he airy?'

I shook my head as I lowered myself onto the couch. Even that hurt like a bitch. 'I don't know a lot about him, honestly. You probably know more.' I paused for a second as the realisation sank in.

'Hunter is air,' I said quietly.

Travis stood up. 'You want to call *him*?' His tone was angry and rude.

'He's the only one I know who is an air element. We don't know Tyler well enough, and Hunter loves Lili just as much as we do—he'd want to help.'

Travis growled at me and I held his gaze. 'You can't hold whatever you feel against him, Travis.'

He muttered something under his breath, and I could no longer taste anything metallic on my tongue. I couldn't forget the taste of blood, even if I wanted to. What did they do when I was out of it?

'That might be a good thing, but before we get him on a plane, we should definitely find out if Tyler has an affinity with air. We can save Hunter a trip up,' Kali said, playing peace-maker. A compromise to help soothe Travis, maybe? Sometimes it was easier to pick your battles than to go head-on into them.

'Did you feed me some of your blood?' I flat out asked Travis, and the conversation halted. The room was silent. 'Well?'

Travis looked away, and I swallowed hard, trying to stop the bile rising in my throat.

'Someone talk to me. What happened?'

'You lost a lot of blood. Like, a *lot*. And I couldn't stop it. You were going to die,' Kali said softly.

'So you thought it was a good idea to drug me? To make it so that I didn't have a choice? You put me in danger. What were you thinking?' I could feel the heat in my body rise and my chest swelled with rage. How dare they.

'You were dying! We didn't have a choice,' Travis yelled. 'I would rather cut my arm and feed you my blood and deal with the fallout than have to bury your cold and lifeless body.'

'Travis.' Kali stood up and moved between us. 'You don't need to even think about that. She wasn't going to die. We weren't going to let it happen.' She turned around to face me, and I could see a flash of hurt in her eyes, almost like she couldn't believe what was happening. 'Lucy, you don't mean that. You aren't going to die, not now. Not when you know your siblings are still alive. You can't do that to them. Not after all this time.'

She was too good at listening, and all I wanted to do was throw something at her head because she was right. I didn't want to admit it but she was, and that was what hurt the most.

After the years of dealing with her torment at school, I knew she was meticulous about saying things that she shouldn't. Not as someone who had hurt me for so long.

'Look, we have history and it's shit and we're going to have to deal with it at some point, but right now? We're here, we're doing this. You were going to die, Lucy. I know that means something to you because you're fighting about it, but we've got bigger things to deal with.'

I sighed and I swallowed past the lump in my throat. It was hard to admit that, but I could do it. I was doing it.

'Just ...' I looked at Travis. His eyes welled with tears he wouldn't shed, and I let down my shields to find the pain that he felt. 'I'm sorry for jumping at you, you just know how I feel about it. But ... thank you.'

Without words, Travis closed the distance between us and pulled me into a hug. He squeezed hard, and I had trouble breathing. 'I don't want to lose you … ever. I wouldn't do anything like that if it was serious. You know it.'

All I could do was nod, but he felt that and pulled back. Underneath the bravado, the idiocy and the wolf was my best friend. He loved me—maybe more than I wanted him to, but he cared.

'Shit, I'm holding too tight. Are you okay?'

'Yeah. I'm okay.' Kali moved into view. 'Do you know if we have everything that the spell would need?'

'I'll have to have a look, but what if we do need something?'

'I know a magick shop that would help us,' I said.

'I'm driving,' Travis said.

'No way, José. You drove on the way back from the pyramids. It's my turn.'

It was a place that was near and dear to my heart, and I didn't want to take the fun out of actually going there. Travis could drive another time.

'You can barely walk, how the hell do you think you can drive?'

I smiled at him. 'I don't need to be able to walk. It's not like my legs aren't working, and I've taken pills to dull the pain. I'm driving. Get over yourself,' I said and took a deep breath to brace myself to get up. I would be fine as long as I didn't stay in one place for too long.

As I PULLED up in front of the magick shop, I took a moment and stared. It felt like I was coming home to an old friend's place. The old rustic porch, the shuttered windows that were open to let the light in and the beige paint colour had me nostalgic over my childhood. The sign hadn't even changed.

'Are we going in?' Travis asked, bringing me out of my thoughts.

'Yeah.' I caught Kali's eye in the rear-view mirror.

She looked at me like she knew what I was thinking. I could feel heat rising up my back and I wondered if it was because I was nervous or because it was trying to get used to her being here.

'Does this place have a memory?' Kali asked.

She was looking to bond, which was weird for me, but it was her olive branch and I was willing to take it.

'Yes. I used to come here as a kid, quite a bit.'

'Good memories?' she pressed.

'Very much so.'

Mystical Happenings had always been a staple in my life until I was big enough to decide for myself not to go.

We got out of the car and walked into the shop. The smell of palo santo and sage lingered in the air and I inhaled. The memory of running through the aisles as a kid and making sure that I didn't knock anything off the shelves was more vivid than I'd thought possible.

'Welcome.' The word was said with a singsongy voice and belonged to a woman who was so familiar. Her face was one I remembered from my childhood; she had smile lines, grey hair and piercing blue eyes. She wore loose clothes and crystals around her neck, on her fingers and in her hair.

'Lucy? Little Lucy Ryder. Oh my goddess, look at you.' With both arms extended, she walked over to me and I resisted the urge to back away. She may have been familiar, but she was still a stranger in my books.

'Yes. Hello,' I said.

'You don't remember me. Well, you do, but not as much as I'd hope. That's okay. I'm Andromeda, but you have always called me Meda. Vayla and I are good friends. Inseparable as children and even to this day.'

Vayla, my grandmother, was ultimately where the witchy gene came from on Mum's side, but Dad had it too, so it was sort of like a double witchy-gene thing. I wasn't quite sure what that meant. I didn't spend a lot of time in Egypt, and when I did, my grandmother always had tabs on Devin, Destiny and me.

'Hello,' I said again.

'Oh goddess. I can't believe how big you are.' She paused to really look at me, her eyes sweeping over my body before they settled on mine. I saw tears welling in her eyes. 'I wish that there was more I could do for your brother and sister. How are you?'

She brushed her fingers against my elbow and I shrugged. The simple movement pulled at the stitches and I hissed. She didn't seem all that surprised by that either.

'Relax. I know you don't trust me, but if I wanted to hurt you, I would have done so already.'

'That's not really comforting,' I said and she laughed.

'You sound like your father. That's amusing. Did I see Kali too?' Meda glanced behind me.

My heart plummeted into my stomach and it felt like someone grabbed it, hard. 'Kali? You know about her? Does *Savta* know about her too?'

'Your father was never good at shielding. I knew before Vayla, but only because he asked me for a na—'

I shook my head to stop her. 'I really don't want to hear about it. I'm still adjusting to the knowledge at the moment.'

'Understandable. What happened here?' She touched my shoulder and I hissed again. Kali's sutures held up, thankfully.

'Nekhbet. She decided to tear up my shoulder.'

Meda muttered to herself and the area started to feel a lot better. 'There. That should help some. I hope I'm not overstepping my boundaries, but I don't think you liked being in the amount of pain you were hiding.'

I wanted to test my shoulder and roll it, but I was too scared to find out about it still hurt. 'Thank you,' I replied to Meda.

'You're welcome, but there is something more. You're ... why are you hexed? And ... the wolf, he is not good for you.'

'Excuse me?' I was taken aback. 'He can hear you, you know.' Travis and Kali were roaming the shop to look for ingredients, so he would be able to hear everything being said. Kali, not so much.

'The wolf. He is dangerous and far from someone who should be in your life, or at least with the way that his control is. He will hurt you.' She seemed to move her hands over my aura and handed me a selenite rod. The milky crystal sat in my hand like it was meant to be there. 'But you two broke something. I can feel something shifted.'

Meda was confirming what I already felt. Bile rose in my throat. 'What do you mean something has shifted?'

'The Bond you hold. It's different. You need to find your Watcher. She will fix everything. Where is she?'

I shivered. How did she know more than I did? How was that even possible?

'I'm sorry, but this is too much. Lili has been taken and we don't know where she is.'

'You need to find her. And soon. You're hexed—I haven't seen spell work like this in years. Someone has placed a hefty hex on you,' she reiterated.

Was it Nefertiti? Or Karrept? Was this why they were back? 'What ... how can I remove it?'

Meda shook her head and clicked her tongue. 'I think they used the opening in your aura to lace it in. It's not too hard to get rid of.'

'I ...' Words couldn't come to mind. Instead she handed me a book, and I ran my fingers over it. 'Wow, this is ...'

The book was ornate, but not as detailed as the Book we had at home. It was covered in gold detailing, lattice and vines, and *Lebashky* was written in hieroglyphics. It felt like home. It was no bigger than an A4 notebook, but it felt meaty and bigger than it was. Almost as though the contents were ready to bust out of the bindings holding them between the comfort of the covers.

'Yours,' she finished for me. 'It's your family tree and a little more. It might help you. Now, let's get rid of this tricky hex. It's manifesting as a darkness, as something that wants to hurt you. Take my hands.'

I glanced at the book before I put it down on the shelf next to us. She held out her hands for me and I hesitated. She wiggled her fingers and smiled, like she was silently reassuring me. She had a lot of power and that movement had my hands reaching out. I took her hands and she wrapped her fingers around my palms. Her hands were soft, young, and I thought about how old she was. She was radiant for her age.

'Why, thank you. I'm glad I don't look as old as I am,' she said, and I had to hold my jaw tight or it would have dropped.

That was unnerving. I knew I could read the thoughts of my family, and Lili and Travis, but that was because we had a connection. I'd never known what it felt like to have someone else do the same thing to me.

'I'm sorry. Sometimes I forget that I'm not always the norm.' Her accent shone through in those simple words, and I blinked at her as I had a flashback of who she was. Of who I had grown up laughing with.

'You used to have purple hair. I remember. You were the Lady in Purple,' I murmured.

She let go of my hands and wiggled her fingers again before she ran them over her hair. It turned to purple and I gasped. The glamour was so seamless, it was beautiful. Seeing her purple hair, I remembered the warmth in her smile that I had loved so much as a child and how enamoured I had been with her freedom, in a country like Egypt.

'I was a little bit obsessed with colours back in the day.' She winked before she shook out her purple hair. Back to grey, the glamour gone, her eyes laced with playfulness.

I nodded and put my hands back in her outstretched ones. She squeezed them and closed her eyes. I followed her example —and that's when I felt the switch.

I wheezed as her power rushed through me. It was like there was a knife cutting me straight down the middle, but only for a moment before it was replaced with heat. It radiated from her hands first and then spread to the rest of my body.

It was like I was sitting in the sun on a beautiful spring day.

Then it crashed and I could feel the heaviness of whatever was around me and I struggled to breathe. I dropped down to one knee from the sheer power of it, and Meda kept going. Through her eyes and with mine still closed, I saw a wall of darkness. It was full of fear, anger, and it was slowly crushing me. I wanted to touch it.

'Meda,' I panted and she kept chanting softly, or so it felt. The chant meant nothing to me, but the words seemed to make complete sense in a way I couldn't put into words. I felt Travis move closer but he hovered just out of reach.

He distracted me for half a second before I gave in to the temptation and touched the wall. It was sticky, black and despair-ridden. I could feel Meda through the wall; she put her hands up against it and I mimicked her motion. I could feel the heat from her palm and I watched as it melted away the barrier. As it did, she laced her fingers through mine and pulled me through it.

The wall shattered into pieces, and something inside me shifted, like it had when I walked through the door of the house. This time it was the opposite; it felt like I was walking into a heated space after being out in the cold for too long.

'Follow me,' Meda whispered.

Without letting go of her hands, I did exactly as she asked, and I slowly opened my eyes as I felt her push me to do so. I blinked a couple of times before I looked into her warm blue eyes and processed that we were still in the shop. She smiled and held up a hand before she walked away.

'How do you feel?' Her voice was coming from somewhere— she had been right in front of me, but now she was nowhere to be found.

I tested my feet as I rose to meet them and nodded to myself. Everything was in place. Everything was okay. I felt Kali hovering close by but she gave me space. Good, that was all I wanted right now. Space.

Meda handed me a glass of water and I took it.

'Lighter,' I said. 'I didn't trust my gut. There were signs and I missed them.'

'That is the beauty of hexes. Silent killers. I'll make a talisman for you to keep it at bay if it comes back; it'll be something small and it'll take me next to no time. Promise me you'll leave the wolf alone, though? You don't need that kind of energy in your life.'

Travis was my best friend and it wasn't like I could just cut him out of my life. I knew that he wouldn't stand for it. Was the energy from him? Was that what she was saying?

'I can't make any promises.' I scratched the back of my neck and sighed. 'Do you think you could maybe ... not tell *Savta?*'

'You and I both know that Vayla is perceptive. If you don't tell her, I won't, but she'll find out.'

She was right. *Savta* always knew more than she would ever say—perhaps that was her all in her power—but I never knew how or why.

Suddenly, there was twinge in my head, and I knew it was Lili. She was reaching out, and it was the first real sense of her that I had felt since we lost her. I choked back a sob, and Meda caught me as I fell forward.

'What is it?' she asked.

'It's my best friend. She's in danger. As long as she isn't with us, she's in danger, and I don't know how to get to her.' I stepped back from Meda to compose myself.

'You will find her. I know you will. Just have some faith. I think you need to make sure you guard your heart.' Meda winked at me before I heard my name. 'Perhaps a certain man who's name starts with *H* will be better to guide you. Hmm?'

Hunter. Everything was leading back to him.

'Lucy! There you are. We've got everything and we're ready to pay,' Kali said. I knew that she had overheard the whole conversation—probably Travis too—but she was trying to get us out so that no one got hurt.

I knew that I had to call Hunter to have him help.

'Thank you,' I said to Meda. Kali and Travis joined us to pay for what we needed. I couldn't help looking over my shoulder at a smiling Meda as we left. It was like she knew my decision before I did.

BACK AT THE HOUSE, Kali turned the crown over. She seemed to be the only one who had the ability to touch the crown without getting burned. I'd picked it up and as a result was running my hand under cold water. Travis had jumped out of his skin, but with his superhuman healing he was not even nursing any pain. Jerk.

'This is really cool,' she said.

I looked over my shoulder from the sink as she turned the crown around in her hands.

She kept trying to put it on, and Travis and I kept coming up with reasons to stop her.

'Are you sure that I can't put this on?' she asked, her eyes shimmering with excitement.

'Kali. Travis can see dead people and could be slowly going crazy if he thinks he can start talking to them. Let's not take a chance here.'

'Hey!' he piped up from the couch.

'You keep muttering to yourself. Trav, you're pretty close to going there,' I pointed out.

Guilty, he looked down at his feet.

'So maybe just wait, Kali,' I said as I shut the tap off, feeling like the cold water had negated the burn. 'Did you come up with anything in your search?' I asked as I dabbed my hand with a towel.

'Bits and pieces. Nekbhet was a protector of children and had a whole bunch of other things attached to her, but nothing really significant and nothing about the crown. I really just want to put it on. Let me,' she begged.

'Kali, come on, work with us here. What if it puts you in some weird coma and we need you or something?'

She frowned down at the crown and gently put it on the couch. 'That is a good point.'

I nodded. 'Maybe we can find someone to help get more information about it. If we know more, then we can definitely figure out what we can do with it.'

'What about Tyler?' Kali looked up and her eyes seemed even brighter. She really liked him.

'He might know something about it. You can call him and see if he knows anything?' I said.

'Yes!' She got off the couch and left the room.

I stared at Travis, who was looking right at me.

'So it's really not going to happen?' he said and pointed to himself and then to me. I nodded.

Since coming back from the magick shop, I'd made a practiced effort to keep my distance, and he could feel it. I took what Meda said to heart. I loved Travis as a friend, and I wanted to keep it exactly that. I had to, for my own sanity.

'Not going to happen, Trav. I don't want to lose you as a friend.'

He muttered something I didn't hear and excused himself. I

was hit by a wave of anger and sadness before he shut the feelings door on me. I also detected a hint of hurt.

I wasn't going to take back what I felt. I didn't want to change our relationship any further than we had. It was something that, while I didn't regret it, I didn't want to actually take it further now. We broke the Bond. Meda confirmed it and I wanted to fix it. I wanted to stay firmly on the side that was familiar.

We couldn't be working with a broken Bond. It wasn't going to help anyone.

I picked up my phone and called the one person I knew who could help me with all of my magick problems. The time difference wouldn't worry Hunter as much as this call would hurt me.

CHAPTER TWENTY-SEVEN

Nefertiti
Epep 2014

I WAS PLUNGED INTO DARKNESS. I screamed, but nothing came out of my mouth. I punched at the darkness and it didn't budge. It was like something was keeping me in place, and I didn't know how to get out. I screamed again, and this time the darkness dissipated.

I shot up in bed, breathing hard and clutching the sheets against my chest. I was not naked, but I must have fallen asleep and it was just a natural reaction. I blinked and searched the room.

Nothing was out of place, but Karrept and Khaldun were gone. They would have gone to the bar to make sure that the wolf was ready for what was to come. But now they were gone, I wanted them back. Being alone had never been something I was good at. Even now. I swung my legs off the bed and walked to the mirror that ran up to the ceiling. The strawberry blonde locks were unruly and my golden eyes stared back at me with disbelief, like I was trying to figure it all out. My mouth seemed to refuse to smile.

The darkness. I felt it before, two years ago, when I tried to get Lucy's—no, the descendant's body and she took over, but I didn't think it could happen again. Not in this body.

'What are you doing to me?' I asked my reflection. But then, it was not really my reflection.

What do you mean?

'You took over, did you not? What did you do?'

Maybe. Why would it matter?

'You are not supposed to be able to do that. What is happening? You feel different. And all I can think about is Lucy and Travis. I did not before.'

In the reflection, my face remained unchanged, but there was a flicker in my eyes; I could see the caramel, just a flash away.

I know how you really feel about Karrept.

Lili's words cut like a knife to the back. Could she really know that? Could she really know what that felt like?

'You are lying.'

Lili didn't answer but I could feel that she was not. She knew. She knew that I would do anything to stay alive, even if it meant going on without him. The scratch that was wasting his strength and would eventually kill him. There would be no way around that, and our spell, the one that we cast and was the reason why we were here and why Lucy, Lili and Travis had the Bond, wouldn't last. With his death, everything would change. Or it would have, if Lucy and Travis hadn't fractured it with their carelessness. But Lili also knew that. She knew that it would never be the same and they would have to live with it now. There was no way around that.

CHAPTER TWENTY-EIGHT

Lucy
Parmuthi 2012

I CLOSED my eyes as I felt Hunter shift gears and floor it. The car sped along the track with ease. If I couldn't see the way he cruised around the corner at such a high speed, then I could believe that I wasn't really doing this. Or the fact that I was in a car that could kill me. Better yet, I could be dead right now, floating somewhere and replaying my death over and over again.

'Lucy, you're not meant to have your eyes shut. I thought you trusted me.' His voice was like a sweet song in my ears. I couldn't see him smirk with his helmet on but I could feel it.

'You never said you were going to be this *crazy*.'

I was strapped in tight. Hunter had checked to make sure that everything was secure, even after the assistant had. I knew, logically, that nothing could happen—I wasn't going to suddenly fall out of the seat or something—but it didn't stop the way my heart plunged into my stomach.

'This is nothing. Watch this.'

No, don't want to see, I thought to myself, but he spun the car anyway. We twirled in what felt like a clumsy circle, but I knew it was elegant and graceful, even in this deathtrap of a car. Why did I agree to this again?

I couldn't say no to a cute boy asking me out, regardless of the fact that he was Devin's best friend.

He straightened up and we went around another sharp turn. I held on to the 'oh shit' handle and willed it to finish. I heard him hooting and laughing before the car came to a slow stop. My insides rattled around, and I felt the love in the way he eased the car down to an acceptable speed before he stopped the car. He took off his helmet and I saw his brown hair flicking out every which way. Helmet hair. My hands shook as I tried to undo my helmet so I could see him and not be restricted by a layer of plastic. He laughed again and carefully took over. He pulled the latch out and helped remove the helmet, his fingers brushing over my chin.

'How about that. Look at your hair,' he said as he smoothed strands that had escaped from my ponytail. I swallowed hard and tried to think of puppies or rainbows. Something other than his whiskey coloured eyes staring back at me. 'Are you okay?' he asked.

I nodded and somehow found my voice. 'Yeah, holy shit. How are you allowed to even do that?'

He laughed at me again. His laugh was soft and amused, almost a tangible thing. I liked it and wanted to hear more.

I'd had a crush on Hunter for a long time, but Devin had always told me no. No to his friends, which was why I was surprised when Hunter asked me out.

'Practice. I'm just good. You know I don't want you to be here just because I'm Dev's friend. He's not even a factor.' It was like Hunter had read my mind.

The pads of his fingers brushed against my cheek and we

leaned into one another. My heart hammered harder in my chest the closer we got.

'Man, Wyatt, you are a firecracker. No wonder your grandfather is so excited to get you on the track ... oh.'

We broke apart and I felt my cheeks burn. I was sure they were the colour of a ruby-red apple. Hunter chuckled and kissed my cheek.

'Barry always has the worst timing. Outcha get.'

I nodded and let Barry unbuckle me. I couldn't get out of the car fast enough. I turned my attention to the track and let my eyes graze over where Hunter spun the car out. I couldn't understand why people would do things like that; why they would put their lives in the hands of a car that could spin out and kill them.

I felt a hand wrap around my wrist and pull me around. In the moment before I closed my eyes, I saw Hunter. His lips pressed against mine, cutting off any more morbid thoughts before they started. I could hear faint catcalls in the background, but none of that mattered. When he broke away, I looked up at him—he was almost a head taller than me—and sighed.

'You were definitely as good as I thought.'

I scoffed and pushed at his shoulder with a few fingers. 'You didn't think I was good? Thanks.'

'Hey, hey. You're my best friend's little sister ...'

'By three minutes!'

'Still little.' He grinned.

'Shut up,' I mumbled, and brushed my lips against his to try to wipe that cheeky grin off his face. 'You're going to have to tell me some other time why and how you can get onto a track like this in a car like that and not end up dead.'

'Shhh. You're talking too much,' he said, and kissed me again.

THE MEMORY of Hunter and my first date always came to mind when I rubbed my fingers over the love heart shaped bead on the bracelet he gave me on our first anniversary. It was now joined by the talisman Meda made for me. Each bead signified a date or a moment in our relationship, and Hunter had enchanted it so that when I touched any of them, I would relive it. The bracelet tied in with our abilities. I didn't think it would work anymore. We had no good memories left. I was half waiting for a breakup charm.

The doorbell rang and I closed Nefertiti's Book to answer it.

I stared at the door and lifted a hand to press against it. I could feel Hunter mirror the motion before I opened it. He was wearing a striped shirt, shorts and Ray-Bans, his runners physique on full display. His hair was cut shorter than usual, but it was always cut that short in summer.

'Hi Lucy,' he said.

I shut the door and leaned against it. All of the feelings I had pushed under the surface flooded back and I had to close my eyes. He made things better. He always had—until he stomped all over my heart.

'I do make things better. You're just good at getting in your own way,' he said through the door.

'Hunter,' I said.

'Yeah, yeah, open the door. I'm melting over here and I don't want to be a puddle of goo.'

I snorted and opened the door. He looked me over and I resisted the urge to kiss him. I really wanted to. He smiled and the urge rose higher. Jerk.

'Hey, don't call me that.'

He pulled me into his arms and I tried not to break down.

Hunter was safe, he was home. He was everything I ever wanted and yet so far away.

'Are you okay?' he asked and I shook my head.

In his arms, I felt like sleeping with Travis was more of a mistake now.

'What? You slept with Matthews? I was wondering why you called me. But now I know ... do you need me to beat him up?' He was doing the mind-reading thing again, like nothing had ever happened. Like he'd never broken up with me.

'There's more to it than that, but get out of my head.'

'Not a chance,' Hunter murmured and pulled out of the hug. He grabbed his bags and walked down the foyer into the living room without needing to be prompted. He had been here before, just before we broke up, and knew where everything was. It was refreshing. He grabbed some water from the fridge and poured it into two glasses.

Hunter held out a glass to me. I took it and raised an eyebrow.

'You look like you need a drink. Well, you look like you need something strong, but this will have to do for now.' He took a drink and focused on me. 'Are you going to tell me the details now? Or do I have to wait for someone else to tell me? And I'm sure they won't be so forthcoming. Your cryptic call in the middle of the night was all I needed to get on a plane, but you know I need more.'

He was always ready to jump any time I needed him.

'We needed your magick expertise. There are some ... things that have sort of cropped up.'

Hunter stared straight through me. He tilted his head forward, put his glass down and leaned over the bench. He was on the other side of it, closer to the sink, while I was on the bar stool opposite him.

'Luce, the cryptic shit you're spewing won't work with me. I could find out exactly what it is if I wanted to, but you and I both know that I wouldn't do that.'

There was a bond that we had between us. It was why he was so magnetic and I was drawn to him. We were soulmates. *Adelphi Psychi*, as Hunter had called it. But we were on the soulmate break right now, and had been for three agonising months.

'We have a magick problem that involves us needing someone whose predominant element is air. It's for a spell.'

Hunter licked his lips before he pressed them together and pushed himself off the bench. His fingertips were dancing on the counter, something he only ever did when he was processing.

'Okay, well that part is doable. You know that my element is air. What do I need to do?'

I would have replied but Kali came in.

'Oh, look, Hot Legs is here,' she said. 'You look better than the time you did when I hit on you.'

'Kali Shaw, you always fail to surprise me with your wit.' Hunter grinned at her as he leaned forward to flick my wrist.

'Aww, that must be why we never made out.' She smiled sweetly and I tried not to choke.

Hunter raised his eyebrow at me. *Long story, explanation later.*

'How is Travis?' I asked.

'Tiring. He just doesn't stop. It's driving me to drink. Where is the strong liquor?'

'I can hear you, you know?' Travis said as he came into the living room.

'I know perfectly well you can hear me. I dated you, remember?' She masked the pain in those words well.

Hunter rose to his full height and stepped away from the bench when Travis rushed him and decked him. Hunter recovered and punched him back.

'Ouch. That *hurt*. What is your problem?' Hunter asked.

'You're my problem,' Travis growled, and I watched his eyes bleed to purple and his claws spring free.

I jumped between the two of them with my hands up in front of me, trying to appease the wolf. And Travis.

'Trav, back down. Now,' I said.

'Move out of the way,' he growled.

'Claws need to go away. Don't make me ask you again. You can't hurt him, we need him.' He had called Kali and I wasn't so much pissed about that anymore, but it was still not an ideal situation. I hadn't driven a knife through her back.

Yet.

Hunter snorted, and I reached for his wrist and squeezed, a sign to keep quiet. *Don't do anything that the wolf would interpret as bait, even if Hunter was laughing at me.*

'I don't like him,' he said.

'I'm well aware of that, Trav, but we need him. We need him to get Lili back. Now. Back. Down.'

Travis growled and didn't do as he was told. It made me angry.

You know what? Screw you. Get out of my face, go and fuck someone else, get me out of your system and cool down. Now.

I don't trust him with you, he said back.

You don't have the right to talk to me like that, remember? We're not a couple.

He put the claws away and grabbed his wallet and stalked out of the room.

'Well, that's just perfect, isn't it? You really have a way with men, Lucy,' Kali threw out.

'Kali,' I said, letting my irritation lace her name. I was starting to feel like she really was my annoying sister.

'Yeah, yeah. I'm going.'

I watched her exit the room before I caved in. I sagged against Hunter and he caught me. He always did.

'What was that?' he whispered.

'Me wishing Travis away. I told him to get out,' I whispered back. I turned in his arms and hugged him tight.

'He'll always be in your life, Luce. He'll always come back.' He squeezed me into a hug and I could feel our heartbeats starting to synchronise. 'What is Kali doing here?'

I pushed back and stared at him. 'You don't know?'

'Nope. What am I meant to know?' He walked to the bench and picked up his glass.

'Kali and I share a sperm donor.'

Hunter choked on the water he had just sipped and I snorted.

'Your dad? He cheated on your mum? What the hell? That is in—what?'

My gaze drifted to his biceps and my train of thought halted; on the inside was a tattoo. It hadn't been there when he had walked in the door. Hunter had mastered the art of glamour and covered it up. That was something he had been working on when we broke up three months ago.

'What's that?' I pointed at it.

Fos Kounidon. Lucy-Bell.

Hunter came from a line of witches who were deeply entrenched all things Greek, and I had learned enough to know what various words meant. This one I knew off by heart because his whole family called me it when they wanted to annoy me. He had three older brothers.

He had my nickname tattooed on his biceps.

Hunter remained silent. 'What is *that*?' The tattoo was magickally gone when I blinked. 'Hunter.'

'It's *nothing*. Okay?'

'It's my *name*. It's not nothing. When did you get it? It wasn't there a few months ago.' Which was the last time that we slept together.

'Just after,' he said quietly.

My head spun. He had broken up with me because he couldn't do it anymore. I shut down the connection between us in that second, and it took everything in me to do it. Hunter had made it obvious that he couldn't trust me enough after Antony. I never told him that he had nearly raped me because I hoped I wouldn't need to. I was too proud and I had thought that he would just believe me because I loved him.

'God. I hate you right now.' I cradled my head in my hands.

'Lucy.' He came towards me and I held up a hand and stepped back.

'Don't. You broke up with me, told me that you didn't love me anymore, and I've been trying to fill the hole you left but I can't. You know why? Because I love you and you know it. I feel bruised and battered on the inside, and it's all because you left me with some stupid excuse. I shouldn't feel this way, Hunt.'

'I left you because loving you was the hardest thing to do after you cheated on me. Do you know how broken I was on the inside?' He looked at me and I could see his green eyes start to water. Goddess, if he started, I was going to cry.

I had held my silence long enough. 'Antony tried to rape me, Hunt. Dev was in the house and stopped him.'

That made him sober up. He straightened and closed the distance between us.

'What? I...why didn't you tell me?' he said before he pulled me into his arms. I tried to resist out of spite, but his hugs were something I missed.

I shivered. 'I thought I didn't need to tell you. I thought you would have believed me. I never had any feelings for him. Nothing beyond he was pretty to look at.'

'Oh god. I'm an idiot.'

Something inside me unfurled and I took a deep, cleansing breath. I sighed and bunched his shirt in my hand.

'I've always loved you, Hunt,' I whispered.

'I know,' he replied and looked down at me. He pressed a soft kiss into my hair and I let him soothe me. After three months of no communication, this was ... everything I had wanted and more.

'We might as well watch some TV. Are you hungry?' Deflection from anything that could come. I was good at that.

'Sure. I can help,' he said and I waved him away.

'It's okay, I can do it. Sit down. Watch TV. All is fine.'

He blinked and hesitated with what he was thinking about saying. The look on my face must have said it all because he nodded and went to sit on the couch. I could stay away from him and do what we needed without putting myself in danger of falling back into old habits. He had a long way to come before that happened.

AT SOME POINT, we made it upstairs and I fell asleep in Hunter's arms. I would've still been there if the vibration from my phone hadn't woken me up.

'Turn it off,' Hunter moaned and covered his eyes.

I shuffled around to find it and answered it without looking.

'Hello?' I said groggily.

'Looooosaaaaay. Oh Looosaaaay.' The drunken slur was familiar.

'Travis?' I sat up and Hunter moved with me.

'Looossaaay. Where are youuuu? What are you dooooing?'

He's drunk, I mouthed to Hunter. He got off the bed and switched on the bedside light. My eyes were assaulted by the brightness for a moment before they adjusted.

'I was sleeping at home. Where are you?'

He snorted and I heard muttering in the background. 'Don't knoooow. A bar. They gave me drinks.'

'I can hear that. Trav, can you let down your shields so I can find where you are?'

'Wolf is too close to the surface. No can doooo. He will rip everyone to shreds,' he said in a singsong voice before he laughed.

'Fuck.'

We had devised a fail-safe in case anything like this ever happened. It shouldn't have; he had a fast metabolism, so he couldn't get drunk no matter how hard he tried. If I could get Lili on the phone, I would be able to find out where she was by breaking down the barrier, but with Nefertiti in charge now, it was left to me.

'Fuck.' He giggled. Oh god, it was like he was twelve all over again.

'Travis, can you see the yellow brick?'

'Oh, Loooosaaay. Don't do that.'

'Travis, the brick. You can see it?'

'Yeess.'

'Break it. And just the one, no other.'

He did what I asked, and in that instant I could feel where he was. I jumped off the bed and found shoes, then grabbed the keys. 'I'm coming. Stay where you are.'

'Looossaaay. You don—'

I didn't hear the rest of what he said because I hung up on him. Kali was up and bleary-eyed. She tried to rub the sleep out of her eyes as I moved into the hallway.

'What happened?'

'Travis is drunk. I'm going to get him.'

'I'll come,' she said without hesitation.

I shook my head. 'His wolf is too close. We can't afford to have him hurt you.'

'Lucy—' Kali started.

'Trust me. I know how to deal with this.'

Her shoulders dropped, and I gave her a small smile before I bolted down the stairs, with Hunter at my heels.

'I'll wait up. I'm thinking that going back to sleep will be a death sentence,' he said.

'Probably a good idea. I'll be back soon.' Then I was out the door.

CHAPTER TWENTY-NINE

Nefertiti
Epep 2014

IT WAS DONE.

Karrept and Khaldun had spent time together and chosen a bar close to the house, one that would be obvious enough for Travis to go to. It would be spelled hard, using a simple concoction laced with the alcohol that would even make a rhino drunk and would work on the werewolf. It would be a good distraction for what was to come. I was giddy with the thought of what we were about to do.

'Are you sure you are ready for this, my love?' Karrept asked.

'You know I'm ready. I am more than ready. Do you have the ingredients prepared?'

'I have ground the walnut shells and the clove together; all we need to do is add the cinquefoil and the eyebright.'

'Goddess, I love you,' I said and grinned because we could do this. I would get my book back, and Karrept and I would be able to start the next part of the ritual. There would be order to the chaos. Magick would be worshipped, not feared. The spell would help Karrept stay in this world, with me, but it would also help the world.

Karrept was shirtless, his golden skin just the way I remembered it, and I was infatuated all over again. Nothing had changed with his death. He still looked the same as he had before he died. I changed the bandages and with the wound taped up, I knew it would still fester. I could tell by the way the decayed skin moved that the infection was eating through his muscles to his bones. Once it got to that point, there wouldn't be any way to save him.

Khaldun had gone to sleep; he had the couch since we had the bed. The magick he and Karrept used took the strength out of him. It was late, but I couldn't sleep—who could with this kind of excitement?

'Let us check the crystal ball,' Karrept said, and with a swipe of his hand, we saw Travis at the bar. He was taking a drink, and even from here I could see just how much the alcohol was taking a toll on his metabolism.

'What did you add to the liquor with the enchantment?' Karrept's and Khaldun's powers wouldn't be able to do much damage without the binders.

'Liquorice and tarragon. I think it was a nice touch. He does not know what is going on and thinks that it is just the drinks. But the magick that I laced through the whole building—oh, my light, you will never believe how much is in there. I could not believe it. Our son is so powerful. We did the best thing that we could have done.'

As the words left his lips, I felt a pang of guilt. If I had been stronger or wiser, I could have raised him. My love for him swelled in my heart as I watched his chest rise and fall. I couldn't stop looking at him. I had longed for a son to raise, but I had to watch from the sidelines as someone within the dynasty —a real nice family—raised him. I'd hated myself for it, but it was in his best interest. He had too many features that were reminiscent of Karrept, and if Aten had found out ... I would have been dead at his hands and not my own.

'It's just a shame we had to watch from the sidelines,' I murmured.

As if he knew I was watching, Khaldun stirred in his sleep and his eyes blinked open. It was time to take what was ours.

Karrept covered my hand with his, a gesture that tugged at my heart. I looked him in the eye and sighed.

We were wearing dark clothing, long-sleeved tops and pants Khaldun had secured for us while we were working on the semantics of the spell. We'd learned from him that it was the best way to blend in, especially at this time of the night. It was late. Closer to 4.00 a.m. than we would have liked, but we couldn't wait any longer.

Karrept took a pouch with all of the ingredients; it would get stashed in the walls so that it would be impossible to locate. The magick would fizzle out when the spell was done, but we only needed it to be there for a couple of hours at the most.

'Are we walking, or ...'

I laughed. 'My love, we are not walking. We both know this.'

He took my hand with his free hand and closed his eyes. He looked so peaceful when they were shut, like nothing could bother him. I took a moment to take a breath before we were wrapped up in a dust storm. It was invisible to most, but with my practiced eye, I could see the dust. When we stopped, we were outside Lucy's house, right where we had been the last time—in the backyard. I knew they wouldn't keep the door unlocked, but we hoped they did.

Karrept took a deep breath and pushed through the magick barrier. Yes, it was strong, but he was stronger. As he held my hand, I let him borrow my magick, the one deep down under Lili's Watcher ability. It was innate and it pulsed, wanting to be used. Like it always had been. I was a queen for a reason, and this power was part of what made others fear me.

There was a magickal click, like a key unlocking a door, then he blasted through the wards and all of the magick. It felt as though a window shattered. It would be our access point in and out of the house, over the magickal shards of the spell that was once in place.

I turned to look at Karrept and saw he was breathing hard. My stomach twisted. The more he used his power, the more it hurt. He wouldn't show his weakness to anyone and even in that moment he hid it from me, but I knew it. I could see it all and that was what scared me the most. He was going to use up all of his reserve and kill himself before we could finish the spell.

'We need to be careful,' I whispered.

He smiled, hiding the worry I knew he felt. 'I am always careful, my light.' He cupped my face with his hand before he moved. He was ready for what was to come, and I knew that this could go either way.

Lucy wasn't home—she was the one who would have been the hardest to get past. The house was tied to her energy, and as long as she was home, it would protect her; with her gone, the others didn't stand a chance.

Through the back door, which we opened with a simple unlocking spell, I could see the haze of light from the kitchen. The light from the digital clock was enough to view the basic layout. As I slipped into the room I was careful to avoid the dining table in the dark.

'What are you doing here?'

I turned to find myself staring right at Karrept. Eerie, to say the least. I felt Lili reach for him. But even in the dark, I could see by the way he moved and spoke that he wasn't Karrept.

It was Hunter.

'You should be in bed,' I sang, then whispered an incantation under my breath. It would wipe his memory and make him remember only what I wanted him to remember. With a tap on the head, he dropped to the ground.

'All you will remember is that you were free, then you weren't. And nothing in between.' The words sealed his fate. I bent down to pick him up but was interrupted.

'Do you actually think you can pick up a grown man all by yourself, Mother?' Khaldun walked into the living room from the hallway.

'I could definitely try.'

'No way,' he said and picked up Hunter like he was a sack of potatoes. I got a chair from the table and Khaldun magickally tied him up.

'What are you doing here?' I asked.

'Can't let you guys do it on your own. No way, José.' Khaldun winked at me and my heart swelled. There were no words for how he made me feel. Or how I felt to see him so grown up.

'Tyler? What are you doing?' Another voice came from the doorway on the right.

'Kali, holy shit. I was just about to find you. I felt the wards break and came to check on you. I found—'

'That's Nefertiti. They're after the Book.' She tried to make a run for it, but Khaldun pulled her to him and muttered the same incantation I used on Hunter. She went limp in his arms.

'That was smooth,' Karrept said as he stood behind them, the Book in his hands. My heart raced. *It's back. I can feel it.*

'The Book,' I marvelled and held out my hands to him. 'I need it. Give me it.'

He handed me the Book and I held it up to my chest. 'They broke the spell on it, but that does not matter. I do not think they got very far.'

It was like a part of me was finally back and I could breathe again.

'Get out of here, I'll finish tying Kali up. Lucy will be back any moment, I am sure of it. I don't want you guys to get caught up in it all.'

He didn't need to tell us twice. Karrept took my free hand, the other hugging the Book tight against my chest. Almost like I was afraid I would lose it again. I willed him some of my power, and when I opened my eyes again, we were back in the hotel room and the Book was with us.

'Finally, we can get this done,' Karrept said and I smiled.

Everything was right in the world with the Book in my hand and Karrept by my side.

CHAPTER THIRTY

Lucy
Epep 2014

I PULLED up to the bar, some trashy place a few blocks away from the house, and caught enough of a glimpse of Travis adjusting his belt and Midriff Girl pulling up her flimsy panties. My brain tried to shield me from what I'd seen, but it failed and anger rattled through my body. I gripped the steering wheel until my knuckles turned white. Travis laughed as he got into the car.

'Loooosaaaay. Hiiii.'

Hi, you arse.

'Get in. Shut the door.' As soon as the words were out of my mouth, Travis was vomiting. He missed the car by centimetres. I stared straight ahead and steeled myself through the noises. The bile rose in my throat and I swallowed hard, but that didn't stop my body from dry retching. Travis shut the door and looked at me, wiping his mouth on the back of his hand.

'All better.' He giggled and sniffed the air.

A growl slipped from his lips and I held up my hand. 'No.

No. You do not get to comment about smelling Hunter on me. You don't even get to ask what happened. You are going to keep your mouth shut because you just fucked Midriff Girl out there. And I'm trying to be the better person about it.' I put the car into gear and sped home.

He was quiet until we got out of the car. He was unsteady on his feet, so I let him use me as a leaning post. He sniffed my hair.

'I hope he was a good fuck.' The venom dripped from those words and made me see red.

I stopped supporting him and let him stand on his own two feet. He was shaky, but in that moment, I didn't care. He was being an arsehole. My hand moved on its own and slapped Travis hard. His eyes widened and his jaw dropped.

Good.

As I tore my attention away from him, I saw the door slightly was ajar. I'd left it closed. 'You, of all people, do not get to say that to me. And I will yell at you more about that later. Bury the drunken idiotic man that is you right now and bring the wolf out. I don't need to deal with you right now.'

I also expected the wolf to know more about what was going on with Travis than Travis himself. He didn't get that drunk. Ever. Being a werewolf meant that he had a faster metabolism than a human. Something or someone had to have magickally intervened for him to be this drunk.

The wolf was also a better offence than drunk Travis. I knew that I hadn't left the door open like that, and it meant that someone was in the house. Or they had been.

I watched as Travis' demeanour shifted; he became sober, his eyes harder and his jaw set tightly. He had the aura of a predator around him.

'Someone was here,' he said quietly. There was still a slight slur to his words. Whatever happened really got him good.

I nodded and walked to the door. I was quiet as I pushed it open and wished like crazy that we still had the bat lying around the house. But after accidentally breaking your father's fingers with it, we no longer had a bat in the house anymore.

I didn't need to tell the wolf to be quiet, and together we moved into the foyer. We carefully moved to the cusp of the foyer and saw the room overturned. Furniture in the wrong places, some broken, but what really caught my attention was Hunter and Kali. They were tied to the chairs.

I ran, not caring if there was anyone still in the house, to Hunter, and kneeled as I ripped the duct tape off his mouth.

'What happened?' I asked.

He shook his head. 'I don't know. One minute you were here, the next I'm tied to a chair. I don't remember anything else. It's like someone stole the memory from me.'

I swallowed hard and glanced at Kali. Her eyes went wide when she saw Travis.

'He's drunker than a sailor. How's he still walking?' Kali asked.

'The wolf's in charge for the moment. Do you remember anything?' She shook her head in response as Travis pulled at the rope and tugged it free.

'Lucy. How did you do that?' she asked, her attention still on Travis. She was mesmerised. 'I could never get the wolf to come out when I wanted him to.'

I was about to say something when the wolf spoke up. 'You wanted me out to fuck me. Not to use me. There's a difference.'

I raised an eyebrow and shrugged. She had her answer.

Hunter's eyes filled with concern. 'Relax,' I muttered. 'He didn't hurt me or do anything.'

Hunter already knew, without words, that Travis had hurt me emotionally. Not all scars were physical. I gave up with the knots—no matter how much I pulled, I couldn't grip them enough to loosen them. 'I'm a weakling. I can't undo the knots. Travis?'

He didn't wait for a second request and he snapped the

knots like they were nothing. Hunter got to his feet and brushed himself off and looked around, almost like he could see through the haze but couldn't quite get there. He shook his head, like he was trying to clear the fuzz in his brain.

'Fucking hell,' Hunter cried out, and I jumped.

He wasn't the sort of person who had much of a temper; I was the hot-headed one and he was the cool, calm and collected one. This was out of the norm for him.

'What?' I asked.

'They took the Book. Motherfuckers. I remember that much. They were here, they came and took the Book, but they used magick and I can't remember who it was or why. It's just there under the surface and I can't figure it out,' Hunter said.

'What do you mean?'

'I mean that there is a block and whoever put it there is good. Really good and … normally this would mean that I would go for a run. Or something of the kind. But … dark … and Egypt. I mean, I could do it.'

'You definitely could,' I reasoned with him.

We both stared at each other before we looked at the room. It was trashed. More furniture to replace, but it wasn't as irreplaceable as the Book. We were screwed.

'If I went, would you leave everything alone and let me help clean?'

'You and I both know the answer to that.'

'Dammit, Lucy,' he muttered. He looked so torn between bolting to the door and cleaning. But I knew that the clarity he would get from the run would help even out his emotions. It would help him deal with the missing memories, because he could try to unpeel the layers.

'It's okay. Go clear your mind, we can do this. We'll be okay,' I said.

'I'll help,' Travis said and I snorted.

'Okay, you're going to bed. The wolf can go now and you can

stumble up the stairs alone.' His eyes widened as the wolf did as it was told. Travis' demeanour completely changed and he was glassy-eyed and giggly.

'I'll help him up the stairs,' Kali said.

'No. You won't. He can do it himself.'

'Lucy—' she countered.

'He needs to learn. You're helping me clean.'

Kali dropped her head, defeated. Travis looked from her to me and back to Kali before he left the room. I heard him stumble up the stairs and I didn't care.

'That was harsh,' Kali said.

'Was it, though? I caught him pulling up his pants after he was done with some whore of a woman. I have little to no sympathy left for him.'

Kali's eyes widened and she looked at me with compassion. It wasn't an emotion I was used to seeing on her face, but people grow up, and we could be better people than we were as children. We had to be.

She walked to the kitchen and pulled a rubbish bag from under the sink. 'I guess cleaning this will be more therapeutic than it would be otherwise?'

Sometimes being busy was a better way to run from your feelings.

I STARED at the screen in front of me, my laptop keeping my bare legs warm. I needed to release some of the stress in my body, and unlike Hunter, running wouldn't help me. Running made it worse. But I could try to write it away. Sometimes that was even better than exercise.

'You always were a run hater,' he said as he walked into the room with wet hair and clean clothes.

'I'm not a run hater, I just hate how repetitive it is. I don't get how you can feel less stressed after one.'

'You're not doing it right, Luce.'

I laughed. 'Yeah, clearly I don't know how to run.'

'It's okay. I can forgive you. Sometimes your way is better,' he mocked.

'Oh, what? You mean having sex to melt the stress away.' I grinned.

'Are you propositioning me? Because I can talk you out of those clothes before you realise what I've done.' He was messing around with me, but part of me wanted it. We fell right back into our flirty ways, no matter what had happened, and I missed it. I missed the way he made me smile.

Even when he was just Devin's best friend, he caught my attention and it was always a part of our dynamic. We had flirted with each other forever before I caved and Hunter asked me out for real. Rinse and repeat.

Hunter was familiar; he was home. He was my one. But it would be tactless to sleep with him just to get back at Travis for sleeping with Midriff Girl. I wasn't like that. I hadn't been in a long time.

I waved him off. 'You think I'm that easy, do you? Psh.'

'Oh, come on, I know you are.' He grinned and I laughed at him.

I went back to tapping away at the keys of the laptop. I closed out of the screen I had been writing in and instead opened a web browser to find information on what I needed. The internet was full of answers—surely it could help with the crown, Anubis, Nekbhet and Karrept. It didn't make sense that there was information missing about Karrept and about what was happening. I couldn't find anything on him. Either he wasn't in history or he was so far hidden from it that it made him look invisible. Even the Illuminate Year was missing. How could something so big be so hidden? There had to be some sort of information on it. And now that we were without the Book, the internet was our best bet.

228

'Are we going to talk about why you called me?' Hunter asked.

I wanted to ignore him because that was what I did best, but I couldn't. I shut my laptop and sighed.

'Yeah, I guess we should.' I put the laptop down and Hunter walked over to the bed and sat down. I crossed my legs under me and it took all my strength to look at him. His whiskey-coloured eyes were darker in the artificial light and he looked tired. We were both tired and wired at the same time. 'We need your help to do a spell that involves people with predominant elements. I'm earth, Kali is fire, Trav is water and you're ...'

'Air.'

I nodded. 'But we're not even sure on where we're going with it. It's not like it's something that we have organised properly, because there's a bit of an issue.'

Hunter leaned forward and I saw his hands hesitate. He wanted to reach out, and I wanted nothing better. But we weren't there yet. Just because we had been cuddling in our sleep earlier didn't mean much right now.

'Your magick, right? I felt it when I walked in, but I didn't quite get it. Not until now.' Hunter held out his hands, an invitation for me to take them if I wanted to.

I reached out and put my hands in his. He closed his fingers around them and held them carefully, like he was afraid I would break, but I wouldn't. He closed his eyes, and I watched his peaceful face, the way his brown hair stuck up every which way and his chiselled cheekbones.

There was a hand that grabbed my heart just looking at him, and I knew that I was doomed. I had always been doomed when it came to Hunter. His aura, magnetism and energy always drew me in.

My hands started to sweat under the warmth of his hold.

'You have some sort of block. I can feel another witch's protection. I'm assuming it's the bracelet you're wearing now?'

Hunter opened his eyes and searched my face before his gaze went to the bracelet that Meda made for me.

'Do you know what kind of block it is? I can't seem to figure it out.'

'It has something to do with the house, I know that much, but there's also something else there ... Luce, did you finish any of the training after we broke up?' His fingers tightened around my hands and guilt settled in the pit of my stomach.

'I didn't. I couldn't do it after we broke up. It was like magick wasn't as colourful without you and I saw no point in doing it.'

Hunter let go of my hands and inched closer. He took my face in his hands and leaned in close. 'That wasn't part of the deal,' he murmured. 'You were meant to finish it and you were meant to get through the initiation. It would have all been fine.'

I didn't want to do it without him. It was the truth, but it also just made me miss him more when I tried.

'There was an ache in my chest whenever I tried. You were missing from everything I did. Everything I have done. I just couldn't.'

It sounded like a weak excuse but I couldn't lie to Hunter, even if I wanted to.

'But, Luce, that magick was so important.'

'I know, I *know*. But magick never felt the same without you.'

Without saying anything, he dropped his hands from my face and wrapped his arms around my shoulders, pulling me in for a hug. I buried my nose into the crook of his neck and inhaled his scent. It was just as I remembered: soft, woody, with a hint of citrus. I could never get enough of that smell.

'Do you want to try working through it together?'

Like I was going to say no to him. I never could, even when he gave me the out.

'How good is it going to be here?' I asked as I pulled back.

'Lucy-Bell, it's always going to be good when you're by my side.'

'Why did we break up?' I whispered. It was totally off topic, but it was enough to make me wish it all away.

'Because I'm an idiot.'

I shook my head. 'Let's try and get this magick under control. Do we start with the meditation?'

Hunter admitting that he was an idiot was the confidence boost I needed to make sure that I could do this. That I would be able to do this without second-guessing my own abilities.

'Yeah. Do you want to be lying down or sitting up?'

'Lying down.'

He got off the bed and took my laptop with him. He placed it on the ottoman at the end of the bed and I lay back. Hunter made sure there was a pillow under my head. 'Just don't fall asleep,' he cautioned.

If I fell asleep during the meditation, I might not wake up; a careful warning from previous times echoed in my mind after Hunter spoke. The bed moved beside me and I knew that Hunter had sat down. It moved again as he got comfortable, but I kept my eyes closed and focused on my breathing. The key to getting the meditation right was to slow down your breath. I used to try to take long, deep breaths, but I learned that the real trick was to breathe normally. Eventually it would even out and deepen on its own.

I forgot when my body switched modes because it was second nature to me.

In and out. In and out.

'Starting at your toes, you're going to relax each one as you step onto that sand. Your happy place always was the beach. Give them a bit of a wiggle so you can feel the sand between your toes.'

I sighed and let myself sink into his voice as I dug my toes deeper into the sand. Fresh, salty air filled my nostrils as the sun warmed my skin. The beach always had a special place in my life, but not as much as the feeling of the sand grounding me in the moment and in my place. It was the only reason why, whenever I meditated for power, I came back to this very place.

The sand crept up my legs and I felt each granule scrape against my skin.

'Focus on the way it feels and not the way it is trying to be. You are in control of what happens here. But only if you believe in it.'

Hunter was right, but he was on the outside and I was deep in this. The sand climbed higher and was covering me from my shorts down. The weight of it pulled me down and I sat in the sand, or more adequately, plopped my arse in the sand. With each breath, the sand rose higher. As it hit my waist, my heart beat a little faster and I could feel it pulse in my throat.

'You can keep your breath under control. Don't let the sand dictate what it can do to you,' Hunter whispered.

The image of me in my mind shut my eyes and leaned into the meditation. I let it soothe my soul and my body. The sand was going to find the weak spots of my magick. It wasn't going to take me away; it couldn't. The morsels of sand reached my chest and I jolted in the meditation. My hands came to the centre, where my heart lay, and I could feel the void. The sand refused to touch it. And it wasn't just the sand, nothing wanted to touch it. My fingers were sand-free and I knew that the problem wasn't my magick—it never had been. It was that my heart was too used to keeping out the hurt.

It was painful losing my Devin and Destiny, and more painful that no one believed me when I said that they weren't dead. I chose to believe that when no one else did. And then when Hunter broke up with me, that faded the fragments of what my grief for my siblings meant. I held tight on to the reality of what could happen and not what was happening in the present. I pulled my hands away from my chest, and just as I was about to get to my feet, I saw hands, much like my own, held out to me. The sun shone behind her and her brown sea-tousled hair whipped around her face. Even though I couldn't see her face, I trusted her.

I took her hands and she pulled me to my feet, the sand crumbling and dissipating away from my clothes and my skin. As I came to eye level with her, I saw myself looking back at my own storm-coloured eyes—before they shifted to the brightest blues I was used to so regularly seeing on another face.

She gripped my hands tighter and pulled me towards her. Without a word, she melded into my body and I gasped as her being collided with mine. I saw Nefertiti and our line as it spread over generations. Her daughters, and their daughters, and their daughters, on and on right to *Savta*, Mum, Destiny and, finally, myself.

We were all one.

Each and every one of us were a part of the next, and it was our blood that connected us all together.

Our blood was the catalyst.

I gulped for air as my eyes opened in the flesh and I saw Hunter staring down at me, his whiskey-coloured eyes filled with concern. I grabbed his shoulders and pulled him into a kiss. Our lips melded together and I put every intention I felt into that kiss. The way I loved him and the way that I wanted him here.

He broke the kiss first, and I brushed a finger over my kiss-swollen lips. 'It's our blood. All of our blood. My blood, Destiny, Mum, *Savta*; all of it. We're the key to it all and that's why Nefertiti had the upper hand.'

'What do you mean?' he asked. I searched his face as he tried to process the kiss. I was past that now. I knew I had to talk to Travis again and it would be a completely different conversation to the one he hoped for.

'I'm a descendant of Nefertiti, Hunt. I'm the one who can find her and stop all this. That's why she wants me. I'm the most familiar body. We look exactly alike. It's taken thousands of years to get the right body, the right face, to make it all work. I can find her with my blood and stop it all.'

'Blood ... wait, you're not thinking about blood scrying, are you?' Hunter put distance between us and rubbed a hand through his hair. I saw the tattoo on his biceps again and resisted the urge to bite my lip, because it was so damn hot.

'I am, yes.'

'Luce ... that's dangerous, and it's not something *you* should be trying after that meditation.'

I shook my head and slowly pushed myself up into a sitting position. I folded my legs under me and held his gaze. 'That's exactly why, though. I saw her. I saw a vision of what happened through the years, and while it doesn't mean that I actually can comprehend everything properly, I know I'm on the right track here. Hunt, Nefertiti wants the world to be different. She just didn't realise that by waiting for so many years it would be so diverse and different to what she knew. Look at what we have to do.' I waved a hand to the room.

'Kali had to do a memory spell to erase any memories of the gods and Travis out of the minds of the patrons at Tamari. Have you seen anything on the news?'

He shook his head.

'That isn't right. We shouldn't have to hide the magick, but we do. Do you think Nefertiti really understands what that means for her?'

'I don't think she gets it, but she has been planning for this for longer than you and I have been alive, Luce, and we know that she wants you. I'm not going to let her have you.'

'And I'm not letting her have Lili a second longer. We need to find them and we're taking the fight to them.'

'What?' Hunter pressed his lips together. 'We have a drunk werewolf who is our only viable weapon right now and you want to go on the offence?'

'Yup. But we need to find them. And we need Kali for it.'

Hunter tilted his head and sighed. 'You got all of that from the meditation to fix your magick?'

I smiled at him. 'There was a hole in my heart. She fixed it. You and I both know why that is, and I'm done playing coy and letting you have your time. We're going to fix this because we know our future. And I'm not taking no as an answer. Get the candles. I'll take Kali.'

KALI RUBBED her sleep-riddled eyes and stared at me like I had grown an extra head. 'You want to do what at this hour?' She yawned and covered her mouth.

'Scry for them using blood. My blood.' I wiggled my fingers in front of her.

'That's what I thought you said. It's dangerous and I never thought that would be an option for you.'

'Why? Because everyone thinks I'm Little Miss Perfect? There is a lot you don't know about me, Kali, even if you think you know everything.'

'I can say the same for you. I'm not as shallow as you think either.'

'This isn't the right time of morning for an argument and a pissing contest,' Hunter said. 'For the record, I think this is a bad idea. Blood magick is dangerous. It's not something you should dabble in.'

He had been adamant about this for the last twenty minutes, and I had heard every single argument but wasn't going to budge. This would work.

'I know, Hunt. But I have this knowing ... and it came to me in the meditation. I want to find Lili, and by using my blood to find Nefertiti and Karrept, it's going to give us the upper hand. I want the spell that's in the Book. The one that we need to end all of this. I don't want any more surprises.'

'Luce, I get it, I do. But I'm going to say it again, it's danger-ous. Can't we find another way?' he asked.

'What, and wait for the wolf to be up and go sniffing about when he's hungover as fuck? No. I'm not waiting for him. I'm not waiting for anyone. We're doing this.' I needed to do this too. I had all of this power and now that the disconnect was gone, I wanted to test to see what that really meant for me and my magick.

'I like this side of you,' Kali said to me.

I looked at Hunter and his jaw was set stubbornly. I needed him to help. Magick with him always felt so much more natural. I held his gaze the warmth spreading through my body.

'Fine. I'll help, but you need to know that I'm not doing this willingly. I'm helping out to make sure that you don't get hurt. Kali, no offence, but I don't care if you're hurt.' He moved beside me and picked up the chalk. Mum was going to have a heart attack after we finished with all of these spells, which required us to mark her decor. All the marks would be gone but she would still know. She had a funny sixth sense about activities that ruined her aesthetics.

'None taken. You love Lucy and you'll do anything for her. I'm used to coming second to her.' The venom in her voice made my stomach drop. I opened my mouth to retort but she shook her head. 'Save it. It's fine. Let's get this going. Hunter, if you can cast the circle, I'll do the rest.'

'On it.' He drew a perfect circle. One that was careful, prac-ticed, never-ending; maybe his best yet. When both ends met one another, I touched his back. He looked at me and anger flashed in his eyes. He didn't like being goaded into things, but this was different. I was taking control and he was mad at me. I tried to hide my surprise but I knew I failed. He clicked his tongue and started to fiddle with the ingredients.

'Stop it, Luce,' he murmured as he stood up straight. 'Just

stop thinking. If you're going to do this, *you* need to clear your mind.'

Even with his anger, he was still a teacher and a guide.

'Lucy, so what we're going to do is—' Kali spoke up and broke me out of my thoughts.

'No, we're going to do it my way.'

Kali's surprised gaze felt good, but I tried to brush that away. I hated being micromanaged, I hated when people didn't believe in me, and I had a deep knowing that this was going to work. I was testy because of Hunter, and because of Travis, and maybe a mix of everything else.

I took a deep breath and tried to clear my mind, but with every breath, an image of Hunter or Travis popped into my mind's eye. What I had to tell Travis ran through my mind but so did the fact that Hunter was begrudgingly doing this, even that Kali was here. That I was getting her to help. This was a clusterfuck of a situation and if I didn't want the answers I deserved I wouldn't be doing this. They wouldn't all be here. Destiny and Devin were alive, and if I found Nefertiti, I'd find out where they were. I could bring them home. And the world would be right again. Or at least my world would be.

Hunter wrapped his fingers around my wrist and raised an eyebrow.

'Stop thinking. You're not centring yourself and it's making your energy erratic. It'll be harder to do the spell.' His voice was soft and he paused. 'Get a grip, Ryder. You can do this.'

I nodded, closed my eyes and took a centring breath. I let it travel down my body before I opened my eyes and rolled my shoulders. It was going to have to do because I couldn't take any more time. The sun was peeking through the blinds by now. I held out my hand to Kali, and she handed me the athame. It was black obsidian with a bone handle. It was smooth but sharp. Hunter spread the map out on the ground, which had been surprisingly hard to find because everyone could just pop a location into Maps and it would give you directions. He nodded at me.

It was time.

I steeled myself and sliced my hand with the athame. I hissed at the immediate pain and curled my hand into a fist. Blood dripped onto the map, and I raised my gaze to Hunter and he started the chant. Whispered words filled the space and I followed their lead.

'Blood of my blood. Take this offering. Show me what I am seeking the most. Show it to me now.' My voice was clear now that my intent was sincere. I pictured Lili's face in my mind, her strawberry blonde hair, blue eyes and her smile when I said something stupid—which was often. It was the image I held on to. I willed the magick to find her. To find Nefertiti.

The droplets of blood on the map coalesced and formed a pattern that I wasn't familiar with. Hunter stood beside me, his hand on my elbow, the only support I needed. I watched as the droplets scattered and joined again in the spot that I least expected them to be.

Looking at the map, I began to laugh. It started with disbelief and stemmed into hysteria. I fell to my knees and clutched my belly. Hunter was trying to reach my bleeding hand, to clean it before wrapping it in gauze.

This whole time they were closer than we realised.

'I think I broke her,' Trav said.

I sucked in a breath and saw Travis looking down at me. I waved him away and Hunter hovered around me, worried. Quickly, he disbanded the circle, but I couldn't stop the tears that ran down my cheeks. Maybe it was the sleep deprivation or a stress reaction but I was hysterical.

Hunter snaked an arm around my waist and brought me to my feet. It was like I didn't weigh anything at all. He guided me to the couch, where he forced me to sit and finished wrapping my bleeding hand before he kneeled in front of me and held my face in his hands.

'What is wrong? Luce, you need to talk to me. Tell me what happened. What does that mean?' He nodded to the map but didn't take his eyes off me.

'Look at the map,' I managed to wheeze out, my fingers gripping at his shirt.

He looked over his shoulder and frowned. 'I don't get it, Luce. What does it mean?'

'Hotel,' I choked out.

Hunter took another look and stared in disbelief. 'Are you fucking kidding me? The hotel? This whole time?'

I nodded and laughed harder.

'I don't get it,' Kali said.

Travis was just as perplexed and I laughed even harder. Shit. I needed to stop. But I couldn't. It was like when you finally cried for the first time in a long time—like floodgates had opened. Hunter sucked in a breath and slowly massaged my shoulders, trying to calm me down.

Finally, I came to a stop and took a deep breath. I remembered when my brother and sister went missing, I had been livid. Inconsolable and barely present. It was such a surreal feeling and I almost felt that way now.

'Luce, what do you mean?' Travis said, swaying. He was still drunk.

'They've been at Dad's hotel the whole time. That's why they were able to take us by surprise so many times. They're literally down the road. Or around the corner, whatever. I actually picked you up from the bar that's connected to the hotel.'

'Oh,' Kali said.

'Oh indeed,' I said. 'I'm sure that they're going to know that we're right on their tails, so we'll need to make sure that we're ready. I need a weapon.' Travis was our best fighter, which reminded me ... 'Travis, what are you even doing up? You need to sleep off the alcohol.'

'I'll be fine,' he said before he ran out of the room to vomit.

'Real fine,' I muttered. Hunter chuckled and Kali chased after him.

'What's the plan?' Hunter asked.

'Sleep. Let's get some because we can't do anything if we're tired, but tomorrow we're on the offensive. They'll be coming for us.'

CHAPTER THIRTY-ONE

Nefertiti
Epep 2014

THE BOOK WAS as beautiful as I remembered. It felt like home and felt right in my hands. I pulled away the fake covering that made it look like a Book of the Dead. The cover was covered in gold hieroglyphics and had an image of Karrept and me on the back. The layers of papyrus were thick so that the cover was sturdy, the individual pages marked with letters of love, spells and everything in between.

In these pages were our hopes.

And the details about the Illuminate Year.

A year when light would take over.

A year when Karrept and I could live without Aten and out of the clutches of what he symbolised.

Or at least, that had been our hopes. Until Karrept was scratched.

'My light, what are you doing?' he asked.

I looked up from the Book and glanced over my shoulder at him. He was stretching, moving carefully to make sure that he didn't tear anything. The scratch was getting bigger; it was starting to eat at his skin faster the more power he used. I was sitting cross-legged on the floor and he made his way over to me. The sun had long set and since being in Liliana's body, sleep came during the daytime hours and I was alert during the night hours, or that was what I liked. Karrept sat next to me. One hand covered mine while the other guided my face to his. 'You know there is a lot that we could be doing right now. Instead, you choose to read over what you already know.'

I smiled and held his chestnut-coloured eyes. 'My love, we need to find a way to get rid of the scratch. Maybe, in the modern age, we can figure it out. We couldn't back then, but we can now and I think that is worth studying over. It's been too many millennia since I last saw what was in here.'

'I can tell you everything in it from memory. There is nothing in there that will stop it. We both know that.'

Maybe something had changed.

Or maybe I was just wishing that something would change.

'There has to be—maybe we're just not looking in the right place. I need you alive and this is not really helping. Why didn't we think this through?'

Karrept gently took the Book out of my hands, almost as if he was scared that if he ripped a single page, I would lose it.

'My light.' He cupped my face in his hands and held my gaze. 'Nefertiti, we did not expect that Aten would find out about us.' He never said my name. He was trying to be serious right now.

'But we had an inkling; we knew we wouldn't be able to sneak around for long. It doesn't matter that it went on for years or that we actually managed to bear children together. This wasn't in the *plan*, we should be free of him, of the wound. How come, in over three millennia, there isn't a cure for this?' I wanted to scream at him, this wasn't fair.

'Because werewolves are tricky by nature and we don't know any more than that.'

'There has to be something more. I refuse to take that as an end-all answer. Where is the tiny contraption that I can find anything I want at the touch of my fingers?'

It's called a phone, Lili chimed in my head. I'd almost forgotten she was there. *Yeah, I haven't forgotten about you, but you can forget about me when you're wearing me?*

Her tone made me stop in my tracks. She was upset. More than before.

'You mean this?' Karrept held up the phone. I nodded and he handed it to me.

'Yes. Thank you,' I said as I took it from him and unlocked the phone.

Do you know something? I asked Lili.

Liliana was quiet and I didn't think that was a particularly good thing because it meant that she did.

'You should sleep,' Karrept said.

I shook my head. 'No, I'm okay.'

As I tapped on the icon with the coloured circle, I gasped; magick swirled around me and took me by surprise. It wrapped around my body and I could see the descendant: Lucy. She was in a circle and she was searching for me. I stared down at my hand as pain seared it and saw the slightest of cuts. She …

'Karrept. She's using blood magick,' I choked out before he took my wrist and slammed his other hand into the air. It put up a barrier that would cut her off, but it still wasn't enough—she knew where we were now.

'They know.'

Karrept's eyes widened and I knew that this was going to be bad.

'We need to prepare,' Karrept uttered.

'With what? We have three witches against us. What are we going to do?'

'We need to kill her. I will raise the army, you find the supplies.'

You know you can give up anytime. I don't think that you'll be able to get what you want.

I didn't say anything because I didn't want Karrept to know I was talking to Lili. As far as he knew, she was deep down in the confines of her own body. But that was so far beyond the truth I didn't even know how to bring that up. It was a lost cause.

CHAPTER THIRTY-TWO

Lucy
Dreamland

I'D NEVER SEEN purple fields before, at least not in person. I marvelled at their beauty. There was a way that the flowers swayed that tried to tell me a story. Like they were trying to whisper secrets to me. I was wearing an A-line gown that was covered in lace. It made my cleavage look amazing and was not something that I owned. In fact, it looked like a wedding dress.

'Oh good, you're here.' I turned to find myself staring at the last person I expected. Her normally strawberry blonde locks were dark and her blue eyes burned bright.

'Li-Nephthys?'

'Thank the gods, I *do* look close to what you think I resemble.'

To her words, I simply nodded. But seeing her made me ache for my best friend, who was cooped up in my family hotel, not far from the house. She was so close but so far away.

'Good. Okay, you need to listen up. You've done something bad, haven't you?'

Blood scrying. There was always a consequence for using the wrong kind of magick.

There was a twinkle in her eyes and the corners of her mouth tweaked into a smile. She knew but she wanted me to admit it. 'You've angered them. Your spell, they know what you did. You need to be prepared.'

'Prepared for what?'

'I think you know what is coming. Do you know who your Guardian is?' She took a step closer to me.

'Guardian?' No. I didn't think those were even a thing. I mean, there was always an inclination that Guardians were real, but ... I didn't think that they were *real*.

'Oh, for goddess' sake. It's the one you call on in times of need, she'll protect you. I can't tell you who she is, but I know that when you meet her, you'll love her. But she's a little delicate. She doesn't like sudden movements, so treat her like she's a precious flower.'

'What? How is she a Guardian then? I don't know what she looks like and I have to treat her like she's fragile piece of Mum's China?'

'You'll find her when you need her. Trust me on that.' Nephthys ran her fingers over the ornate chunky gold necklace around her neck. She opened her mouth and closed it again. Like she didn't want to tell me something. Her body paint was pristine, not a mark out of place, and her shift clung to her body in all of the right places.

'What? What do you want to say?' I was so tired of people keeping things from me.

'The mutt, he's going to punish you if you don't look out for yourself more.'

'Travis is my best friend. He wouldn't hurt me.' Why did everyone keep saying that?

'Won't he?' she asked and raised an eyebrow at me. 'I knew what he was like in his past life. He wasn't a very nice man to you. Well, to Nefertiti. I watched the way he controlled her. Why do you think the curse is in place? It's to keep the two of you apart so he won't ever get that sort of power over you.'

Travis wouldn't hurt me. I wouldn't let him. He knew what it meant if he did.

'Does he?' she asked.

'Get out of my head,' I growled at her. It was getting frustrating that everyone was able to read my mind. I just wanted a chance to have some privacy in my own head, was that too much to ask for? I was used to the boundaries I had in place with Lili and Travis.

'Sorry, you're in my world now. It's easy to do this.' Nephthys shrugged.

Is that why Devin was so good at using dreamland? It ran in our bloodline.

'What do you want?' I said, annoyance showing in my voice.

'To warn you. Karrept is after you. He wants your blood. I'm not sure how far he is willing to go for it, but trust me when I say just arm yourself. Steel is your best bet. Obsidian would be better, but steel will do. Nefertiti isn't as easy as you think she is. She and your ... friend are changing the game. She is cunning. She is going to get you. In the way you least expect it. I have something for you. It will help.'

'What is—'

She took my face in her hands and kissed me. It was soft, caressing and unlike anything I'd ever experienced. And I loved kissing.

Something passed between our lips.

'Luce. Lucy, wake up. It's just a dream.'

Gasping for air, I clawed at the body that was holding me down as I came out of the dream.

'Shhh. It's okay,' he whispered.

I pushed back and found myself in Hunter's arms. He held me against his chest and I heard his beating heart in my ears.

'It's okay. You're safe. I'm here,' he cooed.

'Hunter?' I gasped and clung to his naked chest. Where was his shirt? What was going on?

'I'm here. It's okay,' he soothed. 'What happened?'

'Dream. Nephthys. I ... she gave me something. I don't know what it was.'

'Nephthys was in your dream?' He brushed hair out of my face and tried to catch my gaze but I couldn't meet his.

'It was more than a dream. I can still feel her lips on mine.'

'I didn't think that was something you actually could do,' Hunter said.

'It's not. Devin was ... is the dream guy. I just have them ... or have been. It's the house. Or the energy here. She gave me something,' I said and ran my fingers over my lips.

He looked at me with curiosity. My body ached for more. With Hunter around, I always wanted to be next to him. I felt like we were magnetic and there was a connection between us. It was why we kept sleeping with each other even after we broke up. It was hard not to because I knew he felt it too. But we had decided cold turkey was the best way. We needed the distance to get past the feelings.

Without thinking, I leaned up and kissed him, hard. My fingers laced around his neck and I pulled him closer. I breathed him in, before his hands on my shoulders pushed me back, and I whined.

'Luce,' he said softly, not a hint of change in his tone.

'I'm sorry. I'm sorry,' I said as I tried to get my heart rate down to a normal speed. I covered my mouth with my hand and avoided his eyes. 'Put on a damn shirt.'

'Stop saying you're sorry every time you kiss me, but just know that I can't give what you want and need right now. By the goddess, I want to but I can't. And that kills me. Now, explain it to me slowly. What happened?'

I took a deep breath. 'She said that we made them angry and that they'd be here to retaliate.'

'Retaliate how?' he breathed.

'They're going to attack us. We *need* to be ready.' I pushed myself off the bed and to my feet. It was partly a distraction because Hunter looked so good I could devour him, but I just had the wolf pop into my brain and I understood. 'I need to talk to Travis. We need the wolf. I need the wolf.'

'Lucy—what?' I heard the confusion in his voice. 'What do you need the wolf for?'

'He's the only one who is good with a sword.' I knew I was rambling now, but my mind was running at a hundred kilometres an hour.

'What do you need a sword for? Do you even own a sword?'

I shook my head. 'Well ... not yet, but I will. We need to start right now.' I paced up and down the carpet.

Hunter got off the bed, his footsteps over to me not as silent as I'd thought, and he grabbed my shoulders to stop me pacing. He turned me around to face him. 'Are you sure you don't need more sleep?'

'Yes,' I confirmed.

Maybe I was in shock or something, but it all made sense to me. I was a fast learner and I could get the basics down no problem. A sword could stop Karrept and Nefertiti. I was sure.

'I have to see Travis,' I said again.

'He's still drunk. You might want to wait,' Hunter said, his gaze searching my face.

And that was all I needed to remember drunk Travis, Midriff Girl and the blood scrying. I stumbled and was about to catch myself but Hunter was there and he wrapped his strong arms around me. I let him hold me tight, his warmth and scent more than enough to steady me.

'Whoa there, Luce. You are trying to do so much. You need more sleep. This is too much for your nervous system. I'll stay with you, I promise, but you need to sleep.'

I wanted to fight him but he was right and I knew it. Things made more sense when he took control and I didn't fight him. I liked when I didn't have to think about everything all the time.

'That sounds like a good idea,' I mumbled into his chest, and he led me back to bed in his so very strong arms. I fell asleep as soon as he laid us down.

I HUNCHED over a bowl of granola that Hunter had hastily put together. I added a final dollop of coconut yoghurt to it and stirred it around. Okay, maybe it was more than a dollop, but it was so damn good. Hunter sat across from me, his eyes glued to the book he was reading, but he felt my gaze on him and looked up at me.

'What?' He swiped a finger at the corner of his mouth. 'Do I have yoghurt somewhere?'

I shook my head and took another spoonful to stop myself from saying anything. I felt him try to poke around in my mind, and I smiled a little harder. I checked my magick barrier was in place and felt that the protection was there, even against Hunter. He was curiously cute when he didn't have all of the answers.

'Luce, what is it?' I could tell that it was torture for him to not know what I was smiling about. There was no reason, no logic behind it at all.

'Not a damn thing, you're just fun to mess with.'

He groaned and threw a date at me. I caught it and ate it with a laugh. Hunter grinned, but it slowly slipped from his face as we heard another groan, this time from behind me.

Travis was awake.

Hungover and in what looked like a world of pain, Travis

stumbled to the table and sniffed the air, almost like he was testing it to see if he was hungry or something. I heard a growl from deep in his throat and anticipated the swipe. I lifted a hand and held Travis' fist in the air. His werewolf strength shook me and threatened to throw me off balance, but I pushed back with the magick I now had access to. Hunter jumped out of his chair, his eyes wide, but he didn't move. No sudden movements and the wolf would be okay.

'Lucy,' Hunter said calmly, his attention not straying from Travis and his fist.

'Yeah, Lucy,' Travis mimicked. 'When did this happen?' He nodded at his hand and I knew he meant the magick.

'Last night,' I said without hesitation.

'And you smell like Hunter. When did that happen?'

I laughed—I couldn't help it. His reaction to Hunter's scent all over me was comical after I caught him with his pants down in the alleyway.

'All we did was sleep,' Hunter answered quickly.

'Lies. You fucking smell like her too.' He growled again. His eyes bled from green to purple, and the jealousy in them was enough to make me want to slap him. Instead I let go of his hand and put myself more firmly between Hunter and Travis.

'Travis,' I said, my gaze not wavering from his. 'We just slept.' *And I kissed him*, I added behind the wall of my mind. 'I'm not yours. You don't *get* to claim me.'

His shoulders slumped and he relaxed. And I thought that it would be fine, but Hunter took a step to the left and Travis was faster. He tried to hit Hunter but he ducked. Travis hit a wall of power and let out a frustrated growl.

His wolf was still too close to the surface. I didn't know what happened but the alcohol had to have been laced with magick. There was no way that a werewolf could have gotten drunk, not with their metabolism, and still be so in control. Most were-wolves learned how to hide their wolf early on, so that the world didn't persecute them. Travis was a master at it, and this was out of character for him. If there was no magick in the alcohol, then there had to be a hex, one put in place to make sure that he got drunk.

'Back away from Hunter and get your wolf under control. Or I will do something about it.' I stood my ground. 'And I'm sure you won't like that. You know how much you hate magick intervention.'

'Whoa. What a cocktail of testosterone and magick. I didn't think that was something I'd be privy to so early. Good morning, guys,' Kali said with a yawn. Her gaze flitted between Travis, Hunter and me, and she shrugged. 'I can see the power thing. I like this version of you. How's your palm?'

She moved into the kitchen and it was all that Travis needed to calm down. I watched him take a deep breath before he sank into one of the chairs.

'Itchy actually, but I guess it's healing. How could you sleep through a show like this?'

Kali laughed. 'I was so wiped after last night.'

Silence descended around us and all that was heard was the clinking of spoons and rattling of bowls. The silence in the room was enough to make anyone cringe. I watched as Hunter picked up his bowl of granola and put it in the sink.

'Okay, what's up?' Kali asked first. Her attention moved to Travis and then me.

'Nothing,' Travis said.

'That's bullshit. You two are like the coldest people in the room and I've never seen that from either of you. What is it?'

'It doesn't matter,' I said, my eyes avoiding Travis'.

More silence.

'I think Lucy had an idea,' Hunter spoke up, breaking the awkward silence that kept growing.

'Oh?' Kali said as she slid into the chair next to Travis and started eating her breakfast.

Now was the time to speak up. 'We're going to attack Karrept. At the hotel.'

'What?' Travis said as Kali choked on her cereal.

'Did I stutter?' I asked.

Both Travis and Kali blinked at me.

'We're going to attack them. And you're going to help,' Hunter finished for me, his gaze burning a hole in Travis' skull. He seemed surprised by Hunter's bold words but maybe it was because it was my plan.

'Yeah?'

'Yup,' I said. 'You know how to fight with weapons that I don't. And I'm ready to get Lili back.'

'What do I need to do?'

'Teach us what you know.'

His face said yes without a single word leaving his mouth. He was just as ready to get our best friend back. Because without her, our Bond was incomplete and we were so terrible to one another. I was done with it.

And so was he.

CHAPTER THIRTY-THREE

Nefertiti
Epep 2014

KARREPT SAT IN A MEDITATIVE STATE, his legs folded under him, his eyes closed. His lips moved with words I could barely hear. He was raising his power and energy levels, or trying to. I was about to drop down into the same position and give him some of my strength, but I felt Khaldun at the door. Before he could knock and interrupt his father, I opened the door. His hand was closed in a fist raised in the air.

'Mother, that is freaky. I was just about to knock.'

I smiled and moved out of the way to let him into the room. The bed was a mess and there were plates all over the place, but he took no notice. 'It's an added gift I have. Plus, I know your aura; I felt you before you knocked. Your father is chanting and power syncing. I couldn't let your knock interrupt that.' I closed the door behind him carefully so that all was heard was the soft click. Khaldun walked deeper into the room and sat on the edge of the messy bed, watching Karrept.

'Why does he need to do that?' he asked and I sighed.

'His power is waning. It takes a lot of energy to control everything that is happening, and the more he uses his power, the quicker the scratch seems to fester. We need to stop that or we're going to lose him before we can finish what we came here to do.'

'And what is that?'

I tucked strands of hair behind my ear and looked him in the eye. 'We just want to be together. We never got the chance to. This is our chance. We want to peacefully exist.'

He tilted his head. 'But you took Lucy's siblings. You didn't do that peacefully, and it doesn't look like you have any plans to give them back. Doesn't that put a kink in your plan?'

I sighed and sat down on the floor, directly in front of Karrept, who hadn't stopped chanting. He was known for his concentration and could drown out anything happening in the room for as long as he wanted, but there would come a time when he would stop and it would melt away.

'Because we needed Lucy. Still need Lucy. I can't stay in this body. She is me. It's my body as it was all those years ago.'

'Why can't Father jump into his descendant?'

A very legitimate question. The magick that coursed through Karrept's blood was pure, it wasn't going to ever not be, but Hunter was different.

Hunter is going to be the one who changes it all, isn't he? He's too strong for Karrept because he's a direct descendant and he has power that Karrept doesn't. He can better shield himself from attack. It's why you went to Lucy and then me. Because we're the weaker links. Lucy being without her siblings and me without my brother. The losses we have are the way in. Aren't they? Lili's voice vibrated in my head with the words I didn't dare speak.

I did not know how to put it into words so I said nothing to Khaldun. It was like there was something that stopped me, or maybe it was pride.

'Let me help,' Khaldun said. 'Let me be a vessel for Father. I can get into the house and past the wards they've probably put up now. I can do it.'

Karrept's eyes opened, his chestnut-coloured irises looking more like whiskey as they swirled with magick. It made me lean closer to him, because this was when I wanted him the most. There was something about that look that stirred feelings deep down inside me. I could devour him whole right there as he sat.

'Do you know what that entails?' he asked Khaldun.

Khaldun straightened his shoulders and looked his father squarely in the face. I wondered what it would have been like to have watched him grow up and how he had carried himself. What had he done to make his extraordinary life ordinary because he was given to a family that wasn't royalty? I had told Aten that his birth had ended in a stillborn, and we mourned him.

The kingdom mourned him, but Karrept and I knew the truth. He had been watched. Karrept had kept a keen eye on him and I asked never to be told a word. Because Aten would know I lied. His bloodline … our bloodline … was fated to only bear girls. And I had given him three girls of his own, two of which had been Karrept's. Their saving grace was that their features were like mine and not Aten's so no one was the wiser when they looked at them.

'Tell me.'

Slowly Karrept rose to his feet and I watched from the floor as he walked over to our son. Khaldun stood up to meet his gaze. They were the same height, but Khaldun was in the body of a skinny boy—well, Lili would call it scrawny.

'I would take over the body you are in now. I would also sound like me, not you. You would be there but you would not be. I would be able to go where you went.'

'Will you have access to your magick?' he asked.

Smart boy.

Karrept looked back at me, a sly smile on his face, pride shining in his eyes.

'Yes. But I need you …'

'I give you permission. Do it.'

'Nefertiti.' Karrept held out a hand to me and I took it. My insides shook with fear. Khaldun could get hurt, like seriously hurt. As I took Khaldun's hand, I saw a flash. Karrept's lifeless eyes stared back at me and I cried out, but it was too late. In that instant, his body fell to the floor, and I looked into Khaldun's eyes to see them taken over by Karrept's. His face smiled like he did and he pulled me in close.

The urge to kiss him was strong but he was in the body of Khaldun; it didn't matter that I didn't know what he had looked like when he was alive in our time, it was enough to make me think twice now.

'We're ready, my light. Let's go get ourselves a witch.'

'Be careful,' I whispered and tried to say more, but my body was stuck. It knew what was about to happen and already mourned my son.

CHAPTER THIRTY-FOUR

Lucy
Epep 2014

'ARE you sure that we can do this?' Kali asked as she twirled her sword in her hand. The motion made me think of picking up a softball bat and how with the roll of a wrist, it arched in a circle; it was a beautiful motion and one I never forgot. She threw the sword my way and I made it float, just as the doorbell sounded.

'I think so. We're picking up everything relatively quickly, which is a good thing. Are you doubting what we can do?'

'That's cheating, by the way. Magick isn't supposed to catch it. You're meant to catch it.'

Maybe she was right. It was hard to think about how we were going to pull this off. If we did make it a surprise attack, we had to plan it to a tee and ensure that nothing went wrong. I was going to call the hotel to find out what I could and then get us in there. I had to call Sam too. I needed to make sure that, as a Guardian, he would want to have a hand in Karrept's demise. It was a vendetta he could take joy in. Karrept had a hand in the death of his father, that was the only reason why he was activated a tomb Guardian It would give him some closure.

'Tyler. What are you doing here?' Kali said when she opened the door.

'I came to see you guys. What are you up to?'

I peeked my head down the hallway, the sword now in my hand, waiting for what would come. I lowered the sword when I saw Tyler at the door.

What was he doing here?

I focused my attention on Tyler and took a deep breath and cleared my vision, I couldn't see aura, that was Kali's ability but I could try and see a familiarity in Tyler. What I saw was dark, there was no golden light, nothing that was the playful stranger at the bar two years ago. I swallowed past the lump in my throat and I kept the sword loose by my side.

'Kali. I think you need to step away from the door.'

'What? Why? It's Tyler?' Kali said. The look on her face said more than I wanted to touch, but she had to believe me.

'I don't think that's Tyler,' I said. 'Look at this aura, Kali.'

'Don't be stupid,' she said.

'You little wench.' Tyler's voice became distorted.

Kali finally listened to me and took a step back. 'Luce?'

'Yeah. I'm here. Hello, Karrept.'

'Lucy, you are leaving me with no choice, but we need you.' Karrept's twisted voice came out of Tyler's mouth and it made my insides shake. 'If you will not come to us, we will take you by force.'

There was silence and Kali backed up slowly. I took her hand and squeezed it.

'Wh-what? What's going on? Lucy?' Tyler's voice made my heart ache, the change from Karrept's was jolting. Kali tried to go to him, but I gripped her wrist tight to make sure she didn't move. As long as he was hosting Karrept, he wasn't going to come into the house. We wouldn't let him. I almost wished that we had had the time to put up a spell that wouldn't let him in unless he was invited. Like the myths about vampires entering a house. If they were real.

'Tyler, what do you remember?' I asked.

He shook his head, trying to clear it. 'I—I don't remember much. I remember the club and being here and then it's blank. All of it is blank.'

There was something in the way that he looked at me that told me he was lying. I could feel it and that was the scary part. I always thought that Tyler was innocent and just in the right place at the right time, but this was too much of a coincidence.

'Lucy!' I jumped as Hunter's voice came from the other end of the house. I stared at Kali.

I let go of her wrist. 'Watch him,' I said. 'And, Kali? Don't let him in, whatever you do.'

'Let me in, Kali.'

I knew that Karrept was back, I just hoped that Kali was strong enough to keep him out.

I watched from the living room as the crocodile-headed god pushed at the barrier, the jaws snapping wildly like it would be able to snap right through them. From the animal I could tell that it was Sobek. There was no mistaking that snout for anyone else. I looked past the god and saw Karrept and Nefertiti standing in the background. There was a smile on both of their faces, like they were sharing a private joke. But when I looked at Karrept, I could see he was a shadow of who he was. How much magick was it taking to be in two places at once?

'What happened?' Hunter said. Travis came up beside me and I could feel the wolf shimmering just under his skin.

I turned to him. 'Don't shift,' I said quietly. 'The wolf is our only advantage.' Karrept knew Travis was a wolf, but he didn't know he was stronger in his wolf form than in his human form. I wanted to keep at least one surprise for them.

'Karrept is possessing Tyler. They want me,' I said.

'Well, it is really your power we are after, and the necklaces. But I am happy to take you for all of that,' Karrept said.

He expected me to be weak.

'Watch out for Tyler,' I murmured and walked out onto the deck, Hunter just behind me. I watched as Sobek's jaws tried to chomp at the barrier to no end. Kali was stronger than I was and damn good at what she did.

Hunter took a hold of my hand and squeezed. Travis growled and I tried to relax. If he felt me tense up, I was sure he would go for Hunter's throat.

Are you ready, Trav? I whispered the words into his mind without taking my eyes off Sobek. His attention shifted from Hunter to the goddess.

Ready as I'll ever be.

Hunter's hand went into the air and I mirrored him. Together, through our clasped hands, we focused our energy and pushed it out through our minds. We threw Sobek, Karrept and Nefertiti out of the way with our joint power to give us some breathing space. Travis quickly found a weapon, a garden shovel, and flew at Sobek. Hunter and I broke through the barrier; he went to Sobek and I went towards Karrept. I had no issues with the goddess—Karrept was my only real problem.

He laughed. 'It's like you play directly into my plans, Daughter of Nefertiti.'

'I have a name,' I said as I swung at him. My fist connected with his cheek. He didn't stop laughing, and as I went to sweep his legs out from under him, I felt someone sweep out my own.

I hit the grass, the air ripped from my lungs. I rolled instinctively and found myself staring at Tyler. 'Ty,' I wheezed out.

'Wrong again.' He pulled me to my feet with his power, a power I hadn't known he possessed. I clawed at the air, trying to break his hold. I saw his left hook coming at me and blocked it before I twisted his arm behind him. He yowled in pain.

'Wh-what's going on?' Tyler stuttered. But I wasn't so sure it was him. Or if he was putting it on.

'Ty? Is that you?' I turned so that I could see Karrept in my eyeline and watched as the cocky look drained from his features. In a blink of an eye, something cool pressed against my temple.

'I would let go of him, if you want to keep your pretty little head.' Lili's voice filled my ears, and with those instructions, I did as I was told. Tyler stumbled away and I watched as Karrept filled his face.

What the hell just happened? Why did I even do that? I was so sure I had a tight grip on him.

'You really need to stop being so indecisive, Karrept,' I said as I felt the prick of the blade break the skin. I whimpered at the sliver of pain.

'Your friend doesn't want me to hurt you, but she is not the one in charge,' Nefertiti whispered in my ear.

'Lucy!' Hunter's voice waded through the fuzz. He came into my vision and I smiled.

'Hey, Hunt, have you met Nefertiti? She's in Lili's body.' He could see that very clearly himself, but I was trying to buy some time.

'She looks wrong in there.' He got the hint.

'I know. And your doppelgänger is just to the left of you, but he could be in Tyler's body.'

'What is he wearing? That doesn't even work,' Hunter said. He was trying to stall. I could work with that.

'Maybe he found it at a thrift shop?' I smiled a little wider at him. I hated being put in this position, but if I had to look weak, I would. Lili would know that I wasn't, but just how much did Nefertiti know? I wanted, so badly, to ask her. To confirm what Nephthys had said in the dream.

'Call off your dog,' Nefertiti said.

It was in that second that I saw Travis had Sobek by the

throat. 'Let go of her, Nefertiti. I know that Lili is in there and she would be screaming bloody murder at you for hurting her,' I said.

I couldn't see her face, but I felt the pressure on my temple lighten. In that moment, I thrust my arm up and wrenched the blade out of her hand. I held it against her throat. 'Back away from me now. I don't want to have to hurt you, but I will if you keep pushing me. Trust me.'

She swallowed hard and stepped back, her hands up in the air in defence. Like it would help. But Nefertiti had a wicked smile on her face and I followed her gaze to see Karrept stab Hunter in the chest. It happened in slow motion and it was as if he came out of nowhere.

'No!' I screamed and tried to get to him, but Karrept was now Tyler and he was in between us. I lashed out, my fists finding nothing but air. He kicked my legs out from under me and I was on my back again. 'Travis, Hunter!' I called out. I couldn't see where he was or what was going on. My vision tunnelled and focused on Tyler. I pushed him back with my strength and he laughed.

'There it is. That's the power I want. Give it to me.' I kip flipped to my feet and was making a beeline to him when Sobek blindsided me.

I stumbled and swung my arm out. Sobek ducked and laughed. 'You humans, you are oh so breakable.' He twisted my arm behind my back.

I swung my head back and connected with his crocodile jaw. He stumbled back and I took the opportunity to shove the dagger into his throat with all my strength. He gurgled and stumbled back. Travis snapped his neck and he fell to the ground.

There was no time to celebrate the victory as Karrept/Tyler appeared, the blade now pressed against my chest, his strength keeping Travis away.

'Lucy!' Travis cried.

'Hunter, look after Hunter.'

In the back of my mind, it registered that Kali should have been there too. I didn't know where she was.

'Look at this. I'm going to kill you now,' Karrept said. He turned the blade into my chest and I cried out from the pain. My world flashed before my eyes. Hunter's smile and his laugh would be the things I missed the most. How would they explain to my parents that they were childless?

'You wish,' I choked out—and flipped the dagger and shoved it into Tyler's chest. Just before it slid in, his eyes flickered.

'Lucy?' Tyler's hoarse voice came out.

Then it clicked. 'Oh fuck, Tyler.' But as I said his name, another pricked in my mind: Khaldun.

'Noooooooo.' Kali's scream came out of nowhere. My fingers clawed at the blade to try to wrench it out, but Kali pulled him off me; she ran with speed I didn't know she had.

Travis sank to his feet and I scrambled towards Hunter. My fingers went to his wound and I choked back a sob.

'Lucy, my light,' he coughed. The sound made my soul feel like it was ripped in two.

'No, don't you dare die on me. Help me help you. What do I do?' I was livid. Grief clouded my vision and tried to take away my motor functions, but I kept pressure on the wound. He couldn't leave me.

'Tyler. Is he hurt?' he asked. Hunter was worried about another man when he was hurt just as bad.

He was dying. I could feel it. 'Yes. He's really hurt.'

'You need to help him first, me second,' he wheezed.

'Tell me what I need to do,' I said again. Hunter wasn't going to die on me. Not after I had decided that I needed him in my life.

He was silent.

'Hunter,' I screamed. My hands were bloody, as were my

clothes, but whose blood was a mystery. Was it mine? Hunter's? Or was it Tyler's?

It could be all three.

Hunter coughed and I sobbed. 'Hold your hand'—he coughed again—'over the wound and say this: "Take the pain, e-eaase the rain."' He paused and swallowed hard.

"'Heal this wound of flesh and blood, make it whole, sew it well. Hel…"' He trailed off, and his eyes fluttered shut.

'Hunt, stay with me,' I whispered, tears trickling down my cheeks. I couldn't lose him too.

My voice anchored him back and he opened his eyes. "'Help my lover, my one, be whole again." Envision the skin knitting back together and it'll happen.'

I didn't think twice and dropped the barrier between Travis and me.

Travis, you need to get Kali to do this. Get her to hold her hand over Tyler's wound and say this: Take the pain, ease the rain … I repeated Hunter's instructions. *Hurry.*

I felt a nod of acknowledgement before I focused on Hunter. He had stopped breathing. I panicked.

'No! You don't *get* to leave me.' I placed both hands over his wound and said the incantation, chanting it like it was the last thing I would ever say. I envisioned the skin knitting together, repeating the words over and over again until my mind memorised them and the words blended together. I felt my power rise and pushed it into him. I watched, my hand pressing down firmly on the wound, and waited. He still wasn't breathing and I held my breath.

I felt someone hover behind me and Travis knelt down next to me. I refused to look at him and take my eyes away from Hunter. Seconds stretched on for hours as I watched Hunter die in front of me. I hadn't been too late with the spell. I couldn't have been too late—I knew I had timed it right.

I heard Kali sobbing and my stomach sank. I looked over my

shoulder and watched as she clung to Tyler; that could only mean one thing.

Hunter gasped and I ripped my attention away from Tyler.

'Oh god,' I whispered and kissed him hard. His fingers threaded through my hair for a second before he pulled me back so he could see my eyes.

He was alive. Nothing else mattered.

'Lucy. You—what did you do?' he choked out.

'I healed you,' I whispered. His fingers brushed my cheeks and wiped away the tears.

'What about Tyler?' he said.

I shook my head, my body starting to shake.

'Luce.' Hunter sat up and pulled me into his arms.

I had killed someone I knew. A man who helped me, who had been there when Hunter hadn't been. Hunter knew about him. He was a friend—who had ultimately tried to kill us. Maybe he had been working with Karrept the whole time. What possessed him to do that?

Kali was inconsolable now. I blocked out her sobs and buried my nose into Hunter's neck as the shivering got worse. What was a little shock too?

FINGERS SCRAPED down a chalkboard and I jumped to attention. Shivers tingled up my spine as I looked around at the room. I took in every aspect of it, like I was studying for a test. I was in a school classroom, one that was familiar to me. The desks were still lined up neatly, with the teacher's desk front and centre. Behind it, a whiteboard with symbols, scribbles and Nephthys' name in hieroglyphics. Next to the whiteboard was the chalk-board—and I couldn't mistake the figure next to it, but in an instant it was gone.

'You know you don't belong here, Lucy.' I couldn't mistake Devin's voice no matter how much time passed.

'Dev,' I whispered and looked around. In the corner, right at the back of the class in the shadows was exactly how I remembered my brother. 'What are you doing here?'

'I had to find a way into your dreams, but you're a lot harder to get to when you're next to Travis versus Hunter. I always liked Hunter better because of it.'

'What do you mean?' I pushed my chair back and got to my feet.

'Stop, Luce.' His voice sounded strained, like it hurt him for me to move.

'What? What did I do?' I asked. I desperately wanted to run up to Devin and wrap my arms around him. I ached to find out if his hugs were the same as I remembered.

'It's taking a lot of energy to keep this up, but you need to stay still,' he said. 'I can dream walk, but not like I used to. Right now you're not really sleeping but more in a shocky state of sleep. Kill anyone lately?' The cold tone of those last three words sounded wrong coming from Devin's mouth.

He seemed ... harder.

Like there was a part of him that had changed in two years.

Flashes of Tyler's face flickered in my vision and I cried out.

'I'm sorry. I didn't mean for that to happen.' The quiet undertone of his voice soothed me. It was like the time he picked me up off the ground when we were ten, after I'd skinned my knee because he pushed me off my bike. 'I forget that sometimes I can make things appear. It's been a long time since I've actually been able to do this the way I am.'

I sat down on the table with my feet on the chair, staring into the shadows. I could see a flash of his torso; it wasn't as skinny as I remembered, but I hadn't seen him in two years. 'Dev. You're really alive. I didn't believe it until now, but I didn't want to not believe it either. Where are you?'

He was quiet. And so unlike him. At least with me. Devin and I were like two peas in a pod because we were twins. We always had something to say, but his silence told me something had changed him. And I wanted to get him back. I needed to save him from whatever it was. Because this was not the brother I'd hung on to.

'Devin?' I asked again, and I watched as the shadow of my brother held his head in his hands.

'Lucy, Lucy. You're not ready for that yet. There's more that you need to face before you find me. Did you get a visit from anyone else in your dreams?'

How could he know about that?

'I know about a lot in here. If you think about it in here, then I will know it. It's as simple as that.'

'I ...' The lie was on the tip of my tongue, but I shook my head and sighed. 'Nephthys. She told me that Travis is dangerous and that we did something with the Bond ... we broke it.'

Devin laughed. It was colder and darker than I remembered. I rubbed my hands up and down my arms for warmth as goosebumps covered my skin.

'She's trying to scare you into fixing it ASAP, what a smart woman.' He was speaking in riddles. I was confused.

'What are you ... Dev?'

He pushed back his chair. I jumped at the scrape of metal against wood, and he appeared in front of me. He gripped my biceps and I gasped. His eyes were hollow and his face thinner. Dark circles under his eyes made him look haunted. His cheekbones protruded from his face. He didn't look like the brother I remembered and it scared me.

'Good,' he said. 'It should scare you. You need to not worry about the Bond. Just be careful of what you ask one another to do. Your orders are like commands that a soldier can't break. Travis won't hurt you unless you tell him to. And vice versa. You both have the power to hurt one another equally, but, Lucy, you need to understand.' He licked his lips and stared at me with the ferocity of a wild animal. There was no hint of my brother left in those grey, dead eyes. 'Luce, you need to play it smart when it comes to Karrept. He's more cunning than you think.' He dug his nails deeper into my arms and pain radiated through them. 'You can attack him and take something of his, but you won't be able to keep it. Use what you need from it and then give it back. Don't hold on to her.'

'Her?'

'Lili. Nefertiti. She can hurt you, and will now. You killed their son. Karrept could truly hurt you with Nefertiti at his side. I don't know how, I don't have that ability, but you need to watch out for yourself. Okay? I may look different, but I still care for you. You're my baby sister and even if you hate Destiny, she was just looking out for you too. You have to understand that—everything we did was to protect you because we knew how important you were to their plan.'

'What? What does that mean?'

'You have to go; they're calling you back. Just remember to be careful,' he said, and everything blurred out of focus.

I GASPED for air and the room came back into focus. A gross smell lingered in my nose. Travis and Hunter were both hovering over my face and I pushed them back.

'I need some air,' I cried out and they pulled back. Travis got to his feet and stared at me. His fingers were cracking at his sides, like his claws were rubbing against one another. The sound was inside my skull, and I closed my eyes to try to silence it.

Hunter didn't make a move and stared right at me. I didn't need to have my eyes open to know the intensity of his golden eyes staring back at me. A shiver ran down my spine and my body shook. I opened my eyes and he moved to come closer, but I held up my hand to stop him.

'Luce?' Hunter's voice was unsteady. It was like he was using all of his self-restraint to not dive deep into my brain. He studied my face. I forgot about Travis for a moment, and there was just me and him.

He was trying to make sure I was still here.

'I'm here. Barely,' I choked out.

'You were crying Devin's name out,' Travis said quietly, and it brought the rest of the room back into the spotlight. I was in my room. The shutters were closed. Did I trust myself to use my powers to open them? I wanted to check if there were bodies outside. Could they still be there? Sobek and Tyler, lying in a pool of their own blood?

Devin's words swam in my head. I wanted Travis to get out of my face, wanted to tell him to get out and not come back, but I wasn't sure what would happen. I didn't think I trusted myself.

'What was I saying?' I asked. My attention slipped from Travis back to Hunter. What did that mean?

Hunter took it as a sign and held my hand in his. I let him and squeezed gently. It was more comforting than I remembered it being. My heart skipped in my chest, and Travis growled. I would have let go, but I was done playing around.

'Just his name,' Travis grunted. 'Do you have to do that?'

'Yes. I ...'

Tyler's face filled my vision again, and I looked down. His blood was on my hands, and I couldn't bring him back. There were splatters of blood. It was all over them. I ripped my hand free from Hunter's and cried out, scrambling back into the headboard.

'Get it off. Get it *off*,' I screamed and tried to scrub the blood from them. It wasn't coming off. I scrubbed harder and tried to get up off the bed, but my body wouldn't move.

'Luce. Lucy! You need to calm down,' Hunter cried out.

'Get it off me, right *now*.' The blood coated my hands and dripped down my arms. I screamed.

And hands gripped my biceps, in the same place Devin had gripped. I looked into Travis' eyes; they were pulsing purple but were full of pain.

Like he wished he had done the job so that I didn't have to go through this.

I wished he had.

'I killed him,' I whispered before my body shut down and the world went dark.

It was better that way.

CHAPTER THIRTY-FIVE

Nefertiti
Epep 2014

KARREPT HELD me tight and I couldn't move. I couldn't sleep, think or even eat. My body didn't know what sort of loss this was. I hadn't lost a child before; I'd left the world before my daughters, and that meant they'd had to mourn me instead, but this pain ... it was incomprehensible.

'He's gone. He's gone,' I chanted over and over again.

My teeth chattered and my body shivered. The shock of losing him was too much. It didn't matter that I was covered in goo from Sobek or that there was blood in places there shouldn't have been, it was just there. All of it was there.

I didn't feel him move, but he picked me up and into the bathroom we went. I distantly heard the water running, and he was careful to undo my pants and slowly pull them down. Like I would shatter into a million pieces if he pressed too hard. But that couldn't happen. It was like someone had taken my insides and thrown them into a blender.

I felt raw.

Like there was nothing left.

'He's gone,' I sobbed.

'I know, my light, but he will always be here,' Karrept said as he touched the place between my breasts. Right where my heart was.

It was not the same.

It could not be the same.

'We took our chances and our time with every inch of the plan, but he paid the price.'

He was going to kill Lucy. She did what she needed. Liliana's words weren't comforting, and maybe she meant them as an attack, but they were the truth.

'Hands up,' Karrept murmured and I did as he asked. He lifted the shirt over my head. He unhooked the deathtrap of a bra and left me, for a moment, to check on the water. My teeth chattered and I wrapped my arms around my naked body.

Breathe, you need to remember to do that, Liliana reminded me, but I didn't know if I wanted to be reminded. Maybe I could fade away. *Don't do that! You're in my body, we need to stay alive.*

'I feel numb,' I said through the chattering. Karrept clicked his tongue in response, then his warm hands led me towards the shower.

His gentle touch soothed me as he slowly guided my body under the warm stream of water. I gasped and closed my eyes as I let him tip my head back into the water. It rushed over my hair and down my face and my body.

'I have you now,' Karrept whispered and I nodded.

Because he did. It was all I could do.

You know, you could let me take over if you want. You can go and hide. It sounded like a good idea but if I let that happen, I would wake up standing in front of Lucy. Away from the comfort of Karrept. I cried at the thought of not being close to him, and he pulled me to him. His body felt bigger than normal, or maybe I just felt smaller. Silent sobs wracked my body before they became stronger, louder. Karrept didn't try to stop them, and he didn't say a word, he just held me. A luxury we never had when Aten had been around. The stolen moments were fleeting and nothing like this.

'You are my world. And Khaldun was just as much. We will remember him, always. And we will get our revenge,' he murmured.

Those words were music to my ears, and I looked up at him, through the tears and through the steam. He caught my gaze and held it; the love in his eyes was what I longed for. Millennia had passed and that was all I craved.

He kissed me. First it was slow, soft, almost like he was unsure of me or if I would. I wrapped my arms around his neck and let the warmth of the water run down my back. I kissed him back and pulled him closer, feeling every inch of his body against mine. I moaned as his hands slid down my back. He broke the kiss and found my gaze; the heat in his eyes made my body quiver.

'Are you sure you want this, my light?' he asked.

My body knew the answer, but did my heart want it?

When had it ever said no to him? I had always wanted him, and there was nothing in this world that could stop that from being true. Was that me making the decision? Or was it Liliana?

'Yes,' I whispered and twisted my body, pressing against the shower screen. His hands ran down my shoulders and over my breasts. He kissed his way down my neck, starting just behind my ears and trailing his lips down. He got to my neck and stopped to suck at the skin. I shivered, even with the warmth of his body and the water. It was enough to drive me crazy.

My mind focused on his body and his growing hardness at my back. I ached to feel him deep inside me, the need so fierce and so consuming.

Our lives together had always been like this. We always

wanted more out of one another, pushing and pulling until we got it. Stealing moments where we could.

The shower was a new place.

My nails scraped at the glass before he took a step back and I felt his fingers fill me. They moved in and out without any effort at all. I moaned and wished that it was a thicker part of him but he didn't stop. In and out, in and out they went, while his other hand cupped my breast and squeezed.

'I want you to beg for me,' Karrept whispered in my ear and my eyes fluttered shut.

'A queen does not beg.'

I felt his smirk against my skin before his fingers left me. I was about to complain, but he replaced his fingers with his girthy member and I cried out. He felt so good, so strong. Like he was always meant to be there. I wished I was in my own body again, the one that was a mirror image of mine, because to feel him again in that body …

'My love,' I moaned. 'Just there.'

His hips moved harder, faster, deeper, and he hit the right place and all I could think about was him. I pushed my hips back and the glass rumbled with the weight of our bodies. The all-too-familiar rise of up the mountain my breath quickened and I gripped his hips as my breasts jiggled.

His moans filled my ears just as I exploded, crying out. Tears slid down my cheeks, mixing with the water, and I knew that this was all I needed to feel whole.

The death of our son was enough to bond us together for eternity, always and forever.

'Always and forever,' Karrept whispered and held me close as he pulled me under the water. It washed away the pain, but his embrace helped more than any word or action. We were linked, ready to take on what was about to come to pass.

CHAPTER THIRTY-SIX

Lucy
Epep 2014

I GROANED as I came to. As I opened my eyes, I realised two things: one, it was fucking bright, and two, this wasn't my room.

'Hunter?' I called out of habit.

'Here,' he said. I turned to face him. He was shirtless and bleary-eyed, sitting in the armchair. I must have woken him up because he looked rough around the edges.

'Why am I on the couch and not in my room?'

He pushed himself out of the chair and moved over to the couch. He crouched down next to me and I tried to look at him, but my skull felt like it was splitting in two.

'Well … after you blacked out, you sort of came to and started to act weird. Like your body wasn't sure what was going on and, well … you started throwing anything that was near you. We moved you down here to watch over you.'

'But why?'

He didn't say anything and leaned over the couch to gently rub my temples, the pressure just enough without being too overbearing. I sighed in relief as it helped with the throbbing in my head.

'I don't know. We think that it might have had something to do with killing Tyler. Your body didn't have the greatest reaction. Maybe there was a spell on Tyler and it backfired. Only you'll be able to tell us what happened to you, when you retreated into your mind.'

I had nothing to say and leaned into his touch. It soothed in ways I couldn't explain, but there was a part of me that felt sick to my stomach. 'I did. I killed someone. I killed Tyler, but he wasn't Tyler. Not in the end.'

'What do you mean?'

'When ... I had the name "Khaldun" come into my consciousness after I ... stabbed him. Didn't Kali say something about him?'

'I don't know,' Hunter said. He stopped massaging my temples and lifted my torso up. He carefully sat where my head had been and guided my head into his lap. It gave him better access to play with my hair.

Part of my brain was all muddled. It was trying to process what was happening and why I was here. Who was Khaldun? Why was this happening?

'Wait ...' I pushed myself into a sitting position, mourning the loss of Hunter's fingers at my temple, but something clicked. 'How long was I out for?'

He stared out into the backyard, avoiding my question.

'Hunter,' I said, and this time he looked at me.

'Four days.'

'*What?*' He had to be joking.

'I wish I was,' he said and his finger guided my chin up. 'You had us all scared.'

I wanted to run, but I wanted to know more. This was going to be awkward.

'How ... what happened?'

'I had to get some help. We didn't know what was going on, even Kali wasn't sure, so we did the next best thing we ...'

I gasped and pulled back from him. 'You didn't. You asked the Elders for help, didn't you?'

He looked guilty, but before he could answer, Kali walked into the room. 'We had to. You weren't waking up on your own, and it seemed like there was a deeper connection with Tyler than we all knew and it's triggered some sort of reaction. When you were lucid, even if it was for a moment, you weren't making any sense. There was something about a Khal something ...'

'Khaldun,' I finished.

'Yeah! Wait. Nefertiti's son. How does that even work?'

It didn't make sense, because Tyler was someone who had always been around, always a shoulder to lean on, and the last time I'd seen him was when Devin and Destiny were here.

'Tyler was never ... Tyler,' I said and picked at the cushion I'd moved into my lap.

'Tyler was Khaldun,' Kali said quietly and I looked over to her. 'That is why he was there in the times when he shouldn't have been. Realistically, he shouldn't have been around at all, but they must have done something with his soul to bring him back. Or maybe he was here the whole time and they brought him back to the surface.'

'He wasn't who he was supposed to be and is probably part of why Dev and Dest aren't here. That bastard.' I knew I should have felt guilty, but I couldn't feel anything for someone who could have been an instrument in my siblings' disappearance.

Hunter slipped his fingers in between mine and helped me sit up. He didn't let go and I stared at the back of his hand. It was smooth and his grip was warm.

He chuckled and squeezed my hand. 'We're going to need to find a way to keep you from hurting yourself all the time. You had us all worried. So we put in a barrier for the memories and they will be released slowly, but we don't know if something could set you off.'

I nodded at him and intertwined my fingers with his.

'I saw Devin. In a dream, or, well, whatever that was.'

Did I want to tell them how he warned me about Nefertiti?

'What? How?'

'Can I get some water?' My mouth felt so dry and I didn't trust my legs to support me right now. Hunter got up without a second thought and got me a glass of water. He handed it to me and I took a sip. I had a thought about Travis, but I could feel that he was upstairs, giving me space.

'So?' Hunter asked.

'He came to me and told me that Nefertiti would hurt me in some way, but she already has Lili, so I don't know how else she could hurt me.'

I mean, there were many ways she could make it so that Lili no longer existed, and that would be the worst thing I could ever imagine because I didn't know what I would do without her. I didn't want to even think about what that would look like. Lili was more down to earth and caring than anyone I knew. She was a quiet achiever and was always way too hard on herself. Harder than I was on myself, and that was saying a lot.

'Luce, you killed Nefertiti's son. He might have had answers about your brother and sister,' Travis said now that he was finally downstairs. He must have overheard us.

'Trav!' Kali said. Her tone said that she was afraid of what those words could do to me. But I was too busy thinking about Devin. He was wherever he was and not in a good way. Whatever Nefertiti, Karrept and Ty—Khaldun had done to him had cost him two years of his life.

He was alive. That was all that mattered to me. I had seen him. Even if he looked different and sounded ... harder, he was alive. Finding where he was suddenly was what I itched to do most, but Hunter had done something I hadn't wanted him to do.

'Hunt, what did you ask the Elders to do?'

He pressed his lips together and sighed. 'You weren't really responsive, and when you were, you were talking in gibberish, so ... we ... I asked to put some barriers up so we could get you back. Karrept and Nefertiti know. We know where they are, but they won't stay there for long, so we need to use the element of surprise while we still have it.' He paused and rested his hand on my thigh. 'We made the decision to ask for help. To give you the time to feel the grief but not be debilitated by it.'

'Can you undo it?'

Hunter shook his head. 'It's beyond of my abilities, and Kali's, but they did promise that they would release it slowly when they felt you were ready.'

'But how will they know when I'm ready? It's not like they took much interest in helping before. Like where were they when I needed help with Devin and Destiny?'

The Elders were a council of witches who I tried my best to forget about. They had more power as a collective than anyone knew, but they were the governing body to make sure that witches stayed inside the lines. Or the lines they set.

'That's not really how they work, but they made a special case for you. Let me guess, you only started exploring magick when Hunter came around?' Kali asked.

I didn't want to give her that info, but she could tell from my face.

'It's okay, but our ... your dad should have told you about magick or the Elders. Or something of the like.'

I had known about magick because that was unavoidable, but beyond that, there wasn't a lot of the natural witch upbringing because of the way the world was. Dad couldn't spin us being sent to our deaths when he had an empire to build.

'Luce, we didn't have a choice, it was either lose you to your brain or put in the blocks so that you can get Lili back and we can stop Karrept and Nefertiti.'

When he put it like that, he was right to do it. I didn't like the Elders because of all of the rules they policed, but that could have also been because I was the youngest daughter of a powerful man and woman.

You make it so hard to love you sometimes, Luce, but you are worth it, Hunter said in my brain, and I jumped. It was ... it had been too long since I had heard his words so clear. And maybe it was because I was starting to accept that he wasn't going anywhere and that I couldn't push him away.

I held his gaze. *You can make a woman's heart flutter like that*, I replied, and he just grinned. I guessed that was the exact reaction he'd wanted.

'I'm glad that you're awake, Luce.' Travis' voice pulled my attention and I looked away from Hunter. Travis' green eyes clouded with jealousy for half a moment before they were wiped clean of emotion.

'Even with the silence that's no longer around?'

He chuckled. 'Humour will not make it easier. We could have lost you and I personally don't want that to happen. You definitely aren't allowed to do that again, yeah?' He paused and looked at Kali. 'Not sure we could handle it again.'

'I promise I won't go and kill someone again,' I murmured.

Sarcasm as a coping mechanism was a go. I groggily tried to think about what was next. Hunter squeezed my thigh to bring me back to my body. I was tired, but he had a point; I couldn't idle for too long. Karrept and Nefertiti would move and we would lose our edge. Devin cautioned me against going, but I needed to. I couldn't wait for them any longer.

'We're going to go tonight,' I said and pressed my lips together as Hunter, Travis and Kali all looked at me with wide eyes.

'Tonight? But, Luce, you're just coming out of it,' Travis said.

'You know I'm not one to agree with Travis, but he's right here,' Hunter said.

'I'm all for it,' Kali said. 'Why wait?'

'I need to find Devin and Destiny and I'm not waiting anymore. We need to bring the fight to them.' I squeezed Hunter's hand, and he moved it from my thigh. 'I'm okay. Let's get everything we need together. Where is my phone? Or a phone?'

Travis used his preternatural speed and left the room. When he re-entered, he handed me my phone. I called the hotel's number, one I knew off by heart, and waited for it to connect.

'Good afternoon, thank you for calling Ryder Hotel Cairo. This is Mustafa, how can I help you?'

I took a deep breath to prepare for the story I was about to tell.

RYDER HOTEL LOOKED the same at every location. The glass windows, double-glazed to keep both sound and heat out, were standard; each room had sheer curtains and block-out blinds, to ensure that everyone had a comfortable stay. There was a scent that was a mixture of citrus and florals, which always reminded me of a beautiful spring day, and every location had it, from the US to Greece to home in Australia. From the second you stepped into the hotel, you knew you would be living in luxury and pampered like a queen. The only difference that set each location apart?

The lobbies.

Each was unique to the country or the state. The stained-glass atrium lobby here in Cairo was covered in hieroglyphics, which had been individually blessed by a priest who was a descendant of the ancients and were written by scribes whose job it was to make sure that nothing was damaged. It was heritage-listed, and Dad had purposely done so to keep the culture alive. The hieroglyphics were one of a kind and trying to replicate them would be near impossible.

As we walked up to the concierge desk, I smiled at Mustafa, the ever-kind man on the other end of the phone. He grinned back, like the cat that got the cream. Next to him was a woman, she was the manager. Her dark curly hair stood out against her dark skin – it was the colour of a coffee with a dash of milk, she had intense green eyes so close to those of a cats, and she had ruby colour lips. Antonia was twenty-eight and had been managing Cairo for as long as I could remember.

'Miss Ryder, it's a pleasure to see you and have you here. I have the penthouse suite ready for you.'

The lie was in booking a room, because no matter who I was they wouldn't give me information on a guest. And Karrept and Nefertiti were here. It wouldn't be too hard to find then when we started the search.

'Amazing work, Mustafa.'

'Miss Ryder, it's so good to see you again,' Antonia said. 'Oh, and is that Mr Wyatt?'

Hunter smiled and waved. 'It's me, hello Antonia. I hope you've been well.'

Antonia smiled, her face filling with colour that tried to rival her lipstick. She leaned over and Hunter leaned into me, my fingers brushed against his arm and resisted the urge to wrap my hands around his arm and pull him away. Hunter had a charm that drew so many in, men and women. I drummed the fingers of my free hand against the hilt of the sword that was wrapped up and sitting just off my hip. It was a distraction tool; I needed to stop thinking about the jittery butterflies dancing in my stomach.

They handed us a key, and we were on our way to our room. Kali muttered a spell under her breath so they would forget that I was here with other people besides Hunter. A small feat to make sure that whatever happened here couldn't be traced back to anyone else but me. Kali also added a small thought of "go hide" into their minds to keep them safe from what was to come.

The lobby was unusually quiet for the time of day, but it was closer to sunset, so there would be a lull in hotel goers coming back from their activities for the day and going out to dinner. The perfect time to check out the hotel and find the best outcome for the confrontation to come.

'Weapons as such will not hurt me.'

I heard his voice; the heavy lilt of an accent that was centuries old was still there and this time the voice was in English. It sounded out of place, like he was just learning how to say the words. Maybe Lili had taught him some. Hunter tensed up beside me as he came face to face with his doppelgänger. Or ancestor. Whatever he wanted to be called.

Where did he come from? We were supposed to have the element of surprise, but I guessed the hotel had been buzzing with the news of my arrival. Or maybe there was more to his abilities than we knew. Maybe he has the gift of foresight, that would mean we were fucked.

I pulled the sword from its hiding place on my hip and used both hands to hold the hilt tight. Maybe too tight.

'In some shape and form, they wi—'

Karrept knocked my legs out from under me and the sword went flying out of my hands. I didn't see where it went as I hit the ground hard and the wind was ripped from my lungs.

'I told you, they will not hurt me.' Karrept sneered and I heard an inhuman roar.

Tufts of fur flew over me, skimming my body. I couldn't see but I heard Travis collide with Karrept. I didn't tense up or fight because I knew Travis would be more attracted to that fear rather than Karrept. I looked up to the ceiling and watched through the mosaic stained glass as cracks of lightning illuminated the sky and lit up the lobby.

The weather change was instant. When we had walked in, it was hot, dry and not a cloud in sight. Now it was dark, almost like the thunderstorm was made by Karrept.

Could he do that?

I tried to move but I couldn't. My legs just ... didn't want to work.

'Lucy. You need to get up!' Kali screamed over the howling wind.

I touched my legs and I couldn't feel my touch—it was like they were there but they were missing. Panic swelled in my chest and my breath quickened. My heart raced and all I could hear was the static pounding in my ears. Was this a result of splitting the necklaces?

'Just breathe, Luce,' I said to myself. The reminder was enough for me to take a deep breath in, then let it out again.

Travis howled and it filled the whole room, the sound vibrating through my whole body. I heard a cracking sound through the haze and looked up in time to see the stained glass collapse. My arms shielded my face from the shards, but I felt the cuts as the pieces dragged down my arms. The pain was minimal in comparison to trying to get the panic to ease up. It gripped my heart and no matter how much I tried to tell myself to calm down, that my legs were still there. I couldn't unfeel the void of them not being there ...

'Lucy!' Hunter screamed.

He skidded next to me on his knees and took my face in his hands, any other time this would have been enough to snap me out any funk I was in. 'They're gone,' I murmured and tried to squash the panic.

'What's gone?' In the corner of my eye, I saw him throw up a hand to push zombie-like flunkie back before it resumed its resting place against my cheek.

'My legs. They're gone, they were here and now they're not.'

'Luce, my light, they're right there. Can you feel this?' He took away his hands from my face and pinched me.

I felt nothing. I shook my head.

'It's a hex. I can feel it. Do you trust me?'

How could I not? I nodded at him, and he smiled before he leaned over and pressed his lips to mine. He kissed me like it was the last thing he would ever do. I gripped his shirt and pulled him closer. The warmth of his hand seeped through my skin, and the heat of his lips made me melt into the embrace. It was like coming home after a long journey and life had been so barren without his rain. He broke the kiss and I tried to catch my breath as he rubbed his nose against mine. Then I felt it—a sharp pinch and then the pain.

'*Ouch*,' I cried out. 'Hunter!'

'Good, it worked. Now, get your arse up. We need you.'

With no time to dwell on the kiss or what he had done, I got to my feet and saw the chaos around me. Winged creatures dived from above, and mummies wrapped in bandages fought from the ground. Travis was holding a cat-like creature in his snout while it mewed and tried to kill him. Hunter guided me aside but he didn't need to. Karrept's magick had intended to keep me out of the battle to make the fight fair. Or that was what he thought.

He was scared.

Good. I was glad that he was scared.

He had taken my brother, sister and best friend from me. He was going to pay for every bit of pain I felt.

I shifted my weight and turned to the right as a gurgling sound pulled me out of my trance. A mummy rushed at me, it tried to punch me. I ducked to the left and it missed me by millimetres. I felt the rush of air against my face as it came at me. They were faster than I'd realised, but I dropped to my knees and swept out its legs from underneath it. The mummy like creature screamed and dropped back with a thump. Its legs had split off by the motion and landed in the other direction to its body. With a human that would have maybe winded them. It proved that creatures, especially old ones, didn't really stand the test against time.

I picked up a shard of stained glass, careful to not grip at it too hard and risk cutting myself. Dad's booming voice was in the back of my head as I held a piece of the irreplaceable mosaic glass and stabbed it in the mummy's face before it could grab at me. It puddled into bandages and dust.

Kali grunted and I saw she was in constant movement, ducking as best as she could and getting hit by a ... being. It looked like a god. It had the same build as Anubis and Sobek but they moved too fast for me to see who they were. I scanned the room and saw Karrept make a move towards Kali. He was faster than her. He would kill her.

'Karrept,' I screamed in an attempt to derail him. I made a beeline to him but an arm wrapped around my waist and pulled me back. I fought against the hold, but they were stronger than me.

'Lucy, you must not.' The voice was familiar; it was soft, kind, caring and out of place on the battlefield. Another crack of lightning lit up the sky, and I glimpsed the damage so far. Travis was bleeding, and Kali was trying desperately to keep herself on her feet. And Hunter. Hunter pushed monsters out of the way and made a direct line to Karrept with a look on his face that said it all: he was going to kill him.

One more rapid flash of lighting danced through the sky and I saw Sam, he was in better shape than everyone else, but he was too far away. Sam. He was the defence that they didn't know was coming. Being the Guardian of the tomb meant that his strength was far superior, but he had his own agenda: he wanted revenge for his father. Karrept had killed him. It was the only viable reason as Sam had come in power with Destiny and Devin's disappearance. After I called the hotel, I'd called on Sam for help. He left the tomb without protection to make sure he could witness Karrept's death.

'Let go of me.' I struggled in the embrace and tried to pull away. The voice tsked at me and I stopped struggling. I breathed in deep and steadied myself because Hunter was on a mission. 'Freeze,' I whispered and threw my hand up to set a barrier in place. Hunter came to a hard stop and hit the wall. He cursed at it and looked at me, then his eyes widened.

I couldn't lose him and killing Karrept could do that. Not only was Karrept faster than him and he could kill him in an instant, but he could also delve deeper into it and hurt him.

'Lucy!' He screamed. Hunter wasn't the kind of person to harm a single being, he made sure that spiders were released and not skilled, so it was out of character for him. He took a step back and threw his own power at my barrier. I hissed at the pain; it was like being punched in the stomach. Hunter glanced over his shoulder, with his hand up ready to do it again, but he stopped when he saw the pain I was in.

'I'm a Guardian, Lucy. We can stop this. Do you trust me?' the being who held me said.

I froze. Guardian. Nephthys hadn't lied. She was right. But I didn't think that I would find her mid-battle.

'Isis,' I whispered as it all clicked.

'Yes. Calm down. There are bigger battles to come. Pull back and see what is really happening.'

Why did no one just say what they actually meant?

I hated the riddles and the words that swam around the actual point. I stopped and looked, and I mean really looked, at the room. I saw my opportunity: Nefertiti was in the corner, her eyes lit up with excitement, waiting to see the outcome of the battle. It was like she was getting a kick out of watching some kind of sports game. I pulled myself out of Isis' grip, and she let me. I faced her.

Osiris was at her side, and Bastet's fingers brushed over my arm. Something slipped between us, and I felt a familiarity that I couldn't put into words. It was as if she'd been watching over me my entire life. And she had been. That was why I'd always loved cats.

'Do you understand?' Isis said, pulling my attention, unwillingly, from Bastet.

I nodded. 'Can you distract them all? I need to get to her.' I tilted my head towards Nefertiti.

She smiled at me. 'I can. Be careful.'

Without acknowledging her, I jumped over the corpses of mummies that hadn't disappeared into dust, narrowly missing being pecked at by a bird-thing.

'Save my hide, protect my side.' I threw my hand into the air to put up a protective spell to keep the bird-like thing at bay. And by doing so, I also removed the barrier that held Hunter in place. I ran at full speed towards Nefertiti. The sword Karrept had flung out of my hands was just off to the right, I dodged some glass and picked it up. I wanted to look over my shoulder to see if it was Isis' idea, if she had planted it there, but that would have been a distraction. As I ducked out of the way of another bird, I came to a stop in front of Nefertiti.

I extended my blade to her throat. My brain yelled at me, but I pushed through that because even though her face was Lili's, she was Nefertiti.

'You think that standing back and watching is the best thing you can do, hmm, Nefertiti?' I wondered if Lili could see me or hear me. I wanted to reach out to her. To make sure she was okay.

'It seemed to be. I would lower your sword, Lucy,' she said calmly. I watched her swallow hard, her fingers smoothing invisible creases on her skirt.

The Bond ... the faded fragments of what it used to be were there. It was the tether that kept us all together and being so close to Lili, I could feel her right there and I knew that she could feel the difference.

'I don't think so.' I slipped behind her and held the sword to her throat. 'Whistle for me,' I whispered into her ear.

Nefertiti did as I asked; Lili could wolf whistle, so there was no way no one would not hear her.

Everyone stopped, and Karrept's eyes widened, Hunter was just behind him to the left and he stopped what he was doing, dagger in hand and all. Karrept took a step closer, and I dug the sword harder into Nefertiti's throat. She whimpered and he took it as a sign to stop moving.

'I wouldn't try anything if I were you, Karrept, not if you want her alive,' I said and pushed her forward. Nefertiti was the weakest link, and as a rush of lightning lit up the sky, I could see ancient gods and goddesses lining the room. We had three on our side. Not nearly enough, but with Nefertiti in my arms, I guessed that they were ready to rethink that position. Travis padded over to me and was by my calf, just to Nefertiti's right. It was also the hand that held the sword against Lili's neck. Almost like he was waiting for me to drop it.

'She has your friend inside her. You aren't going to kill her,' he said, but his voice wavered. He didn't seem to believe that I had the same morals anymore.

'Won't I? You took people from me and Lili can be collateral damage if I needed. Back down, Karrept, and you won't have to find out,' I said.

Karrept blinked and nodded his head at a god.

Set screamed and came at me. Isis was there in a heartbeat and ripped his head clean from his shoulders. 'Revenge is a bitch,' she murmured, and the battle started all over again.

Gods and goddesses clashed, but Karrept kept his attention trained on me. 'Travis. Go,' I commanded and the wolf, who was bleeding and breathing heavily, did as he was told and rushed at Karrept. His jaws connected with his leg, and Karrept screamed and batted Travis away like he was a toy. Travis whimpered and Karrept growled at Hunter, who got in his way, he had his hand up and was ready to fight.

'You never learn,' he said to him and pushed him away like he was a rag doll. His body slammed into the reception desk with a hard thud.

'Hunter!' I screamed and held on to Nefertiti tighter. I wanted to go to him and make sure that he was okay.

In the blink of an eye, Isis was there, and she had Karrept's heart in her hand. It kept beating because he was undead.

'Noooo!' I screamed. Nefertiti fell from my arms and tried to crawl towards him. She didn't care about the broken glass or bodily fluids on the floor. 'Isis, we need him. You … we need him.' He had knowledge I needed, like the whereabouts of Destiny and Devin, and I wanted to be the one who got rid of him.

'I thought that it would help you,' she said.

'It does, it would, but—look, everyone is dropping. What's going to happen to you? We need to figure out where he put Destiny and Devin. I need them back.'

Her face didn't flicker. There was no emotion in her expression. 'He knows where they are?'

I nodded. 'Yes. I think so. I hope so. We need their location. Please help him.'

She clicked her tongue and shoved his heart back into his chest. I watched the arteries knit back together and the skin close up as Isis pulled her hand out. 'I will nurse him back to health. This will take some time to heal from. I will contact you when it is done.'

With that, she, Osiris and Bastet disappeared. The remaining gods and goddesses were in various stages of goo and decay. But there were some that were alive. I couldn't distinguish who they were in their different forms – they must have split from their original form when Karrept's heart was pulled from his chest.

The smell of death hit my nose and I swallowed hard, forcing myself to breathe through my mouth.

'Karrept,' Nefertiti whimpered, and we all stared at her before she fainted, her body falling into mine and the sword dropping to the ground with a clang.

'I think they're linked,' Kali said, wiping blood from her own cheek.

'It looks like they are,' I commented as I slid down to the ground, Nefertiti in my arms, her weight too much to hold onto on my own.

It was time to go home.

TRAVIS and I sat on the stairs, trying to block out Nefertiti whimpering and crying from the living room. She had begged us to let her go, and it was hard to listen to her beg and whine in Lili's voice. Trav's knuckles were white as he held on to the banister. His body was still healing from the fight.

'She's hurting.'

'We're all hurting,' I reasoned. 'She's trying to bait us into letting her go.'

'It's working,' he said. 'It's Lili.'

I shook my head. 'It's Nefertiti. She's smart and cunning.'

Kali came down the stairs, her steps quiet but sure. She sat a stair up from Travis and me, and leaned forward. 'Someone needs to go in there and shut her up. Or I'm seriously thinking of doing it myself.'

'Kali,' I hissed.

'What? I'm just saying what everyone else is thinking.'

We were all silent for a moment as we listened to her sobs. Hunter was in the room with her, thinking that seeing him would ease her pain a little.

It just made it worse.

He sighed and gave up. He left the room and leaned against

the wall. He stared at me and shrugged, before his shoulders sagged.

'You need to do something. She's not going to tell me anything. I seem to make her keep crying. I've never had that response before.' Hunter didn't do well with tears, especially when it was someone he knew in pain. When he couldn't do anything to fix her, it made him antsy. He rubbed his jaw.

'She can't keep crying the whole time,' I said, exasperated.

'She sure can try,' Hunter said.

I sighed and pushed myself to my feet. I guessed it was time to make this work and push her buttons, on my terms.

'Nefertiti,' I said.

She sniffed. 'Lucy.'

I rolled my eyes and grabbed the box of tissues from the coffee table and held them out to her. She took a few and struggled to blow her nose. I watched her like she was prey as she made extremely slow movements.

'Are you done?' I asked, referring to the crying.

'You killed my lover,' she spat out.

'Actually, that was Isis, not me. You can't blame me for something that she did.'

'You killed my son!' she cried out.

That rattled me. I stared at her and tried to form the words. I opened my mouth before I shut it again. My brain tried to process the images those words brought to me.

'You sent him to us. It's your own fault,' I hissed, but it was a weak response. She'd hit a nerve.

'He was innocent.'

'No one is innocent. Not even you. Or you wouldn't be hiding in Lili's body. I have some questions,' I said and I squared my shoulders.

'You won't get anything from me.'

I'd hoped she wouldn't say that. Dammit. I came down to her level and looked her in the eye. The golden eyes that had replaced the blue I loved. 'Listen,' I said quietly. 'I'm going to treat you with respect until you give me reason otherwise and I will make sure that Travis bites you.'

'You would not dare!' she said.

'I would. Don't test my patience.'

I wouldn't let Travis actually bite her, because his poisonous bite would kill Lili, but Nefertiti didn't know that I was bluffing.

Lili would know, though. I saw a flash in her eyes, like Lili's blues were right there, but it was gone in an instant.

'Now, tell me what you and Karrept get out of being back?' I continued.

'You were never supposed to be born. If your father had stayed with Kali's mother, you would never have been born.'

'Kali is younger than me, how does that work?' I was puzzled and curious as to what that would mean to her.

'You and your brother were never meant to survive the pregnancy. You were supposed to die within your mother's womb to stop this war, but your father came back; he nurtured the love between your mother and him and saved you both. You are not allowed to live. Not supposed to be living. But you are. So the Illuminate Year was to take you back. To have you. To help magick return.'

She wasn't making any sense, and I took this moment to study her. Lili's good-hearted nature was gone. There wasn't even a hint of the woman who was my best friend. It was surreal, but there was something more. Something dangerous, and I was happy that she was tied up for the moment. I didn't know what she could do. Especially if she was free.

'I don't think I like that answer. I am of your line. Why do you want to kill me?'

'We need you to feed Karrept' was all she said.

'Feed Karrept? Why? Is he dying?' I asked, my mind racing with the possibilities.

Would killing me make him whole? Would he be able to live

off my essence? Why did they wait this long? Why did they need my brother and sister?

'Nefertiti. Answer me.'

She turned her head away from me, and that's when I knew that she was done with conversation. I growled and stormed out.

Point one to Nefertiti.

CHAPTER THIRTY-SEVEN

Nefertiti
Epep 2014

MY HEART ACHED.

I didn't know that it could hurt any more. Losing Khaldun and then watching Isis rip Karrept's heart from his body brought a new level of despair. My stomach rolled and knotted in pain. It felt like there were knives stabbing in my abdomen, and I was surprised that there was no blood. I was tied to a chair against my will and I wanted to leave. But even if I could, I wouldn't return to our room. Karrept wasn't … he was … I didn't know what. He was gone. Isis had taken him. Maybe it was some sort of joke, but the bitch goddess had taken his life before she brought him back, and she wasn't going to bring him back the same. There was a hole deep in my chest and I felt raw, like someone had just ripped out my own heart and stomped all over it.

'Hi. I've got some food for you.' A voice pulled me from my thoughts, and I laid my eyes on Aten's reincarnation.

I could see the wolf in his movements; his broad shoulders

moved with grace and an air of royalty. He was built to lead and if he did already lead a pack, he would do it in the future. He moved the same way Aten did, and it was unnerving to see it again. After all this time, part of my brain rejected that he was there or that we were in the same room.

I never wanted to marry my brother, but I didn't have a choice so I made it work. We made it work. Travis was … not a sibling. He was a friend.

He is our best friend. He won't hurt us. I promise.

Lili's voice in my head was confident but I wasn't. I didn't trust him. No matter what incarnation he was in, he was still Aten.

Still irresistibly Aten—green eyes, piercing gaze, high cheek-bones … kissable lips. Dammit.

'I'm not hungry,' I said softly.

Which was a lie. I was starving. My stomach rumbled as I caught a whiff of the toast. Scrambled eggs too. Oh goddess.

'Are you afraid?' Travis asked.

I stared at him and tilted my head to the side. His spirit was broken. There was a strong wolf under there, I could feel it, but the human part of him was broken. Like there was a piece of him missing.

'No. But it's unnerving how much you look like my ex-husband. He was a wolf too.'

'Are you trying to have a conversation with me now?' He held a forkful of eggs to my lips, cupping his hand underneath it. I opened my mouth and took the eggs. I couldn't help the moan of delight that slipped from my lips.

He is a good cook, always has been. The woman he ends up with is going to be way lucky, because he's good-looking and he's kind and can cook. That's rare.

I didn't understand what Lili meant. Everyone was destined to be with their opposite. The one that had the exact qualities but was also different. So very different. It was why I was picked to marry Aten. We did good together.

'I figured that by having a conversation with you, it might be easier than trying to force-feed food down your throat. You're in Lili's body and that makes me want to be gentle, so you have the upper hand because I know that if I tried to force-feed you, she would have something to say.'

He's right, Lili said.

'What do you get out of it?' I asked him, trying to ignore Lili in the background. Her voice was starting to sound just like mine and that was worrying.

'Nothing, but I do get to spend time with my best friend. I mean, I know that you're wearing her, but she's still in there and I know what she likes. I know who she is and I know how to talk to her. You're the one who is the anomaly here and we can't change that. But you're here.'

He cut a small piece of bacon and stabbed more of the egg before bringing it to my mouth. I opened up and he gently fed it to me. I chewed the food and delighted in the texture. There had been nothing quite so delectable. Food was prepared so differently now and that did so much for the taste and the texture. In that moment he also took a bite, almost like he was scared I would think that he was trying to poison me.

If I wasn't in Lili's body, I would have worried about it, but I was safe.

'You could let me go. I can do this myself,' I reasoned, but I was looking for a way out. I didn't know where I had left to go, but that didn't stop me from wanting to leave.

'I wish I could. But until Kali works on the boundary spell around the house to include you in it, you're stuck tied up. I'm sorry.' He paused. 'We can't take any chances now that we have you.'

His face told me that he was sorry. Maybe it was because he

was staring at his best friend. Or maybe because Lili was sitting back there, loud. Louder than before. Why?

The Bond, she said.

'What do you mean?' I said out loud before I realised I had. I didn't know if I could answer Lili without speaking. I saw an image of her; she had a hand on a jutted-out hip, the other holding the bent elbow. She was annoyed.

'The magick. It has to go back up,' Travis answered and it distracted me.

The Bond is what keeps us together, you know it, and you know exactly what has happened with it. Lucy and Travis broke it because of their indiscretion, and it was why Lucy was able to get you here. Why you're tied to a chair. They can do whatever they want to you because you're in my *body. If you were in your own, they couldn't. Your knowledge is actually pretty handy.*

She was not supposed to know that. None of that was meant to see the light of day, but she knew it. And she would tell if she got the chance.

I will, yes. So either you say something or I try and make you say something.

A deck of cards caught my eye and I looked past Travis to see them better. They were tarot cards.

Lili saw them and her whole demeanour changed.

'They're Lili's,' Travis said when he followed my gaze.

'I know. She knows,' I said and then instantly regretted it.

'What do you mean she knows? Is she actively there?' He seemed panicked but his eyes flashed purple.

Just like Aten's did when he was angry.

'I ... I ...'

'Nefertiti.' His voice gave me chills; it sounded just like Aten's when he was angry.

I shook my head and pressed my lips together. I was done talking.

CHAPTER THIRTY-EIGHT

Lucy
Epep 2014

I TRUSTED Travis not to do anything drastic with Nefertiti because she was in Lili's body. He loved her just as much as I did, if not more. There was something between the two of them that had always been there. Maybe it was a deeper understanding of each other, or maybe the sexual tension between Travis and me had made me miss it. They had been friends longer than Travis and me … by a few days.

Hunter watched me, his whiskey-coloured eyes not straying from me as I paced. The kiss on the battlefield had changed so much; I knew that he loved me now, and had never stopped. Sleeping with Travis broke the friendship wall, and I knew that I needed to get through that. Because Hunter was the one I'd always wanted to be with. Even from that first moment we met, that first day Devin brought him over to hang out, I knew that I wanted to be with him. I needed to be with him.

'You know, you're so cute when you pace up and down like you are,' Hunter said and I stopped to look at him.

'What? Why?' I said with a smile and he grinned back at me. That grin made me want to kiss him stupid. Like I needed an excuse.

'Your thoughts are all over the place,' he said quietly.

I sighed. 'I don't know how to feel. It's all a mess. That kiss ... Hunt, I keep thinking about it and then I think about Destiny and Devin and all of the shit that has happened to get us here. Why me? Why didn't Karrept and Nefertiti find a different way to bring themselves back? Technology is changing and evolving, surely stealing my body isn't their only option. I don't want to end up being some sort of offering and he's going to chop me into little pieces and eat me like Hannibal Lecter. No one is eating me. Would he eat me? Do mummies eat brains? Wait, that's zombies.'

'I have. You're quite tasty,' Hunter said, my brain completely halting.

Did he just ...

Hunter got off the bed and pulled me into his arms, his whole face alight with mischief. He was waiting for me to challenge him.

'That's how easy it was to change your thoughts and your rambling so that all you can think about is me. I've been doing this wrong the whole time.' He laughed and I looked up at him. His gaze was filled with heat, almost like he wanted to devour me.

I leaned up and kissed him. He sighed against my lips, and my whole body sighed with him. We were terribly good at being bad to each other, but we were also so good together.

I broke the kiss quickly because I heard someone.

'Hey, what was that for?'

'There's a werewolf about to open the door,' I said. Hunter took a step back but it wasn't quick enough.

'Sorry,' Travis mumbled as he tried to close the door but I caught it.

'Trav, no. It's okay.'

'Your cheeks are flushed. I interrupted something.'

I wanted to argue but he was right. He had, but right now it didn't matter.

'What's wrong?' I asked.

'Nefertiti and Lili ... I think they've done something weird.'

At those words, I shivered, cold settling deep in my bones. If Nefertiti hurt her, so help me. I was going to lose it.

'What do you mean?'

Travis scratched the back of his neck and shrugged. 'Like, she was excited about the same food that Lili would be ... which I guess is good, but she saw Lili's tarot deck and she ... she acted like it was the most precious thing in the world to . Like, she had the same reaction that Lili would have.'

I'd left her cards out there on purpose, just to see what would happen. I wanted to test to see if there was any of Lili still in there and if there was, I wanted to see what it would take to bring her out.

'I guess that's not really all that bad. But did anything else happen?'

He shrugged. 'I asked her about it and she clammed up. She knows something but she's not telling us. I don't know what it has to do with Lili, but what happens if there is more to this than just the whole Lili and Nefertiti situation? What happens if they're, like, bonded or something? Would that make it harder to get Lili back?'

If Lili and Nefertiti had done some merging-together thing, it was a weird side effect that I hadn't seen coming. How were we going to separate the two if they had merged?

'Shit. I didn't ... this is a lot more complicated than we realised, Trav.'

He cracked his knuckles. 'I just want her back, Luce, and I'm tired of not having her here. She is so important and it feels like we're spiralling without her. We need her more than we realise.'

I looked down at my feet. I wriggled my toes, which were covered in a chocolate-brown polish. Lili's would have been pink, because she loved pink so much. 'We do. Okay, I'm going to talk to her. We need some serious answers. Because we need Lili back more than ever.'

Travis just nodded and turned on his heel.

'Where are you going?' I asked him.

'I don't need to see you and Hunter kissing again, or even acknowledge what's about to happen. I love you too much to be able to stomach that.'

I opened my mouth to say something but I didn't have the words. And I let him walk away. Hunter came up behind me and wrapped his arms around me.

It'll be okay, he whispered into my mind. I wanted to believe him, but it was far from the truth.

NEFERTITI LOOKED straight at me and I tilted my head. She was studying me. Maybe she was trying to figure out how to get me back—or she was just staring for the hell of it.

'Do I have something on my face?' I asked.

She shook her head. 'It's odd to see my face ... not on my face.' She clicked her tongue.

We were sitting at the table and there were plates of food to the side. Nefertiti had eaten most of the food that was put in front of her, but she was still hesitant. It took all of us eating to make her comfortable.

I had untied her and she had full use of her hands, but Kali had made a charm that dampened her abilities, no matter what they were. I didn't want to have some random power flying around without some protection. Hunter had helped Kali with a boundary spell to make sure that she was covered. It would work like an alarm system if she tried to leave, sirens and all. It made me breathe a little easier knowing that she couldn't just run out of the door.

'Well, it's strange to see my best friend in front of me and not be ... well, her. Do you think you can help me out here? I want her back and you want Karrept. But I need your help.'

She crossed her arms over her chest and clicked her tongue again. Maybe it was a tic.

I was taking that as a no.

'I don't know how you want me to fix this. I don't know what you want, nor do I care. Karrept is ... gone.'

'Actually, Isis said that she was going to fix that.'

Nefertiti snorted. It was weird coming from Lili. 'You think she's actually going to help you? She has her own agenda. She won't hold up her end of the bargain. She never has.'

I raised an eyebrow. 'What did she do to you? You sound so jaded.'

'I don't know what that means.'

I was about to get up and give her a piece of my mind, but Hunter covered my hand with his and it soothed me.

'Nefertiti.' Hunter said her name slowly, and her attention shifted from me to him. The way she looked at him made me uncomfortable. There was a level of want, of need, that I didn't like seeing in her eyes. And it was a weird expression on Lili's face and part of me was jealous. 'We just need to know what you know. I know that I don't particularly like to have you here, tied up like a prisoner.'

'I am,' she interjected.

'You're not. We're looking out for our friend and you happen to be in her body. That is where this really lies. We need answers. You want to be free. Help us help you.' His voice was even and quiet. Like he was trying to soothe her. And maybe he was.

Nefertiti sat a little straighter and leaned in. 'What do you want help with?'

'You know where Devin and Destiny are. I need their location,' I said before Hunter could ask.

Her gaze shifted from Hunter to me. It was like I had told her something sour and she didn't want a part in it. At all.

'I only know the location of one. I don't know where the other is. I don't know which one I know. I just have the location. That's all.'

'Where?' I asked without hesitation.

'I need a pen and some paper.'

Travis was there with what she needed. He held them out to her and she was careful not to touch him as she took them. Like she didn't want the memories that came with him. I almost didn't blame her.

She wrote down what looked like a hybrid of hieroglyphics and numbers. What the hell? As I opened my mouth to ask her, there was a knock at the glass door and I jumped, my attention ripped away from Nefertiti to see Isis and Bastet standing at the door.

'I'll get it,' I said and pushed myself out of the chair to let them in.

Isis tried to step in and a sharp sound filled the air. We covered our ears and Isis chuckled. 'This is a good spell. Do you think you can let us in?'

'Kali?'

She smiled. 'With pleasure.' I wondered why she was smiling but I didn't ask.

Bastet was silent as she walked across the threshold of the house, but her amber lion eyes shifted between Nefertiti and me, as if trying to figure out if I was in danger. Or she wasn't sure who she was to look out for. Bastet leaned closer to me. I touched her arm, completely by accident, but I felt a shiver of power run up my arm and settle in my chest. It took me by surprise and I gasped. She didn't look away but instead took my hand as I tried to pull it back. Bastet didn't say a word, but she didn't need to. I understood everything she wanted to say without her actively voicing it. She was here to look out for me. And she would die to make sure I was safe.

'Here. This is all I have.'

Isis didn't move and I pulled myself away from Bastet. She was like a magnet and all I wanted to do was stay close to her. I forced myself to take a step away from her and move back over to Nefertiti.

I took the paper from her. 'What is this?' The numbers were jumbled and sort of looked like coordinates, but there were also some weird roman numerals and letters thrown in there. Hieroglyphics too.

'It's the location.'

'Of what?' I asked.

Isis came up behind me and took the piece of paper from me. 'This is gibberish. Has something broken you, Nefertiti?'

'It's there. Can't you see it?' Nefertiti pointed to the paper in Isis' hands. I looked back at it and couldn't make anything of it.

'Isis, can I have the paper?' She gave it to me and I took a pen and sat at the island bench.

'How is Karrept?' Hunter asked Isis, and Nefertiti whimpered at his name. Isis turned away from me and I heard her speak to Hunter.

'He is okay, but he is fading fast. Whatever needs to be done, needs to be done soon or he will die. I am good at what I do, but I do not have the ability to bring back the dead.'

She wouldn't. She was the goddess of healing and magick. Osiris was the one who would be able to bring back the dead. But Karrept was already dead …

Nefertiti sobbed and covered her face. I wanted to take away the pain because she was in Lili's body but there was more to it, she was hurting emotionally. Her lover was fading and there wasn't much we could do. Or at least that we knew of, anyway.

I scribbled at the bottom of the piece of paper; there was

some room, but all I could see was a bunch of random numbers in different languages. There were also some hieroglyphics. I would have expected it to be all in hieroglyphics or at least in some sort of code that made sense, but this didn't.

I turned on the stool to look at Nefertiti. Her body had slumped forward; there was a heaviness to it that wasn't there ten minutes earlier. Isis' news had been too much for her to bear.

'Nefertiti.' She looked up from her hands and stared me in the face, her eyes red and teary. 'What does he need? I can stay here all day until you tell me, because it doesn't faze me, but he will die and you won't have him. Everything you have done will be for nothing.'

She didn't say a thing, but instead stared at me like she was staring a hole into my body.

'Nefertiti, I want to help you, but you need to meet us halfway.'

'You want him dead. He has taken so much from you, why would I believe anything you say?'

She wasn't wrong. I sighed and rubbed the back of my neck. I wanted him dead, but I also really wanted Lili back. I wanted to have my friend's blue eyes looking back at me. Instead of the light gold I was staring at.

'Do I want him dead? Very possibly so, but you're in the body of my best friend, and I'd dare say someone that I see as a sister. I can't stand the hurt on your face, and I know that you would rather be feared than pitied, but I want her back and I want to find a way to make it so you can coexist if I have to, but I can't do that without your help.'

I hoped that I could barter with her; maybe if I could get information about what Karrept needed, I could get an answer about the location.

'He needs more than what she can give him,' Nefertiti said.

'And what's that?'

She shook her head and I resisted the urge to throw my hands up in frustration.

'Nefertiti, I want to help you, but I can't do this if you aren't going to help me. I already have to decode what your numbers mean and that's half the battle when I don't know what the code is.'

'Can I touch Lili's cards?' Nefertiti asked abruptly.

I glanced over my shoulder at the cards on the coffee table. I pushed myself off the stool and walked over to the deck. I picked it up. There was a surprising amount of weight to the cards. Maybe it was the box or maybe it was the things that this deck had seen. Or the power it held.

'What do you know about them?' I said as I held them out for her.

'These are special to her. I can see it from here. There's an aura around them that I can see. There are numbers on them too.'

I handed the cards to her, and she took them and held them with care. Almost like she wasn't sure if they would crumble in her hands. She looked the box over, turning it in her hands, before she settled it on her knee and gently pulled the box apart. Inside, the cards, so ordinary with their coloured backs, waited to be held. Nefertiti took them out of the box and started to shuffle them. Her technique mirrored Lili's and I could have sworn Lili was in charge.

As she shuffled the tarot deck, a card slipped out.

Everyone in the room stopped and stared down at it.

Death.

There wasn't a grim reaper on this card like many traditional decks had; this one had a girl dancing, almost like she was liberated, and above her was a moth.

Next to the name was a roman numeral that looked familiar.

I walked over to the kitchen island and picked up the paper and right there was that exact roman numeral. The card was the thirteenth in a deck, which would mean that thirteen would be …

'Trav, I think you might be right about what you said. And that's so dangerous.'

Lili and Nefertiti were merging, and the number on the card matched the number on this piece of paper. Maybe the others would correlate.

'Isis. I think I'm going to need some time, but I have an inkling about how to crack this.'

'What are you cracking?'

Hunter looked at me with a smirk. *How are you going to explain that one to a very old goddess?*

'Um … it's like … trying to uncover what the code means.'

'But how does that crack it?' Isis asked.

I stared at her and bit my nail, like the very gesture would make the question go away, because trying to explain modern nuances to a goddess was just not something I had energy for. Not when all I could focus on was the puzzle Nefertiti had given me.

'I think Kali can explain that. Kali …?'

'What—no.'

I took the piece of paper and dashed out of the living room. I was going to go to the one place where I could think without any distractions: Dad's office.

I RAN my hands over the mahogany captain desk that was a safe haven for me, or it was now. There had been a time when it wasn't, and although magick had always been a part of my life it, I never understood how dangerous it was until I was coerced magickally and almost raped as result. It was enough to rattle me and I had to keep my head down to not let another flashback consume my vision. I focused on Dad. This was the place where he made a lot of deals when we vacationed here. He would leave

MANDI KONTOS

us watching a movie to go to his office and close his door. We could never hear those deals being struck but we knew, by the way he opened the door, how well it had gone.

The piece of paper had the start of coordinates. Nefertiti's scribble was unlike Lili's neat handwriting, which was unmistakable with its cursive edges, but so far I had made out 23.4113°N. Even when it looked like 23.4—roman numeral for thirteen and the hieroglyphic for north, which was a lot different than just a letter. I rubbed the palm of my hand against my forehead and leaned my head into it.

Why was this so difficult? I was so close to finding the location of one of my siblings. Devin would be the one who I found first. I had the closest bond to him because he was my twin, but after the dream all I wanted was to find him, to save him from the torture he seemed to be living in. The man in the dream was a far cry from my brother, who was lighter, brighter and a jokester.

I was pulled out of my thoughts by a shuffling of feet to find Nefertiti standing in front of me. Her hair was dishevelled and her eyes were puffy. I was sure if she could see herself in the mirror, she would be shocked.

'I can't tell you what I don't know. Or maybe that I can't tell you, but I will tell you that he needs your blood. It was why we were going to use your body. He has to break a curse and that curse is linked to my line. To our line. To the last of the Lebashky women.'

'What does that even mean? Why is my blood different from anyone else's, and why wasn't Destiny a candidate?'

Nefertiti tucked strands of hair behind her ear and turned away from me. 'She wasn't my descendant. Her body wasn't my reincarnation. Like you are.'

'But why is that important?' I wanted to know why we were here. Why my siblings were gone. Wait did she just say reincarnation? What I her reincarnation?

310

'Because I need your body. We need your body.'

'If I'm your reincarnation, why is it so important now? Why didn't you strike two years ago?'

'Because we had to wait for The Illuminate Year. It's the catalyst.' She pressed her lips together, almost to stop her from saying more. 'When I was with Aten ... he performed some magick on me. Blood magick. It was done long before our wedding and started from birth. He was 8 years older than me.'

I got up out of the leather chair and walked around the big desk to stand in front of her. Nefertiti's eyes never left mine, like she was worried I would strike back or something. I motioned for her to keep going.

'He infused my blood with the cure to his bite.'

My jaw dropped. I realised that all he wanted was a way to heal himself and that Nefertiti had been the answer, all those years ago. But she must not have known ... or she would have saved him then.

'You're telling me that you had the cure to his bite all those years ago and you didn't use it, and now you're here?'

She shook her head. 'No, I didn't know that until it was too late. I knew I was immune to his bite and his scratches, because he ... liked to use them during sex.'

I scrunched up my nose at the image of werewolf teeth and nails being involved. Ouch. No thank you.

'So he needs my blood to heal him. He could have asked.'

She looked down. 'No, he couldn't have. You look like me, Lucy; he wants me back inside you so that we can have our life back.'

'But it doesn't work like that. You aren't me and I'm not you. Just our bodies are similar, and even then, they're not a carbon copy. Why did he go after my siblings and take them from me?'

Nefertiti sighed. 'You would be weaker and easier to inhabit. He took what he needed from you to get you to where you are. We both didn't realise that the Bond we forged was the balance for the spell. It's what linked us all. Linked you with Lili and Travis. There's a curse that is attached to it all as well. You've seen that the Bond changed once you slept with Travis.'

'How do you—'

'Lili, she is here, she knows and can feel it too. You broke it and there isn't a way to fix it, but being madly in love with Karrept and married to Aten must have put a dent in the Bond and required that you never break the lines. Karrept needs your blood and the wolf to break the curse properly. He already had Lili's seeing abilities.'

I swallowed hard. Lili had never mentioned any seeing ability. I mean, beyond the tarot she was obsessed with ... 'What do you mean? Lili doesn't have that ability.'

'She does. It's untapped and she uses the tarot to work it, but there is more there. More that you won't ever be able to understand. I don't know if she ever will. But she was placed here to make sure that the Bond was never broken. But by Karrept taking her out of the equation and breaking your spirit, you did exactly what he wanted.'

'Is she hurt?' I asked. I didn't want to hear any more of this.

'Lili?'

I nodded.

'No, she's here. Sometimes she talks to me, and that is harder to hide.'

'Hide from who?'

'Karrept,' she said.

I raised an eyebrow. 'Why?'

'He doesn't want me to grow attached because he knows this isn't my final body, but I'm afraid that it might be. In some form. I don't know what is happening but she feels different now.'

The hair on the back of my neck stood on end and I wanted to rip her apart. She was taking Lili away from us and that was not going to happen. I couldn't live without her and I didn't want to try.

'Why are you telling me this?'

Before she could say another word, the door burst open and Isis was standing in the frame.

'Karrept wants to meet. In the markets, to trade Nefertiti for the Book.'

'When?' both Nefertiti and I asked. We looked at each other briefly before turning to Isis.

'In half an hour.'

It wasn't enough time to get more information. I needed to know what the Illuminate Year was and what this time and space meant to them, but part of me had an inkling that it was just because they wanted to find a time they could finally be together.

CHAPTER THIRTY-NINE

THEY WERE GOING WITHOUT ME. That was all I could think about. Bastet stayed with me and while she looked calm, I knew that it rattled her to be with me. Together we were sitting not far from the Cairo Marketplace on a bench that was hidden by the signage of the entrance. Bastet was quiet as I tried to think of things to say. Or so I'd thought.

'You know, you are much more palpable in that body, Nefertiti.'

That was such a perplexing thing to come out of her mouth. I stared at her. Her face was soft, hidden by the magick that made her look human, but her eyes—they were a deep chartreuse that wasn't quite green but wasn't yellow either. So much like the colour of a cat's eyes, which wasn't surprising, seeing as she was part cat.

'You seem to like Lucy,' I said back.

'She is a lot nicer than you are.'

I snorted. 'Is she now? She put us together because you are her Guardian and she wants you to watch over me.'

Bastet just shrugged. 'She does not seem to have the same thinking that you do and it is nice. It is softer and I like it. You were always ... so entitled.'

'I am a queen.'

'Were.'

'Still am.'

'No, you are just dead.'

'That's rude.'

'It is the truth.'

We both let the silence hang in the air as we looked at each other. It was weird that I was here and wasn't with Lucy. I ached to see Karrept but I knew that if I did, I wouldn't come back. There would be no way that I would, because I needed him more than I'd realised.

You know, that is a bit unhealthy when it comes to a relationship. And too co-dependent. Were you like that when you were alive? I didn't want to answer Lili's question because, deep down, I knew she was right and that was scary. How much of this wouldn't have happened if it was a healthier relationship, or what if we had been together from the beginning? That was too much.

'You know that this wouldn't have happened if I didn't marry Aten,' I said out loud. Bastet looked up at me and shielded her eyes from the sun.

'You were fated to marry Aten. It was predestined, but you were the one who broke that sacred vow because you could not keep your legs shut.'

I resented that.

'Give me all of your money and your jewellery.' I heard a foreign voice; it was raspy, sure, calculated.

'What?' I said as I turned around and came face to face with the barrel of a gun. Lili panicked and together our hands went up into the air. 'I don't have anything to give.'

'Lies.'

I felt Bastet stand behind me. She mirrored my motion, mostly just following my actions than actually believing him. She could break him half if she wanted to, but she was given orders to just keep an eye on me.

'Liar. You've got a necklace on. Take it off.'

My hand went to my neck, to the necklace I hadn't even realised was there. A thin dainty chain, no doubt a lighter gold because I would prefer gold, but at the end of it was an ankh. I knew that Lucy had the same one around her neck. A symbol of their friendship.

'Surely I can give you something else, anything but this,' I begged, and this time it wasn't me begging. It was Lili. I knew how much this necklace meant to her and she would fight tooth and nail to keep it.

'Just give it to him,' Bastet whispered in my ear. Logically, I knew that I should, but I didn't want to. I needed it. Lili needed it and for the first time, I wanted her to keep something that was hers.

A weird feeling.

'Now!' the guy said. He didn't take his attention off me as he cocked the gun. I swallowed hard, and with defeat, I carefully undid the necklace. It was like removing a sacred part of me. As soon as I did, I held it up in one hand, while the other one was still raised in the air. The thief snatched it before he started stepping backwards. It was like he knew where he was going by memory because he didn't take his eyes off mine and kept the gun trained on me.

When he was far enough away and out of sight, I collapsed and sobbed.

'Why did you fight so hard for that necklace?' Bastet asked as she held me in her arms.

I wondered what it was like to not worry about emotions and feelings; I had always thought that I felt like I didn't have a care. I wanted the necklace back because it wasn't mine and it was an item that was far more important to Lili. And because of that I fought for it. Lili was supposed to be expendable, and she would have been but there was a part of me that liked having her around. The descendant was always the goal but I missed my sister and Lili filled that void.

CHAPTER FORTY

Lucy
Epep 2014

THE CAIRO MARKETPLACE was where vendors came to sell to the tourists, but the history that was here—you could feel it in the walls, in between the cracks in the mortar that held the stone in place. If the walls could talk, they would tell of the many trades that went down between them and the secrets that were told here. The arched entrance just to the left of us was bustling with people looking for a bargain and trying to immerse themselves in the culture Egypt had to offer. To the right of me was a stall with Arabic lanterns in colours of teal, magenta and green, accented with bronze. As a kid, I had always been fascinated by the lanterns' colours and begged my parents to buy me one. I was never old enough to get one, though.

The market itself was packed, but none of those people mattered, none except the man who sat in front of me. Karrept's eyes were dull and tinged with pain, and although he tried to hide it from me, I knew that face better than I knew my own. I knew what Hunter's cues were like, so I could pick up Karrept's just as easily.

'Such a good market,' he said. Without the accent, his voice would have sounded just like Hunter's.

He stiffened next to me and I reached under the table to squeeze his leg. I was thankful, in that moment, that Nefertiti was in Lili's body and didn't look like me.

'It's busy today,' I commented. My cheek throbbed and together with the heat, I could feel a headache coming on. We were sitting in the heart of the market, on bench seats that were outside the only tavern. It was crowded with other patrons who were eating, chattering and drinking like there was nothing big happening right next to them.

Karrept put the Book on the table and slid it across. I wrapped my fingers around it and opened the cover to make sure that it was the real Book. It was.

'It is, yes. A perfect time for a trade. Where is she?'

'Safe.' He started to say something but I held up a hand. 'You'll get her when the trade is done.'

'What do you want?' He leaned over and cringed.

'Are you in some pain?' Travis said from behind me.

I shot him a look over my shoulder and he wiped the stupid grin off his face. *Don't antagonise the mummy, Trav*, I whispered into his mind.

'I want the location of my siblings. You know it. Nefertiti said you did.' Before he could answer, I added, 'And what is the Illuminate Year?'

He laughed. It was melodic and I wanted to reach across the table to see if it felt as good as it sounded. 'You want to know where they are? I cannot give you them. They are not finished yet.' He smirked. 'As for the Illuminate Year, look around you; you are sitting right in it.'

I hit the table with my fist and his smirk broadened. 'You are not getting Nefertiti back until you give me more.' I stood up and climbed over the bench. I had every inclination to walk away from him but he grabbed my arm. Electricity ran up my arm and I turned to face him. 'Let. Go. Of. Me,' I said, my tone low and dangerous.

'You will give me what I want,' he said. Almost as if he expected it to be handed to him.

I almost snorted.

'You are not in any position to negotiate with me, Karrept. I have what you *need*. I can find the spell to expel Nefertiti's soul from my best friend's body, and I will not be sorry to see her go. Ancestor or not, nobody is allowed to mess with my family.'

Lili was just as much family as Destiny and Devin were; no one would change that.

I ripped my arm from his grip. Hunter grabbed my free wrist and I looked at him. He felt compassion for Karrept and was trying to get me to look at it from his perspective. We held his lover in metaphorical magickal chains and he was dying. I shook my head at him. Maybe Travis should have been the one to sit next to me.

'Fine,' Karrept finally choked out. 'I need some papyrus and a quill. I will give you the location.'

Isis manifested them in an instant. Karrept scribbled down something on the paper. I sat down again and he slid the papyrus across the table to me. I picked it up and studied the numbers before I handed them to Isis.

'Are these the same numbers?' I asked Isis.

She studied the papyrus like she was memorising it. After what felt like eons, she finally looked up at Karrept and then to me. 'No.'

'You give me coordinates that don't match and you expect me to deliver your lover to you when she's inside the body of my best friend. Do you actually think I'm that stupid?' Heat rose in my body and a cloud of burning-hot rage pierced my judgement, and I knew that it was a piece of the wolf locked inside

Travis, bleeding out to me. 'Isis is going to take some time to verify these. And if they check out, maybe you'll find Nefertiti back in your arms.'

Karrept slammed his fist on the table, and I watched as small chips of wood danced over the surface. 'No! That was not the deal. Give me Nefertiti.'

A hush settled over the patrons, and every one of them turned their attention on us. I wanted to hide from the spectacle, but humans were curious by nature and we always looked for good goss.

'Getting angry won't help you.' Calm and resigned, I held his gaze. His eyes were a different colour to Hunter's, whose were the colour of whiskey held up to the sun. Karrept's were muddy and they looked ... wrong on his face. He stared back at me with anger and defiance. He knew he could drag Nefertiti home with him, but he wouldn't. Not when we now had the Book too.

'I have given you what you have asked of me; give me what I have asked of you.'

Osiris squeezed his shoulder as a warning.

'We'll verify that it is where my siblings are, but until I get that verification, you won't be getting her. I'll be in touch.'

I got up again and took Hunter's hand. He followed me. Karrept roared and flipped the table before I felt him raise power. There were screams.

It all happened fast. Kali was stepping in front of us with Nekbhet's crown. Karrept's power deflected around her.

'Kali!' I cried out. She looked over her shoulder at me and grinned.

'I figured it out. The crown. It protects us as children of people passed. You're a daughter of Nefertiti, Hunter is Karrept's double, Travis is Aten's double, and me? I'm just me.' She pushed the power back at Karrept, who stumbled. He stopped throwing his power at us and everything was quiet.

'You are a Ryder,' I said. The words truer than anything I'd ever said.

I gripped her hand and smiled, before Karrept snuck in between the cracks and hit me in the face. He jolted my cheek and more pain swirled in the same spot. What was with him and my face? Before I could retaliate, Osiris was there—his bird-like beak apparent to me but I was sure that everyone else around us could only see a human face—and he knocked Karrept unconscious. Karrept slumped into Osiris' arms and Kali let go of my hand. Probably to do some damage control on the crowd. I couldn't tell. I was leaning forward into Osiris.

'I think it's time for you to go,' Osiris said. I was spellbound by his beauty and seeing spots.

'Yes ... we should ... go.' I couldn't take my eyes off him as he hoisted Karrept to his feet.

He laughed at me. 'I think you may need to get Lucy out of here before she tries something neither of you men would appreciate.'

Hunter's arm came around my waist and he pulled me away. He didn't need to be told twice.

'OUCH, OUCH,' I hissed as Hunter gingerly skimmed his fingers over my cheek. It still ached from the battle and the fresh hit had made it even worse. We were on the couch and I had my legs crossed under me.

'Stop squirming. I need to know if he's given you a concussion. That's twice that you've been hit there.'

The Book was on the coffee table. I didn't want to leave it anywhere else. I wasn't above taking it with me into every room I went. It seemed safer that way. Also, it was calling my name. I didn't know if that was because I was a descendant or because the Book knew that Nefertiti was in the house and it needed both of us.

'I think he cracked your cheekbone. You might need to go to the hospital, or you can let me …'

I pushed his hands away as he tried to heal it with magick. 'No way, you need to back up.'

'It's a simple spell.'

'That doesn't mean it's going to stay simple.' I gave him a look, and he took a second to stop before he touched the spot with his fingers and I felt the cool rush of magick.

'Hunt!' Anger clouded my voice.

Even the slightest of touches made my heart race, and I could feel the throbbing in my cheek lessen.

'There, now you won't end up with a killer headache. We will still have to look out for the concussion, seeing as you don't want to go to the doctor.' The buzz of power made me want to do wicked things to him. I pulled him closer so that he had to straddle my lap and leaned up. Our noses brushed against one another, his lips so tantalisingly close. Without waiting another second more, I kissed him. His lips hungrily crashed against mine. He kissed me like he was drinking me up like rain after a long drought. And I needed every part of him.

'Lucy! You need to get in here,' Kali cried out.

Hunter broke the kiss and I groaned. I wanted to keep going because it felt so normal to me. It was everything I'd wanted. But he helped me to my feet and together we ran up the stairs and into the hall. Lili was on the floor, convulsing. Kali pushed her onto her side and held her tightly. A lump formed in my throat, and I had half a second to panic before I dropped to my knees and brought my head down to the floor. My cheekbone throbbed harder and shot a bolt of pain through my head, but that didn't matter. Lili did.

'Lili, can you hear me?' I asked her.

Her eyes opened at the sound of my voice and instead of the golden circles I was now used to, they flashed hazel for a second. I gasped and reached out to touch Lili's cheek, and then the colour was gone.

'What happened?' Nefertiti asked and my hand stopped in its tracks.

'I'm not sure. Can you tell us what is happening?'

'Lili is trying to push through. She is screaming at me. She says that today is important.'

'Today?' There wasn't anything special about today. 'Trav, what's the date?'

He frowned. 'The seventeenth. Oh *shit*.'

Today was not a good day. It was the anniversary of the day she was tortured and her twin brother was killed in front of her eyes. It was a bad day.

'We need her phone. Nefertiti, where is her phone?' I didn't know if it was here or if she'd had it on her when she was originally taken.

Just as I said it, I heard her ringtone and scrambled to my feet to get the phone. It rang through and I stared at the screen in horror. Griffin, her boyfriend, was calling, and if anyone knew Lili as well as we did, it was him. If he heard Nefertiti, he would know something was wrong and he would have our arses. Griffin was also a witch hunter, and he would put *all* of us in danger to save Lili.

'We need Lili, Nefertiti. Can you please let her come forward?' If it happened, it would confirm what I already suspected.

I shook my hand and tried to keep my heart from bursting through my chest. The phone was going to stop ringing soon and we needed Lili.

She closed her eyes and I waited as Nefertiti retreated and Lili came forth. Her features softened and when she opened them again, they were blue and confused.

'What? Luce? What's happening? Where am I?'

'Safe, you're safe here, and I wish I could say more, but Griffin is calling. It's the seventeenth.'

Her eyes widened and she answered the ringing phone with poise. I got to my feet and stared at Hunter and Travis. I motioned towards the door and they left the room. My gaze strayed to Kali, and she nodded at the silent question. She was going to stay with Lili.

I noticed in that moment that Lili was missing her necklace. It was the sister piece to mine. A dainty chain that was white gold with an ankh, it was tuned to our energetic auras and was our protection piece. She hadn't said anything and Bastet had disappeared with Isis as soon as we got home from the market, which was … weird. What had happened while they waited for us?

While Lili and Griffin were speaking, I stepped out of the room and closed the door quietly behind me. I stepped around Hunter and leaned against the wall and sobbed. This was all my fault. All of it. I put Lili in danger, I did this to her. I knew I should have stayed home, but my curiosity and the faded fragments of my soul needed me here. I was losing my best friend to my ancestor—this wasn't the holiday I'd wanted for her. I'd wanted it to be fun, wanted us to explore the tombs and temples and stay up late watching movies, talking about everything that was about to happen when we started university. It wasn't supposed to put their lives in danger. That stupid Book better have answers or I was going to kill Karrept and burn the Book so nothing like this could ever happen again. I didn't care if he looked like Hunter, he had done more damage to my best friend than anyone was allowed to.

I looked past Hunter, whose eyes were concerned. Lili and Nefertiti were warring for control now, which meant that they were doing something I hadn't thought possible. It shouldn't have been possible, but Lili's Watcher powers were untested; we didn't fully understand them because she'd only been working with them for a few years at the most. After Marco's death, in fact. After this day three years ago.

'Lili and Nefertiti are merging,' I whispered.

'I can't believe it.' Travis murmured.

'How long has she been in Lili's body?' Hunter asked. He didn't tell me I was stupid. Because I could feel that I was right and he could feel it too.

I shifted my attention away from the wall and looked at Travis, who blinked. 'Um ... nearly two and a half weeks, I think? Does that sound right?'

'I think so.'

'Then, yeah, it's definitely possible. If that's the truth, then it's going to be harder to separate the two of them.'

'We can't hurt her. And we can't give her to Karrept. Lili and Nefertiti are too close to each other,' I mumbled.

We were all quiet as we heard Lili speak to Griffin. She laughed, and I felt a deep ache inside my chest. I missed her laugh. I missed talking to her more than anything, and I knew that once she was done talking to Griffin, Nefertiti would be back.

I opened the door, holding on to the doorknob for support as she hung up the phone.

'I did good, did I not?' Nefertiti said.

'You did great,' I replied. She was like a child who wanted a star for excelling at something in school. 'Nefertiti, what happened to Lili's necklace? The one that was around your neck.'

Her free hand rested on her chest and she couldn't look me in the eye.

What was going on?

'I was mugged.'

'*What?* How?' I was furious. Bastet was supposed to look after her. I knew she didn't like Nefertiti, but my best friend was in her and I needed her to be in the same headspace that she had gone in there. The stress of what happened would have triggered this.

'With Bastet, while we were waiting for you to finish with meeting with Karrept at the market. I thought he was lying, but then there was a gun shoved in my face. They are new to me, but Lili knew that it was scary enough to listen to. I gave him the only thing I had on me: the necklace.'

'Are you ok?' I asked. Maybe the stress from that had brought on the attack? Maybe they weren't merging and it was a stress-related reaction.

Deep down, I knew that wasn't true, though. Lili and Nefertiti were changing.

'I am ok. But I'm starving.'

'That's where I come in. I can cook. Nefertiti, I think you should try something new.' I watched Travis guide her out of the room. I had to close my eyes; it was too much to watch the two of them slip in and out of the same body.

'I can't do this,' I whispered, and Hunter wrapped his arms around me. 'I can't see her do that again. We need to figure out what to do and I want to do it soon. She is not going back to him.'

'I'll work on the spell,' Kali said.

I stared at her. Did I hate her any less? Yes, but I was worried that she would go back to being the same Kali who made my life hell. I didn't want that. 'Check the Book to see if there's anything that can help. Kali, they're merging and we need to find a way to make it so that Lili doesn't get hurt in the process. We can't give her to Karrept.'

She nodded and walked down the stairs. I stared at Hunter and shook my head. This was all too much.

'We're going to fuck this up royally, Hunt, and Lili is going to suffer.'

'It won't happen. I won't let it.' For a second there, I believed him. 'Are we going to talk about that kiss?'

I pressed my lips together. 'Do we have to?'

He smiled. 'Yeah, we do. I miss you. You know it.'

'I miss you too. It ... it felt like things hadn't changed. Like we were still who we used to be.'

'We are those people, just older. I'm ready to try again, if you are.'

Try again. Travis was downstairs making a meal for Lili/Nefertiti and I was up here with my soulmate, talking about us getting back together. It felt so surreal.

'I'm ready. But it has to be different from last time. We need to be better at this,' I said and waved a finger between us.

'We will be. We know what's at stake if we don't.'

My life was empty without Hunter in it and I made bad decisions as a result. I knew it. He knew it. This had to be different.

NEFERTITI SAT at the table with a plate of eggs in front of her, with bacon and some French toast to the side. I didn't know how Travis managed to do it all so quickly, but she was eating and she was happily doing so. The whole Lili and Nefertiti merging thing was swept away, and Travis was watching her like a hawk. I wasn't sure if she understood, but it made me feel a little better knowing that one of us was watching her every move.

'Your cheek looks a lot better,' Hunter commented, drawing my attention to him.

'Yeah, yeah. Don't brag about it.'

He grinned and reached out to me. Our fingers touched, and a spark of electricity ran through them. There was a knock on the door. I stared at him and wanted to take a moment to consume him completely, but if I did that, I would forget about everything else I had to do.

'Have you managed to finish decoding the numbers?' he

murmured, and I pressed my lips together because the urge to kiss him right then was too much.

'I can't get the last symbol, or number. Want to help me?'

'I'm always up for a challenge.'

I had the numbers memorised, but I didn't need to retrieve the paper because I had an image of the numbers on my phone.

'This is what I have so far. They're coordinates and after Karrept's was different, I don't know what to believe anymore.'

Hunter took my phone and studied it. The way his brows furrowed made it hard not to drink him up. What was going on with me? It was like I had a thirst for him. Meeting Karrept at the market and seeing the uncanny likeness of the two ancestors was unsettling. Could Hunter become someone so powerful?

'This last one, is it not something that you can decode?'

'I don't know what I'm even looking at. The numbers made sense, the roman numerals I finally put two and two together, but this last symbol ... it's not a hieroglyphic.'

Hunter got up off the couch and walked over to the bench. I raised my eyebrows as I watched him search for something. He rattled around for a moment and came back with some scrap paper and a pen.

He sat down and drew out the last image I couldn't understand: two triangles that were upside down. They were connected and looked like notches.

'What the hell is it?' I muttered and picked up the paper from under Hunter's hand and laid it down on the coffee table, like it would help.

But realistically, it wouldn't. I had been staring at it for close to three days now and nothing was clicking. It was the final piece of the puzzle, and when we figured it out, we would be able to find Devin. Because it had to be him. I loved Destiny but she wasn't Devin. She wasn't my twin.

'Aren't they notches? Like, there are two of them? Like in sewing,' Nefertiti said from the island.

I blinked at her for half a second and realised that while those words may have come from Nefertiti, the tone was all Lili.

'What?'

'Notches.'

'I got that. How do you know that?'

'Isn't it common knowledge, though?' Nefertiti shrugged and went back to eating her food.

I stared at Hunter, then wrote down the other numbers I had and put two down where the notches were. The coordinates were complete and I googled them.

'Holy shit,' I murmured.

'Is that what I think it is?'

'*Isis*,' I yelled. I knew she was close by, but I didn't know if she was still in the house.

'What is it, Lucy?'

'I know where one of them is. We're going to get them.'

'Where are they?'

I showed her the screen. 'The Sahara Desert.'

Without saying a word, Isis took my hand and pulled me close to her body. 'Close your eyes or you are going to get sick.'

CHAPTER FORTY-ONE

Nefertiti
Epep 2014

I LAUGHED. Travis was very funny, and Lili was so happy to be with her people again. There was a feeling inside that I couldn't put into words because she was listening. To everything. After having a gun to the face, something had changed. Almost like she was done fighting, but there was more to it.

Being a Watcher meant that she not only watched, she could be altered. That was something I kept locked away, and not even she knew about that. I had separated that part so that she couldn't know. Nephthys was the original Watcher. She knew much, much more than I did, and because of that, she was the anchor in the spell. The stitching that kept it all together.

The separation was just like the way Lucy, Lili and Travis separated themselves from one another. It had taken some time, I knew that, but they had barriers up to stop them from feeling everything that came with the Bond. I could keep information away from Lili and I had.

Being a Watcher also meant that she had the ability to sway

people's wills, to get them to do whatever she wanted if she put enough feeling into it. Her calm energy was why the three of them were so level-headed. It all stemmed from her. Travis was a hot-headed werewolf and Lucy was ... reckless. She followed her feelings. It would be detrimental to the three of them if that ever went unchecked. The Watcher's influence held that at bay, and while they could research and research all they liked, it would be left out of the journals. Nephthys' original journal was fused with the Book. It was what made it so special.

The Book was within my grasp, and I could take it, wipe it all, but they would know. They would look to me and I wouldn't be able to tell them what was there.

'Nefertiti, are you okay?' Travis said, pulling me right out of my thoughts.

'Yes, sorry, I was just thinking about the flavours in the food. They're delicious.'

Travis didn't believe and it surprised me. It seemed he was the weakest link when it came to the metaphysical things, because he was a wolf and didn't like anything metaphysical. But it was so disconcerting to be looking at a carbon copy of Aten and for him to not have the same characteristics that Aten had.

'I don't buy it. What is happening with you and Lili? You know more than what you're letting on and that makes me nervous. Lili better not be leaving us, and you better not be replacing her.'

I shoved food into my mouth. The mixture of flavours was weird but I made do. I made sure to chew longer than I needed so that I didn't have to answer, but something told me Travis was waiting for this and he wasn't swayed in the least.

'I asked you a question, Nefertiti. No amount of shoving food into your mouth is going to stop that. Lili used to do that when she didn't want to tell me something, so you're not doing anything new here.'

I stopped playing with the food and looked at him. This wasn't something I would do. I didn't beat around the bush, but it seemed like I was taking on some of Lili's habits.

'What do you think is happening?'

'I don't know, but there is something off about you. You're starting to smell like Lili, I can't ignore that with my wolf senses. When you first took over her body you didn't smell anything like her. What does that even mean?'

'Take a guess, little wolf cub.'

His eyes flashed purple and I knew that I'd pushed his buttons.

'How do you ...' he growled.

I tapped my brain and he stopped. Lili knew a lot and she was now sharing that almost freely.

'You and Lili are doing something to each other. Aren't you?'

'Oh, so very close.' I pushed the chair out and stood up. 'I need to go to the bathroom,' I announced and left the table, but not before I glanced at the coffee table and saw Lucy looking at the upside-down triangles.

They're notches. You use them to help the material sit right, especially when it's on a curve. Two triangles means that there are two.

'Notches.' The word was out of my mouth before I could think it.

CHAPTER FORTY-TWO

Lucy
Epep 2014

WHEN I OPENED MY EYES, we were in the desert and the sun was beaming down. There were mountains of sand everywhere. The experience of rushing through time and space had been enough to make my stomach flip. I was glad I couldn't see how we got here. I didn't think I would have felt the same.

'You could have warned me. I would have put more clothes on.' I wasn't prepared for the blazing heat and I could feel the hairs on my arms sizzling.

'But you called for me,' Isis said. She shielded her eyes from the sun with her hand and stared at me.

'I know but also I could have done more to get ready.' Shoes … it was lucky I even had them on. The canvas shoes weren't the best protection against the hot sand, but they were better than none.

Isis didn't say anything as she looked around us. I raised both of my hands to block the sun and squinted through the shade. There was sand everywhere. I turned to the left and there was sand; turned to the right and there was more sand. But in the distance, straight ahead, I could see water, or the illusion of water.

'Isis … where are we?'

'The Sahara Desert.'

'Yeah, I got that, but where exactly?'

'The coordinates led us here,' she said as her hands on my shoulders guided me around and I saw the entrance to a cave.

I stumbled back against her and stared at it.

'Isis. This is a cave.'

'Yes.'

Did I want to go into the cave? No. Not in the slightest, but Devin would be inside there, and after two years of knowing that he wasn't dead, I could hug him. I could find the balance in my life that had been off for twenty-three months. We trekked across the sand to get a closer look. I stumbled over a mound before I got to my feet and dusted myself off.

I looked into the cave but I couldn't see anything. Just darkness. All I could think was that I wanted to get away from it, like there was something dangerous inside that would hurt me. The hair on my arms stood up, and my skin was covered in goosebumps. I rubbed my hands over my arms but that didn't do anything. A heavy feeling settled in the pit of my stomach, and against my body screaming at me not to, I took a step into the darkness. I was hit with suffocating nausea and doubled over.

Isis pulled me back and that feeling went away. I blinked. 'What is that?'

She touched the invisible field. Her fingers seemed to get stuck, and as she tried to pull them back, it was like there was a force that was keeping her fingers attached to it.

'It's a power or protection field. It's there to keep people out, and whatever in.'

Devin would hate being inside with no sun. His powers were

335

passive, so he wouldn't be able to use them to get out. That's why he was stuck. Or at least that's what it seemed.

Isis could blast through it. She was a goddess and that was a huge advantage. She could get us through the barrier, but she could also hurt Devin on the other side. I wanted to scream his name and warn him we were there, but at the same time, I didn't want to give us away.

'Isis, what if this isn't safe?'

She pressed her lips together. Her raven black hair was pulled back in a messy bun and her eyes stared right at me, like she was studying me. Her skin seemed accustomed to the heat, like the desert was her natural habitat, because she looked so at home. She seemed to glow in the sun.

'It is safe. I would not be here or let you be here if it was not.'

A tap on my shoulder made me jump. I looked at Bastet's yellow cat eyes and she nodded.

'Bastet would not let you be here if it was not safe.'

Did Bastet come here the same way Isis and I did? And how did she do it so quietly?

'How do I get through this? I imagine that, with you, it just tried to pull you in, whereas with me, I could feel it was trying to crush me. But I want to get through. I need to get to my sibling.'

'You are going to have to use some magick, Lucy. It is the only way to get through.'

Magick?

I tried to centre myself, but the heat was making it hard to think. I inhaled and my throat was full of thick, hot air. It was different to the cool taste of the air conditioner at the house. With a nod, to myself more than anything, I stepped forward into the barrier again. I put my hand on it and felt it pulse under my skin. When I touched it, it didn't have the same reaction as it did to Isis, so I raised my other hand. My palms flat against the power, the colour vibrated under my fingers. It was a vivid teal and I pushed power into it.

It didn't move.

I opened my eyes and could see the wall was very much like a net. I pulled at the netting with a closed fist and tugged it down. It pushed back, and I growled at the way it tried to hold its ground, but I was stronger. I wanted it more.

I yanked at the net and pulled it towards my body, shoving power into it. There was some resistance, but my will to get through was stronger and it shattered. I fell to my knees, breathless at the amount of power it had taken.

'Lucy.' Bastet wrapped an arm around my waist and hoisted me to my feet. 'Are you okay?'

I shook my head almost to clear the cloudy feeling from it. I was dizzy and I leaned on her for support and let her walk me into the cave.

Isis kicked the mirror that was at the entrance and it refracted light through the cave, just like it had in Nefertiti's tomb. 'That was a grand show of power, Lucy. You should rest.'

'I can't. I need to find my brother.'

Still weak as a result of the power push, I leaned on Bastet more, and she let me lead her in.

Cobwebs covered the entry, and as we walked through it, I held my hand out so it hit the webbing first. It was thicker than normal webbing, and I shivered at the thought of a huge spider staring at us from a corner. One step in front of the other. It was all I could do to keep myself vertical.

Webbing stuck to my hand, and I wiped it down my leg to get rid of it, but then it was on my pants—something I could worry about later. The deeper we walked through the cave, the colder it became and I wished I was back out in the sun.

'Is that a ladder?' I asked as I looked at the hole in the floor.

'Yes. The cave must go underneath the earth. We are going to need to go down,' Isis said.

It was not enough that we were in the middle of nowhere in the Sahara Desert, but we were also going deep underground. Whoever did this was prepared to make sure that no one found where they were.

Bastet let me go, and with wobbly legs, I crouched down to hold on to the ladder that led below the surface. With careful placement of my footing, I got to the bottom and tried to adjust my eyes to the darkness. I couldn't see anything, but I waited for Isis and Bastet to make it down to me. Bastet immediately wrapped an arm around my waist and made sure I stayed on my feet, which I really appreciated.

'I can fix this,' Isis said. She snapped her fingers and the room was lit.

I cried out as I saw there were skeletons and scarabs. Lots of dead and alive scarabs. We walked around them, delicately making sure our steps didn't accidentally crush anything. I didn't want to risk anything coming out of the bones if they were shattered by our feet.

In the cave, there was no sound. The wind, the temperature, all of it was different, and while there was pure silence, I realised there was a soft whimper coming from a corner.

'Isis. Over there,' I murmured and Bastet automatically took me over to the corner. It was so dark, but as Isis came closer, her light lit it up—and that was when I saw a flash of red hair and my stomach sank.

My heart raced as I stepped closer and the whimpering intensified. I kicked a rock and it rattled in the cave. Wild eyes stared at me. Their lustrous green was missing; instead, they were sunken and haunted. Her lips were thin and almost blue.

'Destiny,' I whispered.

The ache in my chest didn't go away and disappointment rattled through my bones. The sadness that it wasn't Devin was all I could think about in that moment. Isis didn't hesitate and she floated over to Destiny. She wrapped an arm around her, but as she touched her, Destiny screamed. It was ear-shattering. I cried out and covered my ears with my hands. The intensity of the scream and the pain that came with it was too much to handle. How long had she been here?

Was the howl joyful or was it scared?

'Dest ... it's *me*. It's Lucy,' I screamed at her, but she didn't stop.

My stomach twisted at the agony in her wail. I wondered if that was what banshees sounded like. Isis tapped a finger to her forehead and my sister crumpled in her arms, the screams rudely cut off. I breathed a sigh of relief.

I could see how emaciated she was. The rags that clung to her body were too loose and the once muscular and vibrant redhead of a sister was a sore memory. This was someone else who was fragile, weak and scared. All things Destiny Hope Ryder never was until today.

'We need to get back to the house. She might do better there.' Isis looked from me to Bastet, and something passed between them.

'Close your eyes, Lucy. This is going to hurt.' Bastet pulled me in close and I did as she said. Instead of the flawless transit that Isis had provided, this was like my skin was ripping off and trying to knit back together.

It hurt like a bitch.

WITH THE DIRT and gunk out of her hair and off her skin, there wasn't much of an improvement. Her protruding ribs and sunken eyes haunted me when I closed my eyes. How could something like this happen to her? I gingerly touched her hands; her fingers looked like they had been worked down to the bone, as if she had been a worker bee in some mine. A far cry from what they had looked like two years ago. Destiny was still cold to touch but seemed to be

339

warming a little. Or maybe I was hoping that that was the case.

None of my clothes or Kali's fit her, so we had to make do with pins to keep everything from falling. If Nefertiti wasn't house-sitting Lili's body, she could have fixed it for us. Lili had a way with material.

'Good as new,' I whispered as I pushed a few strands of her hair out of her face. She would have batted my hands away if she was still the sister I knew, but she didn't.

I helped her down the stairs and into the living room. Travis was in stress-mode, so I could smell different scents floating through the air. I guided Destiny onto a bar stool and she looked at me, lost and dazed. I smiled and Travis put a bowl of rice and a spoon in front of her, we didn't know what her stomach would be like so starting with something easy and bland would help us gage what to give her next. She looked at it, then at me, and then tried to pick up the spoon. She grasped it but didn't seem to know what to do with it. Destiny stared at me and I gently took the spoon from her and scooped up some of the rice. I held it up for her to take it back and when she did, everyone watched in silence.

The loud, bitchy and exuberant sister I had learned to loathe was gone, replaced by a dull shell of who she once was.

As she chewed, she seemed excited at the prospect of doing something for herself. She even took the spoon from me and tried to have a go herself. She did it and beamed at me, but the smile on her face dropped faster than I could blink and she screamed. The spoon rattled against the counter and I jumped off the seat, ready to spring into action. Her attention was focused solely on Hunter. His eyes widened and I took Destiny into my arms. She screamed into my shoulder and I held her with all of the strength I could muster.

Inside me, I could feel the subtle shifts and the urge to kill Karrept crept to the surface. 'Destiny, shhh, it's okay, it's just

Hunter. He's not going to hurt you.' I turned the both of us around so I could look at Hunter. His shoulders rose to his ears and he looked away. The guilt he felt was tangible and through our connection, I could feel it flowing into my body.

'Don't let him hurt me. He hurts so bad. He gets inside and hurts so, so, so bad.'

I watched Hunter's face harden; his eyes narrowed and lips pressed together tightly. Travis was suddenly next to him, whispering something I couldn't hear. Isis walked in and her face crumpled, instantly taking Destiny out of my arms and into hers. She soothed her better than I did and she quietened down. Maybe it was something in the way that she spoke or the words she said to her.

'I think it is best if Hunter stays out of the room when she is around. I do not want to have to watch this again and again. I have done too much watching already.'

I swallowed past the lump in my throat. 'I'm going to kill him for touching her,' I murmured.

There were whipping scars on her back, they weren't new, but still there nonetheless. It was a weird sight, the way the scars marred her skin, skin that she had always exfoliated and moisturised and taken the utmost care with. Even in the middle of winter. Karrept had hurt my sister, my older, bitchy and annoying sister, and broken her. She was a shell of the person she had been, and he had hurt her, emotionally and physically, in ways that I couldn't comprehend.

He was going to pay for that.

Even if it meant I was going to kill him.

'I'm going to help,' Hunter said softly. 'She's as much my sister as she is yours.'

A tingling sensation ran down my spine. I looked at Hunter, really looked at him, and he was staring back at me. He knew what he wanted. And I knew that I wanted it too.

I was going to marry this man one day. And he was going to be part the family. Destiny was his sister-in-law.

I nodded at him, but I wanted to say more. I wanted to tell him how much I loved him and how much it hurt being away. All of the bad things I'd done. Instead I pressed my lips together and turned to Isis.

'Isis. You watched over her? Why couldn't you do anything?'

'It is the same reason as to why you nearly killed yourself. We Guardians can only watch. We do not have a corporeal body to act with, Karrept brought us into the now with his remaining power.' The pain in her voice almost knocked me off my feet. I stumbled but Hunter steadied me.

'It's not fair.'

'It is not, but it is how we have always been. I will look after her and make sure she eats. Go and sleep, you are looking tired.'

Gee, that made me feel great. 'I'm not tired,' I argued, but it was a lie. I was exhausted. Pulling the net down from the cave had taken more out of me than I'd let on.

Travis spoke up. 'You are.'

He and Hunter cornered me and with raised eyebrows, both faces seeming to say the same thing.

'Fine. I'm going to bed, but watch out for Destiny, or I'm going to kill you,' I said to Travis.

'I'm not going to let her roam around the streets, Luce, have some faith in us.' Travis looked at Hunter and he nodded.

My gaze searched between them, and I just hoped that they wouldn't kill each other. I didn't know how I was going to explain that.

I promise not to harm a hair on his head, Travis whispered into my mind as Hunter guided me up the stairs.

Travis! There were plenty of other places he could hurt him. Or ways.

I heard laughter in my head before Hunter distracted me with his hand at the small of my back.

. . .

Egypt
Epep 2012

DEVIN ZIPPED up his backpack before he picked up his phone and tapped it against his palm. He was leaving me and spending time with Destiny.

'Come on, can't you just blow it off? You can't leave me alone for that long. Do you know how it's going to make me feel to be alone with Mum for a whole week?'

'You're being melodramatic. Dest and I are only going for, like, a night. What is so bad about that?' His dark grey eyes, so much like mine, stared down at me and I sighed.

'People die on expeditions like yours. What if you don't come back?' I had already told him about the bad feeling I'd had. I didn't want to be left alone.

'Don't be silly, Luce. I told you I'm never leaving you. As much as you get on my nerves and test my patience, you are pretty all right for a sister.' He wrapped an arm around my shoulders. 'Even if you make me want to strangle you for being an idiot. Do me a favour and call Hunter back, will you? I don't want him blowing up my phone because he's stressing out that he's made you mad or something.'

I rolled my eyes and poked him in the side. 'Yeah, yeah.'

'I'm serious. I can't handle this, and you know how I feel about getting in the middle of your relationship. It's just weird and wrong.' Devin sat down on the end of the bed next to me and pulled on his boots. He was quick with the laces, tightening each of the sections so that he could get out of answering any further questions.

'Shut up. But seriously, you're changing the subject.'

'Lucy-Bell, I'm not leaving to go and join the circus or something. It's just a small trip. I'll be back before you know it.'

I scoffed and pushed myself off the bed, then started to pace across the carpet. Devin sighed and watched me. 'You know that if you leave me alone with Her Highness,' I said, 'I'm going to come and find you and drag you back and kick your butt. You know I can win. I did last time.'

He stopped me pacing with his hands on my shoulders, forcing me to pay attention to him. 'Are you okay? Like, seriously? I'm worried about you after what happened earlier in the week. The blood thing?'

Devin was scaring me with the intensity in his eyes. 'I'm fine. I must have bit my tongue, because I had a taste in my mouth very close to blood.' I shrugged it off. I had to, even if it scared me. I didn't like the way he was looking at me.

'Are you sure?' I nodded and he continued, the tension visible in his shoulders. 'Good. I was worried. We both were.'

'We were both worried about what?' Destiny said as she came into the room.

'Lucy's thing earlier in the week.'

Destiny paled a little but caught the fumble. 'Yeah. Worried. Glad you're okay.'

'Can you guys just tell me why I can't come? I mean, it's not fair. Just because I'm the youngest, and it's only by three minutes, why don't I get to go?' I wasn't going to let it drop, not yet. I deserved to go.

'You're like a bull. Honestly, Lucy, just drop it. We want to go and check things out and we'll be back, then we'll take you.'

'That's not good enough. You both suck.' I crossed my arms over my chest.

'Tell us something that you don't always say,' Devin said and ruffled my hair. I glared at him and he laughed.

'How about when we get back I'll steal some booze and we'll

make margaritas. I know you love those,' Destiny said. It was weird that she was offering to do something with me.

'Did you get dropped on your head or something?' I asked her.

She laughed. 'See, that's what I get for trying to make things better for you. Whatever. Dev, we have to go or we're going to be late.' Destiny left the room and Devin picked up his backpack.

'Please don't leave me alone with Her Highness. I need you,' I repeated. I loved Mum, but not enough to spend more than a few days alone with her.

'I won't be going anywhere. I promise.' He hugged me tight. 'Try not to kill Mum while we're gone, okay? You're her baby.'

'Yeah, yeah.' I waved him off and he smiled and left the room. I sat on the bed and held my head in my hands.

When I looked up, the scene had faded and I could tell that the time changed. The room was the same but I could see Travis' things all over it. His clothes and his shoes, the bed was messy too. The room shifted again and Devin was standing in front of me, in 2014. I jumped and he smiled at me. This time I could see his face. And the rest of him.

'What ... what is this?' It was almost like the classroom but it was different. The air was lighter and there were no shadows in play here.

'Your dream. Well, sort of. I can dream walk, remember, Luce?' He touched my arm and without thinking, I threw myself into his chest and clung to him, a sob escaping from my lips. This was a different Devin, the one that I loved and missed. This was a sign that he was alive. More so than last time.

I pulled back and punched him in the arm.

'Ouch. Luce!'

'Where the hell are you? I'll come and get you, just tell me where I need to go. I can send Osiris right now.'

'Osiris is there?' He sounded surprised.

'Yes. Karrept summoned all the Guardians and he's here, right in the house.'

'Isis and Bastet too?'

I nodded at him. 'Is that a problem?'

'Maybe. I don't know. Listen, we don't have much time. As you can see, my moods swing all over the place and the happier the memory, the better and stronger I am. I don't want you to see the dark classroom again. You have to trust me when I tell you that Karrept is on his way to get me.'

'What? Why would he be doing that? Isis said he was coming to the house. He wants me and he isn't going to stop until he gets me.'

'He was, then he realised that you found Destiny. I'm not strong enough to take him. Not with my power being so low. I'm ...' He paused and looked around; the room flickered. '... weak. Weaker than I should be. But I've been watching out for Destiny, helping her with energy. You'll have to find someone to help her with that. You can't let her get too cold.'

'What does that even mean? You know I don't understand your riddles.'

'Lucy, just trust me, okay? You need to get Karrept back to you. Finish the spell. You'll get a weapon out of it. I'll tell you where I am later, I promise. For now, I need to reserve my strength.'

I punched him in the arm again and his eyes narrowed. 'Ouch, what was that for?'

'You left me alone with Her Highness. I hurt myself and Hunter broke up with me, a number of times. How dare you leave me!'

He rubbed his arm. 'Luce, if I could have stopped this from happening, I would've. You weren't supposed to come back to Egypt, you were supposed to go on like nothing had changed.'

I snorted. 'Fat chance that was ever going to happen. I told you that I would kick your butt for leaving me.'

He sighed. 'Not now. When you find me, you can do it, I promise. Just help me, okay?'

'I couldn't say no even if I wanted to, Dev. I'm going to get you back.'

'God, I'm glad that you're strong. Now, wake the hell up and make it happen.'

I jolted out of sleep and tried to take deep breaths, but I was panting. It was like the shock of it all was setting in.

I could feel Hunter moving my way and I forced myself out of bed. There was so much to do.

I took the stairs as fast as I could and as soon as I entered the living room, everyone's eyes stared back at me with surprise.

'What the hell?' Hunter said as he met me halfway.

'Devin ... he came to me in my dream. We need to move the spell forward, the one to get Karrept, because he's after him.'

Osiris jumped to his feet and I shook my head. 'He didn't tell me where he was the scribble he gave me was just that, scribble, so we can't get to him. Not yet. We need to move the furniture and make space. Be careful we don't scratch the floor. Mum will kill us.' Not an exaggeration either.

Destiny was in the corner watching, but with every sound and movement, she kept jumping. It was starting to test everyone's patience, mine included. We didn't have time to baby her if we wanted to save Devin. Thankfully, Isis guided her into another room.

'You have to move the chair against the door. Come on, we don't have much time,' I said to Travis.

'I'll have you against the door,' Travis said. I stopped in my tracks and blushed.

His words shouldn't have made my stomach clench and the air rush out of my lungs. He smirked and Hunter rolled his eyes. I bit my lip, locking eyes with Hunter. He shrugged at me because he knew that even though I had a visceral reaction to those words, I wouldn't act on it. I couldn't.

'Okay, why isn't Osiris helping?' Hunter asked, trying to break the tension that had started to rise in the room.

'Nobody asked,' Osiris said, matter of fact.

'Oh, come on, Travis, you're a bloody werewolf. Why are you playing human?' Kali said, the impatience showing in her voice.

Travis shrugged and picked up the couch with two hands. All by himself. He pushed it against the wall and dusted his hands. Osiris lifted the other couch without much effort as well.

'It's not moving again, Luce, so don't even dare think of asking,' Hunter said.

'I wasn't going to.' Yet.

'Yes, you were,' Travis said.

Why were they on the same page all of a sudden?

Because we know you, Hunter said to me.

'Osiris, do you know what you need to do?'

The god with the perfectly chiselled jaw nodded. 'We must keep Karrept from harming you until the spell is done.'

'Excellent. Isis, are Destiny and Nefertiti safe?' I called out to the other room. She confirmed, and like that, we were ready.

Kali handed me the chalk and smiled. 'I think this is your circle to finish.' Maybe, after everything, she wasn't so bad.

Travis was smiling smugly at me. Jerk.

I snorted at Hunter. Standing behind him was a tall man; he had black curls, was wearing studded leather, and on his chest was an emblem with small shield and an axe in the centre. 'Ares? Really? Ares is your Guardian? That surprises me.'

'What? He's pretty to look at and has a great sense of humour,' Hunter said.

Ares winked at me and I pointed at Hunter. 'Hey, don't go sharing your feelings with him.'

Ares laughed and I couldn't help but smile.

I turned around and forced the smile off my face as I closed the circle. Kali stepped into her corner with her Guardian, Astarte, behind her.

'If you wig out, Travis, just focus on me and I'll help you get through it,' Kali said. He didn't have a Guardian because he was a werewolf, but he did have the entire pack and its power behind him—even if his father had been reluctant to allow it.

Together in the circle, in step with one another, we picked up an item that represented our element. Kali was fire, Hunter air, Travis water, and I was earth.

'All hail the Guardians of the Watchtowers of the East, I summon thee, fill our circle with your presences,' Hunter said.

Kali was next. 'All hail the Guardians of the Watchtowers of the North, I summon thee, fill our circle with your presences.'

'All hail the Guardians of the Watchtowers of the West, I summon thee, fill our circle with your presences,' Travis said, his voice shaky.

'All hail the Guardians of the Watchtowers of the South, I summon thee, fill our circle with your presences,' I finished. 'We invoked the goddess and god into our circle with perfect light and peace, so mote it be.'

I felt a breeze rustle through the room as the Guardians filled our circle with perfect love and trust. 'Okay, Kali, you're first. We don't want Karrept here too early.'

Hunter should have gone first, being at the top of the circle, but his element was dangerous and tied to Karrept faster than the rest of ours.

'As I summon thee, fire from the well, take that which has been given a new lease on life.' Kali pushed the flame into the cauldron in the middle of the circle and it fizzled out as soon as it hit the iron. It would be warm to touch but it wouldn't ignite until the last element was added.

'To quench your thirst, I give you water from the lake of those who have watched over us. It has travelled far, taken more than needed and has waited patiently.' The water slipped through Travis' fingers as he poured it into the cauldron. It hissed as it met the sides, steam rising from within.

Hunter took a deep breath. 'With this feather, we offer you the air of wisdom. It has seen many, taken most but never has it failed. It's forever flying and forever travelling.' The feather fluttered through the steam and settled at the cauldron's bottom. The intent was to bring Karrept to us while we undid the magick that kept him whole.

'Soil and toil, grounding and humbling earth, we take from it. Bury that which is unnatural, take back what was stolen.' I trickled the earth into the cauldron and with a flash of light, the room filled with power. Travis growled and Kali took his hand. On the other side of him, I took Kali's other hand and then Hunter's. We all closed our eyes and focused on the cauldron.

Winds whipped around us, and I could feel sand hitting my calves. Karrept's voice carried over the wind's howling. 'All together, is there some sort of offering to come?' We all ignored him—that's what the Guardians were here for.

As we each took turns to pour our own personal power into the cauldron, I broke away and picked up the blade. It was plain, simple and black. I held it over the rim in both hands before I dropped it in. Together we chanted: 'Forge this blade, harden its steel. Take that which we want and give it a life of its own.' Each of us stepped back to the edge of the circle and the fire ignited. I shielded my eyes from the glow, careful about the circle's edge.

Karrept's arm circled my neck and I jumped. 'I could kill you right now,' he whispered in my ear. Hunter finally opened his eyes. They widened and he took a step closer. Karrept threw up his arm and held him in his spot with his magick.

How did he get through the power that was wrapped around the house? Had we let our guard down without realising it?

'I would choose your next steps very carefully, descendant of mine.'

'You can't scare me anymore,' I murmured.

I was careful to make sure that my feet stayed inside of the circle as his arm tightened around my neck.

'I am most displeased at that. Can you enlighten me as to how that would be?'

'I know what you want. And I know how to kill you. The blade? It'll look familiar soon enough.'

Kali took a step forward, and I held a hand up for her to stop. She did as I asked, but the necklace she'd kept hidden under her top slipped into view. Her eyes widened and I felt Karrept's arm slacken around my throat as he centred all of his attention on Kali.

'Why does she have the necklace around her neck? Lucy, what have you done?'

With him so focused on Kali, I thrust my elbow back into his solar plexus, and I heard him gasp before he doubled over. I wrenched free of his grasp and stumbled close to the altar. Hunter helped me to my feet and held me close. Without words, he asked if I was okay. I nodded and saw the blade hovering over the cauldron. With speed, I snatched it. It hummed with power and ownership. It was mine. The blade longed to be used for what it wanted the most.

Karrept's final death.

The blade was the same make as the blade that had sealed the spell and started the Illuminate Year and all of the destruction that they had brought forth. It would end it.

The spell had forged the dagger again, after all these millennia. I looked over to Karrept, who was still doubled over, trying to catch his breath. We had some time before he regained his composure.

'Can we leave the circle now?' Travis asked, twitching nervously.

Kali shook her head. 'We need to thank the Guardians and the elements so we can undo the circle.' Just as she finished,

Ares hit the circle and rebounded off it, the noise deafening. I clung to Hunter.

'That wasn't me,' Kali said.

'It wasn't me either,' Hunter and I said in unison.

The Guardians were in battle mode as they formed a wall around us. Travis bent down and touched the circle drawn on the ground. 'There's something extra here. I can't differentiate it like you guys can, but there's something other than salt here.'

Hunter let go of me and looked down at the circle, clicking his tongue. 'They put a ring of protection and it settled in after Karrept grabbed you. They needed him to that. Those sneaky Guardians.' Hunter glanced over his shoulder and shook his head, a smile on his face. 'Wait where is Karrept?' he asked.

When we really looked at the Guardians, they were fighting creatures that Karrept must have summoned while he was down. The noise had been muted with the extra line of protection.

'Okay, we need to get this gone,' Hunter said and pulled my attention away from the battle at hand. 'Repeat after me: Fire, earth, water, air, thank you for your gifts, thank you for your time, we release thee back to your watchtowers. Be free. Goddess and god, we thank you for gracing our circle with your presence, you are free.'

Together, we chanted the words in hushed tones. I felt each of the elements leave the circle and it was a soft rumble as earth left, the distinct brush of air again my cheek, the splash of water before and a flash of fire all singled before us. I hastily broke the circle rubbing out the chalk line. The Guardians were still around us and I watched as Sam walked next to me. I didn't know how long he had been here, but I knew that he was here to avenge his father. He held out his hand and nodded at the blade in mine. He had sensed Karrept's proximity to me and came as close as he could because he wanted to be the one to get Karrept and be over with the Illuminate Year.

'I can't give it to you,' I whispered.

Sam tackled me to the ground. I hit it hard and for a second my vision blurred. I was about to yell at him, when a ball of power narrowly missed us.

'If you will not give me the blade, then I will still protect you. Do you remember the game we used to play when we were children?' He rolled off me and stood. I nodded as he held out his hand and helped me to my feet. 'Good, we're going to put that into play. You need to make sure you duck if it happens.'

Sam was tricky. He had access to power now that he didn't have when we were children, and playing around with energy balls was the hardest part of our game. They had never been moving.

Karrept sensed that there were more of us than there was of them, and he manifested footmen, decaying soldiers who were fierce. And smelled gross. There were enough of them to make the house feel too small. He made a beeline to me and smiled.

'What are you smiling about?' I said, the blade out and ready to play. It wanted to taste his blood.

'You think that you will be able to stop me? Your sister may be back, but you do not know what has happened to her. Did she scream when she saw your beloved? I bet she did.'

His fist came flying at me and I ducked, the knife slicing his arm. The skin hissed and bubbled. Though Karrept didn't show that it hurt, I could see the way the magick ate through his skin.

'What did you do to her?' I grunted as he quickly punched again, this time connecting with my shoulder.

'You will have to keep me alive to find out or wait to see what happens. Where is Nefertiti?' he growled as he caught my leg. He pushed me to the wall. My back hit it with a hard thump, and the blade flew from my hand. I felt like a yo-yo that had just come back to life after years of being packed away.

'No!' I cried out, my vision blurring. How hard had my head hit the wall?

'Where is she?' he asked again.

'Safe. Away from you. She told me that you needed my essence, but you forgot that Devin wants to see you dead. You can't keep me from winning this.'

I felt him. For the first time in just over two years, my brother filled my being and it was like we were whole again. Since he left, I'd felt empty, like he'd cut off his ties to me— which I now knew was because he wanted to keep me safe—so to have him back, even for a moment, was bliss.

'Most excellent.' With that, Karrept kissed me, his hands holding my face in place.

I felt him pull at the strings of my life, sucking my essence into his body. I could feel Devin panic in my head, and everyone who was tied to me stopped dead in their tracks. Time stood still, my head becoming hazy. I pushed against Karrept, my life draining from me, and I could hear him laughing. Devin fled, with an apology, but I understood; he needed to gather his strength. I needed to find him and I didn't want him to get lost —I'd already lost him once.

Karrept was wrenched from my grasp and I slid down the wall, my vision spotty and my body aching. A cold had settled deep in my chest and I wheezed for air.

It hurt to breathe.

But that wasn't where the cold stopped. It filled my head and made me think of the snowy mountains of Mt Buller back home.

Karrept's beautiful face was marred with pain. He turned and I saw the dagger lodged in his back. He stumbled towards Hunter, who was now far from his grasp. I felt rather than saw Hunter pick me up and help me to my feet, one hand held protectively against my hip, the other holding us up against the wall. Through the haze, I saw Karrept burst into an array of bugs and bandages. Hunter covered my body with his to make sure that none of them splattered on me.

Then, before I knew it, he was kissing me. His lips were just as soft as Karrept's, but there was a familiarity and love that Karrept couldn't even compete with. I felt warmth flow into my mouth, and I pushed him away as I realised what he was doing.

'No,' I wheezed.

He had tried to give me his life essence.

'Luce,' he whispered. 'Your lips are blue. I can't lose you. You need more.' He tried to kiss me again. Even in my weakened state, I turned away.

He took a step back, bugs crunching under his shoes, and looked at me. 'Lucy, don't make this any harder than it already is.'

'I am going to kill you with the'—I wheezed and bent over, trying to get more air into my lungs—'amount of life I need. No.'

Hunter looked stricken and turned to Travis, who came to a stop next to him. 'Oh, look, I guess I get to save the day, Ryder,' he said with a smirk.

'No. Not even you. I think I need to sit down.' I slid down the wall and closed my eyes. It was bliss.

Shaking. Someone was shaking me. 'Luce. Lucy Fate Ryder, you open your eyes right this—oh.'

I blinked and Hunter's face came back into focus. 'You can't do that to me,' he said.

'Do what?'

'Black out like that. Come on, Luce, don't make me beg. You need to take some of his essence, please.' His voice broke.

Sam came into view, and I smiled at him.

'Hi, Sam.'

'Hello, Lucy. You need to listen to them.' The worry on his face was out of place and I just laughed—maybe I was broken. Sam had a deep cut on his cheek from the battle and there was dried blood caked on his skin.

'Fuck it.' I heard Travis swear. 'Lucy, kiss me now.' He took my face in his both hands and kissed me after the order. He pushed his life into me and I resisted at first, before I wrapped an arm around his neck and kissed him harder, taking more of him.

Warmth flooded through my body; it was akin to lying in the sun and letting its rays take away the chill on a cold day. He wrenched his lips away from mine, his eyes violet glowing with danger. Like he wanted to devour me whole.

'Hello there, pretty wolf,' I whispered and touched his cheek. Travis turned away from me and nodded at Hunter before he ran out of the room.

I was drunk on Travis. Hunter frowned and helped me to my feet.

'Are you okay?' There was the unasked question of why I had done that.

'He tasted really good.' I giggled.

'She is drunk on his essence. I have a fix for this.' Sam pulled something from his pocket and blew it at my face.

Instantly, I sobered up and let go of Hunter. 'What the fuck?' I could feel Travis and his wolf; he had run away to keep himself safe. Around us, the place was a mess: there was blood and goop I didn't want to know about everywhere, Kali had a cut across her cheek and Destiny was shivering next to her, while Nefertiti sat in the pile of bugs, sobbing. I looked back at Hunter and saw he had a bruise on his cheek and a cut on his arm. Sam looked like he'd run into a wall—his nose looked shattered.

'I missed a lot, huh?' I said finally as I looked at Hunter. He laughed.

'Yeah. Come on, let's go and get cleaned up and then we can deal with this. The Guardians were all sent back too, so don't worry about looking for Isis and co.'

'Destiny won't stop shaking,' Kali said, 'and I don't know how to make it stop.'

Devin had said that she needed something. What the hell was it?

'Devin warned me about this, but I can't remember what it was.'

'So cold,' Destiny whispered. Her gaze found mine and I saw her eyes mist over, almost like someone put grey contacts over the vivid green that used to stare back at us. 'Need life.'

'Warmth. She needs energy,' I whispered. Just like I had, but this was on a whole different level.

'Oh. *Oh.*' Kali realised what I was talking about and took Destiny's hands. She chanted under her breath, transferring some of her warmth to Destiny.

Destiny smiled at her, warm and content, before she slowly lay back and her eyes fluttered shut. My own widened at the sight and Hunter held me tight as Kali leaned over her.

'She's just sleeping, I think.'

I breathed a sigh of relief. That only left one problem.

CHAPTER FORTY-THREE

Nefertiti
Epep 2014

I STARED at the remnants of Karrept, the bandages and the bugs, and sobbed. I covered my face with my hands to give myself some sort of dignity. He was really gone. After all of these years. After all the time we had spent plotting what would happen and how it would happen this year. We hadn't thought that we would be here. Or at least I didn't. Lucy was supposed to be the one to house me, but instead it was Liliana and she was different. Not as broken, but also not as compliant. There was a fire in her, one that would come back to burn her if she left it unchecked.

But I liked her. There was this part inside me that wanted to keep her close. Closer than anything. And I knew that there was no way they would be able to make it without me in their lives now. Not with how close Lili and I were. That was going to be the drawcard for them.

Or I was going to die. That was ultimately what would

happen, and right now? I welcomed it. I would be at peace and maybe find Karrept. I had to find him. My life didn't matter without him, and that was a feeling I had never thought too much about when I was alive. He'd always been *there*. Always been in the background as we bore children together and let Aten raise them with me. That would have hurt him the most, but he was always there. Always in their lives when it mattered, even if they didn't know he was their father all along.

You know, you guys have a really unhealthy relationship when it comes to being together. It's not at all natural, but I guess you being here, in my body, isn't exactly natural either.

'You aren't wrong,' I whispered because I didn't want the others in the room to hear me. They would have thought I was crazier than I was. But I was taking on more and more of Lili's nuances the longer I was inside her.

I picked up the bandages, which were oddly warm to the touch, and stared at them. There was a part of him still here in it, and I knew that they would try to take this away from me. Karrept had been more than just a man to me. He was the one who had made things make sense. Even as a young queen, I didn't have the experience I had as I rose to the throne, but with his guidance and his ability to soothe the bad and teach me what I needed to do to be the best Queen I could be..

'Nefertiti, we need to clean up,' a voice said. I looked over my shoulder and saw Hunter, his face so much like Karrept's. It hurt harder to look at him.

Unshed tears threatened to trail down my cheeks and I shook my head. 'You can't take him away. You wouldn't. You already took him from me.'

I had seen it all happen. Isis had held me back as Hunter drove the knife into Karrept. Almost fitting that his own descendant would be the one to kill him.

'We need to do it,' he said again, and I shook my head. With the Guardians all gone, there was no one to hold me in place and I lunged at Hunter. He wasn't expecting it and I dropped him to the floor.

'Nefertiti!' Lucy yelled, and before I realised it, I was held in place by power that was once my own.

'Let me go. He killed the only man I have loved, and you— you should understand.'

Lucy looked at me, her hand in the air as she kept me in place. 'One, he just tried to kill me, so I don't understand, but that doesn't give you the right to kill the man that I love. If you wanted to do something useful, you'd clear it up, but you're not and instead you squat in my best friend's body like it's a haven. We are getting you out of there and you won't have any choice in it. Travis, take Nefertiti to her room and lock her in. When we're ready, we'll get her out.'

'You can't do that!' I yelled.

'I just did.'

And like that, Travis picked me up and slung me over his shoulder like a caveman. Karrept had done that to me once, but it was for a very different purpose. The magick that held me in place was gone as he touched me and he carried me up the stairs. I beat at his shoulder with my fists.

'Put me down.'

'I'm sorry, Nefertiti, this is for your own good. We need Lili and we're going to get her out of there, but we need to make sure that you're safe and you're not in the way, causing any harm. And we can't have that.'

I could hear the regret in his voice, but I knew he was more worried about his friend in this body than me.

'You'll regret this,' I threatened, and I could feel Lili sigh. She knew that it was an empty threat.

'We're keeping you safe, and you don't need to see what's about to happen.'

They were going to burn the rest of him, I knew it. And that would be the most painful thing to watch, but maybe being so lonely and away from people who could comfort me—even if they were the ones who had put me in this position—was even worse.

CHAPTER FORTY-FOUR

Lucy
Mesore 2014

TWO AND HALF WEEKS AGO, I didn't think I would be trying to find a way to save Nefertiti. But she had bonded with Lili; Sam had confirmed that when he'd done a reading on her. He had used the surface of a sword to read her aura and what had happened to her. And because of that, we couldn't just tear Nefertiti away without ripping into Lili's psyche, and that was a part of her we needed. A part I needed more. Lili would help us fix the mess Travis and I broke with the Bond when we slept together.

But most of all, I needed my best friend back. I needed to talk to her.

'He's gone. Why not just let me go with him? Kill me now— use the blade, shove it into my heart and we can call it even.'

I clicked my tongue. 'You are in my best friend's body; you really think I'm going to kill you?'

'Yes.'

The look I gave her wasn't one that was nice and she knew it.

'No,' she followed up.

'You know that I won't kill you, even Lili knows that, but you need to have a will to live, otherwise this won't work. I won't risk her life to save you, do you understand, Nefertiti?'

'I'm an ancestor of yours. Why do you care less about me?'

I sighed and pressed the heel of my hand against my forehead. 'Because you are the whole reason we are in this situation. You couldn't leave well enough alone and you had to take my siblings, and you had to try and kill me.'

She was quiet … in fact, everyone was quiet. I looked around the room. I had three pairs of eyes staring at me.

Nefertiti opened her mouth and I shook my head. 'No, you don't get to say anything. You are the one who put us here. We are taking Lili back and you're going to deal with it.'

We'd made the decision on what we were going to do. In order to bring Lili back, we had to split Nefertiti so that each of us girls could take a bit of her into us. At first, when Hunter had brought up the solution, we all vehemently disagreed—why would we risk that for ourselves? I didn't know how to feel about the thought of having a piece of my ancient great-grandmother merge with me. Would it be weird? Would she know things about me that I didn't? Or would she just be like a foreign passenger in my body?

Travis had sat me down and put forth all of the pros to my cons, and with his guidance, which surprised him more than me, I realised that this needed to happen and that there was no way around it. I mean, besides the fact that Nefertiti was in Lili's body, we needed to keep her. We could use her if anything else should crop up and that was all that mattered. For a guy who didn't like werewolf politics very much, he was good at thinking on his feet.

And using that to his advantage in times of need.

'Don't you want to feel less, Nefertiti?' I held my ground, strong and steady. Even if this scared me.

'I'd give anything to feel like my heart isn't breaking in my chest right now. There's not enough room in here. Not enough.'

She sounded crazy, like she was losing a bit of herself every second that we stood there waiting for her to give us permission. I wished I could tell her I knew how it felt, but I didn't. I'd only lost Hunter to a breakup. Not to death. She was already inside a circle that was salted and protected; all we needed was her say and we would be ready to go.

'I know,' Kali crooned. She stepped up to her and brought herself down to Nefertiti's level. She was sitting on a chair, her eyelids fluttering as she tried to stay with us. 'Let us help, really help, and I promise you that everything will be okay.'

She was nodding and I was moving my hands about quickly, slipping everything we needed into the circle with my magick. There was a plate with a block of clay—the clay was cut into four pieces and would bind the spell—as well as each of the elements sitting in a bowl. There was an incense stick for air, a candle for fire, a small chunk of dirt for earth and an ice cube for water above each piece of clay.

I came up behind Kali and touched her shoulder. She stood up and took one of Nefertiti's hands. I took the other and Kali and I joined hands. We chanted under our breaths, louder and louder as we grew confident with the wording. Our words blended together and latched on to Lili, the magick pulling Nefertiti's soul out of her body and splitting it in the air above us. I watched the sliver of her soul that was going to inhabit my body hover around me. It shimmered before it dived into my chest. I let go of everyone and gripped my shirt right over my heart. I felt her settling inside me, but it was almost like she was home and it didn't make much of a difference.

'Lili?' I said softly. Her attention snapped to me, and instead of the vivid golden orbs that I had steadily gotten used to, I found her blue eyes. I rushed up and hugged her. 'You're really here. Oh god.'

'Luce,' she breathed and held me tight. I buried my nose in the crook of her neck and tried not to let the emotions that swirled in my body show, but with the Bond the way it was, it was impossible.

'You are not allowed to leave me again,' I murmured.

'Me leave you? You left me!' she said with a laugh and I pulled back. I had missed that laugh the most. There was a warmth and a kindness that had been lost with Nefertiti.

But now it was back.

'What did you do?' Destiny flung open the door and stared at me, her eyes alert and her hair brighter than it had been in days. I could see a hint of the red that it used to be.

I looked at the pieces of clay and saw that each piece was now strong, hardened and no longer raw.

'What we had to. You needed energy and we couldn't keep letting you borrow ours, Destiny,' I said.

'Get it out. Get her *out* of me. I can feel her there and I don't want it.' She stomped into the room, and I held her with my power before she stepped into the circle and would ruin it all just by putting her foot down over the line. Eyes wide, she looked from me to Kali, then to Lili and back to me. 'You have no right to do this.'

'You better back up, I'm not going to have you hurt our half-sister because you're about to step on the circle she made.'

She took a step back. 'I'm sorry,' she murmured and I had to do a double take. Destiny never apologised to anyone, and it was surreal to hear those words come out of her mouth.

'I—I want this out of me. She's there, eating at me.' She clawed at her arms and Kali quickly disbanded the circle. I stepped over the line and held Destiny's arms.

'It will get better, I promise, but we had to do it. We needed to do it. Devin said we needed to find another way to give you energy, even if I don't understand ...' I pulled her into a hug and held her so close. She was warmer than she had been this morning, her skin less pale. There was more of a humanness to her skin colour. She didn't look so ... dead.

Destiny sagged in my arms and I sighed softly into her hair. At that moment, Hunter walked past the room. He pushed open the door and saw all of us.

'Lili, you're back.' He smiled and she beamed at him.

'You bet. Look at you, all back again. Didn't I tell you it'd happen?'

'You say a lot of things, Lili. You know that much to be true.'

She laughed at him and dusted herself off. 'I'm starving. Has Travis been stress cooking? Because I sure as hell need some of that food.'

'He's about to put the brownies in the oven.'

With Destiny still in my arms, I looked to Lili and our eyes gleamed. 'He's making brownies?' we both said in unison.

'I'm licking the bowl,' Lili called first.

'That's not fair!' I countered and felt Destiny shift in my arms. She pulled back to look at me.

'Are they the brownies that have the little chunks of crunchy stuff in them?' She seemed a little warmer at the mention of chocolate. Good.

'Yup. It's the only kind he makes, and they get better the more stressed out he is,' I said.

The excitement in the room was so foreign after everything that had happened, but it was like normal was returning to us. Kali was packing up, and I eyed Hunter as Lili and Destiny left. He walked into the room and we stood in front of Kali. The spell was her bright idea after Hunter had suggested it—she deserved some slack.

'Go fight over the bowl, Hunter and I will clean up,' I said.

Her eyes widened with shock and she sighed. 'I'm not used to this "being nice to you" thing and the more I do it, the easier it is. I'm sorry for being such a bitch when we were growing up.'

I shrugged. 'It happens. Kids are mean growing up, it's a fact of life.'

'That's true. Thank you.'

With that, she turned around and left. Hunter pulled me against him and smiled.

'What?' I asked.

'You are one of a kind, Lucy Fate Ryder.'

'Shut up,' I said with a smile as he kissed me.

Things would be okay. They had to be.

LILI's long strawberry locks were no more. Her hair was short and up in a ponytail. It was also no longer strawberry blonde but a russet colour that looked damned good on her. I hadn't anticipated that she would suffer with nightmares. Last night she woke up screaming and somehow managed to hack her hair off with a knife she found. I found a hairdresser close by and we fixed it. It would be something to get used to, but she seemed happier for it. Maybe she needed a small change to help her move forward. I don't know, but whatever she needed, I wasn't above giving her exactly that. She had been through enough trauma and I knew that the nightmares weren't going to stop for a while.

'Okay, thanks, Mum.' Her voice distracted me from my thoughts and I raised an eyebrow at her.

'So?'

'Mum is such a hard arse. She rambled on about wanting to wait to tell me and that with everything that had happened it just slipped her mind, blah, blah, whatever. Anyway, she said that it's not hard to fix the Bond. The curse is forever gone, but we have to put up, like, a sort of buffer to make sure that we don't actually hurt one another, because at the wrong moment, ordering one of us to do something could be harmful, and there really isn't a way to put stipulations or a limit on the order.'

That was dangerous. In the heat of the moment, one of us could order the other to jump off a cliff and we'd have to do it.

'What do we need to do to get it back into shape?'

'Well, it's not really a lot, but we do need some of our blood and we sadly have to ingest a bit of the mixture each.'

'No way!' I wasn't squeamish about much, but the thought of drinking blood, no matter how little, was a whole world of no. Mostly because Travis' blood was a drug. Literally.

'Luce.' Travis came up next to me. 'It's not like we're going to enjoy it, but if we need to do it to get the Bond back, we need to do it.'

'Speak for yourself, wolf. I don't want the high your blood gives.'

He had been reaching for my hand but he stopped. 'Wolf. After everything, you call me wolf?'

I was staring at my hands one moment and the next I was looking at Travis, who had his hands on my arms and had spun me to look at him. His hands wrapped around my biceps to keep me close.

'I'm sorry. I didn't mean to.' In all honesty, I hadn't. I'd never uttered those words before and couldn't figure out why I had then. Nefertiti giggled in my head and I groaned.

'What?' Travis must have seen something in my eyes because he let me go.

'Nefertiti,' I whispered.

He looked stricken and turned to Hunter. 'You said that that wouldn't happen, you assured me it wouldn't.' Anger vibrated off his body, and I wrenched my arm back from him.

'Travis,' I said quietly. His eyes bled to purple and I said his name again, this time with a little more force. 'Don't blame Hunter. We knew there would be some side effects, and it's only been a couple of days. Okay? Calm down. Shut down the wolf and get rid of those violet eyes, please.'

Saying *please* didn't make it a command. There were so many little loopholes we had to learn to cope with, but it was useful to know them, especially in moments like this.

'Dammit.' He pushed back and took a deep breath before he closed his eyes. He counted under his breath and when he opened them, they were back to their normal green.

'Thank you,' I murmured to him and he nodded.

'What else goes into the spell?' Hunter asked. He had been calm and unmoving as Travis laid the blame on him. He was level-headed and wanted to see what would happen from all sides. I liked that about him the best.

'Well, I have to do this alone, without either of them, but beyond their blood, I need to speak whatever chant comes to mind and then bind the rest of it in three identical handwoven bracelets that we'll wear for one year and a day and then tentatively take them off and see if it worked. If it doesn't, I repeat the whole thing and we try again. It's a never-ending cycle until we get it right.'

'So you're not going to be able to guarantee that it'll fix the Bond the first time round?' Hunter looked from Lili to Travis and then to me. His eyes silently told me that he wanted to fix this for me so that Lili didn't have to, but he couldn't. This was part of what it meant to be a Watcher.

'No. Mum said that we shouldn't hope too much that it'll work the first time. Because I've only just found out about the fact that I'm the real reason the Bond even happened and this whole Watcher mumbo jumbo. We just have to assume that it'll go pear-shaped and in a year and a day's time, we'll have to re-spell the bracelets and go through it all again.' She sighed and stood up off the stool. She grabbed a bowl and a knife and handed it to me.

'Oh, come on. Really?' I took the hilt of the knife. I sighed and sliced my hand in one quick swipe. It hurt and I closed my hand into a fist. 'Someone better wipe this down before Lili cuts

369

herself,' I said out loud and tried not to stare at the blood trickling into the bowl.

Kali was there with wipes—I didn't even hear her come in—and she wiped the blade down before she gave it to Lili.

'Wait a minute. Travis is a werewolf; won't his blood make you both sick?' Kali said.

Lili shook her head and pushed my hand up. I unfurled the fist and Hunter was there with a towel to stop the bleeding. 'No, it's a small dose and we're immune to it or at least that's the gist of it, because of the Bond. Although there might be a little bit of a high. That's a benefit I learned from Nefertiti which is wired back to you, Luce, you're immunity makes it harder for me too.'

I wanted to add that my blood was also the one thing that muted Travis' blood. Instead I sighed and tried to squash the nausea that rolled in my belly. Hunter put a hand on my shoulder. His touch helped but not by much. His presence soothed me, but knowing that my blood could fix the damage that Travis' blood could do and not telling Lili and Trav made me feel gross.

I watched Lili hand the knife to Travis. 'Do you have the bracelets?' I asked Lili.

Kali produced three bracelets and handed them to Lili. 'Yup. I made these for you guys. I'll go and set up.'

'Do you need a circle?' Hunter asked.

'No. Well … I'll have a salt circle, but that's all I need. It's really pretty simple. I'll be back soon,' she said and took the bowl with our mixed blood. Travis looked wild, his attention and his nose all on the blood that passed him by. He started to follow, and Kali intercepted him, holding him back with a hand on his chest, over his heart.

'I wouldn't do that if I were you, Trav,' she muttered. 'Your wolf is all out of sorts, isn't he?'

'Yes,' he breathed and she hugged him.

'I think it's time to go for a good run, you actually need it.

Don't even bother making out that you don't, I can see that you do, and while Lucy and Lili know you best, I do know when you need to go for a run. Or something of the like.'

'Yeah, you're probably right.' He turned to me and stood up straighter. 'Luce, can you call me when Lili is done? I'll come back. Remind her that she needs to make sure that my bracelet will fit around a paw.' He held up his arm and I watched the nails sharpen and lengthen. I nodded at him and he was off.

'That was smart,' Hunter said to Kali.

She shrugged. 'It was better than having him lose control. I'm not sure what would have happened, but I'm sure his wolf would have gone for you first. You've got what he wants.' She pointed at me and I rubbed my arms. I didn't want to have to see that fight happen.

'I most definitely do,' Hunter murmured and tilted my chin up so I could see his eyes. They were filled with lust, and the heat and the need in his gaze made my lower belly tighten as images flashed through my mind. I remembered what it was like to feel him deep inside me and I couldn't wait to make new memories. Hunter knew that we would be inseparable when we got back and he wasn't running away from it.

And neither was I. I was ready for this. He felt it, and with a knowing smile, he sealed that acknowledgement with a kiss.

LILI WAS DONE with the spell and she was sitting at the breakfast counter with the chalice full of our blood and the bracelets. I didn't want to know what else was in it. I was happy to be ignorant about it.

'Okay, these should work, but if not we'll have to find a witch that isn't involved in our lives at all. Outside sources are best, it seems. Apparently, when I was done, Mum was compelled to tell me more. While the Bond was fate waiting to happen, the curse was put there because Aten and Nefertiti were married and Karrept wanted to make sure you guys wouldn't get a chance to be together. Karrept and Nefertiti were very specific with the curse, so unless the bits of Nefertiti that we have within us can maybe work together and find out why, then we'll never know.'

Destiny walked in. Her hair was still duller than usual, but her eyes were bright and I hadn't realised I missed seeing that. Maybe she would go back to her normal self. She had stopped complaining and screeching about Nefertiti being inside her. She finally understood that it was necessary and she wasn't cold all the time.

'Dest, how are you feeling?' I asked tentatively.

She blew up at me when I asked yesterday, but that wasn't going to stop me today. Her mood swings were a real bitch to deal with.

'Okay,' she mumbled.

We watched her for a second before Lili looped a bracelet around my wrist. 'There, that's yours, do mine.' She held it out and I slipped it around her dainty wrist. I adjusted it and we turned to Travis, whose eyes were still wolf violet but we trusted that he wasn't going to hurt us. We looped it around his wrist and tightened it. Together Lili and I took a step back and we felt the power float around the room. Lili picked up the chalice and handed it to me.

'You have to sip this three times, then give it to me and I'll do the same and then Travis will have the rest, because he's the wolf.' *And he enjoyed blood more than the two of us,* I finished for her.

I did as she told me and took my three sips, I focused on my breathing to make sure that I didn't vomit it back up. Lili took her sips and passed the chalice to Travis, who took his two sips and then threw his head back and downed the rest of it.

'So? How do we know that it's worked?' he said.

'Slap yourself, Travis,' I said. He slapped himself and I giggled.

'Okay, so it might take some time, but I don't think we should be baiting it right now. Lucy, stop that.'

I was attempting to poke at the bracelet when something weird passed through me and I shivered. Nefertiti laughed at me and I had to take a step back. I knew no one else could hear her laugh, because I was the only one she would torment. She believed that I was an easy target because she thought she knew me better than she knew the rest, but I was sure that Lili had learned to filter her out. She'd had some practice with it before.

You should have killed me when you had the chance. I was weaker because I didn't get what I wanted, but part of me is in you now. And I'm right where I want to be, her voice whispered in my mind. I stumbled back and gripped on to Hunter, who chased her voice away. I clung to him.

'Nefertiti. She … she was talking to me. And I could feel her right *there.*'

I didn't sign up for this. I knew that if we hadn't done the spell, we wouldn't have gotten Lili back, but I could feel the pain that Nefertiti felt over losing Karrept, and it was like going through a breakup all over again. I'd already done that; I'd done the time for it. I looked at Travis and he was staring at me, the intensity in his gaze forcing me not to look away. Nefertiti stirred inside me, and I knew that she still felt something for the man who looked like her ex-husband. It was hard not to. Hunter must have felt something because he pulled me closer and it chased her away again. It also gave me the strength to look away from Travis.

'This is going to be a bit of a problem,' Kali murmured. 'We're going to have to try and figure out a way to help keep her back.'

'You don't have her trying to come through, do you?' I asked Kali and she shook her head.

'She doesn't seem to have that same effect on me. Lili?' Lili shook her head. 'I don't know about Destiny, but I'd imagine you two would have the most trouble with her because you are blood relatives of hers. I'll try and figure out if there's something that I can do to help.'

The thought of Destiny going through this too made me want to curl up and cry. She'd been through enough and having to add to that trauma with Nefertiti lurking around in her head was too much. What had we done? If we could deal with this and we were stronger than she was, how was she coping?

'Can you work on something for Destiny asap?' *I don't want to be responsible for making her crazy*, I followed in my mind. I wasn't going to admit that out loud, not with Destiny still within earshot.

'I'll work on something now. I'll have to do some searching on the net to try and find the necessary items I need,' Kali said. The net would be out of the question; that would leave too much of a trace.

'I can give you the number to the magick shop. Andromeda, or, well, Meda, was more than happy to help when we were in there. I'm sure she would be happy to assist us now that we have Destiny back.' Maybe it would help speed things up a little.

'That would be great. Are you going to be okay?' The care in Kali's voice made me look up, surprised.

'I—I … yeah, I'll be fine.' Hunter squeezed my shoulder and I resisted the urge to cover his hand with mine.

'All right. I'll get on to that straight away.'

I broke away from Hunter and went to find the index cards with numbers and found Andromeda's name. It was lucky that the magick to do this even existed here. But Kali took the card from my fingers and programmed the address into her phone and left to get supplies.

CHAPTER FORTY-FIVE

Lucy
Mesore 2014

KALI FINGERED the necklace around her throat, and I watched her from my seat on the plane. She was nervous and I wasn't sure if it was because the necklace didn't want to go back to Destiny or because we were on a plane. Destiny was holding my hand hostage, and it felt like every bone was fusing together. I didn't think she'd be such a nervous flyer. She never had been.

'Dest,' I whispered. Everyone else except Hunter and Kali were sleeping, so I kept my voice down. 'Do you think you can lighten up your grip a little?'

'What?' She looked down at our hands and let go. 'Oh. I'm sorry,' she mumbled. I rubbed my thumb across the back of her hand before stretching out my hand.

'Are you okay? I mean, you seem really worried about the plane and you never were an anxious flyer.'

'Things changed, Luce, but I'm nervous about going home. What are Mum and Dad going to say? And what about Josh? I imagine he didn't keep in touch.'

Actually, he'd made the effort to come over when he could and sat down and chatted with Dad and Mum. While he seemed to steer clear of me—I was afraid that was because he didn't like me—he was always there for them.

'He came around often enough, Dest, give him some credit. What else is there?'

The plane bumped with some turbulence and her hand squeezed mine again. Ouch.

'The metal. I don't like it, not anymore. How long to go?'

If she was still just human, then the metal wouldn't affect her. But there was something about her, something that made it harder for her to think, even function.

'Still a while,' I murmured.

'Make it stop. I can't handle this.' She pulled at her seatbelt and I had to unlock mine to make sure that hers stayed put. Hunter got to his feet and made sure that she wasn't about to run past him. She was remarkably stronger than I remember her being and it was harder for me to keep her calm. Magickal force had to be used and it made it harder to be alone with her.

'Destiny. You have to calm down, remember we spoke about this? You have to stay calm or you're going to hurt everyone.'

The lights started to flicker and my heart leapt into my throat. We didn't need the plane to go down.

'Calm down, Destiny. You're stronger than this, remember that.' Kali was up too, and not bothering to keep quiet. There was no way either Lili or Travis could keep sleeping with the rocking of the plane.

'Miss Ryder, what is happening? We're having some issues here,' the captain said over the aircom.

'Destiny Hope Ryder, calm the fuck down. I'm sorry to yell, but you are not the only one on this plane, and we need to get back in one piece. You can freak out when we get on the ground, but don't you dare bring this plane down on us. I will not forgive you, Mum and Dad won't forgive you either. Don't you want to go home and see Josh?'

'Miss Ryder?' the captain asked.

'We're just having a little talk, try to keep her steady,' Hunter said for me. I couldn't afford to take my eyes off my sister.

'Dest?' I asked. She pressed the heels of her palms to her eyelids. 'Just breathe.' She took a deep breath and I held mine. It was safe to say that she was not going to last the whole trip, but we had to. We'd given her anti-anxiety drugs and even sleeping pills, but her body metabolised them too quickly. I leaned closer and touched her. Her skin was ice cold and she was shaking. 'Hunter, can you get some blankets for her?'

'Sure,' he said and shuffled off to get some. Kali looked at Travis, whose sleepy eyes were peering at Destiny.

'I can give her some energy. Not a lot, given we're on a plane, but I can give her enough to help warm her.'

'That would be great,' I said and stepped out of the way. Lili came to stand with me and we watched Travis help my sister.

'This was not meant to happen,' Lili murmured to me.

'I know. Nefertiti was supposed to help with this, but I think it might be a fight for survival thing. Her body thinks she's in trouble so it's shutting down. I didn't think this would happen on the way home.'

'We didn't see this happening. We couldn't have, really. Don't beat yourself up for it.'

'She's my sister. I can't help her. This is frustrating as fuck.'

Kali came over to us as Hunter placed blankets on Destiny's lap. 'We need to figure out what is happening with her. She's anxious and cold but she's here—well, sort of. There's something that she needs, but we don't know what it is. Any more dream visits from Devin?'

'Um ... guys,' Travis said and the tone in his voice made me look at Destiny. 'I don't think what I just felt from her is good.'

'What do you mean?' I said as I watched her fall into a fitful sleep. The energy that Travis shared was different.

'She's not ... I don't think she's actually alive. She's too cold for that. And I felt something ... dead.'

'What the hell did he do?' I bit my nail out of habit. I didn't think I was going to sleep much more this flight.

I wanted to ask Devin what he meant, but I hadn't seen him in three weeks. He said he wasn't strong enough. I needed to see him in my dreams to help me understand. Needing energy wasn't normal, and she needed someone who was like a battery for her or this wasn't going to work. Travis, being a wolf, had an infinite amount of heat, but he couldn't sustain her.

Not for the rest of her life.

THE LANDING WAS smooth and Destiny dropped to her knees as soon as her feet touched the ground. She didn't care that there was a light drizzle of rain, the kind that Melbourne was known for. She scraped her knees, tearing her jeans. Blood and torn skin covered her knees, as well as the pavement where she'd fallen. I saw something wriggle and did a double take. It didn't wriggle again, so I shook my head. I must have been delirious from the lack of sleep on the plane.

'Did you just see that?' Travis asked and confirmed what I'd seen.

My stomach sank.

'See what?' Hunter asked.

Travis bent down and picked up the wriggling thing attached to the piece of skin on the ground.

'No,' I breathed and stepped closer. Attached to the skin was a maggot.

'What the hell?' Lili said.

Collectively, we looked at Destiny, who was staring at the skin. Through the hole in her jeans, I could see the skin reknitting slowly. It pushed the other maggots back into her body and I saw her eyes glaze over, a dull white sheen covering them.

'Travis,' I warned as he stepped closer and held his hand out to her. The instant he touched her, her complexion brightened and her eyes were back to their usual green. She breathed a sigh and looked down at her feet. Almost like she was ashamed of the secret she had been holding on to. For weeks. For years, even.

'Um, so, the plan is to have Destiny and me walking further back. The hat should hide her hair; the sunglasses, her eyes. No one will recognise her,' Kali said. She was right. 'Enjoy your coming-out party, Lucy.' She winked at me and took Destiny's hand.

I smiled at her but all of my attention was still on Destiny, who was refusing to look me in the eye. She let Kali drag her off and didn't give me a second look.

'Good luck, guys. Come on, Trav.' Lili pulled Travis further in front. He discarded the maggot and skin and looked over his shoulder as he walked away.

'Are you okay?' Hunter asked as he stopped me, cupping my cheek with his hand.

'Living dead. That's the only reasoning I have,' I whispered to him.

Destiny was cold to the touch; she needed warmth and energy; she was cranky and metal ... the metal didn't make any sense to me. Maybe it was the air.

'What are you talking about?' Hunter said.

'Destiny. She's, I don't know, not a vampire because vampires don't exist ...'

'Just like werewolves aren't meant to.' Hunter smirked.

'Shut it. I mean, what else could she be?'

'Zombie. She could be a zombie. It would make the maggot thing fit and the lack of warmth and energy.' Hunter dropped his hand from my cheek and kissed my forehead before taking my hand.

'That's just impossible. We'd need to find a necromancer, then, and I'm pretty sure that they don't actually exist. Voodooist, yes, but not necromancers.'

'I don't know what to say, Luce, but we won't be able to know for sure. Not unless Destiny is willing to tell us what it is,' Hunter murmured.

'I know. And I can't wait that long. Shit, it's freezing.' I hugged my jacket closer to my chest. In the short time away, I had forgotten how cold Melbourne was in winter. The sharpness of the air made me flick my collar up and huddle further into my clothes.

'Let's get our bags. We have to prepare for what's going to happen.'

I sighed. Hunter and I were going to be coming back as a couple, which meant that there would be photographers galore, not to mention questions. *Why are we back together? When did we break up? Did he fly out to surprise you?* Being an heiress was tiring and anyone who said otherwise was lying.

Once we collected our bags, it was time for the moment of truth. I watched as Destiny and Kali went one way. Destiny tilted her head at me and smiled. There was something in that smile that made me worry.

Lili sighed. 'Some days I wish they stayed in bed. I'll see you guys in the car.'

I did too. I watched Travis and Lili go off towards the car, following the driver who had been waiting patiently for us to arrive. I squeezed Hunter's hand and out we went.

Flashes of light blinded us, questions all blended into one, but the most disconcerting thing? The clicks I heard that didn't have flashes attached to them. Hunter stopped us before the car and pulled me against his body. He kissed me hard and I forgot about the world for a second and kissed him back. His mouth explored mine and when he pulled back, I grinned.

'What was that for?' I whispered as he opened the car door.

'It looked like I was going to lose you and I needed to make sure that I wasn't going to.'

'You are such a media whore,' I murmured. He laughed and let me slide into the car. Our bags were put in the boot, and while we waited for the driver to take us home, Hunter squeezed my hand. We were finally going home.

I saw Travis glaring at Hunter, but when he caught me looking, he wiped the sour look off his face. It was going to be a long drive home.

WE WERE FINALLY outside our house and I looked at Destiny, whose whole attention was outside of the car instead of with us. Did things look different since she was last home? The car had stopped in front of our house and Hunter was the only one left with us, because he had refused to leave.

'Destiny. Before we go in there, what is wrong? What happened to you in the Sahara Desert? Why won't you talk to me?' Holding my tongue only lasted for so long.

She was silent and had been since we dropped Lili home. Destiny didn't want to open up, and I was so close to smacking her over the head with everything I had to make her talk to me.

'For fuck's sake, you can't give me the silent treatment. Everyone saw it. What happened? Why do you keep needing energy? Travis is not going to be around forever and Devin can't keep supplying you with whatever he was. He's too far now. Tell me.'

'He killed me,' she said softly. 'He raped me and then killed me and brought me back before I sent him away because I was going to eat him. I need energy to keep me alive.'

I swallowed past the lump in my throat. I was hoping that

she would tell me something else, but she didn't and I wasn't sure I could breathe.

'So you're a zombie or something?'

'Ye-es.' Her voice cracked at the truth. 'You can't tell Mum and Dad. Please. I'll find some way to keep my energy up. Devin obviously helped keep me alive, but it cost him. I don't want them worrying more than they already are.'

'They're going to find out when you start rotting or something.'

She looked stricken. 'Ew. No. I don't rot, I just ... get duller. I ... Luce, don't make me go over this, please. Not now. I need time. Give me time.'

'I can't. We have to find someone to help you.'

'A necromancer. They'll help.' She stared at me blankly.

'They don't exist,' I said.

Hunter was quiet and he took my hand as I glanced out the window and saw Mum and Dad standing at the mouth of the door.

'They do. I'll have to find one. Luce, please don't tell anyone.' She leaned across and touched my knee. Involuntarily, I flinched away and she looked hurt. 'I can't infect you.' Her voice was quiet.

Just then, the door opened and Hunter got out and helped me out. Destiny followed and shielded her eyes from the sun that peeked through the heavy cover of clouds. I walked up the steps to our parents and hugged them tight. When they pulled away, they glanced from me to Hunter and I saw Dad grin, before they looked past me and saw Destiny. The hat was off, so her red hair, in all its glory, was shining in the sun. Mum sobbed and ran to her. Dad pulled me into a hug.

'How did you ...? What happened in Egypt?' he asked.

'I'll tell you all about it later, just go and make sure that she's real. I know you want to squeeze her.' He rubbed my shoulder and flew down the stairs. When Mum finished hugging her, he pulled her into his arms and held her tight. Dad didn't cry often, but I could definitely see tears from where I was standing.

'You know, even with everything, I'm proud of what you've done. I know you hated your sister, but here she is,' Hunter commented.

'Only she's not the sister I always knew,' I muttered.

'I know, but maybe she'll be better.'

Maybe she would be.

I TWIRLED on the path leading up to the house, and Hunter laughed as he sat on the step with his iPad. 'You know, you need to stop looking so tantalising with your book smarts,' I said and joined him on the step.

'Shut up. It's just an iPad. I'm searching Google to see if there's anything to help us. It's nothing special.' He laughed and rubbed my knee. 'The coordinates that you gave me are really hard to find. I can't seem to pinpoint it. Maybe you wrote down a number wrong because it keeps pointing me to somewhere in Africa, then somewhere in Turkey. Have you had any more dreams?'

I shook my head. 'Nothing. We can try a scrying spell now that we know he's alive and Karrept is gone, but I'm not sure how much that will do. It's not like we haven't tried that before, right?'

We were trying to figure out if the other numbers that Karrept gave us were real, we'd brushed it off because they weren't the same ones as Nefertiti's but if she had Destiny's location maybe Karrept had Devins. Now that we were home I needed to know if they had been a ploy to throw us off Destiny's scent or if he really did give up Devin's location. Now that I knew he was alive, I wasn't stopping. I would bring him home too.

Hunter frowned. 'Right. This is going to be a lot harder than I thought.'

'You're telling me,' I muttered.

The sun was shining and even though it was the middle of winter, the day didn't have the same chill to it as you would expect. Something about the weather changing made the heat from the sun weird. We were silent as I watched him type in the coordinates again.

'Hunter, you haven't been home since we got back. Mum and Dad are starting to worry about you,' I said softly.

He sighed and held the iPad to his chest. 'I can't bring myself to leave you. I'm scared I'm going to lose you again. I've had enough of that happening in my life to last a very long time. You're not allowed to do anything stupid, not again.' He kissed my cheek and I smiled.

'I can't promise anything. Trouble seems to follow me. Are you going to try for the fire department?' He had been talking about joining the Metropolitan Fire Bureau. I didn't know if I wanted the stress of worrying about him, but I wouldn't get in his way.

'I think so. I've been going for runs and hitting the gym to get my fitness up.' And it was showing. 'But we'll have to see if I can be ready in time for the next selection round.'

'Mm … my man, a firey. That's kind of hot. You'll come home with soot smudges. That's so sexy.'

'I could burn off my eyebrows too. That's not hot at all.'

I laughed and poked his ribs. He scoffed at me before going back to his googling.

'What are we going to do about Destiny?' I asked.

He shrugged and was about to say something but he saw what I felt.

Travis was coming and it gave me goosebumps. He drove up and parked his car. The valets came to try to park his car but he waved them off, which was standard for him. No one touched his car if he could help it.

'Wyatt, Luce,' Travis said. I shielded my eyes from the glaring sun to look at him.

'Hey, Trav, what's up?'

'Not much. I was just wondering if I could talk to you for a second. Do you mind, Wyatt?' The tension between the pair of them was so tight, I couldn't poke at it out of fear it would hit me in the face. I turned to Hunter and he nodded. He got up off the step, squeezed my shoulder that didn't still hurt and walked inside.

'Hey,' I said again.

Travis sat down next to me and sighed. 'Hi. You're looking good. Your cheek has basically healed. And you haven't got many scars.'

'No. I was lucky, I guess. Kali has one on her cheek and Dad said that he'd pay to get it removed but she doesn't want that. She's happy with her war scars. How weird is that?' It was even weirder knowing that Kali was now welcome to come over whenever she wanted. She and Dad were bonding and so was my mum. It was weirder with Destiny, who couldn't wrap her head around Kali being our half-sister.

'She's a hard arse. You'll get used to it soon enough.'

'Yeah, I hope so.' We lapsed into silence and it was strange; I wasn't sure if it was because of what had happened between us or if it was just because we didn't know where to start.

'So you know I'm going away for a bit, yeah?'

The thought hadn't escaped my mind since he told me. 'Yep. Europe, right? What are your plans there?' It was a safe question.

'See the Eiffel Tower, the Catacombs, you know, the usual.' He paused and there was more silence between us. This was getting ridiculous. 'Plus, the sperm donor said it might reflect well on the pack if I go and visit some of the packs there too,' he added.

'Oh, official pack business. That seems so thrilling. You'll have to tell me all about it.' It was easy to lapse back into the friendship we'd had. The one where we told each other almost anything. With that statement, though, Travis tensed up. I looked at him and frowned.

I couldn't feel him in my head—he had the door between us firmly shut on my side. His shoulders and hands held so much tension and it told me that he wanted to tell me something.

'What's up?' I said again.

'Nothing. I'm just … nervous. I have something for you, but you can't peek until I'm gone. Promise me?'

Presents? I raised an eyebrow at him and he handed me a letter. It was light and my name was scribbled in his messy handwriting.

'I promise. What's the deal with this?'

'Just trust me, Luce, please?' He didn't smile at me and I missed it.

I nodded at him and he stood up and pulled me to my feet. He gave me a big hug and squeezed me tight. It was almost suffocating, especially when I was so short in comparison to him.

'I love you. I hope you know that. I'll see you soon.'

'Of course you do. I'll see you soon.'

I was anxious to see what was in the letter. As soon as I was inside, I leaned against the door, madly ripping at the envelope. I saw Travis' familiar script and read the letter carefully.

Lucy,
There are things that I wish I could change.
I wish I could be with you, or I could just

switch off what I feel and we could go back to how we were, but the fact is ... we can't. We can't go back to who we were before we slept together, before we broke the curse. You were right, no surprise there. I'm ... I'm going for a while. It hurts too much to see you with Hunter and I know that if I stuck around the way that I am now ... I'd rip out his throat.

Because you're mine. You've always been mine. Or at least in my heart you have been.

I know that you and Hunter are meant to be. I see it in the way that he looks at you, in the way that he smiles and talks to you. He is so much gentler than I ever could be, and part of that is because he doesn't have a wolf lurking under the surface. He's just human. Whereas I am not.

It's exactly what you need. You don't need a stupid werewolf to complicate your life. So. I'm leaving for a while. I can't tell you when I'll be back or where I'm going, because I know that you'll find me and you'll try and talk to me out of it. Through the wolf, I've learned to shut you out too. Only you, though. And that's what I'm going to do. I'm sorry, Lucy-Bell, but I need to do it to feel sane. To find out what I need and who I am.

Just know that through it all, I love you. I

always will. I just ... I can't be here when you are with him. It's not fair on me and on you.

Love always,
Travis

I scanned every sentence, every word, every letter as I tried to make sense of it. Then it sank in. He was leaving me. He was running. He was using his trip as a reason to do it. I wrenched open the door and ran outside. I could see the taillights of his car. My brain tried to figure out what was going on with him, because I couldn't feel him. It was like he had cut himself off from me. I sobbed. I couldn't stop it.

'Lucy? What's wrong?' The voice was unfamiliar, and after two and a half years of not hearing it, it was hard to remember that it belonged in the house. I turned back to see Destiny at the base of the stairs. I shivered from the cold and forced my legs to take me inside now that his car was gone.

'Trav is ... he's ...' *Gone.* I couldn't bring myself to say the words because then it would be true and he would be gone. Gone for a while, maybe for good. If it was for good, I didn't know what I would do. I held the letter out for her to read and sat down on the stairs with my head in my hands and sobbed again. She held the letter and I could tell she was reading fast because she rattled the page, almost like she was trying to see if there was more to the letter. The sound made me feel hollow. Like I was missing a limb.

'He'll come back, Luce, don't stress about it. He's always been around, so he'll get over it.' She was trying to convince me but I knew that it was half-hearted.

Destiny didn't think that he was going to come back. Ever.

She sat down next to me and wrapped an arm around my shoulders. The simple gesture made me lean into her. I couldn't, in all of my years alive, ever remember her being the one to comfort me, but here she was, doing exactly that.

'I think I got it. I just need ... what happened?' Hunter walked into the entryway and saw me. He hugged his iPad under his arm and dropped to his knees. His hands rested on my knees as he held my teary gaze. I couldn't find the words to tell him, but he knew. 'We'll get through this. He's gone, but you're not. Don't beat yourself up for something that is out of your hands. Travis will realise how much hurt he caused because of this, but it won't make him come back. You need to accept that. It's his way of moving on.'

Hunter was saying all of the right things—of course he was, that was what he did—but it didn't help the ache of missing him. I wanted to reach out to Lili, but I was scared that she would tell me that he was still there and that would seal the deal that he was cutting me off.

'You're not alone. Not anymore,' Destiny murmured. 'We're going to make sure that you get past this.'

And just like that, I was more comforted than I had been in years. My sister was back, and even though she was different, it was the sort of difference I could learn to like, even love. Life had changed, and it was going to keep changing, and I needed every little bit of love in my life.

REFERENCE

Ancient Egyptian Months

Season 1
    December - Choeak (Keek)
    November - Athor (Hatoor)
    October - Phaophi (Babeh)
    September - Thoth (Toot)

Season 2
    April - Parmuthi (Bar-moodeh)
    March - Phamenoth (Baram-hat)
    February - Mechir (Amsheer)
    January -Tobi (To-beh)

Season 3
    August - Mesore (Mesoree)
    July - Epep (Abib)
    June - Paoni (Ba-oo-neh)
    May - Pachons (Beshens)

ACKNOWLEDGMENTS

This story started as an idle idea of a 14 year old who had to come up with something, anything to write for an English class assignment. I never thought that it would come so far and be what it is today. It was the first real story idea that drew me to writing and ignited a passion for exploring what could happen when I sat down and put words to a page.

The real magic came after completing the first draft and I believe that moving the story, moving myself physically and meeting the amazing writers and mentors I have, changed the story for the better.

With any endeavour, and something that is such a long process, one that is also so lonely, it takes a special kind of person to stand by your side. And I could not have had this story be what it is without these amazing souls.

Firstly, my dad, who allowed me the space to spread my wing and move states, not only did he help me do it but also was secretly my biggest cheerleader. It wasn't until after his sudden death did I realise just how much he spoke of my endeavours to those around him. I miss him every day and wish that he could see what this book has amounted to and just how much work has gone into it. I just hope that he has his cheshire grin plastered on his face as he looks down at me.

This book...the drive to finish it, would never have gotten here if it wasn't for one of my very best friends. Peta has helped me get through every stage of this story, from finishing my first complete draft at her magical home in the Victorian Countryside to sharing both an editor and a proofreader, I could not have done this book without. Your willingness to listen and let me ramble about the story in all of it's forms is something that I can not and will not ever not need. Not to mention that last push to get through that very. last. scene. Did you know that she too dwelled on a book for over 20 years? And the best part? She published it too. Please, go buy *Unwinding the Spiral*, you won't regret it.

While I was drafting this through the years, Mum has always been my biggest cheerleader; the one to tell me to hurry up and publish the damn thing, so that she could brag about it to all of her friends. She was always there to listen to my rambles and give me feedback when I read chapters out loud to her. Without her support and her huge heart, this book wouldn't be here. I'm so grateful to have the most selfless mother who, no matter what, puts myself and my brother first. And speaking of my brother, Peter has always listened patiently to the stories I told about my characters and called me crazy before he understood.

Where would I be without some of the most amazing and supportive teachers and lecturers I've ever had. The story started in Mr Richard Hafer's classroom as a task to write a story about anything we wanted, that extended to Mr Wayne Beaumont's senior class, the class that I decided this story and my writing was really worth the effort. But the real MVP's are Dr Alice Robinson and Dr Karen Simpson-Nikakis, who lovingly pushed me past my limits, getting me to explore the different areas of what I could do with the written word and even forcing me to change character names. I am forever grateful to have chosen to study writing under their watchful guidance because it has taught me that the connections we make are far more important than the lessons themselves (and I finally found something I loved to do).

To my husband, Dave, who didn't understand how I could be so consumed with fictional characters and learned that me yelling at my laptop was a form of therapy and not me losing it. He sat through listening to chapters and nodded. The process is something that he doesn't understand, but hopefully does now.

Getting a novel to this point is no small feat, I'm blessed with the keen eye of Emily Marquart, who's patience is unparalleled. She helped me uncover a version of the story that stretched out further than I realised and it's so much better for it. Thank you to Beth Attwood for her keen eye with picking up the things I felt I had - but missed.

Thank you to champions like Chanelle, Sarah, Hannah, Megan and Silvana, you kept me going when I didn't think I was any good. And to Emilia, one of the first of my friends to take me serious and inspires me to do better.

Lastly to my clients at my day job–your continued check ins to see if this book was published, warmed my heart and pushed me forward. Now when you call I'll be able to tell you that it's ready. It's yours to take home.

ABOUT THE AUTHOR

Mandi Kontos is an urban fantasy writer who lives in Melbourne Australia with her husband, tuxedo cat Rajah, a plethora of plants and a collection of journals she never writes in. By day she is a lighting designer and by night a writing mindset mentor and word wrangler.

She has a Bachelor of Arts, Bachelor of Writing and Publishing and a Masters in Creative Writing. She is a perpetual student and loves to learn.

Mandi loves to take the supernatural and blend it with the mundane things of life, taking mythology and spinning it on its head.

Her debut novel *Faded Fragments* has been a labour of love and is the first in *The Nexus Series*.

Join her newsletter to get updates about her writing and books to come.

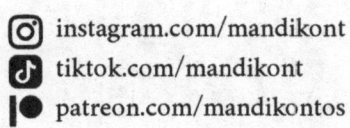

instagram.com/mandikont
tiktok.com/mandikont
patreon.com/mandikontos

SIGN UP FOR BOOK UPDATES

If you loved Faded Fragments, sign up to the email list to get sneak peak behind the scenes at the next book and the others coming in the series. It's your best bet to get a chance to access to special bonuses and pre-order before anyone else does.

Scan the QR code to sign up today